Critical accla...
and the In...

THE SUMMER THAT NEVER WAS

'Robinson's Inspector Banks novels have built up a rising reputation as one of the most authentic and atmospheric of crime series. Procedural details aside, Banks can make Morse look almost philistine . . . Any reader who still misses Morse should promptly resolve to go north with Banks' *Independent*

'Peter Robinson succeeds in brilliantly contrasting the two cases . . . Inspector Banks is making a real mark as one of our most thoughtful and interesting detectives' *Sunday Express*

'As a crime writer, Robinson is not as granite-hard as Ian Rankin, and this is reflected in the crisp yet emphatic narration. Banks is genuinely human, rather than a hard man' *Observer*

'Absorbing' *Sunday Telegraph*

'Peter Robinson is the rising star of the crime scene' *Manchester Evening News*

'As he ascends the international ranks of mystery writers, Robinson quietly and methodically stretches the boundaries of crime fiction, to the point where critics now routinely compare him with P. D. James . . . Robinson handles his story and his characters with all the respectful skill of a fine cabinetmaker' *National Post*, Canada

THE SUMMER THAT NEVER WAS

Peter Robinson grew up in Yorkshire, and now lives in Canada.

His Inspector Banks series has won numerous awards in Britain, Europe, Canada and the United States. There are now fifteen novels published by Pan Macmillan in the series, of which *The Summer That Never Was* is the thirteenth. *Aftermath*, the twelfth, was a *Sunday Times* bestseller.

PETER
ROBINSON

THE SUMMER THAT NEVER WAS

AN INSPECTOR BANKS MYSTERY

PAN BOOKS

First published in Great Britain 2003 by Macmillan

First published in paperback 2004 by Pan Books
an imprint of Pan Macmillan, a division of Macmillan Publishers Limited
Pan Macmillan, 20 New Wharf Road, London N1 9RR
Basingstoke and Oxford
Associated companies throughout the world
www.panmacmillan.com

ISBN 978-1-4472-2304-7

1 3 5 7 9 8 6 4 2

A CIP catalogue record for this book is available from
the British Library.

Typeset by SX Composing DTP, Rayleigh, Essex
Printed and bound by CPI Group (UK) Ltd, Croydon, CR0 4YY

Visit **www.panmacmillan.com** to read more about all our books and to buy
them. You will also find features, author interviews and news of any author
events, and you can sign up for e-newsletters so that you're always first to hear
about our new releases.

For Sheila

The glory dropped from their youth and love,
And both perceived they had dreamed a dream;

Which hovered as dreams do, still above:
But who can take a dream for truth?

Robert Browning, 'The Statue and the Bust'

1

Trevor Dickinson was hung-over and bad-tempered when he turned up for work on Monday morning. His mouth tasted like the bottom of a bird cage, his head was throbbing like the speakers at a heavy metal concert, and his stomach was lurching like a car with a dirty carburettor. He had already drunk half a bottle of Milk of Magnesia and swallowed four extra-strength paracetamol, with no noticeable effect.

When he arrived at the site, Trevor found he had to wait until the police had cleared away the last of the demonstrators before he could start work. There were five left, all sitting cross-legged in the field. *Environmentalists*. One was a little grey-haired old lady. Ought to be ashamed of herself, Trevor thought, a woman of her age squatting down on the grass with a bunch of bloody Marxist homosexual tree-huggers.

He looked around for some clue as to why anyone would want to save those particular few acres. The fields belonged to a farmer who had recently been put out of business by a combination of mad-cow disease and foot and mouth. As far as Trevor knew, there weren't any rare pink-nippled fart warblers that couldn't nest anywhere else in the entire country; nor were there any ivy-leafed lark's turds lurking in the hedgerows. There weren't even any trees, unless you counted the shabby row of poplars that grew between the fields and the A1, stunted and choked from years of exhaust fumes.

The police cleared away the demonstrators – including the old lady – by picking them up bodily and carting them off to a nearby van, then they gave the go-ahead to Trevor and his fellow workers. The weekend's rain had muddied the ground, which made manoeuvring more difficult than usual, but Trevor was a skilled operator, and he soon got his dipper shovel well below the topsoil, hoisting his loads high and dumping them into the waiting lorry. He handled the levers with an innate dexterity, directing the complex system of clutches, gears, shafts and winch drums like a conductor, scooping as much as the power shovel could hold, then straightening it so as not to spill any when he lifted it up and over to the lorry.

Trevor had been at work for well over two hours when he thought he saw something sticking out of the dirt.

Leaning forward from his seat and rubbing condensation from the inside window of the cab, he squinted to see what it was, and when he saw, it took his breath away. He was looking at a human skull, and what was worse was that it seemed to be looking right back at him.

•

Alan Banks didn't feel in the least bit hung-over, but he knew he'd drunk too much ouzo the night before when he saw that he had left the television on. The only channels it received were Greek, and he never watched it when he was sober.

Banks groaned, stretched and made some of the strong Greek coffee he had become so attached to during his first week on the island. While the coffee was brewing, he put on a CD of Mozart's arias, picked up one of last week's newspapers he hadn't read yet, and walked out onto the balcony. Though he had brought his Discman, he felt fortunate that the small timeshare flat had a mini stereo system with a CD player. He had brought a stack of his favourite CDs with him, including Billie Holiday, John Coltrane, Schubert, Walton, the Grateful Dead and Led Zeppelin.

He stood by the iron railings listening to 'Parto, ma tu, ben mio' and looking down at the sea beyond the jumbled terraces of rooftops and walls, a cubist composition of intersecting blue and white planes. The sun was shining in a perfect blue sky, the way it had done every day since he had arrived. He could smell wild lavender and rose-mary in the air. A cruise ship had just dropped anchor, and the first launches of the day were carrying their loads of excited camera-bearing tourists to the harbour, gulls squawking in their wake.

Banks went to pour himself some coffee, then came out again and sat down. His white wooden chair scraped against the terracotta tiles, scaring the small lizard-like creature that had been basking in the morning sun.

After looking at the old newspaper and perhaps read-ing a little more of Homer's *Odyssey*, Banks thought he would walk down to the village for a long lunch, maybe have a glass or two of wine, pick up some fresh bread, olives and goat's cheese, then come back for a nap and a little music, before spending his evening at the taverna on the quayside playing chess with Alexandros, as had been his habit since his second day.

There was nothing much that interested him in the newspapers except the sports and arts pages. Rain had stopped play in the third Test at Old Trafford, which was hardly news, England had won an important World Cup qualifying match, and it wasn't the right day of the week for the book or record reviews. He did, however, notice a brief report on a skeleton uncovered by a construction worker at the site of a new shopping centre by the A1, not far from Peterborough. He only noticed it because he had spent a good part of his early life in Peterborough, and his parents still lived there.

He put the newspaper aside and watched the gulls swoop and circle. They looked as if they were drifting on waves of Mozart's music. Drifting, just like him. He thought back to his second conversation with Alexandros. During their game of chess, Alex had paused, looked seriously at Banks and said, 'You seem like a man with many secrets, Alan, a very sad man. What is it you are running from?'

Banks had thought about that a lot. Was he running? Yes, in a way. Running from a failed marriage and a botched romance, and from a job that had threatened, for the second time in his life, to send him over the edge with its conflicting demands, its proximity to violent death and all that was worst in people. He was seeking a temporary escape, at least.

Or did it go deeper than that? Was he trying to run away from himself, from what he was, or from what he had become? He had sat there pondering the question and answered only, 'I wish I knew,' before making a rash move and putting his queen in jeopardy.

He had managed to avoid affairs of the heart during his brief stay. Andrea, the waitress at Philippe's taverna, flirted with him, but that was all. Occasionally, one of the women from the cruise ships would give him that certain kind of wistful look which led only to one place if you let it, but he hadn't let it. He had also found himself a place where he didn't have to confront crime on a daily basis, more particularly a place where he didn't have to go down into cellars stuffed with the violated bodies of teenage girls, a scene from his last case that still, even here on this peaceful island, haunted his dreams.

So he had achieved his goal, run away from a messy life and found paradise of a kind. Why was it, then, that he still felt so damn restless?

•

Detective Inspector Michelle Hart of the Cambridgeshire Constabulary, Northern Division, entered the forensic anthropology department of the District Hospital. She was looking forward to this morning. Usually at post-mortems she found herself disturbed not so much by the cutting and probing itself as by the contrast between the bright reflective surfaces of utilitarian tile and steel and the messy slosh of stomach contents, the dribbles of blackish blood running into the polished gutters, between the smell of disinfectant and the stench of a punctured bowel. But this morning none of that was going to happen. This morning all that Dr Wendy Cooper, the forensic anthropologist, had to examine was bones.

Michelle had worked with her just over a month ago – her first case in her new posting – on some remains that had turned out to be Anglo-Saxon, not unusual in those parts, and they had got on well enough. The only thing she found hard to take was Dr Cooper's predilection for playing country and western music while she worked. She said it helped her to concentrate, but Loretta Lynn had quite the opposite effect on Michelle.

Dr Cooper and her graduate-student assistant, David

Roberts, were bent over the partial skeleton, arranging the small bones of the hands and feet in the correct order. It must be a difficult task, Michelle realized from the one brief anatomy course she had attended: how you told one rib or one knuckle from another was quite beyond her. Dr Cooper seemed to be doing well enough. She was in her early fifties, a rather stout figure with very short grey hair, silver-rimmed glasses and a no-nonsense manner.

'Do you know how many bones there are in a human hand?' Dr Cooper asked without looking away from the skeleton.

'A lot?' Michelle answered.

'Twenty-six,' said Dr Cooper. 'Twenty-six. And awkward little buggers to make out, some of them.'

'Got anything for me yet?' Michelle took out her notebook.

'A little bit. As you can see, we're still trying to put him back together again.'

'Him?'

'Oh, yes. You can take my word for that. The skull and pubis bear it out. Northern European, too, I'd say.' She turned the skull sideways. 'See that straight facial profile, the narrow nasal aperture? All signs. There are others, of course: the high cranium, the eye sockets. But you don't want a lesson in ethnic anthropology, do you?'

'I suppose not,' said Michelle, who actually found the subject quite interesting. Sometimes she thought she might have chosen the wrong career and should instead have become an anthropologist. Or perhaps a doctor. 'Not very tall, though, is he?'

Dr Cooper looked at the bones laid out on the steel trolley. 'Tall enough for his age, I'd say.'

'Don't tell me you know his age.'

'Of course. Only a rough guess, mind you. By measuring the long bones and applying the appropriate formula, and by simple measuring tape here on the table, we've calculated his height at around five foot six. That's somewhere between a hundred and sixty-seven and a hundred and sixty-eight centimetres.'

'A kid, then?'

Dr Cooper nodded and touched the shoulder with her pen. 'The medial clavicular epiphysis – collarbone to you – is the last epiphysis in the body to fuse, normally in the mid-twenties, though it can occur any time between fifteen and thirty-two. His hasn't fused yet. I've also examined the rib ends and vertebrae. In an older person, you'd expect not only signs of wear and tear, but sharper ends and more scalloping on the ribs. His rib ends are flat and smoothly rounded, only slightly undulating, and the vertebrae show no epiphyseal rings at all. Also the fusion of ilium, ischium and pubis is in its early stages. That process usually takes place between the ages of twelve and seventeen.'

'So you're saying he's how old?'

'In my business it doesn't pay to go out on a limb, but I'll say between twelve and fifteen. Allow a couple of years either way as a fair margin of error. The databases we get these figures from aren't always complete and sometimes they're out of date.'

'That's amazing. Anything else?'

'The teeth. Of course, you'll have to bring in the odontologist to examine the roots and check the levels of fluoride, if there is any – it wasn't introduced in toothpaste here until 1959 – but I can tell you three things right now. First off, there are no deciduous teeth left – that's baby teeth – and the second molar has erupted. That means he's aged around twelve, again give or take a couple of years, and I'd hazard a guess, given the other evidence, that he's older rather than younger.'

'And the third thing?'

'A bit less scientific, I'm afraid, but judging by the general state of his teeth and the look of all these metal fillings in the posterior teeth I'd guess vintage school dentist.'

'How long ago was he buried there?'

'Impossible to say. There's no remaining soft tissue or ligaments, the bones are discoloured and there's some flaking, so I'd say more than a decade or two, but beyond that it's anyone's guess until I've done more rigorous tests.'

'Any sign of cause of death?'

'Not yet. I need to get the bones cleaned up. Sometimes you can't see knife marks, for example, because of the encrusted dirt.'

'What about that hole in the skull?'

Dr Cooper ran her finger around the jagged hole. 'Must have occurred during excavation. It's definitely post mortem.'

'How can you tell?'

'If it had happened before death, there'd be signs of healing. This is a clean break.'

'But what if it was the *cause* of death?'

Dr Cooper sighed as if she were talking to a dense undergraduate. Michelle noticed David Roberts grin, and he blushed when he saw her watching him. 'If that were the case,' the doctor went on, 'you'd expect a very different shape. Fresh bones break in a different way from old bones. And look at that.' She pointed to the hole. 'What do you see?'

Michelle peered closely. 'The edges,' she said. 'They're not the same colour as the surrounding bone.'

'Very good. That means it's a recent break. If it had happened around the time of death, you'd expect the edges to have stained the same colour as the rest of the skull, wouldn't you?'

'I suppose so,' said Michelle. 'Simple, isn't it?'

'If you know what you're looking for. There's a fractured humerus, too, right arm, but that's healed, so I'd say it happened while he was alive. And do you see this?' She pointed to the left arm. 'It's slightly longer than his right arm, which may indicate left-handedness. Of course, it could be due to the fracture, but I doubt it. There are differences in the scapulae that also support my hypothesis.'

Michelle made some notes, then turned back to Dr Cooper. 'We know he was most likely buried where he was found,' she said, 'because the remains were about three or four feet underground, but is there any way of knowing whether he died there or was moved there later?'

Dr Cooper shook her head. 'Any evidence of that was destroyed in the same way the skull and some of the other bones were damaged. By the bulldozer.'

'Where's the stuff we found with the body?'

Dr Cooper gestured towards the bench that ran the length of the far wall and turned back to the bones. David Roberts spoke for the first time. He had a habit of keeping his head down when he spoke to Michelle, and of mumbling, so she couldn't always hear what he was saying. He seemed embarrassed in her presence, as if he fancied her. She knew that her combination of blonde hair and green eyes had a captivating effect on some men, but this was ridiculous. Michelle had just turned forty and David couldn't be more than twenty-two.

She followed him over to the bench, where he pointed to a number of barely recognizable objects. 'We can't say for certain that they're his,' he said, 'but all these were gathered within a short radius of the body.' When she looked more closely, Michelle thought she could make out scraps of material, perhaps fragments of clothing, a belt buckle, coins, a penknife, a round-edged triangular shape, shoe leather, lace eyelets, and several round objects. 'What are those?' she asked.

'Marbles.' David rubbed one of them with a cloth and handed it to her.

It felt smooth to Michelle's touch, and inside the heavy glass sphere was a double helix of blue. 'Summer, then,' she said, almost to herself.

'Beg your pardon?'

She looked up at David. 'Oh, sorry. I said summer. Boys usually played marbles in summer. Outdoors, when the weather was good. What about the coins?'

'A few pennies, half a crown, sixpence, a threepenny bit.'

'All old coinage?'

'Before decimalization, at any rate.'

'So that's pre-1971.' She picked up the small triangular object. 'What's this?'

David polished away some of the grime and revealed a tortoiseshell pattern. 'I think it's a plectrum,' he said. 'You know, for a guitar.'

'A musician, then?' Michelle picked up a chain bracelet of some sort, crusted and corroded, with a flat, elongated oval at its centre and something written on it.

Dr Cooper came over. 'Yes, I thought that was interesting,' she said. 'You know what it is?'

'A bracelet of some kind?'

'Yes. I think it's an identity bracelet. They became very popular with teenage boys during the mid-sixties. I remember my brother had one. David was able to clean this one up a bit. All the silver plating's gone, of course, but luckily the engraver's drill went deep into the alloy underneath. You can read part of the name if you look very closely. Here, use this.' She passed Michelle a magnifying glass. Michelle looked through it and was able to make out the faint edges of some of the engraved letters: GR–HA–. That was all.

'Graham, I'd guess,' said Dr Cooper.

Michelle looked at the collection of bones, trying to imagine the warm, living, breathing human being that they had once formed. A boy. '*Graham*,' she whispered. 'Pity he didn't have his last name engraved, too. It'd make our job a lot simpler.'

Dr Cooper put her hands on her ample hips and laughed. 'To be honest, my dear,' she said, 'I don't think you can have it much simpler than this, can you? If I'm right so far, you're looking for a left-handed boy named Graham, aged between say twelve and fifteen, who once broke his upper right arm and went missing at least twenty or thirty years ago, maybe in summer. Oh, and he played marbles and the guitar. Am I forgetting anything? I'll bet there can't be too many matching that description in your files.'

●

Banks walked down the hill and through the village's winding streets at about seven every evening. He loved the quality of the light at that time of day, the way the small white houses with their colourful wooden steps seemed to glow, and the flowers – a profusion of purple, pink and red – seemed incandescent. The scent of gardenia mingled with thyme and oregano. Below him, the wine-dark sea stretched all the way back to the mainland, just as it had done in Homer's day. Although it wasn't exactly *wine* dark, Banks noticed. Not all of it, anyway. Some of the areas closer to land were deep blue or green, and it only darkened to the purple of a young Greek wine much further out.

One or two of the shopkeepers greeted him as he passed. He had been on the island for a little over two weeks now, which was longer than most tourists stayed, and while he wasn't *accepted* his presence was at least acknowledged. It was much the same as in a Yorkshire village, where you remain an incomer until you have wintered out several years. Maybe he *would* stay here that long, learn the language, become a mysterious hermit, merge into the rhythms of island life. He even looked a bit Greek, with his lean frame, closely cropped black hair and tanned skin.

He picked up the two-day-old English newspapers that came on the last boat of the day and carried them with him to Philippe's quayside taverna, where he spent most of his evenings at an outside table overlooking the harbour. He would have an ouzo as an aperitif, make his mind up about what to eat, then drink retsina with dinner. He found that he had come to enjoy the odd, oily taste of the local resinated wine.

Banks lit a cigarette and watched the tourists getting into the launch that would take them back to their cruise ship and the evening's entertainment: probably Cheryl from Cheadle Hulme dancing the dance of the seven veils, or a group of Beatles' imitators from Heckmondwike. Tomorrow they would disembark on a new island, where they would buy overpriced trinkets and take photographs they wouldn't look at more than once. A group of German tourists, who must have been staying overnight at one of the island's few small hotels, took a table at the other side of the patio and ordered beer. They were the only other people sitting outside.

Banks sipped ouzo and nibbled on some olives and dolmades as he settled on fish à la Grecque and a green salad for dinner. The last of the tourists had returned to the cruise ship, and as soon as he had cleared away his stock Alex would come by to play chess. In the meantime, Banks turned to the newspapers.

His attention was caught by an article on the bottom right of the front page, headed, DNA CONFIRMS IDENTITY OF LONG-BURIED BODY. Intrigued, Banks read on:

A week ago the skeleton of a young boy was unearthed by workers digging the foundations of a new shopping centre next to the A1 west of Peterborough, Cambridgeshire. Information discovered at the scene and provided by forensic anthropologist Dr Wendy Cooper led to a very narrow list of possibilities. 'It was almost a gift,' Dr Cooper told our reporter. 'Usually old bones don't tell you so much, but in this case we knew early on that he was a young boy who had broken his right arm once and was most likely left-handed.' An identity bracelet, popular with teenage boys in the mid-sixties, was found near the scene and bore part of a name. Detective Inspector Michelle Hart of the Cambridgeshire Constabulary commented, 'Dr Cooper gave us a lot to work with. It was simply a matter of going through the files, narrowing the possibilities.' When police came up with one strong candidate, Graham Marshall, the boy's parents were approached for DNA samples, and the testing proved positive. 'It's a relief to know they've found our Graham after all these years,' said Mrs Marshall at her home. 'Even though we lived in hope.' Graham Marshall disappeared on Sunday, 22 August 1965, at the age of fourteen while walking his regular newspaper round near his council-estate home in Peterborough. No trace of him has ever been found until now. 'The police at the time exhausted every possible lead,' DI Hart told our reporter, 'but there's always a chance that this discovery will bring new clues.' Asked if there was likely to be a new investigation into the case, DI Hart would only state that, 'Missing persons are never written off until they are found, and if there's the possibility of foul play, then justice must be pursued.' As yet, there are no clear indications of cause of death, though Dr Cooper did point out that the boy could hardly bury himself under three feet of earth.

Banks felt his stomach clench. He put the paper down and stared out to sea, where the setting sun was sprinkling rose dust over the horizon. Everything around him began to shimmer and feel unreal. As if on cue, the tape of Greek music came to 'Zorba's Dance', as it did every night. The taverna, the harbour, the brittle laughter all seemed to vanish into the distance, and there was only Banks with his memories and the stark words in the newspaper.

'Alan? What is it you say: a penny for them?'

Banks looked up and saw the dark, squat figure of Alex standing over him. 'Alex. Sorry. Good to see you. Sit down.'

Alex sat, looking concerned. 'You look as if you've had bad news.'

'You could say that.' Banks lit a cigarette and stared out over the darkening sea. He could smell salt and a whiff of dead fish. Alex gestured to Andrea, and in moments a bottle of ouzo appeared on the table in front of them, along with another plate of olives and dolmades. Philippe lit the lanterns that hung around the outside patio and they swayed in the breeze, casting fleeting shadows over the tables. Alex took out his portable chess set from its leather bag and arranged the pieces.

Banks knew that Alex wouldn't press him. It was one of the things he liked about his new friend. Alex had been born on the island and after university in Athens had travelled the world as an executive for a Greek shipping line, before deciding to pack it all in ten years ago at the age of forty. Now he made a living from tooling leather belts, which he sold to tourists on the quayside. Alex was an extremely cultured man, Banks had soon discovered, with a passion for Greek art and architecture, and his English was almost perfect. He also possessed what seemed to Banks a very deep-rooted sense of himself and a content-ment with the simple life which Banks wished he could attain. Of course, he hadn't told Alex what *he* did for a living, merely that he was a civil servant. He had found that telling strangers you met on holiday you were a policeman tended to put them off. Either that or they had a mystery for you to solve, the way people always seem to have strange ailments to ask about when they are introduced to doctors.

'Perhaps it's not a good idea tonight,' Alex said, and Banks noticed he was putting the chess set away. It had always been a mere backdrop to conversation, anyway, as neither man was a skilled player.

'I'm sorry,' said Banks. 'I just don't seem to be in the mood. I'd only lose.'

'You usually do. But it's all right, my friend. Clearly there is something troubling you.' Alex stood to leave, but Banks reached out and touched his arm. Oddly enough, he *wanted* to tell someone. 'No, stay,' he said, pouring them both a generous glass of ouzo. Alex looked at him for a moment with those serious brown eyes and sat down again.

'When I was fourteen,' said Banks, looking out at the lights in the harbour and listening to the stays on the fishing boats rattle, 'a close schoolfriend of mine disappeared. He was never seen again. Nobody ever found out what happened to him. Not a trace.' He smiled and turned to look at Alex. 'It's funny because this music seemed to be playing constantly back then: "Zorba's Dance". It was a big hit in England at the time. Marcello Minerbi. Funny the little things you remember, isn't it?'

Alex nodded. 'Memory is indeed a mysterious process.'

'And often not to be trusted.'

'True, it seems that as things lie there they are . . . strangely metamorphosed.'

'A lovely Greek word, *metamorphosed*.'

'It is. One thinks of Ovid, of course.'

'But it happens to the past, doesn't it? To our memories.'

'Yes.'

'Anyway,' Banks went on, 'there was a general assumption at the time that my friend, Graham was his name, had been abducted by a paedophile – another Greek word, but not so lovely – and done away with.'

'It seems a reasonable assumption, given life in the

cities. But might he not have simply run away from home?'

'That was another theory, but he had no reason to, as far as anyone knew. He was happy enough, and he never talked about running off. Anyway,' Banks went on, 'all attempts to find him failed and he never turned up again. The thing is, about two months earlier I was playing down by the river when a man came and grabbed me and tried to push me in.'

'What happened?'

'I was wiry and slippery enough to wriggle my way free and run off.'

'But you never told the authorities?'

'I never even told my parents.'

'Why not?'

'You know what kids are like, Alex. I wasn't meant to be playing down there, for a start. It was quite a long way from home. I was also playing truant. I was supposed to be at school. And I suppose I blamed myself. I just didn't want to get into trouble.'

Alex poured more ouzo. 'So, when your friend disappeared, you assumed it was the same man?'

'Yes.'

'And you've been carrying the guilt all these years?'

'I suppose so. I never really thought about it, that way, but every once in a while, when I think about it I feel . . . it's like an old wound that never quite heals. I don't know. I think it was partly why I—'

'Why you what?'

'Never mind.'

'Why you became a policeman?'

Banks looked at him in astonishment. 'How did you know?'

Alex was smiling. 'I've met a few in my time. You get to recognize the signs.'

'Like what?'

'Oh, watchfulness, curiosity, a certain way of walking and sitting. Little things.'

Banks laughed. 'By the sound of it, you'd make a pretty good policeman yourself, Alex.'

'Oh, no. I think not.'

'Why?'

'I don't think I could ever be certain that I was on the right side.'

'And are you now?'

'I try to be.'

'So do I,' said Banks.

'I'm sure you are a good policeman. You must remember, though, in Greece . . . well, we've had our share of regimes. But please go on.'

Banks tapped the folded newspaper. 'They've found him,' he said. 'Buried by the roadside about eight miles away from where he disappeared.'

Alex whistled between his teeth.

'They don't know the cause of death yet,' Banks went on, 'but he couldn't have got there by himself.'

'So perhaps the assumptions were right?'

'Yes.'

'And that makes you feel bad all over again, does it?'

'Terrible. What if I was responsible, Alex? What if it *was* the same man? If I'd spoken up—'

'Even if you had reported what happened, it doesn't mean he would have been caught. These men can be very clever, as I'm sure you have learned over the years.' Alex shook his head. 'But I'm not foolish enough to believe that one can talk a man out of his guilt when he's set on feeling it. Do you believe in fate?'

'I don't know.'

'We Greeks are great believers in fate, in destiny.'

'What does it matter, anyway?'

'Because it exonerates you. Don't you see? It's like the Catholic Church absolving you of sin. If it's fate, then you were meant to survive and not tell anyone, and your friend was destined to be abducted and killed and his body discovered many years later.'

'Then I *don't* believe in fate.'

'Well, it was worth a try,' said Alex. 'What are you going to do?'

'I don't know. There's nothing I can do, really, is there? The local police will investigate, and they'll either find out what happened or they won't. My bet is that after all these years they won't.'

Alex said nothing for a moment, just toyed with his ouzo glass, then he took a long sip and sighed.

'What?' said Banks.

'I have a feeling I'm going to miss you, my friend.'

'Why? I'm not going anywhere.'

'You know the Germans occupied this island during the war?'

'Of course,' said Banks, surprised by Alex's abrupt change of subject. 'I've explored the old fortifications. You know I have. We talked about it. It wasn't exactly *The Guns of Navarone*, but I was impressed.'

Alex waved his hand in a dismissive gesture. 'You and I can only imagine what life was like under the Nazi occupation,' he said, 'but my father lived through it. He once told me a story about when he was a boy, not much older than you and your friends were. The German officer in command of the island was called von Braun, and everyone thought he must have been an incompetent bastard to be sent somewhere like this. As you say, my friend, not exactly *The Guns of Navarone*, not exactly the most strategic position in the Mediterranean. Nevertheless, someone had to keep an eye on the populace, and von Braun was the man. It wasn't a very exacting task, and I'm sure the soldiers posted here became very sloppy.

'One day, my father and three of his friends stole a German jeep. The roads are bad, as you can see even now, and they couldn't drive, of course, and knew nothing beyond the rudiments, so they crashed into a boulder after they'd barely gone half a mile. Luckily, they were uninjured and ran away before the soldiers were alerted to what had happened, though apparently one soldier saw them and told von Braun there were four kids.' Alex paused and lit one of his Turkish cigarettes. Banks had once questioned him on the political correctness of a Greek smoking Turkish tobacco, but all he'd said was that it tasted better.

'Anyway,' Alex went on, expelling a plume of smoke, 'whatever the reason, von Braun took it upon himself to seek retribution, make an example, in the same way the Nazis did in many occupied villages. He probably wanted to prove that he wasn't just some soft, incompetent idiot sent to the middle of nowhere to keep him out of harm's way. He rounded up four teenage boys – the same number the soldier had counted – and had them shot just over there.' Alex pointed to where the main street met the quayside. 'Two of them had actually been involved; the other two were innocent. None of them was my father.'

The German tourists laughed at something one of the

women had said and called Andrea to order more beer. They were already pretty drunk in Banks's opinion, and there's not much worse than a drunken German, unless it's a drunken English football fan.

Alex ignored them and went on. 'My father was guilt-stricken for not speaking up, as was his friend, but what could they have done? The Nazis would probably have shot them in addition to the four others they had chosen. It was what the Americans call a no-win situation. He carried that shame and that guilt with him all his life.'

'Is he still alive?'

'He's been dead for years now. But the point is von Braun was one of the minor war criminals tried after the war, and do you know what? My father *went to the trial.* He'd never left the island before in his life, except for one visit to Athens to have his appendix removed, but he *had to go.* To bear witness.'

Banks felt oppressed by Alex's story and the weight of history, felt as if there was nothing he could say that would not be inappropriately light. Finally, he found his voice. 'Are you trying to tell me you think I ought to go back?'

Alex looked at him and smiled sadly. 'I'm not the one who thinks you ought to go back.'

'Ah, shit.' Banks lit a cigarette and tilted the ouzo bottle again. It was nearly empty.

'Am I right?' Alex persisted.

Banks looked out at the sea, dark now, twisting the lights reflected on its shimmering surface, and nodded. There was nothing he could do tonight, of course, but Alex was right; he *would* have to go. He had been carrying his guilty secret around for so long now that it had become a part of him, and he could no more put the discovery of Graham Marshall's bones out of his mind than he could all the other things he had thought he'd left behind: Sandra and her pregnancy, Annie Cabbot, the Job.

He watched a pair of young lovers, arms around one another, stroll along the quayside and felt terribly sad because he knew it was all over now, this brief sojourn in paradise, knew that this would be the last time he and Alex spent a companionable evening together in the Greek warmth, with the waves lapping against the ancient stone quay and the smell of Turkish tobacco and salt and rosemary in the air. He knew that tomorrow he had to go down to the harbour early, take the morning ferry to Piraeus and get on the first flight home. And he wished to hell he didn't.

2

Up in Yorkshire, two days later, the sky was far from cloudless, and the sun was definitely not shining. It had not, in fact, shone since Banks had left for Greece, reflected Detective Inspector Annie Cabbot as she pushed yet another pile of paperwork aside and put her feet up on the desk. It was as if the bugger had gone and taken all the sunshine with him. Nothing but cold rain, grey skies, and more rain. And this was August. Where was summer?

Annie had to admit that she missed Banks. She had ended their romantic relationship, but there was no one else in her life, and she enjoyed his company and his professional insight. In her weaker moments, too, she sometimes wished they had managed to remain lovers, but it wasn't a valid option, given his family baggage and her renewed interest in her career. Too many complications involved in sleeping with the boss. On the plus side, she had found far more time for her painting and had started meditation and yoga again.

Not that she couldn't understand *why* Banks had gone. The poor sod had simply had enough. He needed to recharge his batteries, gird his loins before he entered the fray once more. A month should do it, Assistant Chief Constable Ron McLaughlin had agreed, and Banks had more than enough accrued leave for that. So he had buggered off to Greece, taking the sunshine with him. Lucky sod.

At least Banks's temporary absence meant a quick transfer for Annie from Complaints and Discipline back to CID at the rank of detective inspector, which was what she had been angling for. She didn't have her own office any more, however, only a semi-partitioned corner in the detectives' squad room along with DS Hatchley and six DCs, including Winsome Jackman, Kevin Templeton and Gavin Rickerd, but it was worth the sacrifice to be away from that fat sexist lecher Detective Superintendent Chambers, not to mention a welcome change from the kind of dirty jobs she had been given under his command.

There hadn't been much more crime than sun in the Western Division lately, either, except in Harrogate of all places, where a mysterious epidemic of egg throwing had broken out. Youths seemed to have taken to throwing eggs at passing cars, old folk's windows and even at police stations. But that was Harrogate, not Eastvale. Which was why Annie, bored with looking over reports, mission statements, circulars and cost-cutting proposals, perked her ears up when she heard the tapping of Detective Superintendent Gristhorpe's walking stick approaching the office door. She took her feet off the desk, as much so that Gristhorpe wouldn't notice her red suede ankle boots as anything else, tucked her wavy chestnut hair behind her ears and pretended to be buried deep in paperwork.

Gristhorpe walked over to her desk. He'd lost quite a bit of weight since he shattered his ankle, but he still looked robust enough. Even so, rumour had it that he had been heard to broach the subject of retirement. 'Owt on, Annie?' he asked.

Annie gestured to the papers strewn over her desk. 'Not a lot.'

'Only there's this boy gone missing. Schoolboy, aged fifteen.'

'How long ago?'

'Didn't come home last night.' Gristhorpe put the misper report in front of her. 'Parents have been calling us since yesterday evening.'

Annie raised her eyebrows. 'A bit soon to bring us in on it, isn't it, sir? Kids go missing all the time. Fifteen year olds in particular.'

Gristhorpe scratched his chin. 'Not ones called Luke Armitage, they don't.'

'Luke Armitage? Not . . . '

'Aye. Martin Armitage's son. Stepson, to be accurate.'

'Oh, shit.' Martin Armitage was an ex-football player, who in his time had been one of the major strikers of the Premier League. Since retiring from professional sport, he had become something of a country gentleman. He lived with his wife and stepson Luke in Swainsdale Hall, a magnificent manor house perched on the daleside above Fortford. Armitage was known as a 'Champagne' socialist because he professed to have left-wing leanings, gave to charities, especially those supporting and promoting children's sporting activities, and chose to send his son to Eastvale Comprehensive instead of to a public school.

His wife, Robin Fetherling, had once been a celebrated model, well enough known in her field as Martin Armitage was in his, and her exploits, including drugs, wild parties and stormy public affairs with a variety of rock stars, had provided plenty of fodder twenty years ago or more, when Annie was a teenager. Robin Fetherling and Neil Byrd had been a hot item, the beautiful young couple of the moment, when Annie was at the University of Exeter. She had even listened to Neil Byrd's records in her student flat, but she hadn't heard his name, or his music, in years – hardly surprising, as she had neither the time nor the inclination to keep up with pop music these days. She remembered reading that Robin and Neil had had a baby out of wedlock about fifteen years ago. *Luke.* Then they split up, and Neil Byrd committed suicide while the child was still very young.

'Oh, shit, indeed,' said Gristhorpe. 'I'd not like to think we give better service to the rich and famous than to the poor, Annie, but perhaps you could go and try to set the parents at ease. The kid's probably gone gallivanting off with his mates, run away to London or something, but you know what people's imaginations can get up to.'

'Where did he disappear from, sir?'

'We don't know for certain. He'd been into town yesterday afternoon, and when he didn't come home for tea they started to get worried. At first they thought he might have met up with some mates, but when it got dark and he still wasn't home they started to get worried. By this morning they were frantic, of course. Turns out the lad carried a mobile with him, so they're sure he would have rung if anything came up.'

Annie frowned. 'That *does* sound odd. Have they tried ringing him?'

'No signal. They say his phone's switched off.'

Annie stood up and reached for her umbrella. 'I'll go over there and talk to them now.'

'And Annie?'

'Yes, sir?'

'You hardly need me to tell you this, but try to keep as low a profile as possible. The last thing we want is the local press on the case.'

'Softly, softly, sir.'

Gristhorpe nodded. 'Good.'

Annie walked towards the door.

'Nice boots,' said Gristhorpe from behind her.

•

Banks remembered the days surrounding Graham Marshall's disappearance more clearly than he remembered most days that long ago, he realized, as he closed his eyes and settled back in the airplane seat, though memory, he found, tended to take more of a cavalier view of the past than an accurate one; it conflated, condensed and transposed. It *metamorphosed*, as Alex had said last night.

Weeks, months, years were spread out in his mind's eye, but not necessarily in chronological order. The emotions and incidents might be easy enough to relocate and remember, but sometimes, as in police work, you have to rely on external evidence to reconstruct the true sequence. Whether he had got caught shoplifting in Woolworth's in 1963 or 1965, for example, he couldn't remember, though he recollected with absolute clarity the sense of fear and helplessness in that cramped triangular room under the escalator, the cloying smell of Old Spice aftershave and the way the two dark-suited shop detectives laughed as they pushed him about and made him empty his pockets. But when he thought about it more he remembered it was also the same day he had bought the brand-new *With the Beatles* LP, which was released in late November 1963.

And that was the way it often happened. Remember one small thing – a smell, a piece of music, the weather, a fragment of conversation – then scrutinize it, question it from every angle, and before you know it, there's another piece of information you thought you'd forgotten. And another. It didn't always work, but sometimes when he did this Banks ended up creating a film of his own past, a film which he was both watching and acting in at the same time. He could see what clothes he was wearing, knew what he was feeling, what people were saying, how warm or cold it was. Sometimes the sheer reality of the memory terrified him and he had to snap himself out of it in a cold sweat.

Just over a week after he had returned from a holiday in Blackpool with the Banks family, Graham Marshall had disappeared during his Sunday morning paper round out of Donald Bradford's newsagent's shop across the main road, a round he had been walking for about six months, and one that Banks himself had walked a year or so earlier, when Mr Thackeray owned the shop. At first, of course, nobody knew anything about what had happened apart from Mr and Mrs Marshall and the police.

As Banks leaned back in his seat and closed his eyes, he tried to reconstruct that Sunday. It would have started in the normal way. On weekends, Banks usually stayed in bed until lunchtime, when his mother called him down for the roast. During lunch they would listen to the radio comedies on the Light Programme: *The Navy Lark* and *Round the Horne*, probably repeats because it was summer, until *The Billy Cotton Band Show* drove Banks out of doors to meet up with his friends on the estate.

Sometimes, the five of them – Banks, Graham, Steve Hill, Paul Major and Dave Grenfell – would go to the local park, staking out an area of grass near the playing fields, and listen to Alan Freeman's *Pick of the Pops* on Paul's trannie, watching the girls walk by. Sometimes Steve would get bold and offer one of them a couple of

Woodbines to toss him off, but mostly they just watched and yearned from a distance.

Other Sundays they'd gather at Paul's and play records, which was what they did on the day Graham disappeared, Banks remembered. Paul's was best because he had a new Dansette, which he would bring outside on the steps if the weather was good. They didn't play the music too loudly, so nobody complained. If Paul's mum and dad were out, they'd sneak a cigarette or two as well. That Sunday everyone was there except Graham, and nobody knew why he was missing, unless his parents were keeping him in the house for some reason. They could be strict, Graham's parents, especially his dad. Still, whatever the reason, he wasn't there, and nobody thought too much of it.

There they would be, then, sitting on the steps, wearing their twelve-inch-bottom drainpipe trousers, tight-fitting shirts and winkle-pickers, hair about as long as they could grow it before their parents prescribed a trip to Mad Freddy's, the local barber's. No doubt they played other music, but the highlights of that day, Banks remembered, were Steve's pristine copy of the latest Bob Dylan LP, *Bringing It All Back Home*, and Banks's *Help!*

Along with his fascination for masturbation, Steve Hill had some rather way-out tastes in music. Other kids might like Sandie Shaw, Cliff Richard and Cilla Black, but for Steve it was the Animals, the Who and Bob Dylan. Banks and Graham were with him most of the way, although Banks also enjoyed some of the more traditional pop music, like Dusty Springfield and Gene Pitney, while Dave and Paul were more conservative, sticking with Roy Orbison and Elvis. Of course, everybody hated Val Doonican, Jim Reeves and the Bachelors.

That day, songs like 'Subterranean Homesick Blues' and 'Maggie's Farm' transported Banks to places he didn't know existed, and the mysterious love songs, 'Love Minus Zero/No Limit' and 'She Belongs to Me', lingered with him for days. Though Banks had to admit he didn't understand a word Dylan was singing about, there was something magical about the songs, even vaguely frightening, like a beautiful dream in which someone starts speaking gibberish. But perhaps that was hindsight. This was only the beginning. He didn't become a fully fledged Dylan fan until 'Like a Rolling Stone' knocked him for six a month or two later, and he wouldn't claim, even today, to know what Dylan was singing about half the time.

The girls from down the street walked by at one point, as they always did, very mod in their miniskirts and Mary Quant hairdos, all bobs, fringes and headbands, eye make-up laid on with a trowel, lips pale and pink, noses in the air. They were sixteen, far too old for Banks or his friends, and they all had eighteen-year-old boyfriends with Vespas or Lambrettas.

Dave left early, saying he had to go to his grandparents' house in Ely for tea, though Banks thought it was because Dylan was getting up his nose. Steve headed off a few minutes later, taking his LP with him. Banks couldn't remember the exact time, but he was certain that he and Paul were listening to 'Everyone's Gone to the Moon' when they saw the Ford Zephyr cruising down the street. It couldn't have been the first one, because Graham had been missing since morning, but it was the first one they saw. Paul pointed and started whistling the *Z Cars* theme music. Police cars weren't a novelty on the estate, but they were still rare enough visitors in those days to be noticed. The car stopped at number 58, Graham's house, and two uniformed officers got out and knocked on the door.

Banks remembered watching as Mrs Marshall opened the door, thin cardie wrapped around her, despite the warmth of day, and the two policemen took off their hats and followed her into the house. After that, nothing was ever quite the same on the estate.

Back in the twenty-first century, Banks opened his eyes and rubbed them. The memory had made him even more tired. He'd had a devil of a time getting to Athens the other day, and when he had got there it was only to find that he couldn't get a flight home until the following morning. He'd had to spend the night in a cheap hotel, and he hadn't slept well surrounded by the noise and bustle of a big city, after the peace and quiet of his island retreat.

Now the plane was flying up the Adriatic, between Italy and the former Yugoslavia. Banks was sitting on the left and the sky was so cloudless he fancied he could see all of Italy stretched out below him, greens and blues and earth colours, from the Adriatic to the Mediterranean: mountains, the crater of a volcano, vineyards, the cluster of a village and sprawl of a large city. Soon he would be landing back in Manchester, and soon the quest would begin in earnest. Graham Marshall's bones had been found, and Banks damn well wanted to know how and why they had ended up where they did.

•

Annie turned off the B road between Fortford and Relton onto the gravel drive of Swainsdale Hall. Elm, sycamore and ash dotted the landscape and obscured the view of the hall itself until the last curve, when it was revealed in all its splendour. Built of local limestone and millstone grit in the seventeenth century, the hall was a long, two-storey symmetrical stone building with a central chimneystack and stone-mullioned windows. The Dale's leading family, the Blackwoods, had lived there until they had died out in the way many old aristocratic families had died out: lack of money and no suitable heirs. Though Martin Armitage had bought the place for a song, so the stories went, the cost of upkeep was crippling, and Annie could see as she approached that parts of the flagstone roof were in a state of disrepair.

Annie parked in front of the hall and glanced through the slanting rain over the Dale. It was a magnificent view. Beyond the low hump of the earthworks in the lower field, an ancient Celtic defence against the invading Romans, she could see the entire green valley spread out before her, from the meandering River Swain all the way up the opposite side to the grey limestone scars, which seemed to grin like a skeleton's teeth. The dark, stubby ruins of Devraulx Abbey were visible about halfway up the opposite daleside, as was the village of Lyndgarth with its square church tower and smoke rising from chimneys over roofs darkened by the rain.

A dog barked inside the house as Annie approached the door. More of a cat person herself, she hated the way dogs rushed up when visitors arrived and barked and jumped at you, slobbered and sniffed your crotch, created chaos in the hall while the apologetic owner tried to control the animal's enthusiasm and explain how it really was just very friendly.

This time was no exception. However, the young woman who opened the door got a firm grip on the dog's collar before it could drool on Annie's skirt, and another woman appeared behind her. 'Miata!' she called out. 'Behave! Josie, would you take Miata to the scullery, please?'

'Yes, Ma'am.' Josie disappeared, half-dragging the frustrated Dobermann along with her.

'I'm sorry,' the woman said. 'She gets so excited when we have visitors. She's only being friendly.'

'Miata. Nice name,' said Annie and introduced herself.

'Thank you.' The woman held out her hand. 'I'm Robin Armitage. Please come in.'

Annie followed Robin down the hall and through a door on the right. The room was enormous, reminiscent of an old banqueting hall, with antique furniture scattered around a beautiful central Persian rug, a grand piano, and a stone fireplace bigger than Annie's entire cottage. On the wall over the mantelpiece hung what looked to Annie's trained eye like a genuine Matisse.

The man, who had been staring out of the back window over a lawn the size of a golf course, turned when Annie entered. Like his wife, he looked as if he hadn't slept all night. He introduced himself as Martin Armitage and shook her hand. His grip was firm and brief.

Martin Armitage was over six feet tall, handsome in a rugged, athletic sort of way, with his hair shaved almost to his skull, the way many footballers wore it. He was slim, long-legged and fit, as befitted an ex-sportsman, and even his casual clothes, jeans and a loose hand-knitted sweater, looked as if they cost more than Annie's monthly salary. He glanced down at Annie's boots, and she wished she'd gone for something more conservative that morning. But how was she to know?

'Detective Superintendent Gristhorpe told me about Luke,' Annie said.

'Yes.' Robin Armitage tried to smile, but it came out like the twentieth take of a commercial shoot. 'Look, I'll have Josie bring us some tea. Or coffee, if you'd prefer it?'

'Tea would be fine, thanks,' said Annie, perching carefully on the edge of an antique armchair. One of the most civilized things about being a policewoman, she thought, especially working in plainclothes, was that the people you visited – witnesses, victims and villains alike – invariably offered you some sort of refreshment. Usually tea. It was as English as fish and chips. From what she had read, or seen on television, she couldn't imagine anything like it happening anywhere else in the world. But, for all she knew, perhaps the French offered wine when a gendarme came to call.

'I know how upsetting something like this can be,' Annie began, 'but in ninety-nine per cent of cases there's absolutely nothing to worry about.'

Robin raised a finely plucked eyebrow. 'Do you mean that? You're not just saying it to make us feel better?'

'It's true. You'd be surprised how many mispers we get – sorry, that's police talk for missing persons – and most of them turn up none the worse for wear.'

'*Most* of them?' echoed Martin Armitage.

'I'm just telling you that statistically he's likely—'

'*Statistically?* What kind of—'

'Martin! Calm down. She's only trying to help.' Robin turned to Annie. 'I'm sorry,' she said, 'but neither of us has had much sleep. Luke's never done anything like this before, and we really are quite frantic with worry. Nothing short of seeing Luke back here safe and sound will change that. Please, tell us where you think he is.'

'I wish I could answer that, I really do,' said Annie. She

took out her notebook. 'Can I just get some information from you?'

Martin Armitage ran his hand over his head, sighed and flopped down on the sofa again. 'Yes, of course,' he said. 'And I apologize. My nerves are a bit frazzled, that's all.' When he looked right at her, she could see the concern in his eyes and she could also see the steely gaze of a man who usually got what he wanted. Josie came in with tea, which she served on a silver tray. Annie felt a bit embarrassed, the way she always did around servants.

Martin Armitage's lip curled in a smile, as if he had noticed her discomfort. 'A bit pretentious, isn't it?' he said. 'I suppose you're wondering why a dyed-in-the-wool socialist like me employs a maid? It's not as if I don't know how to make a cup of tea. I grew up with six brothers in a West Yorkshire mining town so small nobody even noticed when Maggie Thatcher wiped it off the face of the earth. Bread and dripping for breakfast, if you were lucky. That sort of thing. Robin here grew up on a small farm in Devon.'

And how many millions of pounds ago was that? Annie wondered, but she wasn't here to discuss their lifestyle. 'It's none of my business,' she said. 'I should imagine you're both very busy; you can use the help.' She paused. 'Just as long as you don't expect me to stick my little finger in the air while I drink my tea.'

Martin managed a weak laugh. 'I always like to dunk digestive biscuits in mine.' Then he leaned forward and became serious again. 'But you're not going to make me feel better by distracting me. What can we do? Where do we look? Where do we begin?'

'We'll do the looking. That's what we're here for. When did you first start to believe something was wrong?'

Martin looked at his wife. 'When was it, love? After tea, early evening?'

Robin nodded. 'He's always home for tea. When he wasn't back by after seven o'clock and we hadn't heard from him, we started to get worried.'

'What did you do?'

'We tried to call him on his mobile,' Martin said.

'And what happened?'

'It was switched off.'

'Then what?'

'Well, about eight o'clock,' Robin said, 'Martin went looking for him.'

'Where did you look, Mr Armitage?'

'I just drove around Eastvale. A bit aimless, really. But I had to do something. Robin stayed at home in case he rang or turned up.'

'How long were you gone?'

'Not long. I was back, oh, around ten.'

Robin nodded in agreement.

'Do you have a recent photograph of Luke?' Annie asked. 'Something we can circulate.'

Robin went over to one of the low polished tables and picked up a package of prints. She thumbed through them and handed one to Annie. 'This was taken at Easter. We took Luke to Paris for the holidays. Will it do?' Annie looked at the photograph. It showed a tall, thin young man, dark hair curling around his ears and brow, who looked older than his fifteen years, even to the point of having the fluffy beginnings of a goatee. He was standing by a grave in an old cemetery looking moody and contemplative, but his face was out of the shadows, and close enough to the camera to be useful for identification purposes.

'He insisted on visiting the Père Lachaise cemetery,' Robin explained. 'That's where all the famous people are buried. Chopin. Balzac. Proust. Edith Piaf. Colette. Luke's standing by Jim Morrison's grave there. Have you heard of Jim Morrison?'

'I've heard of him,' said Annie, who remembered friends of her father's playing loud Doors records even years after Morrison's death. 'Light My Fire' and 'The End' in particular had lodged themselves somewhere in her memories of those days.

'It's funny,' said Robin, 'but most of the people making pilgrimages to that grave weren't even born when he was at the height of his popularity. Even I was just a little girl when the Doors were first big.'

That placed her in her early forties, Annie guessed, and still a striking figure. Robin Armitage's golden tresses hung over her narrow shoulders and shone every bit as much in real life as they did in her magazine adverts for shampoo. Despite signs of strain and worry, hardly a line marred her smooth, pale complexion. Though Robin was shorter than Annie had imagined, her figure looked as slender as it had been in all the posters Annie had ever seen of her, and those lips, which had so tantalizingly sucked the low-fat ice cream off the spoon in a famous television commercial some years ago, were still as full and pink. Even the beauty spot Annie had always imagined was fake was still there at the corner of her mouth, and close up it looked real.

Yes, Robin Armitage looked every bit as good as she had twenty years ago. Annie thought she ought to hate the woman on sight, but she couldn't. It wasn't just because of the missing boy, either, she told herself, but she sensed something very human, very vulnerable, behind the exquisitely packaged model's facade.

'This'll do fine,' said Annie, slipping the photograph into her briefcase. 'I'll get it circulated as soon as I get back. What was he wearing?'

'The usual,' said Robin. 'Black T-shirt and black jeans.'

'You say "the usual". Do you mean he always wears black?'

'It's a phase,' said Martin Armitage. 'Or at least that's what his mother tells me.'

'It is, Martin. You wait; he'll grow out of it. If we ever see him again.'

'Don't worry, Mrs Armitage. He'll turn up. In the meantime, I'd like more information about Luke himself, anything you know about his friends, interests or acquaintances that could help us work out where he may be. First of all, was everything all right between you? Had there been any arguments recently?'

'Not that I can think of,' Robin answered. 'I mean, nothing serious. Everything was fine between us. Luke had everything he wanted.'

'It's been my experience,' said Annie, 'that nobody ever has everything they want, even if someone who loves them very dearly thinks they have. Human needs are so various and so hard to define at times.'

'I didn't only mean material things,' said Robin. 'As a matter of fact, Luke isn't much interested in the things money can buy, except for electronic gadgets and books.' Her long-lashed blue eyes blurred with tears. 'I meant that he has all the love we can give him.'

'I don't doubt it,' said Annie. 'What I was thinking though, was, maybe there was something he wanted to do that you wouldn't let him?'

'Like what?' asked Robin.

'Something you didn't approve of. A pop concert he wanted to go to. Friends you didn't like him being with. That sort of thing.'

'Oh, I see what you mean. But I can't think of anything. Can you, darling?'

Martin Armitage shook his head. 'As parents go, I think we're pretty liberal,' he said. 'We realize kids grow up quickly these days. I grew up quickly myself. And Luke's a smart lad. I can't think of any films I wouldn't want him to see, except for pornography, of course. He's also a quiet, shy sort of boy, not much of a mixer. He keeps to himself.'

'He's very creative,' Robin added. 'He loves to read and he writes stories and poems. When we were in France it was all Rimbaud, Verlaine and Baudelaire.'

Annie had heard of some of those poets through her father, had even read some of them. She thought they were a little advanced for a fifteen-year-old boy, then she remembered that Rimbaud started writing poetry at fifteen and gave it up at nineteen.

'What about girlfriends?' Annie asked.

'He never mentioned anyone,' said Robin.

'He might be embarrassed to tell you,' Annie suggested.

'I'm sure we'd have known.'

Annie changed tack and made a note to look into Luke's love life, or lack of it, later, if necessary. 'I don't know how to put this any more diplomatically,' she said, 'but I understand you're not Luke's biological father, Mr Armitage?'

'True. He's my stepson. But I've always thought of him as my own son. Robin and I have been married ten years now. Luke has our family name.'

'Tell me about Luke's father, Mrs Armitage.'

Robin glanced over at her husband.

'It's all right, darling,' Martin Armitage said. 'It doesn't bother me if you talk about him, though I can't quite see the point of all this.'

Robin turned back to Annie. 'Actually, I'm surprised you don't know already, given the inordinate amount of interest the gutter press took in the whole affair at the time. It's Neil Byrd. I thought most people knew about Neil and me.'

'Oh, I know who he was and what happened. I just don't remember the details. He was a pop singer, wasn't he?'

'A pop singer? He'd have been disgusted to hear himself called that. He thought of himself more as a sort of modern troubadour, more of a poet than anything else.'

From singer-songwriter to footballer, Annie thought, the way Marilyn Monroe went from baseball player to playwright. There was clearly more to Robin Armitage than met the eye. 'Please excuse my ignorance and refresh my memory,' she said.

Robin glanced out of the window, where a large thrush had found a worm on the lawn, then sat down beside her husband. He took her hand as she spoke. 'You're probably thinking it seems like an odd combination,' she said. 'But Neil was the first man not to treat me like a complete moron because of my looks. It's difficult being . . . well, you know, looking like I did. Most men are either too scared to approach you or they think you must be an easy lay. With Neil, it was neither.'

'How long were you together?'

'About five years. Luke was only two when Neil walked out on us. Just like that. No warning. He said he

40

needed his solitude and couldn't afford to be burdened with a family any longer. That's exactly the way he put it: *burdened*.'

'I'm sorry,' said Annie. 'What happened? What about your career?'

'I was twenty-five when we met, and I'd been modelling since I was fourteen. It was hard to get my figure back after Luke, of course, and I was never *quite* the same as before, but I still got work, mostly TV commercials, a small and very forgettable part in a slasher film, part fifteen of some series or other. But why do you need to know all this? It can't have anything to do with Luke's disappearance. Neil's been dead for twelve years.'

'I agree with my wife,' said Martin. 'As I said earlier, I can't see what relevance all this has.'

'I'm just trying to get as much background as I can,' Annie explained. 'You never know what might be important to missing persons, what might trigger them. Does Luke know who his father was?'

'Oh, yes. He doesn't remember Neil, of course, but I told him. I thought it important not to keep secrets from him.'

'How long has he known?'

'I told him when he was twelve.'

'And before that?'

'Martin is the only father he has known.'

So for seven years, Annie calculated, Luke had accepted Martin Armitage as his true father, then his mother had dropped the bombshell about Neil Byrd. 'How did he react to the news?' she asked.

'He was confused, naturally,' said Robin. 'And he asked a lot of questions. But other than that . . . I don't know. He didn't talk about it much afterwards.'

Annie made a couple of notes as she digested this. She thought there must be more to it than Robin let on, but perhaps not. Kids can be surprisingly resilient. And unexpectedly sensitive.

'Do you still have any contact with any of Neil Byrd's friends or relatives?' Annie asked.

'Good Lord, no. Neil's parents both died young – it was one of the things that haunted him – and I don't move in those sort of circles any more.'

'May I see Luke's room?'

'Of course.' Robin led Annie out into the hall, up a flight of worn stone stairs to the upper floor, where she turned to the left and opened the heavy oak door of the second room along.

Annie turned on the bedside light. It took her a few moments to register that the room was black except for the carpeted floor. It faced north, so it didn't get a lot of sun, and even with the bedside light on – there was no ceiling light – it looked gloomy. It was tidier than she had expected, though, and almost spartan in its contents.

Luke, or someone, had painted a solar system and stars on the ceiling. One wall was covered with posters of rock stars and, moving closer, Annie noted the names: Kurt Cobain, Nick Drake, Jeff Buckley, Ian Curtis, Jim Morrison. Most of them were at least vaguely familiar to her, but she thought Banks might know more about them than she did. No sports personalities, she noticed. On the opposite wall, written in silver spray-paint, were the words, 'Le Poëte se fait voyant par un long, immense et raisonné dérèglement de tous les sens.' The words rang a bell, but she couldn't quite place them, and her French wasn't good enough to provide her with a clear translation. 'Do you know what this means?' she asked.

'Sorry,' said Robin. 'I never was any good at French in school.'

Annie copied the words down in her notebook. An electric guitar stood propped against a small amplifier under the mullioned window, a computer sat on a desk, and next to the wardrobe was a mini stereo system and a stack of CDs. She opened the violin case on top of the dresser and saw that it did, indeed, contain a violin.

Annie flipped through the CDs. Most of the bands she'd never heard of, such as Incubus, System of a Down and Slipknot, but she recognized some oldies like Nirvana and REM. There was even some old Bob Dylan. Though Annie knew virtually nothing about the musical tastes of fifteen-year-old boys, she was certain they didn't usually include Bob Dylan.

There was nothing by Neil Byrd. Again, Annie wished Banks were here; he'd be able to read something into all this. The last CD she had bought consisted of chants by Tibetan monks, to help with her yoga and meditation.

Annie glanced at the contents of the bookcase: a lot of novels, including *Sons and Lovers*, *Catcher in the Rye* and *Le Grand Meaulnes*, alongside the more traditional adolescent fare of Philip Pullman and short-story collections by Ray Bradbury and H.P. Lovecraft, a number of poetry anthologies, an oversized book on Pre-Raphaelite art, and that was about it.

Other than that, the room revealed remarkably little. There was no address book, at least none that Annie could find, and not very much of anything except the books, clothes and CDs. Robin told her that Luke carried a battered leather shoulder bag around with him, wouldn't go anywhere without it, and anything important to him would be in there, including his ultra-light laptop.

Annie did find some printed manuscripts in a drawer, short stories and poems, the most recent of which was dated a year ago, and she asked if she could borrow them to look at later. She could tell that Robin wasn't keen, mostly, it seemed, for the sake of Luke's precious privacy, but again a little prodding in the right direction worked wonders. She didn't think the creative work would tell her much, anyway, but it might give her some insight into Luke's character.

There was nothing more to be gained from staying up there and the black walls were beginning to oppress her, so she told Robin she had finished. They went back downstairs, where Martin Armitage was still sitting on the sofa.

'I understand you sent Luke to Eastvale Comprehensive instead of a public school, like Braughtmore,' Annie said.

'We don't believe in public schools,' said Martin, his West Yorkshire accent getting thicker as he spoke. 'They're just breeding grounds for effete civil servants. There's nothing wrong with a comprehensive school education.' Then he paused and smiled. Annie got the impression it was a gesture that had worked for him often with the media, the sudden flow of charm turned on like an electric current. 'Well, maybe there's a lot wrong with it – at least that's what I keep hearing – but it was good enough for me, and it's good enough for most kids. Luke's intelligent and hard working. He'll do fine.'

Judging from her body language – the folded arms and lips pressed together – Annie surmised that Robin didn't agree, that Luke's education had been a matter of some heated discussion.

'Is he happy at school?' she asked.

'He's never complained,' said Martin. 'No more than

any kid would. You know, he doesn't like his geography teacher, doesn't like games, and algebra's too hard. That sort of thing.'

'He's not a sports fan?'

'Unfortunately, no,' said Martin. 'I've tried to get him interested, but . . .' He shrugged.

'What about the other boys at school? Even if he is, as you say, a bit of a loner, he must have *some* contact with his classmates?'

'I suppose so, but I've never seen any evidence of it.'

'He's never brought friends to the house?'

'Never.'

'Or asked permission to visit their houses.'

'No.'

'Does he go out a lot?'

'No more than any other boy his age,' said Martin. 'Maybe even less.'

'We want Luke to have a normal life,' said Robin. 'It's hard knowing what to allow and what not to. It's hard to know how much discipline to apply. If you don't give enough, then the child runs wild, and the parents get the blame. If you keep too strict control, he doesn't develop naturally and he blames you for screwing him up. We do our best to be good parents and strike a fair balance.'

Annie, an outsider herself at school because she was brought up in an artists' commune, the 'hippie chick' to the other kids, understood just how alienated Luke might feel, not through any fault of his parents. For a start, they lived in an out-of-the-way place like Swainsdale Hall, a grand place at that; secondly, they were minor celebrities; and thirdly, he sounded like an introverted personality anyway.

'I'm sure you do,' she said. 'What did he do yesterday?'

'He went into the town centre.'

'How did he get there?'

'Bus. There's a good service, at least until after teatime.'

'Did he have any particular reason to go to Eastvale yesterday?'

'Nothing in particular,' Robin answered. 'He just loves hunting for second-hand books, and he wanted to look at some new computer stuff.'

'That's all?'

'As far as I know. It was nothing out of the ordinary.'

'Has he ever stopped out all night before?'

'No,' said Robin, putting her hand to her throat. 'Never. That's why we're so worried. He wouldn't put us through this unless something . . . something awful's happened.'

She started to cry, and her husband held her, smoothing her silky, spun-gold hair. 'There, there, darling. Don't worry. They'll find him.' All the time his intense eyes were looking right at Annie, as if daring her to disagree. Not that she wanted to. A man used to having his own way. A man of action, too, Annie had no doubt, used to running ahead with the ball and slamming it into the back of the net.

'What about the rest of the family: uncles, aunts, grandparents?' she asked. 'Was he close to anybody in particular?'

'Robin's family's down in Devon,' said Martin. 'My parents are dead, but I've got a married sister living in Dorset and a brother in Cardiff. Of course, we rang everyone we could think of, but nobody's seen him.'

'Did he have any money with him?'

'Not much. A few pounds. Look, Inspector,' he said, 'I do appreciate your questions, but you're on the wrong track. Luke has his mobile. If he wanted to go somewhere or do something that meant he wouldn't be coming home, or that he'd be late, then why wouldn't he give us a buzz?'

'Unless it was something he didn't want you to know about.'

'But he's only *fifteen*,' said Martin. 'What on earth could he be up to that's so secret he wouldn't want his parents to know about it?'

Do you know where your children are? Do you know what your children are doing? It was Annie's experience, both through her own memories and as a policewoman, that there was *no one* more secretive than an adolescent, especially a sensitive, lonely adolescent, but Luke's parents just didn't seem to get this. Hadn't they been through it themselves? Or had so much else happened since their own childhoods that they had forgotten what it was like?

There were any number of reasons why Luke might have thought it necessary to go off for a while without telling his parents – children are often selfish and inconsiderate – but they couldn't seem to think of one. Still, it wasn't the first time Annie had come across such an astonishing gap between parental perception and reality. More often than she would have expected, she had found herself facing the parents of missing children who said they had simply no idea where young Sally could have gone or why she would want to go off anywhere and cause them such pain.

'Have there ever been any threats against you?' she asked.

'No,' said Martin. 'Why do you ask?'

'Celebrities often attract the wrong sort of attention.'

Martin snorted. 'We're hardly Beckham and Posh

Spice. We're not much in the public eye these days. Not for the past five years or so, since we moved here. We both keep a very low profile.'

'Did it cross your mind that someone might have thought Luke was worth kidnapping?' she asked.

'Despite what you think,' Martin said, 'we're actually not all that wealthy.' He gestured around. 'The house, for a start . . . it just eats up money. We'd be very poor marks for a kidnapper, believe me.'

'The kidnapper might not know that.'

Robin and Martin looked at one another. Finally Robin spoke. 'No, I don't think so. As I said, we always wanted Luke to have a normal life, not like mine. We didn't want him surrounded by bodyguards and security. Maybe it was foolish of us, unrealistic, but it's worked until now. Nothing bad ever happened to him.'

'And I'm sure nothing has now,' said Annie. 'Look, I realize it's probably second nature to you, but if anyone from the press comes around asking questions—'

'Don't worry,' said Martin Armitage. 'They'll have me to deal with.'

'Very good, sir. And just to be on the safe side, do you think we could arrange to have any phone calls intercepted?'

'But why?' asked Robin.

'In case of ransom demands.'

She put her hand to her cheek. 'But surely you don't think—'

'It's just a precaution.'

'It's an unlisted number,' Martin said.

'Even so.'

He held Annie's gaze for a few beats before nodding. 'Very well. If you must.'

'Thank you, sir. I'll arrange for the technician to drop by later this morning. Do you have a business office?'

'No,' said Martin. 'Not at the moment.'

'You don't have a business number?'

'No.' He paused, then went on as if he'd sensed an implied slight in Annie's tone or manner. 'Look, I might have been just a football player, but that doesn't mean I'm thick, you know.'

'I didn't—'

'I got my A levels, went to Leeds Polytechnic, as it was back then, and got a business diploma.'

So what did that make him? Annie wondered, unimpressed: the 'thinking woman's crumpet'? 'I didn't mean to imply anything,' she went on. 'I'm simply trying to make sure we've got every eventuality covered.'

'I'm sorry,' Martin said. 'It's been a stressful night. It's just, well, being who we are, Robin and I get that sort of thing a lot. People tend to patronize us.'

'I understand,' said Annie, standing up to leave. 'I won't keep you any longer.' She passed her card over to Robin, who was closer. 'My mobile number's on there, too.' She smiled and added, 'When you can reach it.' Cell-phone coverage was spotty in the Dales, to say the least. 'If you do hear anything at all, you won't hesitate to call me, will you?'

'No,' said Robin. 'Of course not. And if—'

'You'll be the first to hear. Don't worry, we'll be looking for him, I can assure you. We're really very good at this sort of thing.'

'If there's anything I can do—' said Martin.

'Of course.' Annie gave them her best, most confident smile and left, not feeling confident at all.

3

DI Michelle Hart locked up her dark grey Peugeot outside 58 Hazel Crescent and took measure of the neighbourhood. She'd been there twice before: once investigating a string of burglaries and another time because of vandalism. As council estates went these days, the Hazels, as the locals called it, wasn't particularly bad. Built in the early sixties before the 'new town' expansion, its terraces of serviceable brick houses behind low walls and privet hedges were now home to a mixed crowd of unemployed people, teenage mothers, pensioners who couldn't afford to move, and a growing Asian population, mostly from Pakistan or Bangladesh. There were even a few asylum seekers. Like every other estate, the Hazels also had its share of shiftless hooligans who took their greatest pleasure in vandalizing other people's property, stealing cars and spraying graffiti over the walls.

It was still raining, and there was no sign of any gaps in the grey cloud cover. The drab street that curved through the heart of the estate was empty, all the kids indoors playing computer games or surfing the web and their mothers wishing the sun would come out and bring a few moments' peace and quiet.

Michelle knocked on the dark green door. Mrs Marshall, a frail-looking woman, stooped and grey-haired, face lined with care, answered and led her into a small living room and bade her sit on a plum velour armchair.

Michelle had met the Marshalls before, during the identification process, but hadn't yet visited them at home.
Everything in the room was so tidy and spotless that she
felt a momentary twinge of guilt over her own unwashed
breakfast dishes, unmade bed and the dust balls in the
corner. Still, who was there to see them but her?

Bill Marshall, incapacitated by a stroke, looked at
Michelle, blanket over his knees, walking stick by his
side, slack-jawed, a little drool collecting at the corner of
his mouth, one half of his face drooping lower than the
other, as if it had melted like a Dalí watch. He had been a
big man, that much was obvious, but now his body had
withered with disease. His eyes were alive, though, the
whites a little cloudy, but the grey irises intense and
watchful. Michelle said hello to him and thought she saw
his head move just a fraction in greeting. Though he
couldn't speak, Mrs Marshall had assured Michelle that
he could understand everything they said.

Among the framed photographs on the mantelpiece
above the electric fire was one of a young boy, aged about
thirteen or fourteen, hair in a 'Beatle' cut popular in the
early sixties, wearing a black polo neck, standing on a
promenade with the sea in the background and a long pier
off to one side. He was a good-looking kid, Michelle
noticed, perhaps a little feminine, soft and delicate in his
features, but he'd probably have grown up to be a real
heartbreaker, nonetheless.

Mrs Marshall noticed her looking. 'Yes, that's our
Graham. It was taken on the last holiday he had. We
couldn't go away that year – Bill had a big job to finish –
so the Bankses took him to Blackpool with them. Their lad
Alan was a good mate of his. Mr Banks took that photo
and gave it to us when they came back.' She paused. 'No

more than a week or so later and Graham was gone for ever.'

'He looks like a fine boy,' Michelle said.

Mrs Marshall nodded and sniffed.

'I don't want to bother you for long,' Michelle began, 'but, as you can imagine, finding your son after all this time has come as a bit of a shock to us, too. I need to ask a few more questions, if that's all right?'

'You've got your job to do, love. Don't worry about us. We did our mourning years ago. Most of it, anyhow.' She fingered the collar of her dress. 'Funny, though, how it all just seems like it happened only yesterday, now you've found him.'

'I haven't seen the reports yet, but I understand there was a full investigation in 1965, when Graham first disappeared?'

'Oh, yes. And I can't fault them. They did their best. Searched high and low. Jet Harris himself was in charge, you know. At his wits' end he was when all their efforts turned up nothing. He even came to search our house for clues himself.'

Detective Superintendent John Harris – nicknamed Jet after both his speed and his resemblance to the Shadows' bass guitarist – was still a legend around divisional head-quarters. Even Michelle had read the small biographical pamphlet published by one of the local bobbies with a literary bent, and she had been impressed by it, from his lowly birth in the Glasgow slums in 1920, to his Distinguished Conduct Medal with the Royal Marines Commandos in the Second World War, his rise through the ranks to detective chief superintendent, and his legendary retirement party in 1985. His framed photograph hung on the wall near the front entrance, and his hallowed name was mentioned only with suitably hushed awe. Michelle could imagine how his failure to solve the Graham Marshall case must have galled him. Harris had a reputation not only for closing cases quickly, but for hanging on and not letting go until he got a conviction. Since his death from cancer eight years ago, he had become even more revered. 'It'll have been done properly, then,' she said. 'I don't know what to say. Sometimes one just slips through the cracks.'

'Don't apologize, love. I've got no complaints. They turned over every stone they could find, but who'd think to dig there, eight miles away? I mean, they could hardly dig up the whole county, could they?'

'I suppose not,' Michelle agreed.

'And there were those missing kids out Manchester way,' Mrs Marshall went on. 'What they later called the Moors Murders. It wasn't until a couple of months after our Graham disappeared, though, that Brady and Hindley got caught, and then it was all over the news, of course.'

Michelle knew about Ian Brady and Myra Hindley, the Moors Murderers, even though she had been only a child at the time. As with Jack the Ripper, Reginald Christie and the Yorkshire Ripper, the horror of their acts was etched into the consciousness of future generations. She hadn't realized, though, just how closely their crimes were linked chronologically with Graham Marshall's disappearance. It might have been natural for Detective Superintendent Harris at least to assume that Graham's disappearance could somehow be linked with the victims of Brady and Hindley. On the other hand, Peterborough was over a hundred and thirty miles from Manchester, and Brady and Hindley tended to stick to their own neck of the woods.

Before Michelle could formulate her next question,

another woman walked into the room. She bore a strong facial resemblance to the boy in the photograph – the same small, straight nose, oval chin and well-defined cheekbones – only the feminine aspects were even more enhanced in her. She wore her grey-streaked hair long, tied in a pony-tail, and was casually dressed in a dark blue T-shirt and jeans. She was a little too thin for comfort, or perhaps Michelle was jealous, always feeling herself to be five or ten pounds overweight, and the stress of recent events showed in her features, as it did in Mrs Marshall's.

'This is Joan, my daughter,' Mrs Marshall said.

Michelle stood and shook Joan's limp hand.

'She lives in Folkestone, teaches at a comprehensive school there,' Mrs Marshall added with obvious pride. 'She was going on her holidays, but when she heard . . . well, she wanted to be with us.'

'I understand,' said Michelle. 'Were you and Graham close, Joan?'

'As close as any brother and sister with two years between them can be in their teens,' said Joan, with a rueful smile. She sat on the floor in front of the television and crossed her legs. 'Actually, I'm not being fair. Graham wasn't like most other boys his age. He even bought me presents. He didn't tease me or torment me. If anything, he was very protective.'

'From what?'

'Sorry?'

'What did he have to protect you from?'

'Oh, I didn't mean anything in particular. You know, just in general. If anyone tried to bully me or anything like that.'

'Boys?'

'Well, I was only twelve when he disappeared, but yes,

there were a couple of over-amorous local lads he sent packing.'

'Was Graham a tough lad?'

'Not really,' said Mrs Marshall. 'Mind you, he never backed away from a fight. When we moved and he first went to school here, there was a bit of bullying – you know, the way they always like to test the new kid – but in his first week our Graham took on the school bully. He didn't win, but he put up a good fight, blacked an eye and bloodied a nose, so nobody bothered him after that.'

Michelle was wondering how difficult it would be for someone to abduct and murder Graham Marshall if he could put up a good fight. Might it have taken two people? Might he have been drugged or knocked unconscious first? Or was it someone he knew and went with willingly? 'You said you moved up here?' Michelle went on. 'Would that be from the East End?'

'It still shows, does it, after all these years? Once a cockney, always a cockney, I suppose. Not that I'm ashamed of it. Yes, we came from Bethnal Green. We moved around a fair bit because of Bill's work. He's a bricklayer. Or he was. We'd only been here a year or so when it happened. Graham had just finished third form at the local grammar school.'

'But you stayed on after.'

'Yes. There was plenty of work, what with the new town business. Plenty of building. And we like it here. It suits us.'

'Mrs Marshall,' said Michelle, 'I know it's a long time ago, but can you tell me what sort of things Graham was interested in?'

'Interested in? Oh, the usual boys' stuff. Football. Cricket. And pop music. He was pop music crazy. We've still got his old guitar upstairs. Practised chords for hours, he did. Mind you, he read a lot too. Graham was the sort of lad who could amuse himself. He didn't always need someone to entertain him. Loved to read about space. You know, science fiction, rockets to Mars, green-eyed monsters. Space mad, he was.' She looked at the photograph and a faraway expression came over her features. 'Just the day before he . . . well, there was some sort of rocket launch in America, and he was so excited, watching it on telly.'

'Did he have many friends?'

'He made quite a few around here,' Joan answered. She looked at her mother. 'Who was there, Mum?'

'Let me remember. There was the Banks lad, of course, they were very close, and David Grenfell and Paul Major. And Steven Hill. Some others, maybe, but those five all lived on the estate, so they'd walk to school together, play cricket or football on the rec, listen to music together, swap records. That sort of thing. Some of their parents still live here. Those who are still left alive, that is.'

'Was Graham a popular boy?'

'I'd say so, yes,' said Mrs Marshall. 'He had an easy-going nature. I can't see how he could possibly have offended anyone. I'm not saying he was perfect, mind you. He was a normal teenage lad and he had his fair share of high spirits.'

'Was he a bright lad?'

'He did well at school, didn't he, Mum?' said Joan.

'Yes. He'd have got to university easily, just like his sister.'

'What did he want to be when he grew up?'

'An astronaut or a pop star, but I'm sure he would have changed his mind about that. He was good at physics and chemistry. He'd probably have made a good teacher.' She paused. 'What's going to happen now, if you don't mind me asking, Miss Hart? I mean, it was all so long ago. Surely you don't think you can catch whoever did this? Not after all this time.'

'I don't know,' said Michelle. 'I certainly wouldn't want to make any rash promises. But when something like this happens, we do our best to go over the ground again and see if we can find something someone missed the first time around. A fresh pair of eyes. It works sometimes. But if I'm to be completely honest with you, I'd have to say we'll not be giving the case full priority in terms of manpower.'

'Believe me, love, there's plenty of crime going on around here now without you police spending your time digging up the past as well.' She paused. 'It's just that . . . well, I think I *would* like to know, even after all this time. I thought about it a lot the other day, when they came back with the DNA results and said it definitely was our Graham. I thought I'd got resigned that we'd never know, but now, well, I'm not so sure. I mean, if you can just find out what happened to him, and why . . .' She looked at her husband. 'I know he'd like his mind set at ease before . . . well, I'm sure you know what I mean.'

Michelle packed away her notebook in her briefcase. 'Yes, I think I know what you mean,' she said. 'And I promise I'll do my best.'

'There is one question I'd like to ask,' said Mrs Marshall.

'Yes?'

'Well, you know, the way things happened, we never . . . I mean, our Graham never had a proper funeral. Do you think we could do that? You know, the bones . . .'

Michelle thought for a moment. 'We might need them

for a few days longer,' she said, 'for tests and such like. But I don't see why not. Look, I'll talk to the forensic anthropologist. I'm sure she'll do her best to release the remains as soon as possible.'

'You do? Really? Oh, thank you so very much, Miss Hart. You don't know how much it means to us. Do you have any children of your own?'

Michelle felt herself tense up, the way she always did when people asked her that. Finally, she got the words out. 'No. No, I don't.'

Mrs Marshall saw her to the door. 'If there's anything more I can tell you,' she said, 'please don't hesitate to ask.'

'I won't,' said Michelle. 'Thank you.' And she walked down the path in the rain to her car taking deep breaths, shaken, flooded with memories she'd been blocking out, memories of Melissa and of Ted. Now Graham Marshall was more to her than just a pile of bones on a steel table; he was a bright, easy-going lad with a Beatle haircut who wanted to be an astronaut or a pop star. If only she could figure out where to begin.

•

Banks met Annie at the Woolpack, a quiet pub in the tiny village of Maltham, about halfway between Gratly and Harksmere. On his way home from Manchester airport, he had debated whether to call her and he decided in the end it would be a good idea. He wanted to talk to someone about what he had just learned, and Annie was the only person he had told about the incident with the pervert down by the river. It shocked him to realize that he hadn't even told his ex-wife Sandra, though they had been married for over twenty years.

It was drizzling when he pulled up in the market square car park shortly before nine o'clock. Annie's purple Astra was nowhere in sight. He obeyed the sign and stepped on the disinfectant pad before entering the pub. Though there hadn't been an outbreak near Maltham itself, incidences of foot-and-mouth disease had occurred in some of the surrounding areas, and as a consequence strict, sometimes unpopular, measures had been brought in by the Ministry. Many footpaths had been closed and access to the countryside limited. Also, as local farmers used the village pubs and shops, many of the owners had placed disinfectant mats on their doorsteps.

Maltham itself wasn't much of a place, though it did have a fine Norman church, and the Woolpack was one of those pubs that did good business mostly by virtue of its being on a busy road between tourist destinations. That meant most of the trade was transient and during the day, so the few grizzled locals who stood around the bar turned as one and gawped when Banks entered. They did that every time. One of them must have recognized him and said something, because in no time at all they turned back to their pints and ignored him. Banks bought a pint of Black Sheep bitter and a packet of cheese and onion crisps and sat down near the door, as far from the bar as he could get. A couple of the other tables were taken, tourists renting local cottages, by the looks of them. Poor sods, they'd be going out of their minds with no footpaths to walk.

Christ, it was a long way from Greece, Banks thought. Hard to believe that at this time just two nights ago he had been drinking ouzo and nibbling dolmades with Alex in Philippe's taverna. They had drunk well into the small hours, knowing it was to be their last evening together, telling stories and soaking up the scented warmth of the air and the rhythm of the sea lapping at the quayside beside them. In the morning, Banks had looked for Alex by the harbour to say goodbye as he caught the early ferry to Piraeus, but his friend was nowhere to be seen. Probably nursing his hangover, Banks had thought, aware of the pounding in his own head.

The door opened, the men gawped again – with a bit more interest this time – and Annie entered in tight jeans and a light blue sleeveless top, bag slung over her shoulder. She pecked Banks on the cheek and sat down. Smelling her delicate grapefruit-scented shampoo and soap, and aware of the vague outlines of her nipples under the thin cotton, Banks felt a momentary rush of desire for her, but he held himself in check. That part of their relationship was over; they had moved on to something different. Instead, he went back to the bar and bought her a pint.

'Look at that tan,' Annie said when he sat down again, her laugh lines crinkling. 'It's all right for some.'

'I'm sure you'll manage a week in Blackpool before summer's over,' said Banks.

'Dancing to the Wurlitzer in the Tower Ballroom? Donkey rides on the beach in the rain? Candyfloss on the prom and a kiss-me-quick hat? I can hardly wait.' She leaned over and patted his arm. 'It is good to see you again, Alan.'

'You, too.'

'So come on, then. Tell. How was Greece?'

'Magnificent. Magical. Paradisiacal.'

'Then what the bloody hell are you doing back in Yorkshire? You were hardly forthcoming on the phone.'

'Years of practice.'

Annie leaned back in her chair and stretched out her legs the way she did, crossing them at the slender ankles, where the thin gold chain hung, sipped some beer and almost purred. Banks had never met anyone else who could look so comfortable and at home in a hard chair.

'Anyway,' she said, 'you're looking well. Less stressed. Even half a holiday seems to have had some effect.'

Banks considered for a moment and decided that he did feel much better than he had when he left. 'It helped put things in perspective,' he said. 'And you?'

'Swimmingly. Thriving. The job's going well. I'm getting back into yoga and meditation. And I've been doing some painting again.'

'I kept you away from all that?'

Annie laughed. 'Well, it's not as if you twisted my arm, but when you've got as little time as people in our line of work have, then something has to go by the wayside.'

Banks was about to make a sarcastic reference to that something being him this time, but he bit his tongue. He wouldn't have done that two weeks ago. The holiday really must have done him good. 'Well,' he said, 'I'm glad you're happy. I mean it, Annie.'

Annie touched his hand. 'I know you do. Now what brings you back here in such a hurry? I hope it's not serious.'

'It is in a way.' Banks lit a cigarette and went on to explain about the discovery of Graham Marshall's bones.

Annie listened, frowning. When Banks had finished, she said, 'I can understand why you're concerned, but what can you do?'

'I don't know,' Banks said. 'Maybe nothing. If I were the local police, I wouldn't want me sticking my nose in, but when I heard, I just felt . . . I don't know. It was a big part of my adolescence, Annie, Graham just disappearing like that, and I suppose it's a big part of me now, always has been. I can't explain, but there it is. I told you about the man by the river, the one who tried to push me in?'

'Yes.'

'If it was him, then maybe I can help them find him, if he's still alive. I can remember what he looked like. Odds are there could be a photo on file.'

'And if it wasn't him? Is that it? Is this the guilt you talked about before?'

'Partly,' said Banks. 'I *should* have spoken up. But it's more than that. Even if it's nothing to do with the man by the river, *someone* killed Graham and buried his body. Maybe I can remember something, maybe there was something I missed at the time, being just a kid myself. If I can cast my mind back . . . Another?'

Annie looked at her glass. Half full. And she was driving. 'No,' she said. 'Not for me.'

'Don't worry,' said Banks, catching her anxious glance as he went to the bar. 'This'll be my last for the evening.'

'So when are you going down there?' Annie asked when he came back.

'First thing tomorrow morning.'

'And you're going to do what, exactly? Present yourself at the local nick and offer to help them solve their case?'

'Something like that. I haven't thought it out yet. It'll hardly be high priority with the locals. Anyway, surely they'll be interested in someone who was around at the time? They interviewed me back then, you know. I remember it clearly.'

'Well, you said yourself they won't exactly welcome you with open arms, not if you go as a copper trying to tell them how to do their jobs.'

'I'll practise humility.'

Annie laughed. 'You'd better be careful,' she said. 'They might have you down as a suspect.'

'It wouldn't surprise me.'

'Anyway, it's a pity you're not sticking around. We might be able to use your help up here.'

'Oh? What's on?'

'Missing kid.'

'Another?'

'This one disappeared a bit more recently than your friend Graham.'

'Boy or girl?'

'Does it matter?'

'You know it does, Annie. Far more girls are abducted, raped and killed than boys.'

'A boy.'

'How old?'

'Fifteen.'

That was almost Graham's age when he disappeared, Banks thought. 'Then the odds are good he'll turn up none the worse for wear,' he said, though Graham hadn't.

'That's what I told the parents.'

Banks sipped his beer. There were some compensations to being back in Yorkshire, he thought, looking around the quiet, cosy pub, hearing the rain patter on the windows, tasting the Black Sheep and watching Annie shift in her chair as she tried to phrase her concerns.

'He's an odd kid,' she said. 'Bit of a loner. Writes poetry. Doesn't like sports. His room is painted black.'

'What were the circumstances?'

Annie told him. 'And there's another thing.'

'What?'

'He's Luke Armitage.'

'Robin's boy? Neil Byrd's son?'

'Martin Armitage's stepson. Do you know him?'

'Martin Armitage? Hardly. Saw him play once or twice, though. I must say I thought he was overrated. But I've got a couple of CDs by Neil Byrd. They did a compilation three or four years ago, and they've just brought out a collection of out-takes and live performances. He really *was* very good, you know. Did you meet the supermodel?'

'Robin? Yes.'

'Quite the looker, as I remember.'

'Still is,' said Annie, scowling. 'If you like that sort of thing.'

'What sort of thing?'

'Oh, you know . . . skinny, flawless, beautiful.'

Banks grinned. 'So what's the problem?'

'Oh, nothing. It's just me. He'll probably turn up safe and sound.'

'But you're worried?'

'Just a teeny bit.'

'Kidnapping?'

'It crossed my mind, but there's been no ransom demand yet. We searched the house, of course, just in case, but there was no sign he'd been back home.'

'We did talk to the Armitages about security when they first moved to Swainsdale Hall, you know,' Banks said. 'They installed the usual burglar alarms and such, but beyond that they said they just wanted to live a normal life. Nothing much we could do.'

'I suppose not,' Annie agreed. She brought out her notebook and showed Banks the French words she had copied down from Luke's wall. 'Make any sense of this? It's awfully familiar, but I can't put my finger on it.'

Banks frowned as he peered at the text. It looked familiar to him, too, but he couldn't place it, either. 'Le Poëte se fait voyant par un long, immense et raisonné dérèglement de tous les sens.' He tried to decipher it word by word, reaching far back into his memory for his grammar-school French. Hard to believe now that he had been quite good at it at one time, even got a grade two in his O levels. Then he remembered. 'It's Rimbaud, I think. The French poet. Something about the total disordering of all the senses.'

'Of course!' said Annie. 'I could kick myself. Robin Armitage told me Luke was into Rimbaud, Baudelaire and Verlaine and all that stuff. What about these?' She named the subjects of Luke's posters. 'I mean, I've heard of some of them, Nick Drake, for example, and I know Kurt Cobain was in Nirvana and killed himself, but what about the others?'

Banks frowned. 'They're all singers. Ian Curtis used to sing with Joy Division. Jeff Buckley was Tim Buckley's son.'

'Used to? Was? There's an ominous past tense to all this, isn't there?'

'Oh, yes,' said Banks. 'They all either committed suicide or died under mysterious circumstances.'

'Interesting.' Annie's mobile buzzed. Excusing herself, she walked over to the front door before taking it out of her shoulder bag and stepping outside. When she came back two minutes later she looked puzzled.

'Not bad news, I hope?' said Banks.

'No, not at all. Quite the opposite.'

'Do tell.'

'That was Robin. Robin Armitage. Apparently, Luke just rang them.'

'And?'

'He says he just needed some space, that he'll be back home tomorrow.'

'Did he say where he was?'

'Wouldn't tell them.'

'What are you going to do?'

Annie finished her drink. 'I think I'd better go down the station, scale down the manhunt. You know how expensive these things are. I don't want Red Ron on my back for wasting our time and money.'

'Scale down?'

'Yes. Call me overly suspicious, if you like, but I'm not going to call off the search completely until I see Luke Armitage, safe and sound at home, with my own eyes.'

'I wouldn't call that overly suspicious,' said Banks. 'I'd call it very sensible.'

Annie leaned forward and pecked Banks on the cheek again. 'It really is good to see you again, Alan. Stay in touch.'

'I will,' said Banks, and he watched her walk out the door, hint of Body Shop grapefruit soap wafting behind her, the soft pressure of her kiss lingering on his cheek.

4

On the surface, it had seemed a simple enough question to ask: where were the Graham Marshall case files? In reality, it was like searching for the Holy Grail, and it had taken Michelle and her DC, Nat Collins, the best part of two days.

After first trying Bridge Street, in the city centre, which served as Divisional Headquarters until Thorpe Wood opened in 1979, Michelle and DC Collins drove from station to station all across the Northern Division – Bretton, Orton, Werrington, Yaxley, Hampton – discovering that some of them were relatively new, and the premises used in 1965 long since demolished and covered over by new housing estates or shopping centres. What complicated matters even more was that the original forces – Cambridge, Peterborough, Ely and Huntingdon – had amalgamated into the Mid-Anglia Constabulary in 1965, necessitating a major overhaul and restructuring, and had become the present-day Cambridgeshire Constabulary in 1974.

As one helpful duty constable after another suggested possibilities, Michelle had begun to despair of ever finding the old paperwork. About the only bright spot on the horizon was that the weather had improved that morning, and the sun was poking its lazy way through greasy rags of cloud. But that made the air humid, and Michelle was about to throw in the towel around lunchtime. She'd drunk a bit too much wine the previous evening, too – something that was happening rather too often these days – and the fact that she didn't feel a hundred per cent didn't help much either.

When she finally did track the paperwork down, having sent DC Collins to Cambridge to make enquiries there, she could have kicked herself. It was deep in the bowels of Divisional Headquarters, not more than thirty feet or so below her office, and the civilian records clerk, Mrs Metcalfe, proved to be a mine of information and let her sign out a couple of files. Why hadn't Michelle thought to look there in the first place? Easy. She had only been at Thorpe Wood for a short time, and no one had given her the grand tour; she didn't know that the basement was the repository for much of the county force's old paperwork.

The noise level was high in the open-plan squad room, phones ringing, men laughing at dirty jokes, doors opening and closing, but Michelle was able to shut it all out as she put on her reading glasses and opened the first folder, which contained maps and photos of the Hazels estate, along with a summary of any relevant witness statements that helped to pin down Graham's progress on the morning of 22 August 1965.

One useful hand-drawn map showed Graham's paper round in detail, listing all the houses he delivered to and, for good measure, what newspapers they took. The poor lad must have had a hell of a heavy load, as many of the Sunday papers were bulky with magazines and supplements.

At the eastern end of the estate, Wilmer Road separated the Hazels from an area of older houses, soon to be demolished. It was at the T-junction between Wilmer and

Hazel Crescent that Graham had delivered his last news-paper, a *News of the World*, to Mr and Mrs Halloran, who lived in the corner house.

The next delivery was supposed to be to one of the houses across the road, but the Lintons there said they never received their *Observer* that day. Nobody else on the other side of Wilmer Road received a newspaper that morning, either.

The anonymous map-maker had also calculated that it would have been around six-thirty a.m. when Graham, who started at six a.m., got to that part of his round – daylight at that time of year, but still very early in the morning for any sort of traffic, including pedestrian. It was a Sunday, after all, the traditional morning for a lie-in after the excesses of Saturday night, and most of the customers said they were still in bed when their papers arrived.

Michelle looked at the old black-and-white photos. They depicted a very different scene from the one she had visited yesterday, after she had talked to the Marshalls. In 1965, across Wilmer Road, there had been a grim row of old shops, all boarded up and ready for demolition, but today a modern DIY centre stood next to the new estate which had replaced the old houses. The derelict shops looked like just the sort of place a kid might want to explore. Michelle checked the file to see if they had been searched. Of course they had. Dogs brought in, too. Not a trace.

Michelle tucked some strands of blonde hair, which had been tickling her cheek, behind her ears and chewed at the end of her pen as she read over transcripts of the initial interviews. Nearly everything was typed, of course, except some of the documents that were handwritten, and the results looked strange, with the uneven pressure of the keys and the occasional blob of a deformed 'e' or 'g'. Such distinguishing features used to be very handy for identifying which machine a note had been typed on, Michelle reflected, before the anonymity of laser printers. Some of the papers were carbon copies, faint and often hard to read. Occasionally, illegible amendments had been made in pen or pencil between the lines, the original words scratched out. All in all, not a promising start.

Detective Superintendent Benjamin Shaw, now one of the senior officers at Thorpe Wood, was named once or twice as a detective constable on the case. Michelle knew that Shaw had started his career in Peterborough and had recently returned from six years with the Lincolnshire Constabulary, but it still surprised her to see his name in connection with something that happened so long ago. Maybe she should have a word with him, see if he had any theories that hadn't made it into the files.

It seemed that the first person to miss Graham Marshall was his employer, Donald Bradford, owner of the newsagent's shop. Bradford lived some distance away from the shop and employed a local woman to open up, not arriving himself until eight o'clock. According to Bradford's statement, when Graham hadn't returned by eight-fifteen that Sunday, half an hour late for his second round on a neighbouring estate, Bradford drove around the Wilmer Road Estate in search of him. He found nothing. Whatever had happened to Graham, his papers and his canvas bag were missing too. Michelle was willing to bet that some of those scraps of cloth found with the bones came from Graham's newspaper sack.

After that, Donald Bradford called at Graham's house to see if the lad had become ill and hurried home without stopping to report in. He hadn't. Graham's parents, now also worried, searched the estate for their son and found nothing. With news of the Manchester child abductions still fresh in the public eye, both Bradford and the Marshalls were soon concerned enough to call in the police, and a short while after that the official investigation began. Preliminary enquiries were carried out in the immediate area, and Detective Superintendent Harris was put in charge first thing the following day, when still no trace had been found of Graham, and the cumbersome but efficient mechanics of a police investigation groaned into action.

Michelle stretched and tried to work out a crick in her neck without success. It was hot in the office and her tights were killing her. DC Collins, just back from Cambridge, took pity on her and said, 'I'm just off to the canteen, Ma'am. Bring you anything?'

'I'd love a Diet Coke, please,' said Michelle. 'And maybe a slice of chocolate gateau, if they've got any left.' She reached for her handbag.

'It's all right,' said Collins. 'Pay me when I get back.'

Michelle thanked him, adjusted her tights as discreetly as possible below her desk and turned back to the files. As far as she could gather from a cursory glance, there hadn't been any leads at all. Police had interviewed everyone on Graham's round, along with all his friends, family and schoolteachers. None of it led anywhere. Graham was described, among other things, as being bright, cheeky, quiet, polite, rude, sweet-natured, foul-mouthed, talented and secretive. Which pretty much covered every eventuality.

Nobody on Wilmer Road had seen or heard anything unusual that morning – no screams, shouts or sounds of a struggle – though one person said he had heard a car door bang around half-past six. There were no convenient dog-walkers, and even the most devout of church-goers, being for the most part Methodists or low Anglican, were still in the Land of Nod. All the evidence, especially the missing newspaper sack, suggested that Graham had most likely got into a car willingly, with someone he knew, someone local. But who? And why?

DC Collins returned with Michelle's Diet Coke. 'No gateau, I'm afraid,' he said, 'so I brought you a Danish instead.'

'Thanks,' said Michelle, who didn't like Danish but paid him anyway, nibbled at it for a while then dropped the rest in her waste bin and went back to her files. The Coke tin was cold and wet, so she pressed it against her flushed cheek and enjoyed the icy sensation, then she did the same with her other cheek and her forehead.

The police at the time didn't neglect the possibility that Graham might have run away under his own steam, dumping the sack of papers somewhere and heading for the bright lights of London like so many young lads had in the mid-sixties, but they could find nothing at all to support this theory. His home life seemed happy enough, and none of his friends suggested that he was at all interested in running away from home. The sack was never found, either. Even so, missing persons reports went out all over the country, and there were the usual sightings, none of which amounted to anything.

The interviews also turned up nothing, and police checks into the records of several estate dwellers drew a blank. Michelle could read a little excitement between the lines when police discovered that one of the deliveries on Graham's route was to the house of a man who had served time for exposing himself in a local park, but subsequent interviews – no doubt involving some very rough business, knowing police methods of the time and Jet Harris's reputation as a tough guy – led nowhere, and the man was exonerated.

Michelle slipped off her reading glasses and rubbed her tired eyes. At first glance, she had to admit that it seemed very much as if Graham Marshall had disappeared into the void. But she knew one thing that the police hadn't known in 1965. She had seen his bones, and she knew that Graham had been murdered.

•

Annie Cabbot drove out to Swainsdale Hall mid-morning to tie up a few loose ends with the Armitages. The sun had come to the Yorkshire Dales at last, and wraiths of mist rose from the roadsides and the fields that stretched up the dalesides. The grass was bright green after so much rain, and the limestone walls and buildings shone clean grey. The view from the front of Swainsdale Hall was magnificent, and Annie could see plenty of blue sky beyond Fremlington Edge, with only a few light fluffy clouds scudding by on the breeze.

The Armitages must be relieved, Annie thought as she got out of her car. Of course, they would be happier when Luke arrived back home, but at least they knew he was safe.

Josie answered the door and seemed surprised to see her. There was no sign of Miata this time, but Annie could hear the dog barking from the back of the house.

'Sorry I didn't phone ahead,' Annie said. 'Are they in?'

Josie stood aside and let Annie walk through to the same large living room she had been in yesterday. Only

Robin Armitage was there this time, sitting on the sofa and flipping through a copy of *Vogue*. She jumped to her feet when Annie entered and smoothed down her skirt. 'It's you again. What's happened? Is something wrong?'

'Calm down, Mrs Armitage,' said Annie. 'Nothing's happened. I came to see if you're all right.'

'All right? Of course I am. Why shouldn't I be? Luke's coming home.'

'May I sit down?'

'Please.'

Annie sat, but Robin Armitage stayed on her feet, pacing. 'I'd have thought you'd be relieved,' Annie said.

'I am,' said Robin. 'Of course I am. It's just that . . . well, I'll be a lot more settled when Luke's back home again. I'm sure you understand.'

'Have you heard from him again?'

'No. Only the once.'

'And he definitely said he's coming home today?'

'Yes.'

'I'd like to talk to him when he gets back, if that's all right.'

'Certainly. But why?'

'We like to follow up on these matters. Just routine.'

Robin stood up and folded her arms, making it clear that she wanted Annie to leave. 'I'll let you know the minute he's back.'

Annie remained seated. 'Mrs Armitage, you told me yesterday that Luke said he needed some space. Do you know why?'

'Why?'

'Yes. You told me he's a normal teenager, and there's nothing wrong in the family, so why would he run off like that, worry the two of you half to death?'

'I hardly think that's relevant now, do you, Detective Inspector Cabbot?' Annie turned to see Martin Armitage standing in the doorway, briefcase in hand. 'Why are you here? What is it?' Despite his commanding presence, he seemed edgy to Annie, like his wife, shifting his weight from foot to foot as he stood there, as if he had to go to the toilet.

'Nothing,' she said. 'Just a friendly visit.'

'I see. Well, thank you for your efforts and your concern. We really do appreciate it, but I can see no point in your coming and badgering us with more questions now that Luke's safe and sound, can you?'

Interesting choice of words, *badgering*, Annie thought. Most families wouldn't see it that way, not with their son missing.

He glanced at his watch. 'Anyway, I'm afraid I have to hurry off to a business meeting. It's been nice to see you again, Inspector, and thank you again.'

'Yes, thank you,' echoed Robin.

Dismissed. Annie knew when she was beaten. 'I was just leaving,' she said. 'I only wanted to make sure everything was okay. I didn't mean to cause offence.'

'Well, as you can see,' said Martin, 'everything's fine. Luke will be back home this evening, and it will be as if none of this ever happened.'

Annie smiled. 'Well, don't be *too* hard on him.'

Martin managed a tight smile, which didn't reach his eyes. 'I was young once, myself, Detective Inspector Cabbot. I know what it's like.'

'Oh, just one more thing.' Annie paused in the doorway.

'Yes?'

'You said Luke rang you last night.'

'Yes. And immediately afterwards my wife rang you.'

Annie glanced at Robin, then back at Martin. 'Yes, I appreciate that,' she said, 'but I'm wondering why Luke's call wasn't intercepted. After all, the technician had set everything up, and we picked up your wife's call to me.'

'That's easy,' said Martin. 'He called me on my mobile.'

'Did he usually do that?'

'We were supposed to be going out for dinner,' Martin explained. 'As it was, we ended up cancelling, but Luke wasn't to know that.'

'Ah, I see,' said Annie. 'Problem solved. Goodbye, then.'

They both bade her a perfunctory goodbye and she left. At the end of the drive, she turned right, towards Relton, and parked in a lay-by just around the corner from the Armitages' drive, where she took out her mobile and discovered that there was, indeed, a signal in the area. So Martin Armitage hadn't been lying about that. What was it, then, that had given her the unmistakable feeling that something was wrong?

Annie sat for a moment in her car trying to figure out the meaning of the tension she had sensed in the room, not just between her and Robin, but between Robin and Martin. Something was going on; Annie only wished she knew what. Neither Robin nor Martin had behaved like a couple who had just heard that the son whose life they feared for was now safe and would soon be home.

When Martin Armitage's Beemer shot out of the driveway spraying gravel a minute or two later, Annie had an idea. It was rare that she got to think or act spontaneously, as so much police work was governed by procedure, rules and regulations, but Annie was feeling reckless this morning, and the situation called for some initiative on her part.

As far as she knew, Martin Armitage had no idea what make or colour car she drove, so he would hardly be suspicious that a purple Astra was following him at a respectable distance.

•

As Banks drove down the A1 and entered the landscape of bright new shopping centres, electronics warehouses and housing estates that had replaced the old coal mines, pit wheels and slag heaps of West Yorkshire, he thought about the way the country had changed since Graham's disappearance.

1965. Winston Churchill's funeral. The Wilson era. The end of capital punishment. The Kray trial. Carnaby Street. The Moors Murders. The first US space walk. *Help!* Mods and rockers. It was a time of possibility, of hope for the future, the fulcrum of the sixties. Only weeks after Graham disappeared, the sexy, leather-clad Emma Peel debuted in *The Avengers*, Jeremy Sandford's documentary-style TV play about a homeless mother and her children, *Cathy Come Home*, caused a major stir, and the Who were singing about 'My Generation'. Soon, young people were taking to the streets to protest against war, famine and anything else they could think of, shouting 'Make love, not war,' smoking dope and dropping acid. Everything seemed on the verge of blossoming into some new sort of order, and Graham, who had seemed so forward-looking, so *cool* in so many ways, should have been there to see it, but he wasn't.

And what came between then and Blair's Britain? Mostly Margaret Thatcher, who dismantled the country's manufacturing base, emasculated the trades unions, and demoralized the working man, leaving the north, especially, a ghost land of empty factories, thrift shops and decaying council estates, where those growing up had no hope of a job. In their idleness and hopelessness, many turned to crime and vandalism; car theft became commonplace; and the police became the enemy of the people. Today, without doubt, it was a softer, easier, more middle-of-the-road Britain, and a much more American one, with McDonald's, Pizza Huts and shopping malls springing up all over the place. Most people seemed to have what they wanted, but what they wanted was mostly of a material nature – a new car, a DVD player, a pair of Nike trainers – and people were being mugged, even murdered, for their mobile phones.

But were things so very different back in the mid-sixties? Banks asked himself. Wasn't consumerism just as rife back then? That Monday evening in August 1965, when the knock came at their door, the Banks family was settling down to watch *Coronation Street* on their brand-new television set, bought on hire purchase just the previous week. Banks's father was in work then, at the sheet-metal factory, and if anyone had predicted that he would be made redundant seventeen years later, he'd have laughed in their face.

Coronation Street was one of those rituals every Monday and Wednesday when, tea over, dishes washed and put away, homework and odd jobs done, the family sat down to watch television together. So it was an unexpected disruption when someone knocked at the door. No one *ever* did that. As far as the Bankses were concerned, *everyone* on the street – everyone they knew, at any rate – watched *Coronation Street* and would no more think of interrupting than . . . well, Ida Banks was lost for words. Arthur Banks answered the door, prepared to send the commercial traveller and his suitcase of goods packing.

The one thing that entered nobody's mind when he did this, because it was such a disturbance of the normal routine, was that Joey, Banks's pet budgie, was out of his cage, having his evening constitutional, and when Arthur Banks opened the front door to admit the two detectives, he left the living-room door open, too. Joey seized the moment and flew away. No doubt he thought he was flying to the freedom of the open sky, but Banks knew, even at his young age, that such a pretty coloured thing wouldn't survive a day among the winged predators out there. When they realized what had happened, everyone dashed out in the garden looking to see where he had gone, but there wasn't a trace. Joey had vanished, never to return.

More fuss might have been made over Joey's escape had the new visitors not become the centre of everyone's awed attention. They were the first plainclothes policemen ever to enter the Banks household, and even young Banks himself forgot about Joey for the time being. Looking back now, it seemed like some sort of ill omen to him, but at the time he hadn't seen any significance beyond the simple loss of a pet.

Both men wore suits and ties, Banks remembered, but no hats. One of them, the one who did most of the talking, was about the same age as his father, with slicked-back dark hair, a long nose, a general air of benevolence and a twinkle in his eye, the sort of kindly uncle who might slip you half a crown to go to the pictures and wink as he gave it to you. The other one was younger and more nondescript. Banks couldn't remember much about him at all except that he had ginger hair, freckles and sticking-out ears. Banks couldn't remember their names, if he had ever known them.

Banks's father turned off the television set. Nine-year-old Roy just sat and gawped at the men. Neither detective apologized for disturbing the family. They sat, but didn't relax, remaining perched on the edges of their chairs as the kindly uncle asked his questions and the other took notes. Banks couldn't remember the exact wording after so many years, but imagined it went along the following lines.

'You know why we're here, don't you?'

'It's about Graham, isn't it?'

'Yes. You were a friend of his, right?'

'Yes.'

'Do you have any idea where he might have gone?'

'No.'

'When did you see him last?'

'Saturday afternoon.'

'Did he say or do anything unusual?'

'No.'

'What did you do?'

'Went shopping in town.'

'What'd you buy?'

'Just some records.'

'What sort of a mood was Graham in?'

'Just ordinary.'

'Was anything bothering him?'

'He was just like normal.'

'Did he ever talk about running away from home?'

'No.'

'Any idea where he might go if he did run away? Did he talk about any particular places?'

'No. But he was from London. I mean, his parents brought him up from London last year.'

'We know that. We were just wondering if there was anywhere else he talked about.'

'I don't think so.'

'What about secret hiding places?' The detective winked. 'I know all lads have secret places.'

'No.' Banks was unwilling to tell them about the big tree in the park – holly, he thought it was – with prickly leaves and branches right down to the ground. If you made your way through them, you ended up hidden inside, between the thick leaves and the trunk, like being in a teepee. He knew Graham was missing and it was important, but he wasn't going to give away the gang's secrets. He would look in the tree himself later and make sure Graham wasn't there.

'Did Graham have any problems you were aware of? Was he upset about anything?'

'No.'

'School?'

'We're on holiday.'

'I know that, but I mean in general. It was a new school for him, wasn't it? He'd only been there one year. Did he have any problems with the other boys?'

'No, not really. He had a fight with Mick Slack, but he's just a bully. He picks fights with all the new kids.'

'That's all?'

'Yes.'

'Have you seen any strange men hanging around the area lately?'

'No.' Banks probably blushed as he lied. He certainly felt his cheeks burning.

'Nobody?'

'No.'

'Did Graham ever mention anyone bothering him?'

'No.'

'All right then, son, that's it for now. But if you can think of anything at all, you know where the police station is, don't you?'

'Yes.'

'And I'm sorry about your budgie, really I am.'

'Thank you.'

They seemed all set to go then and got to their feet. Just before they left, they asked Roy and Banks's parents a few general questions, and that was it. When they shut the door everyone was quiet. There were still ten minutes of *Coronation Street* left, but nobody thought of switching on the television set again. Banks remembered turning to Joey's empty cage and feeling the tears gather in his eyes.

•

Annie waited until Martin Armitage's Beemer had got a respectable distance ahead, then let a local delivery van get between them before she started to follow. The roads were quiet at that time in the morning – they were quiet most of the time, if truth be told – so she couldn't appear *too* conspicuous. At the village of Relton he turned right and followed the B road that ran about halfway up the valley-side.

They passed through tiny Mortsett, which didn't even have a pub or a general store, and Annie got stuck when the delivery van stopped to make a call at one of the cottages. The road wasn't wide enough for her to pass.

She got out and prepared to show her warrant card and ask the driver to get out of the way – there was a passing area about twenty yards further along – when she noticed

Armitage pull over and halt about half a mile beyond the village. She had a clear view of the open road, so she brought out the binoculars she kept in her glove compartment and watched him.

Armitage got out of the car with his briefcase, looked around and started walking over the grass towards a squat stone shepherd's shelter about eighty yards off the road, up the daleside, and she didn't think he was nervous because he was breaking the government foot-and-mouth regulations.

When he got there he ducked inside the shelter, and when he came out he wasn't carrying his briefcase. Annie watched him walk back to his car. He stumbled once over the uneven ground, then glanced around again and drove off in the direction of Gratly.

'Birds, is it?' a voice asked, disturbing Annie's concentration,

'What?' She turned to face the delivery man, a brash, gel-haired youngster with bad teeth.

'The binoculars,' he said. 'Bird-watching. Can't understand it, myself. Boring. Now, when it comes to the other sort of birds—'

Annie flipped him her warrant card and said, 'Move your van out of the way and let me pass.'

'All right, all right,' he said. 'No need to get shirty. There's no one home, anyway. Never is in this bloody godforsaken hole.'

He drove off and Annie got back into her car. Armitage was long gone by the time she reached the spot where he had stopped, and there were no other cars in sight, save the delivery van fast disappearing ahead.

Annie was the one who felt nervous now. Was someone watching her with binoculars the way she had watched Armitage? She hoped not. If this was what she thought it was, it wouldn't do to reveal police interest. The air was still and mild, and Annie could smell warm grass after rain. Somewhere in the distance a tractor chugged across a field, and sheep baaed from the daleside as she ignored the posted warnings and made her way to the shelter. The place smelled musty and acrid inside. Enough light spilled through the gaps in the drystone for her to see the used condom on the dirt, the empty cigarette packet and crushed lager cans. A local lad's idea of showing his girlfriend a good time, no doubt. She could also see the briefcase, the inexpensive, nylon kind.

Annie picked it up. It felt heavy. She opened the Velcro strips and inside, as she had expected, found stacks of money, mostly ten and twenty pound notes. She had no idea exactly how much there was, but guessed it must be somewhere in the region of ten or fifteen thousand pounds.

She put the briefcase back where it was and returned to her car. She couldn't just sit there by the roadside waiting for something to happen, but she couldn't very well leave the scene either. In the end, she drove back to Mortsett and parked. There was no police station in the tiny hamlet, and she knew it would be no use trying to use her UHF hand radio behind so many hills and at such a distance. Besides, it only had a range of a couple of miles. She was driving her own car, as she often did, and she hadn't got to having the more powerful VHF radio installed. It hardly seemed necessary, as she wasn't a patrol officer and, more often than not, she simply used the car to drive to work and back, and perhaps to interview witnesses, as she had done that morning. Before she headed out on foot to find a good spot from which to watch the shelter without being seen, Annie picked up her mobile to ring the station and let Detective Superintendent Gristhorpe know what was going on.

And, wouldn't you know it, the damn mobile didn't work. Out of range. Bloody typical. She should have known. She was quite close to Gratly, where Banks lived, and her mobile didn't work there either.

There was an old red telephone box in the village, but the phone had been vandalized, the wires torn from the cash box. *Damn!* Unwilling to take her eyes off the shelter for too long, Annie knocked on some doors, but the van driver had been right; nobody seemed to be home, and the one old lady who did answer said she didn't have a telephone.

Annie cursed under her breath; it looked as if she was on her own for the time being. She couldn't leave the shelter unwatched, and she had no idea how long she would have to stay out there. The sooner she found a good vantage point, the better. Still, she thought, turning towards the hillside, it served her bloody well right for not calling in *before* she followed Armitage. So much for initiative.

5

Nick Lowe's *The Convincer* ended and Banks slipped in David Gray's *White Ladder*. As he approached the turn-off to Peterborough, he wondered what to do first. He had rung his parents to let them know he was coming, of course, so perhaps he should go straight there. On the other hand, he was closer to police HQ, and the sooner he introduced himself to Detective Inspector Michelle Hart, the better. So he headed for the police station in its idyllic setting just off the Nene Parkway, between the nature reserve and the golf course.

In the reception area, he asked to speak to the detective in charge of the Graham Marshall investigation, introducing himself only as Alan Banks, a childhood friend. He didn't want to appear to be pulling rank or even introduce himself as a fellow copper, at least not at first, not until he saw which way the wind was blowing. Besides, just out of curiosity, he wanted to know how they treated an ordinary member of the public who came forward with information. It would do no harm to play a bit of a game.

After he had been waiting about ten minutes, a young woman opened the locked door that led to the main part of the station and beckoned him inside. Conservatively dressed in a navy blue suit, skirt below the knees, and a button-down white blouse, she was petite and slim, with shoulder-length blonde hair parted in the middle and tucked behind her small, delicate ears. She had a jagged fringe that came almost down to her eyes, which were a startling green, a colour Banks remembered seeing somewhere in the sea near Greece. Her mouth was slightly down-turned at the edges, which made her look a bit sad, and she had a small, straight nose. All in all, she was a very attractive woman, Banks thought, but he sensed a severity and a reserve in her – a definite 'No Entry' sign – and there was no mistaking the lines that suffering had etched around her haunting and haunted eyes.

'Mr Banks?' she said, raising her eyebrows.

Banks stood up. 'Yes.'

'I'm Detective Inspector Hart. Please follow me.' She led him to an interview room. It felt very strange being on the receiving end, Banks thought, and he got an inkling of the discomfort some of his interviewees must have felt. He looked around. Though it was a different county, the basics were still the same as in every interview room he had ever seen: table and chairs bolted to the floor, high window covered by a grille, institutional green paint on the walls, and that unforgettable smell of fear.

There was nothing to worry about, of course, but Banks couldn't help feeling just a little nervous as DI Hart put on her silver-rimmed, oval reading glasses and shuffled the papers around in front of her, as he had done many times himself, to draw out the tension and cause anxiety in the person sitting opposite. It touched the raw nerve of his childhood fear of authority, even though he knew he was authority, himself, now. Banks had always been aware of that irony, but a situation like this one really brought it home.

He also felt that DI Hart didn't need to act this way with him, that she was putting on too much of a show. His fault, perhaps, for not saying who he was, but even so, it was a bit heavy-handed to talk to him in an official interview room. He had come in voluntarily and he was neither a witness nor a suspect. She could have found an empty office and sent for coffee. But what would he have done? The same as her, probably; it was the us and them mentality, and in her mind he was a civilian. *Them.*

DI Hart stopped playing with her papers and broke the silence. 'So you say you can help with the Graham Marshall investigation?'

'Perhaps,' said Banks. 'I knew him.'

'Have you any idea at all what might have happened to him?'

'I'm afraid not,' said Banks. He had intended to tell her everything but found it wasn't as easy as that. Not yet. 'We just hung around together.'

'What was he like?'

'Graham? It's hard to say,' said Banks. 'I mean, you don't think about things like that when you're kids, do you?'

'Try now.'

'He was deep, I think. Quiet, at any rate. Most kids joked around, did stupid stuff, but Graham was always more serious, more reserved.' Banks remembered the small, almost secret smile as Graham had watched others act out comic routines – as if he didn't find them funny but knew he had to smile. 'You never felt you were fully privy to what was going on in his mind,' he added.

'You mean he kept secrets?'

'Don't we all?'

'What were his?'

'They wouldn't have been secrets if I knew them, would they? I'm just trying to give you some sense of what he was like. There was a secretive side to his nature.'

'Go on.'

She was becoming edgy, Banks thought. Rough day, probably, and not enough help. 'We did all the usual stuff together: played football and cricket, listened to music, talked about our favourite TV shows.'

'What about girlfriends?'

'Graham was a good-looking kid. The girls liked him, and he liked them, but I don't think he had anyone steady.'

'What kind of mischief did he get up to?'

'Well, I wouldn't want to incriminate myself, but we broke a window or two, did a bit of shoplifting, played truant, and we smoked cigarettes behind the cycle sheds at school. Pretty much normal stuff for teenagers back then. We didn't break into anyone's home, steal cars or mug old ladies.'

'Drugs?'

'This was 1965, for crying out loud.'

'Drugs were around back then.'

'How would you know? You probably weren't even born.'

Michelle reddened. 'I know King Harold got an arrow in his eye at the Battle of Hastings in 1066 and I wasn't born then.'

'Okay. Point taken. But drugs . . .? Not us, at any rate. Cigarettes were about the worst we did back then. Drugs may have been increasingly popular with the younger generation in London, but not with fourteen-year-old kids in a provincial backwater. Look, I should probably have done this before, but . . .' He reached into his inside pocket and took out his warrant card, laying it on the desk in front of her.

Michelle looked at it a minute, picked it up and looked

more closely, then slid it back across the desk to Banks. She took off her reading glasses and set them on the table. 'Prick,' she whispered.

'Come again?'

'You heard me. Why didn't you tell me from the start you were a DCI instead of playing games and stringing me along, making me feel like a complete fool?'

'Because I didn't want to give the impression I was trying to interfere. I'm simply here as someone who knew Graham. Besides, why did you have to come on so heavy-handed? I came here to volunteer information. There was no need to put me in an interview room and use the same tactics you use on a suspect. I'm surprised you didn't leave me here alone to stew for an hour.'

'You're making me wish I had.'

They glared at one another in silence for a few moments, then Banks said, 'Look, I'm sorry. I had no intention of making you feel foolish. And you don't need to. Why should you? It's true that I knew Graham. We were close friends at school. We lived on the same street. But this isn't my case, and I don't want you to think I'm pushing my nose in or anything. That's why I didn't announce myself at first. I'm sorry. You're right. I should have told you I was on the Job right from the start. Okay?'

Michelle gazed at him through narrowed eyes for a while, then twitched the corners of her lips in a brief smile and nodded. 'Your name came up when I was talking to his parents. I would have got in touch eventually.'

'The powers that be not exactly overwhelming you with assistance on this one, then?'

Michelle snorted. 'You could say that. One DC. It's not a high priority case, and I'm the new kid on the block. New *girl*.'

'I know what you mean,' Banks said. He remembered first meeting Annie Cabbot when she was put out to pasture at Harkside and he was in outer Siberia back in Eastvale. That hadn't been a high priority case to start with, either, but it had turned into one. He could sympathize with DI Hart.

'Anyway,' she went on, 'I didn't know you were a copper. I suppose I should call you "sir"? Rank and all?'

'Not necessary. I'm not one to stand on ceremony. Besides, I'm on your patch here. You're the boss. I do have a suggestion, though.'

'Oh?'

Banks looked at his watch. 'It's one o'clock. I drove down from Eastvale this morning without stopping and I haven't had a thing to eat. Why don't we get out of this depressing interview room and talk about Graham over lunch? I'll pay.'

Michelle raised on eyebrow. 'You're asking me out to lunch?'

'To discuss the case. Over lunch. Yes. Dammit, I'm hungry. Know any decent pubs around here?'

She gazed at him again, apparently appraising him for any imminent risk he might pose to her. When she couldn't seem to think of anything, she said, 'Okay. I know a place. Come on. But I'm paying my own way.'

•

What a stupid bloody decision it had been to take to the high ground, Annie Cabbot thought as she trudged illegally up the footpath, trying to avoid the little clusters of sheep droppings that seemed to be everywhere, and failing, as often as not. Her legs ached and she was panting with effort, even though she thought of herself as pretty fit.

She wasn't dressed for a walk in the country, either. Knowing she was visiting the Armitages again that morning, she had dressed in a skirt and blouse. She was even wearing tights. Not to mention the navy pumps that were crippling her. It was a hot day, and she could feel the sweat trickling along every available channel. Stray tresses of hair stuck to her cheeks and forehead.

As she climbed, she kept glancing behind her at the shepherd's shelter, but nobody approached it. She could only hope that she hadn't been spotted, that the kidnapper, if that was what this was all about, wasn't watching her through binoculars from a comfortable distance.

She found a spot she thought would do. It was a gentle dip in the daleside a few yards off the footpath. From there she could lie on her stomach and keep a close eye on the shelter without being seen from below.

Annie felt the warm, damp grass against her body, smelled its sweetness as she lay flat on her stomach, binoculars in hand. It felt good, and she wanted to take off all her clothes, feel the sun and earth on her bare skin, but she told herself not to be such a bloody fool and get on with the job. She compromised by taking off her jacket. The sun beat down on the back of her head and her shoulders. She had no suntan lotion with her, so she put the jacket over the back of her neck, even though it felt too hot. Better than getting sunstroke.

When she had got settled, there she lay. Waiting. Watching. Thoughts drifted through her head the way they did when she settled down to meditation, and she tried to practise the same technique of letting them go without dwelling on them. It started as a sort of free association, then went way beyond: sunlight; warmth;

skin; pigment; her father; Banks; music; Luke Armitage's black room; dead singers; secrets; kidnapping; murder.

Flies buzzed around her, snapping her out of the chain of association. She waved them away. At one point she felt a beetle or some insect creeping down the front of her bra and almost panicked, but she managed to get it off her before it got too far. A couple of curious rabbits approached, twitched their noses and turned away. Annie wondered if she would end up in Wonderland if she followed one.

She took long, deep breaths of grass-scented air. Time passed. An hour. Two. Three. Still nobody came to pick up the briefcase. Of course, the shepherd's shelter was off-limits because of foot and mouth, as was all open country-side, but that hadn't stopped Martin Armitage, and she was certain it wouldn't stop the kidnapper either. In fact, it was probably why the place had been chosen: little chance of anyone passing by. Most people in the area were law-abiding when it came to the restrictions, because they knew how much was at stake, and the tourists were staying away, taking their holidays abroad or in the cities instead. Normally, Annie obeyed the signs, too, but this was an emergency, and she knew she hadn't been anywhere near an infected area in weeks.

She wished she had something to eat and drink. It was long past lunchtime now, and she was starving. The heat was also making her thirsty. And there was something else, she realized, a more pressing urge: she needed to go to the toilet.

Well, she thought, looking around and seeing nothing but sheep in every direction, there's a simple remedy for that. She moved a few yards away from her flattened spot on the ground, checked for nettles and thistles, then took off her tights, squatted and peed. At least a woman could do that during surveillance in the countryside, Annie thought with a smile. It was a bit different if you were sitting cooped up in your car on a city street, as she had found out more than once in the past. Before she had finished, two low-flying jets from a nearby US airbase screamed over, seemingly no more than twenty feet or so from her head. She wondered if the pilots had got a good view. She gave them the finger, the way Americans did.

Back on her stomach, she tried her mobile again on the off-chance that it might just have been local interference before, but still no luck. The moor was a dead zone.

How long should she wait? she wondered. And why hadn't he come? The money was just lying there. What if he didn't come before nightfall and the lovers returned, more important things than foot-and-mouth on their minds? Several thousand quid as well as a quick bonk would be an unexpected bonus for them.

Her stomach rumbling, tongue dry against the roof of her mouth, Annie picked up the binoculars again and trained them on the shelter.

•

Michelle drove Banks to a pub she knew near the A1, wondering more than once on the way why she was doing this. But she knew the answer. She was bored with routine, bored first with tracking down the paperwork, and then bored with reading through it. She needed to get out, blow the cobwebs away, and this was the opportunity to do that and work as well.

She also had to admit that she was intrigued to meet someone who had been a friend of Graham Marshall's, especially as this Banks, despite a touch of grey in his closely cropped black hair, didn't look old enough. He was slim, perhaps stood three or four inches taller than her five foot five, had an angular face with lively blue eyes and a tan. He showed no great clothes sense but was dressed in basic Marks & Sparks casuals – light sports jacket, grey chinos, a blue denim shirt unbuttoned at the collar – and the look suited him. Some men his age only looked good in a business suit, Michelle thought. Anything else made them the male version of mutton dressed up as lamb. But on some older men casual looked natural. It did on Banks.

'Is it to be DI Hart, then?' Banks asked.

Michelle glanced sideways at him. 'I suppose you can call me Michelle, if you want.'

'Michelle it is, then. Nice name.'

Was he *flirting*? 'Come off it,' Michelle said.

'No, seriously. I mean it. No need to blush.'

Angry at herself for letting her embarrassment show, Michelle said, 'Just as long as you don't start singing the old Beatles song.'

'I never sing to a woman I've just met. Besides, I imagine you must have heard it many times.'

Michelle graced him with a smile. 'Too numerous to mention.'

The pub had parking at the back and a big freshly mown lawn with white tables and chairs where they could sit out in the sun. A couple of families were already there, settled in for the afternoon by the look of it, kids running around and playing on the swings and slide the pub provided in a small playground, but Michelle and Banks managed to find a quiet enough spot at the far end near the trees. Michelle watched the children play as Banks went inside to get the drinks. One of them was about six or seven, head covered in lovely golden curls, laughing unselfconsciously as she went higher on the swings. *Melissa*. Michelle felt as if her heart was breaking up inside her chest as she watched. It was a relief when Banks came back with a pint for himself and a shandy for her, and set two menus down on the table.

'What's up?' he asked. 'You look as if you've seen a ghost.'

'Maybe I have,' she said. 'Cheers.' They clinked glasses. Banks was diplomatic, she noted, curious about her mood, but sensitive and considerate enough to leave well enough alone and pretend to be studying the menu. Michelle liked that. She wasn't very hungry, but she ordered a prawn sandwich just to avoid being questioned about her lack of appetite. If truth be told, her stomach still felt sour from last night's wine. Banks was obviously ravenous, as he ordered a huge Yorkshire pudding filled with sausages and gravy.

When their orders were in, they sat back in their chairs and relaxed. They were in the shade of a beech tree, where it was still warm but out of the direct sunlight. Banks drank some beer and lit a cigarette. He looked in good shape, Michelle thought, for someone who smoked, drank and ate huge Yorkshire puddings and sausages. But how long would that last? If he really was Graham Marshall's contemporary, he'd be around fifty now, and wasn't that the age that men started worrying about their arteries and blood pressure, not to mention the prostate? Still, who was she to judge? True, she didn't smoke, but she drank too much and ate far too much junk food.

'So what else can you tell me about Graham Marshall?' she asked.

Banks drew on his cigarette and let the smoke out

slowly. He seemed to be enjoying it, Michelle thought, or was it a strategy he used to gain the upper hand in interviews? They all had some sort of strategy, even Michelle, though she would have been hard-pushed to define what it was. She thought herself quite direct. Finally, he answered, 'We were friends at school, and out of it too. He lived a few doors down the street, and for the year I knew him there was a small gang of us, who were pretty much inseparable.'

'David Grenfell, Paul Major, Steven Hill and you. I've only had time to track down and speak to David and Paul on the phone so far, though neither of them was able to tell me very much. Go on.'

'I haven't see any of them since I left for London when I was eighteen.'

'You only knew Graham for a year?'

'Yes. He was a new kid in our class the September before he disappeared, so it wasn't quite a full year even. His family had moved up from London that July or August, the way quite a lot of people were already doing then. This was before the huge influx; that came later in the sixties and the early seventies, the "new town" expansion. You probably weren't around then.'

'I certainly wasn't here.'

'Where, if you don't mind my asking?'

'I grew up in Hawick, border country. Spent most of my early police career with Greater Manchester, and since then I've been on the move. I've only been here a couple of months. Go on with your story.'

'That explains the accent.' Banks paused to sip beer and smoke again. 'I grew up here, a provincial kid. "Where my childhood was unspent." Graham seemed, I don't know, sort of cool, exotic, different. He was from

London, and that was where it was all happening. When you grow up in the provinces you feel everything's passing you by, happening somewhere else, and London was one of those "in" places back then, like San Francisco.'

'What do you mean by "cool"?'

Banks scratched the scar beside his right eye. Michelle wondered how he'd got it. 'I don't know. Not much fazed him. He never showed much emotion or reaction, and he seemed sort of worldly wise beyond his years. Don't get me wrong, though; Graham had his enthusiasms. He knew a lot about pop music, obscure B-sides and all that. He played guitar quite well. He was crazy about science fiction. And he had a Beatle haircut. My mother wouldn't let me have one. Short back and sides all the way.'

'But he was cool?'

'Yes. I don't know how to define the quality, really. How do you?'

'I think I know what you mean. I had a girlfriend like that. She was just like . . . oh, I don't know . . . someone who made you feel awkward, someone you wanted to emulate, perhaps. I'm not sure I can define it any more clearly.'

'No. Just *cool*, before it was even cool to be cool.'

'His mother said something about bullying.'

'Oh, that was just after he arrived. Mick Slack, the school bully. He had to try it on with everybody. Graham wasn't much of a fighter, but he didn't give up, and Slack never went near him again. Neither did anybody else. It was the only time I ever saw him fight.'

'I know it's hard to remember that far back,' said Michelle, 'but did you notice anything different about him towards the end?'

'No. He seemed much the same as always.'

'He went on holiday with you shortly before he disappeared, so his mother told me.'

'Yes. His parents couldn't go that year, so they let him come with us. It's good to have someone your own age to hang about with when you're away for a couple of weeks. It could get awfully boring with just parents and a younger brother.'

Michelle smiled. 'Younger sister, too. When did you last see Graham?'

'Just the day before he disappeared. Saturday.'

'What did you do?'

Banks gazed away into the trees before answering. 'Do? What we usually did on Saturdays. In the morning we went to the Palace, to the matinee. *Flash Gordon* or *Hopalong Cassidy*, a Three Stooges short.'

'And the afternoon?'

'In town. There was an electrical shop on Bridge Street that used to sell records. Long gone now. Three or four of us would sometimes crowd into one of those booths and smoke ourselves silly listening to the latest singles.'

'And that night?'

'Don't remember. I think I just stayed in watching TV. Saturday nights were good. *Juke Box Jury*, *Dr Who*, *Dixon of Dock Green*. Then there was *The Avengers*, but I don't think it was on that summer. I don't remember it, anyway.'

'Anything odd about the day at all? About Graham?'

'You know, for the life of me I can't remember anything unusual. I'm thinking perhaps I didn't know him very well, after all.'

Michelle was getting the strong impression that Banks *did* know something, that he was holding back. She didn't know why, but she was certain that was the case.

'Number twelve?' A young girl carrying two plates wandered into the garden.

Banks glanced at the number the bartender had given him. 'Over here,' he said.

She delivered the plates. Michelle gazed at her prawn sandwich, wondering if she'd be able to finish it. Banks tucked into his Yorkshire pudding and sausage for a while, then said, 'I used to do Graham's paper round before him, before the shop changed owners. It used to be Thackeray's until old man Thackeray got TB and let the business run into the ground. That's when Bradford bought the shop and built it up again.'

'But you didn't go back?'

'No. I'd got an after-school job at the mushroom farm down past the allotments. Filthy work, but it paid well, at least for back then.'

'Ever have any trouble on the paper round?'

'No. I was thinking about that on my way here, among other things.'

'No strangers ever invited you inside or anything?'

'There was one bloke who always seemed a bit weird at the time, though he was probably harmless.'

'Oh?' Michelle took out her notebook, prawn sandwich still untouched on the plate in front of her, now arousing the interest of a passing bluebottle.

Banks swatted the fly away. 'Better eat it soon,' he said.

'Who was this bloke you were talking about?'

'I can't remember the number, but it was near the end of Hazel Crescent, before you crossed Wilmer Road. Thing was, he was about the only one ever awake at that time, and I got the impression he hadn't even gone to bed. He'd open the door in his pyjamas and ask me to come in for a smoke or drink or whatever, but I always said no.'

'Why?'

Banks shrugged. 'Dunno. Instinct. Something about him. A smell, I don't know. Sometimes when you're a kid you've got a sort of sixth sense for danger. If you're lucky, it stays with you. Anyway, I'd already been well trained not to accept sweets from strange men, so I wasn't going to accept anything else, either.'

'Harry Chatham,' Michelle said.

'What?'

'That'll be Harry Chatham. Body odour, one of his characteristics.'

'You *have* done your homework.'

'He came under suspicion at the time, but he was eventually ruled out. You were right to stay away. He did have a history of exposing himself to young boys. Never went further than that, though.'

'They were sure?'

Michelle nodded. 'He was on holiday in Great Yarmouth. Didn't get back until that Sunday night. Plenty of witnesses. Jet Harris gave him the third degree, I should imagine.'

Banks smiled. '*Jet Harris*. Haven't heard his name in years. You know, when I was a kid growing up around there, it was always, "Better keep your nose clean or Jet Harris will get you and lock you up." We were terrified of him, though none of us had ever met him.'

Michelle laughed. 'It's still pretty much the same today,' she said.

'Surely he must be dead by now?'

'Eight years ago. But the legend lingers on.' She picked up her sandwich and took a bite. It was good. She realized she was hungry after all and had soon devoured the first half. 'Was there anything else?' Michelle asked.

She noticed Banks hesitate again. He had finished his Yorkshire pudding, and he reached for another cigarette. A temporary postponement. Funny, she'd seen the signs before in criminals she'd interviewed. This man definitely had something on his conscience, and he was debating whether to tell her or not. Michelle sensed that she couldn't hurry matters by pushing him, so she let him put the cigarette in his mouth and fiddle with his lighter for a few moments. And she waited.

•

Annie wished she hadn't given up smoking. At least it would have been something to do as she lay on her belly in the wet grass keeping an eye on the distant shepherd's shelter. She glanced at her watch and realized she had been lying there over four hours and nobody had come for the money.

Under her clothes, and the jacket protecting the back of her neck, Annie felt bathed in sweat. All she wanted to do was walk under a nice cool shower and luxuriate there for half an hour. But if she left her spot, what would happen? On the other hand, what would happen if she stayed there?

The kidnapper might turn up, but would Annie go running down the daleside to make an arrest? No, because Luke Armitage certainly wouldn't be with him. Would she have time to get to her car in Mortsett and follow whoever picked up the money? Possibly, but she would have a much better chance if she were already in the car.

In the end, Annie decided that she should go back down to Mortsett, still keeping an eye on the shelter, and

keep trying until she found someone home with a telephone, then sit in her car and watch from there until
relief came from Eastvale. She felt her bones ache as she
stood up and brushed the loose grass from her blouse.

It was a plan, and it beat lying around up here melting
in the sun.

●

Now that it was time to confess, Banks was finding it
more difficult than he had imagined. He knew he was
stalling, playing for time, when what he should do was
just come right out with it, but his mouth felt dry and the
words stuck in his throat. He sipped some beer. It didn't
help much. Sweat tickled the back of his neck and ran
down his spine.

'We were playing down by the river,' he said, 'not far
from the city centre. It wasn't developed quite as much as
it is today, so it was a pretty desolate stretch of water.'

'Who was playing with you?'

'Just Paul and Steve.'

'Go on.'

'It was nothing, really,' Banks said, embarrassed at how
slight the events that had haunted him for years now
seemed on this bright afternoon sitting under a beech tree
with an attractive woman. But there was no backing out
now. 'We were throwing stones in the water, skimming,
that sort of thing. Then we moved down the riverbank a
bit and found some bigger stones and bricks. We started
chucking those in to make a big splash. At least I did. Steve
and Paul were a bit further down. Anyway, I was holding
this big rock to my chest with both hands – it took all my
strength – when I noticed this tall, scruffy sort of bloke
walking along the riverbank towards me.'

'What did you do?'

'Held on to it,' said Banks. 'So I didn't splash him. Always the polite little bugger, I was. I remember smiling as he got nearer, you know, showing him I was holding off dropping the rock until he was out of range.' Banks paused and drew on his cigarette. 'Next thing I knew,' he went on, 'he'd grabbed hold of me from behind and I'd dropped the rock and splashed us both.'

'What happened? What did he do?'

'We struggled. I thought he was trying to push me in, but I managed to dig in my heels. I might not have been very big, but I was wiry and strong. I think my resistance surprised him. I remember smelling his sweat and I think he'd been drinking. Beer. I remembered smelling it on my father's breath when he came back from the pub sometimes.'

Michelle took her notebook out. 'Can you give me a description?'

'He had a ragged dark beard. His hair was greasy and long, longer than usual back then. It was black. Like Rasputin. And he wore one of those army greatcoats. I remember thinking when I saw him coming that he must be hot in such a heavy overcoat.'

'When was this?'

'Late June. It was a nice day, sort of like today.'

'So what happened?'

'He tried to drag me away, towards the bushes, but I managed to squirm out of his grasp, one arm at any rate, and he swung me around, swore at me and punched me in the face. The momentum broke me loose, so I ran.'

'Where were your friends?'

'Back up by the road by then. A good hundred yards away. Watching.'

'Didn't they help you?'

'They were scared.'

'They didn't call the police?'

'It all happened so fast. When I got free, I ran off and joined them and we never looked back. We decided not to say anything to our parents because we weren't supposed to be playing down by the river in the first place, and we were supposed to be at school. We thought we'd get into trouble.'

'I can imagine you did. What did your parents say about your face?'

'They weren't too pleased. I told them I'd got into a bit of a scrap at school. All in all, I suppose it was a lucky escape. I tried to put it out of my mind, but . . .'

'You couldn't?'

'Off and on. There's been lengthy periods of my life when I haven't thought of it at all.'

'Why do you see a connection with what happened to Graham?'

'It seemed too much of a coincidence, that's all,' said Banks. 'First this pervert trying to push me in the river, dragging me into the bushes, then Graham disappearing like that.'

'Well,' said Michelle, finishing her drink and closing her notebook, 'I'd better go and see if I can find any trace of your mystery man, hadn't I?'

6

Showered and dressed in crisp, clean clothes, Annie presented herself at Detective Superintendent Gristhorpe's office that afternoon, as requested. There was something austere and headmasterly about the room that always intimidated her. Partly, it was to do with the tall bookcases, mostly filled with legal and forensics texts, but dotted here and there with classics such as *Bleak House* and *Anna Karenina*, books Annie had never read, books that mocked her with their oft-mentioned titles and their thickness. And partly it was Gristhorpe's appearance: big, bulky, red-faced, unruly-haired, hook-nosed, pockmarked. Today he wore grey flannel trousers and a tweed jacket with elbow patches. He looked as if he ought to be smoking a pipe, but Annie knew he didn't smoke.

'Right,' said Gristhorpe after he had asked her to sit down. 'Now, tell me what the hell's going on out Mortsett way.'

Annie felt herself flush. 'It was a judgement call, sir.'

Gristhorpe waved his large, hairy hand. 'I'm not questioning your judgement. I want to know what you think is happening.'

Annie relaxed a little and crossed her legs. 'I think Luke Armitage has been kidnapped, sir. Someone communicated a ransom demand to the family last night, and Martin Armitage rang me to cancel the search for Luke.'

'But you didn't?'

'No, sir. Something wasn't right. In my opinion, Luke Armitage wasn't to be considered "found" until I'd seen him with my own eyes and talked to him.'

'Fair enough. What happened next?'

'As you know, sir, I went out to see the family again this morning. I got the distinct impression they didn't want me there, that something was going on.' Annie explained about following Martin Armitage to the drop and being stuck up the hillside watching the shelter by herself for hours, until she went back down to the village and finally found someone at home with a telephone.

'Do you think he saw you? The kidnapper.'

'It's possible,' Annie admitted. 'If he was hiding somewhere nearby and watching through binoculars. It's open country up there. But it's my impression that he'll either wait until nightfall—'

'And risk leaving the money out there all day?'

'It's off the beaten track. And most people follow the government regulations.'

'What else?'

'Pardon, sir.'

'You said "either". To me, that implies an "or". I interrupted you. Go on. What else do you think might have happened?'

'Maybe something has gone wrong, something we don't know about.'

'Like?'

Annie swallowed and looked away. 'Like Luke's dead, sir. It happens sometimes with kidnappings. He tried to escape, struggled too hard . . .'

'But the kidnapper can still collect. Remember, the Armitages can't possibly know their son's dead, if he is, and the money's just sitting there for the taking. If you weren't seen, then only Martin Armitage and the kidnapper know it's there.'

'That's what puzzles me, sir. The money. Obviously a kidnapper who makes a ransom demand is in it for the money, whether the victim lives or dies. Maybe he's just being unduly cautious, waiting for dark, as I suggested earlier.'

'Possibly.' Gristhorpe looked at his watch. 'Who's up there now?'

'DC Templeton, sir.'

'Organize a surveillance rota. I'll ask for permission to plant an electronic tracking device in the briefcase. Someone can put it there under cover of darkness, if the damn thing hasn't been picked up before then.' Gristhorpe grunted. 'Might as well be hanged for a sheep as a lamb. ACC McLaughlin will have my guts for garters.'

'You could always blame me, sir.'

'Aye, you'd like that wouldn't you, Annie, a chance to get bolshie with the bigwigs?'

'Sir—'

'It's all right, lass. I'm only teasing you. Haven't you learned Yorkshire ways yet?'

'Sometimes I despair that I ever will.'

'Give it a few more years. Anyway, that's my job. I can handle the brass.'

'What about the Armitages, sir?'

'I think you'd better pay them another visit, don't you?'

'But what if their place is being watched?'

'The kidnapper doesn't know you.' Gristhorpe smiled. 'And it's not as if you *look* like a plainclothes copper, Annie.'

'And I thought I'd put on my conservative best.'

'All you have to do is wear those red boots again. Are their telephone calls still being intercepted?'

'Yes, sir.'

'Then how the devil . . .?'

'The same thing puzzled me. Martin Armitage said the call from Luke came through on his mobile, so I'm assuming it was the kidnapper's call he was talking about.'

'But why wouldn't he just use the regular land line?'

'Armitage said he and Robin were supposed to go out to dinner that night, so Luke didn't think they'd be home.'

'He believed they would *still* go out to dinner, even after he'd disappeared? And he told his kidnapper this?'

'I know it sounds odd, sir. And in my judgement, Martin Armitage is the last person Luke would call.'

'Ah, I see. Signs of family tension?'

'All under the surface, but definitely there, I'd say. Luke's very much his mother's son, and his biological father's, perhaps. He's creative, artistic, a loner, a dreamer. Martin Armitage is a man of action, a sportsman, bit of a macho tough guy.'

'Go carefully then, Annie. You don't want to disturb a nest of vipers.'

'There might be no choice if I want honest answers to my questions.'

'Then tread softly and carry a big stick.'

'I'll do that.'

'And don't give up on the kid. It's early days yet.'

'Yes, sir,' Annie said, though she wasn't at all certain about that.

•

The old street looked much the same as it had when Banks lived there with his parents between 1962 and 1969

– from 'Love Me Do' to Woodstock – except that everything, the brickwork, the doors, the slate roofs, was just
that little bit shabbier, and small satellite dishes had
replaced the forest of old television aerials on just about
all the houses, including his parents'. That made sense.
He couldn't imagine his father living without Sky Sports.

Back in the early sixties the estate was new, and
Banks's mother had been thrilled to move from their little
back-to-back terraced house with the outside toilet to the
new house with 'all mod cons', as they used to say. As far
as Banks was concerned, the best 'mod cons' were the
indoors WC, a real bathroom to replace the tin tub they
had had to fill from a kettle every Friday, and a room of
his own. In the old house, he had shared with his brother,
Roy, who was five years younger, and like all siblings they
fought more than anything else.

The house stood near the western edge of the estate,
close to the arterial road, across from an abandoned
factory and a row of shops, including the newsagent's.
Banks paused for a moment and took in the weathered
terraced houses – rows of five, each with a little garden,
wooden gate, low wall and privet hedge. Some people had
made small improvements, he noticed, and one house had
an enclosed porch. The owners must have bought the
place when the Conservatives sold off council houses for
peanuts in the eighties. Maybe there was even a
conservatory around the back, Banks thought, though it
would be folly to add an extension made almost entirely
of glass on an estate like this.

A knot of kids stood smoking and shoving one another
in the middle of the street, some Asian, some white, clock-
ing Banks out of the corners of their eyes. Locals were
always suspicious of newcomers, and the kids had no idea

who he was, that he had grown up here, too. Some of them were wearing low-slung baggy jeans and hoodies. Mangy dogs wandered up and down the street, barking at everything and nothing, shitting on the pavements, and loud rock music blasted out of an open window several houses east.

Banks opened the gate. He noticed that his mother had planted some colourful flowers and kept the small patch of lawn neatly trimmed. This was the only garden she had ever had, and she always had been proud of her little patch of earth. He walked up the flagstone path and knocked at the door. He saw his mother approach through the frosted-glass pane. She opened the door, rubbed her hands together as if drying them, and gave him a hug. 'Alan,' she said. 'Lovely to see you. Come on in.'

Banks dropped his overnight bag in the hall and followed his mother through to the living room. The wallpaper was a sort of wispy autumn-leaves pattern, the three-piece suite a matching brown velveteen, and there was a sentimental autumnal landscape hanging over the electric fire. He didn't remember this theme from his previous visit, about a year ago, but he couldn't be certain that it hadn't been there, either. So much for the observant detective and the dutiful son.

His father was sitting in his usual armchair, the one with the best straight-on view of the television. He didn't get up, only grunted, 'Son. How you doing?'

'Not bad, Dad. You?'

'Mustn't complain.' Arthur Banks had been suffering from mild angina and an assortment of less specified chronic illnesses for years, ever since he'd been made redundant from the sheet-metal factory, and they seemed to get neither better nor worse as the years went on. He took pills occasionally for the chest pains. Other than that, and the damage booze and fags had wreaked on his liver and lungs over the years, he had always been fit as a fiddle. Short, skinny and hollow-chested, he still had a head of thick dark hair with hardly a trace of grey. He wore it slicked back with lashings of Brylcreem.

Banks's mother, plump and nervy, with pouchy, chipmunk cheeks and a haze of blue-grey hair hovering around her skull, fussed about how thin Banks was looking. 'I don't suppose you've been eating properly since Sandra left, have you?' she said.

'You know how it is,' said Banks. 'I manage to gulp down the occasional Big Mac and fries now and then, if I've got time to spare.'

'Don't be cheeky. Besides, you need *proper* food. In for tea?'

'I suppose so,' Banks said. He hadn't thought about what he was going to do once he actually *got* home. If truth be told, he had imagined that the local police – in the lovely form of DI Michelle Hart – would find his offer of help invaluable and give him an office at Thorpe Wood. But that clearly was not to be. Fair enough, he thought, it's *her* case, after all. 'I'll just take my bag up,' he said, heading for the stairs.

Though Banks hadn't stayed overnight since he had first left for London, somehow he knew that his room would be just as it always had been. And he was right. Almost. It was the same wardrobe, the same small bookcase, the same narrow bed he had slept in as a teenager, sneaking his transistor radio under the covers to listen to Radio Luxembourg, or reading a book by the light of a torch. The only thing different was the wallpaper. Gone were the sports-car images of his adolescence, replaced by pink and green stripes. He stood on the threshold for a few moments permitting it all to flow back, allowing the emotion that he felt nudging at the boundaries of his consciousness. It wasn't quite nostalgia, nor was it loss, but something in between.

The view hadn't changed. Banks's bedroom was the only one at the back of the house, next to the WC and bathroom, and it looked out over backyards and an alleyway, beyond which an empty field stretched a hundred yards or so to the next estate. People walked their dogs there, and sometimes the local kids gathered at night.

Banks used to do that, he remembered, with Dave, Paul, Steve and Graham, sharing Woodbines and Park Drives or, if Graham was flush, those long American tipped cigarettes, Peter Stuyvesants or Pall Mall. Later, after Graham had disappeared, Banks had sometimes been there with girlfriends. The field wasn't square and there was a little dog-leg on the other side where, if you were careful, you couldn't be seen from the houses. He remembered well enough those long, raw-lipped snogging sessions, pushed up against the rusty corrugated iron fencing, the fervid struggles with bra hooks, safety pins or whatever other contrivances the local girls so inconsiderately used to keep themselves fastened up.

Banks dropped his bag at the bottom of the bed and stretched. It had been a long drive, and the time spent in the pub garden, the pint he had drunk with DI Hart, all conspired to make him feel tired. He thought of taking a brief nap before tea but decided it would be rude; he could at least go down and talk to his parents as he hadn't been in touch for so long.

First, he unpacked his shirt to hang up in the wardrobe before the creases became too permanent. The other clothes in the wardrobe were unfamiliar, but Banks noticed several cardboard boxes on the floor. He pulled one out and was stunned when he saw it contained his old records: singles, as those were all he could afford back then, when they cost 6/4 and an LP cost 32/6. Of course, he got LPs for Christmas and birthdays, often with record tokens, but they were mostly Beatles and Rolling Stones, and he had taken those to London with him.

The records here represented the beginnings of his musical interests. When he left, he had soon gone on to Cream, Hendrix and Jefferson Airplane, then later discovered jazz and, later still, classical, but these . . . Banks dipped his hand in and lifted out a stack, flipping through them. Here they were in all their glory: Dusty Springfield's 'Goin' Back', The Shadows' 'The Rise & Fall of Flingel Bunt', Cilla Black's 'Anyone Who Had a Heart' and 'Alfie', 'Nutrocker' by B. Bumble and the Stingers, Sandie Shaw's 'Always Something There to Remind Me', 'House of the Rising Sun' by the Animals and 'As Tears Go By' by Marianne Faithfull. There were many more, some he had forgotten, and a few really obscure artists, such as Ral Donner and Kenny Lynch, and cover versions of Del Shannon and Roy Orbison hits made by unnamed performers for Woolworth's cheap Embassy label. What a treasure trove of nostalgia, all the stuff he listened to between the ages of about eleven and sixteen. His old record player was long gone, but his parents had a stereo downstairs, so perhaps he would play a few of the old songs while he was home.

For the moment, he put back the box and pulled out another one, this one full mostly of old toys. There were model aeroplanes – Spitfires, Wellingtons, Junkers and a Messerschmitt with a broken wing – a couple of Dinky toys, a Dan Dare rocket gun, and a small clockwork Dalek that said 'Ex-ter-min-ate! Ex-ter-min-ate!' as it rolled along like an upturned dustbin. There were a few old annuals, too – *The Saint*, *Danger Man* and *The Man From U.N.C.L.E.* – along with what had once been his pride and joy, a pocket-sized Philips transistor radio. Maybe if he put in some new batteries, he could even get it working.

The third box he opened was full of old school reports, magazines, letters and exercise books. He had sometimes wondered over the years what had happened to all this stuff and assumed, if anything, that his parents had chucked it out when they figured he wouldn't need it any more. Not so. It had been hiding away in the wardrobe all this time. There they were: *Beatles Monthly*, *Fabulous*, *Record Song Book* and *The Radio Luxembourg Book of Record Stars*.

Banks pulled out a handful of the small notebooks and found they were his old diaries. Some were plain Letts' diaries, with a little slot for a pencil down the spine, and some were special themed, illustrated ones, such as pop-star, television or sports diaries. The one that was of most immediate interest to him, though, was a *Photoplay* diary with a stiff, laminated cover and a colour photo of Sean Connery and Honor Blackman from 1964's Bond film, *Goldfinger*, on the front. Inside, a photo of a different film star faced each page of dates. The first was Brigitte Bardot, for the week starting Sunday, 27 December 1964, the first full week of his diary for 1965, the year Graham disappeared.

•

Michelle took off her reading glasses and rubbed the bridge of her nose, where she sensed a headache beginning to form between her eyes. She suffered from headaches frequently these days, and while her doctor assured her there was nothing seriously wrong – no brain tumour or neurological disease – and her psychiatrist told her that it was probably just stress and 'coping', she couldn't help but worry.

The air quality in the archives office didn't help either. Instead of signing the heavier boxes out and carrying them up to her office, Michelle had decided she might as well look through the material down there. The reading room was just a glassed-in alcove with a desk and chair. It stood at the entrance to several parallel aisles of old papers, some of which went back to the late nineteenth century. If the environment had been a little more comfortable, she might have considered having a browse around the archives. There was bound to be some fascinating stuff.

For the moment, 1965 would have to do. Michelle wanted to get a general idea of the crimes occurring around the time of Graham's disappearance, to see if she could come up with any links to Banks's mysterious stranger, and Mrs Metcalfe had directed her to the log-books that indexed and recorded all complaints and actions taken, day by day. It made for interesting reading, not all of it relevant to what she was looking for. Many of the calls listed went no further – missing pets, some domestic complaints – but the lists gave her a good impression of what daily life must have been like for a copper back then.

In May, for example, a man had been arrested in connection with an assault on a fourteen-year-old girl, who had accepted a lift with him near the A1, but he bore no resemblance whatsoever to Banks's description of the man by the river. Also in May there had been a major jewellery robbery at a city-centre shop, netting the thieves £18,000. In June a number of youths had gone on the rampage and slashed tyres on about thirty cars in the city centre; in the same month a twenty-one-year-old man had been stabbed outside the Rose and Crown on Bridge Street, after an argument over a girl. In August, two alleged homosexuals had been questioned in connection with lewd goings on at the country mansion of local bigwig, Rupert Mandeville, but the anonymous informant couldn't be located, and all charges had later been dismissed for lack of evidence. Hard to believe that it was a crime to be gay, Michelle thought, but 1965 was back in the dark ages, before homosexuality had been legalized in 1967.

There were certainly plenty of incidents before and after Graham Marshall's disappearance, Michelle was fast discovering, but none of them seemed to have anything remotely to do with Banks's riverbank adventure. She read on. In July police had investigated complaints about a local protection racket modelled on the East London Kray gang's operation, allegedly led by a man called Carlo Fiorino, but no charges were brought.

The more she read, the more Michelle realized what a vast chasm yawned between 1965 and today. She had, in fact, been born in 1961, but she was damned if she was going to admit that to Banks. Her own teenage years had been spent in what Banks would no doubt call a musical wasteland made up of the Bay City Rollers, Elton John and Hot Chocolate, not to mention *Saturday Night Fever* and *Grease*. Punk came along when she was about fifteen, but Michelle was far too conservative to join in with that crowd. If truth be told, the punks scared her with their torn clothes, spiky hair and safety pins in their ears. And the music just sounded like noise to her.

Not that Michelle had had a great deal of time for pop music; she had been a studious child, lamenting that it always seemed to take her so long to finish her homework when others were done and out on the town. Her mother said she was too much of a perfectionist to let something be and have done with it, and perhaps that was true. Painstaking. Perfectionist. These were labels she had come to know and hate from friends, family and the teachers at school. Why not just say pedestrian and plodding and have done with it, if that was what they meant? she sometimes wondered.

She hadn't done brilliantly at school despite all her hard work, but she had managed to pass enough O and A levels to get into a poly – again cramming through all the concerts and parties her fellow students went to – where she had studied business and management techniques before deciding on the police as a career. On those rare occasions when she did have time to go out, late in the seventies, she liked to dance. For that, reggae or two-tone was her music of choice: Bob Marley, the Specials, Madness, UB40.

Michelle had always hated nostalgia snobs, as she called them, and in her experience, the sixties' ones were the worst of the lot. She suspected that Banks was one. To hear them talk, you'd think paradise had been lost or the seventh seal broken now that so many of the great rock icons were dead, geriatric or gaga, and nobody wore beads and kaftans any more, and you'd also think that drug-taking was an innocent way to spend a few hours relaxing, or a means of reaching some exalted spiritual state, instead of a waste of lives and a source of money for evil, unscrupulous dealers.

The archives office was quiet except for the buzzing of the fluorescent light. Silence is a rare thing in a police station, where everyone is pushed together in open-plan offices, but down here Michelle could even hear her watch ticking. After five. Time for a break soon, some fresh air perhaps, and then back down to it.

Reading the crime reports for August, she sensed rather than heard someone approaching the office, and when she looked up, she saw it was Detective Superintendent Benjamin Shaw.

Shaw's bulk filled the doorway and blocked some of the light from coming in. 'What you up to, DI Hart?' he asked.

'Just checking the old logs, sir.'

'I can see that. What for? You won't find anything there, you know. Not after all this time.'

'I was just having a general look around, trying to get some context for the Marshall case. Actually, I was wondering if—'

'*Context*? Is that one of those fancy words they taught you at polytechnic? Bloody time-wasting sounds more like it.'

'Sir—'

'Don't bother to argue, Inspector. You're wasting your time. What do you expect to find in the dusty old files, apart from *context*?'

'I was talking to one of Graham Marshall's friends earlier,' she said. 'He told me he was approached by a strange man on the riverbank about two months before the Marshall boy disappeared. I was just trying to see if any similar incidents were on file.'

Shaw sat on the edge of the desk. It creaked and tilted

a little. Michelle worried that the damn thing would break under his weight. 'And?' he asked. 'I'm curious.'

'Nothing so far, sir. Do you remember anything odd like that?'

Shaw frowned. 'No. But who is this "friend"?'

'He's called Banks, sir. Alan Banks. Actually, it's Detective Chief Inspector Banks.'

'Is it, indeed? Banks? The name sounds vaguely familiar. I take it he didn't report the incident at the time?'

'No, sir. Too scared of what his parents might say.'

'I can imagine. Look, about this Banks chap,' he went on. 'I think I'd like a little word with him. Can you arrange it?'

'I've got his phone number, sir. But . . .' Michelle was about to tell Shaw that it was *her* case and that she didn't appreciate his poaching her interviews, but she decided it wouldn't be diplomatic to alienate one of her senior officers at such an early stage of her career in Peterborough. Besides, he might be helpful, having been involved in the original investigation.

'But what?'

'Nothing, sir.'

'Good.' Shaw stood up. 'We'll have him in, then. Soon as possible.'

•

'I know it must seem odd after all these years,' Banks said, 'but I'm Alan Banks, and I've come to offer my condolences.'

'*Alan Banks*. Well, I never!' The look of suspicion on Mrs Marshall's face was immediately transformed into one of pleasure. She opened the door wide. 'Do come in and make yourself at home.'

It was over thirty-six years since Banks had set foot in the Marshall house, and he had a vague memory that the furniture had been made of much darker wood then, heavier and sturdier. Now the sideboard and television stand looked as if they were made of pine. The three-piece suite seemed much bigger, and a huge television dominated one corner of the room.

Even all those years ago, he remembered, he hadn't been inside Graham's house often. Some parents kept an open house for their children's friends, the way his own did, and Dave's and Paul's, but the Marshalls were always a bit distant, stand-offish. Graham never spoke about his mum and dad much, either, Banks remembered, but that hadn't struck him as at all unusual at the time. Kids don't, except to complain if they're not allowed to do something or are discovered in some deception and have their pocket money stopped. As far as Banks knew, Graham Marshall's home life was every bit as normal as his own.

His mother had told him that Mr Marshall had been disabled by a stroke, so he was prepared for the frail, drooling figure staring up at him from the armchair. Mrs Marshall looked tired and careworn herself, which was hardly surprising, and he wondered how she kept the place so spick and span. Maybe the social helped out, as he doubted she could afford a daily.

'Look, Bill, it's Alan Banks,' said Mrs Marshall. 'You know, one of our Graham's old friends.'

It was hard to read Mr Marshall's expression through the distortions of his face, but his gaze seemed to relax a little when he found out who the visitor was. Banks said hello and sat down. He spotted the old photo of Graham, the one his own father had taken with his Brownie on

Blackpool prom. He had taken one of Banks, too, also wearing a black polo-neck 'Beatle' jumper, but without the matching hairstyle.

Mr Marshall was sitting in the same spot he had always sat in, like Banks's own father. Back then, he had always seemed to be smoking, but now he looked as if he could hardly lift a cigarette to his lips.

'I understand you're an important policeman now,' Mrs Marshall said.

'I don't know about important, but I'm a policeman, yes.'

'You don't have to be so modest. I bump into your mum at the shops from time to time and she's very proud of you.'

That's more than she lets on to me, Banks thought. 'Well,' he said, 'you know what mothers are like.'

'Have you come to help with the investigation?'

'I don't know that I can,' said Banks. 'But if they want any help from me, I'd be happy to give it.'

'She seems very nice. The girl they sent round.'

'I'm sure she'll be just fine.'

'I told her I can't imagine what she can do that Jet Harris and his boys didn't do back then. They were very thorough.'

'I know they were.'

'But he just seemed to have . . . vanished. All these years.'

'I've often thought about him,' Banks said. 'I realize I didn't actually know him for very long, but he was a good friend. I missed him. We all missed him.'

Mrs Marshall sniffed. 'Thank you. He appreciated the way you all accepted him when we were new here. You know how difficult it can be to make friends sometimes.

It's just so hard to believe that he's turned up after all this time.'

'It happens,' said Banks. 'And don't give up on the investigation. There's a lot more science and technology in police work these days. Look how quickly they identified the remains. They couldn't have done that twenty years ago.'

'I just wish I could be of some use,' said Mrs Marshall, 'but I don't remember anything out of the ordinary at all. It just came like a lightning bolt. Out of the blue.'

Banks stood up. 'I know,' he said. 'But if there's anything to be discovered, I'm sure DI Hart will discover it.'

'Are you going already?'

'It's nearly teatime,' Banks said, smiling. 'And my mother would never forgive me if I didn't turn up for tea. She thinks I need fattening up.'

Mrs Marshall smiled. 'Better go then. Mustn't cross your mother. By the way, they can't release the body yet, but Miss Hart said she'd let me know when we can have the funeral. You will come, won't you?'

'Of course,' said Banks. When he looked over to say goodbye to Mr Marshall, he had a sudden flash of the big, muscular man he used to be, the sense of physical menace he had somehow conveyed. Back then, Banks remembered with a shock, he had been *afraid* of Graham's dad. He never had any real reason to feel that way, but he had done.

•

She should have packed it in long ago, Michelle realized, but she was loath to give up without finding at least some trace of Banks's mystery man, if any existed. Besides, the material itself gave her an interesting picture of the times, and she found herself becoming quite fascinated by it all.

1965 hadn't been a bumper crime year for Peterborough, but the fast-growing city had its share of some of the more newsworthy national problems, Michelle was fast discovering. Mods and rockers clashed at some city-centre pubs, cannabis was beginning to insinuate its way into the lifestyles of the young and rebellious – despite what Banks had said – and the pornography trade was blossoming in the shape of tons of German, Danish and Swedish magazines covering every perversion you could imagine and some you couldn't. Why not Norwegian or Finnish, too? Michelle wondered. Weren't they into porn? Burglary and armed robbery were as common as ever, and the only thing that seemed new today was the increase in car theft.

Far fewer people owned cars in 1965, Michelle realized, and that made her think again about Banks's statement. Banks said he had been assaulted by a dirty, scruffy 'Rasputin-like' stranger on the riverside near the city centre. But Graham Marshall had been abducted, along with a heavy canvas bag full of newspapers, two months later, from a council estate several miles away. The MOs were different. It didn't look as if Graham had put up a struggle, for example, which he certainly would have done, as Banks had, if he'd been attacked by this frightening stranger and felt that he had been fighting for his life. Besides, the man who assaulted Banks had been on foot, and Graham hadn't walked all the way to his burial site. It was possible that the mysterious stranger had a car somewhere, but not very likely. Given Banks's description, Michelle would have guessed the man was homeless and poor, perhaps a tramp. *The passing tramp.* Cliché of so many detective stories.

The problem was that she still couldn't see any logical connection between the event Banks had described and the disappearance of Graham Marshall. She thought that Banks's sense of guilt might, over the years, have warped his judgement in the matter. It happened; she'd seen it before. But could it have happened that way? Who was this man?

There was a good chance, Michelle realized, that she might not find out anything about him in the police files. Not everyone had a file, despite what the anti-police groups seemed to think. She might have to dig in the newspaper morgue or perhaps the local mental hospital archives. The man sounded disturbed, and there was a chance he had sought treatment at some time. Of course, there was also every possibility that he wasn't a local. Michelle had no idea where the River Nene started, but she thought it was somewhere down Northampton way, and she knew that it flowed all the way to the Wash. Maybe he was walking the riverbank from town to town.

She flipped through file after file and tossed them aside in frustration. Finally, as her eyes were starting to tire, she struck gold.

7

The Coach and Horses, about a hundred yards along the main road, had changed over the years, Banks noticed, but not as much as some pubs. The large public bar had always housed a diverse group, mixed generations drinking there together, and today it was no different, though the racial mix had changed. Now, among the white faces, there were Pakistanis and Sikhs and, according to Arthur Banks, a group of Kosovan asylum seekers, who lived on the estate, also drank there.

Noisy machines with flashing lights had replaced the old bar-billiards area, the scarred wooden benches had been replaced with padded ones, perhaps the wallpaper had been redone and the light fixtures modernized, but that was about all. The brewery had forked out for this minor facelift sometime in the eighties, Banks's father had told him, hoping to pull in a younger, freer-spending crowd. But it didn't take. The people who drank at the Coach and Horses had, for the most part, been drinking there most of their lives. And their fathers before them. Banks had drunk his first legal pint here, with his father on his eighteenth birthday, though he had been knocking them back with his mates at the Wheatsheaf, about a mile away, since he was sixteen. The last time he had been in the Coach and Horses, he had played one of the earliest pub video games, that silly machine where you bounced the tennis ball back and forth across a green phosphorous screen.

Though there were few young people to be seen there, the Coach and Horses still managed to be a warm and lively place, Banks noticed as he walked in with his father just after eight o'clock that night, his mother's steamed pudding and custard – the *proper* food he was supposed to be eating – still weighing heavily in his stomach. His father had managed the walk without too much puffing and wheezing, which he put down to having stopped smoking two years ago. Banks had tapped his own jacket pocket rather guiltily for his cigarettes as they went out of the door.

This was Arthur Banks's local. He had been coming here almost every day for forty years, and so had his cronies, Harry Finnegan, Jock McFall and Norman Grenfell, Dave's father. Here, Arthur was respected. Here, he could escape the clutches of his ailments and the shame of his redundancy, at least for an hour or two, as he drank, laughed and told lies with the men with whom he felt most comfortable. For the Coach and Horses was, by and large a *men's* pub, despite the occasional couple and groups of women dropping by after work. When Arthur took Ida out for a drink, as he did on Fridays, they went to the Duck and Drake or the Duke of Wellington, where Ida Banks caught up on the local gossip and they took part in trivia quizzes and laughed at people making fools of themselves in the karaoke sessions.

But there was none of that at the Coach and Horses, and the piped sixties' pop music was turned down low enough so that old men could hear each other talk. At the moment, the Kinks were singing 'Waterloo Sunset', one of Banks's favourites. After Banks and his father had settled themselves at the table, pints in front of them and introductions made, Arthur Banks first lamented Jock McFall's absence due to hospitalization for a prostate operation, then Norman Grenfell started the ball rolling.

'We were just saying, before you got here, Alan, what a terrible thing it is about the Marshall boy. I remember you and our David used to play with him.'

'Yes. How is Dave, by the way?'

'He's doing fine,' said Norman. 'He and Ellie still live in Dorchester. The kids have grown up now, of course.'

'They're still together?' Ellie Hatcher was, Banks remembered, Dave's first real girlfriend; they must have started going out together around 1968.

'Some couples stick it out,' muttered Arthur Banks.

Banks ignored the remark and asked Norman to pass on his regards to Dave next time they spoke. Unlike Jock and Harry, Banks remembered, both of whom had worked with Arthur at the sheet-metal factory, Norman had worked in a clothing shop on Midgate, where he could sometimes get his mates a discount on a duffel coat, a pair of jeans or Tuf shoes. Norman drank halves instead of pints and smoked a pipe, which made him different, almost genteel, compared to the rough factory workers. He also had a hobby – he read and collected everything to do with steam trains and had an entire room of his small house devoted to clockwork models – and that set him even further apart from the beer, sport and telly crowd. Yet Norman Grenfell had always been as much a part of the group as Jock or Harry or Arthur himself, though he didn't share that ineffable bond that working men have, of having toiled under the same lousy conditions for the same lousy bosses and faced the same dangers day in, day out, for the same lousy pay. Maybe, Banks wondered, Graham had been a bit like that, too: set apart by his background, by his being a newcomer, by his London *cool*, yet still a part of the gang. The quiet one. The George Harrison of the group.

'Well,' Banks said, raising his glass. 'Here's to Graham. In the long run, I suppose it's best they found him. At least his parents can lay his bones to rest now.'

'True enough,' said Harry.

'Amen,' said Norman.

'Didn't Graham's father used to drink here?' Banks asked.

Arthur Banks laughed. 'He did. He was a rum customer, Bill Marshall. Isn't that right, Harry?'

'A rum customer, indeed. And a couple of bricks short of a full hod, too, if you ask me.'

They all laughed.

'In what way was he rum?' Banks asked.

Harry nudged Banks's father. 'Always the copper, your lad, hey?'

Arthur's brow darkened. Banks knew damn well that his father had never approved of his choice of career, and that no matter how well he did, how successful he was, to his father he would always be a traitor to the working class, who traditionally feared and despised coppers. As far as Arthur Banks was concerned, his son was employed by the middle and upper classes to protect their interests and their property. Never mind that most coppers of Arthur's own generation came from the working classes, unlike today, when many were middle-class university graduates and management types. The two of them had never resolved this problem, and Banks could see even now that his father was bothered by Harry Finnegan's little dig.

'Graham was a friend of mine,' Banks went on quickly to diffuse the tension. 'I was just wondering, that's all.'

'Is that why you're down here?' Norman asked.

'Partly, yes.'

It was the same question Mrs Marshall had asked him. Perhaps people assumed that because he was a policeman, and because he knew Graham, he would be assigned to this particular case. 'I don't know how much I can help,' Banks said, glancing sideways at his father, who was working on his beer. He had never told either of his parents about what had happened down by the river and he wasn't about to do so now. It might come out, of course, if his information led anywhere, and now he had an inkling of what the many witnesses who lied to avoid disclosing a shameful secret had to be anxious about. 'It's just that, well, I've thought about Graham and what happened on and off over the years, and I just thought I ought to come and try to help, that's all.'

'I can understand that,' said Norman, relighting his pipe. 'I think it's been a bit of a shock to the system for all of us, one way or another.'

'You were saying about Graham's father, Dad?'

Arthur Banks glanced at his son. 'Was I?'

'You said he was strange. I didn't know him well. I never really talked to him.'

'Course not,' said Arthur. 'You were just a kid.'

'That's why I'm asking you.'

There was a pause, then Arthur Banks looked over at Harry Finnegan. 'He was shifty, wouldn't you say so, Harry?'

'He was indeed. Always an eye for a fiddle, and not above a bit of strong-arm stuff. I wouldn't have trusted him as far as I could throw him. And he was a big talker, too.'

'What do you mean?' Banks asked.

'Well,' his father said, 'you know the family came up from London?'

'Yes.'

'Bill Marshall worked as a bricklayer and he was a good one, too, but when he'd had a drink or two he'd start letting things slip about some of his other activities in London.'

'I still don't understand.'

'He was a fit bloke, Bill. Strong. Big hands, powerful upper body. Comes from carrying those hods around the building sites.'

'He used to get into fights?'

'You could say that.'

'What your Dad's saying,' explained Harry, leaning forward, 'is that Bill Marshall let slip he used to act as an enforcer for gangsters down the Smoke. Protection rackets, that sort of thing.'

The Smoke? Banks hadn't heard that term for London in years. 'He did?' Banks shook his head. It was hard to imagine the old man in the chair as having been some sort of gang enforcer, but it might help explain the fear Banks remembered feeling in his presence all those years ago, the threat of violence. 'I'd never have—'

'How could you?' his father cut in. 'Like I said, you were just a kid. You couldn't understand things like that.'

The music had changed, Banks noticed. Herb Alpert and his bloody Tijuana Brass, just finishing, thank God. Banks had hated them back then and he hated them now. Next came the Bachelors, 'Marie'. Mum and Dad music. 'Did you tell the police?' he asked.

The men looked at one another, then Arthur looked back at Banks, his lip curling. 'What do *you* think?'

'But he could—'

'Listen. Bill Marshall might have been a big talker, but he had nothing to do with his son's disappearance.'

'How can you know that?'

Arthur Banks snorted. 'You police. All the bloody same, you are. Just because a man might be a bit dodgy in one area, you're ready to fit him up with anything.'

'I've never fitted anyone up in my life,' said Banks.

'What I'm saying is that Bill Marshall might have been a bit of a wild man, but he didn't go around killing young lads, especially not his own son.'

'I didn't say I thought he did it,' Banks said, noticing that the others were watching him and his father now, as if they were the evening's entertainment.

'Then what *did* you mean?'

'Look, Dad,' Banks said, reaching for a cigarette. He had been determined not to smoke in front of his father, mostly because of the old man's health, but not smoking in the Coach and Horses was as pointless as swimming in the no-pissing section of a swimming pool, if such a section were ever to exist. 'If there was any truth in what Bill Marshall said about his criminal background in London, then isn't it possible that something he'd done there came back to haunt him?'

'But nobody hurt *Bill*.'

'Doesn't matter, Dad. These people often have more devious ways of getting back at their enemies. Believe me. I've come across more than a few of them in my time. Did he ever mention any names?'

'What do you mean?'

'I mean in London. The people he worked for. Did he ever mention any names?'

Harry Finnegan gave a nervous laugh. Arthur shot him

a glance and he shut up. 'As a matter of fact,' said Arthur, pausing dramatically, 'he did.'

'Who?'

'The Twins. Reggie and Ronnie Kray.'

'Bloody hell!'

Arthur Banks's eyes shone with triumph. '*Now* do you see why we just thought he had a big mouth on him?'

•

For the second time that day Annie turned up at Swainsdale Hall, only this time she felt the butterflies in the pit of her stomach. People like Martin Armitage were difficult enough to deal with in the first place, and he wouldn't like what she had to say. Still, she thought, for all his tough bluster, he hadn't done much but kick a ball around most of his life. Robin was another matter. Annie sensed that she might feel relieved to have someone else to share her fears with, and that underneath her accommodating exterior and her air of vulnerability, there was a strong woman who was capable of standing up to her husband.

Josie answered the door, as usual, holding a barking Miata by the collar. Annie wanted to talk to Josie and her husband, Calvin, but they could wait. For the moment, the fewer people who knew what was going on the better. Robin and Martin were both out in the garden sitting at a wrought-iron table under a striped umbrella. It was a warm evening, and the back garden faced south, so there was plenty of honey-tinted sunlight and dark shadows cast by tree branches. Annie felt like reaching for her sketch pad. Beyond the high drystone wall that marked the property boundary, the daleside stretched up in a patchwork of uneven fields, green until the sere bareness of the higher slopes, where it rose more steeply to merge into the wild stretch of heather moorland that separated the dales.

Neither Martin nor Robin seemed to be enjoying the beautiful evening or the long, cool drinks that sat in front of them. Both seemed pale, tense and preoccupied, the mobile perched on the table like an unexploded bomb.

'What are you doing here?' Martin Armitage said. 'I told you Luke was on his way home and I'd be in touch when he got here.'

'I take it he's not arrived yet?'

'No.'

'Heard from him again?'

'No.'

Annie sighed and sat down without being invited.

'I didn't ask you to—'

Annie raised her hand to quiet Martin down. 'Look,' she said, 'there's no point pissing about any more. I know what's going on.'

'I don't understand what you mean.'

'Come off it, Mr Armitage. I followed you.'

'You did what?'

'I followed you. After I left this morning I waited in a lay-by and followed you to the shepherd's shelter. What were you doing there?'

'None of your bloody business. Why, what are you going to do? Charge me with disobeying government regulations?'

'Let me tell you what you were doing, Mr Armitage. You were leaving a briefcase full of money. Old bills. Tens and twenties for the most part. Around ten thousand pounds, at a guess, maybe fifteen.'

Armitage was red in the face. Still, Annie pressed on.

'And now let me tell you what happened. They got in touch with you last night on your mobile, said they'd got Luke and you were to hand over the money. You told them you couldn't lay your hands on that much cash until the banks were open, so they gave you until this morning to leave it at the prearranged drop.' Which means they know something about the area, Annie realized, or that they've been watching, scouting for some time. Maybe someone had noticed them. Strangers usually stood out around these parts, especially as the tourist numbers were down. 'How am I doing so far?'

'You've got imagination, I'll certainly give you that.'

'They said no police, which is why my arrival scared the living daylights out of you.'

'I've told you—'

'Martin.' Robin Armitage spoke for the first time, and though her voice was soft and kindly, it was authoritative enough to command her husband's attention. 'Can't you see?' she went on. 'She knows. I must admit that I, for one, feel rather relieved.'

'But he said—'

'They don't know who I am,' said Annie. 'And I'm pretty certain they didn't see me around Mortsett this morning.'

'Pretty certain?'

Annie looked him in the eye. 'I'd be a liar if I said I was a hundred per cent certain.' Birds in the trees filled in the silence that followed, and a light breeze ruffled Annie's hair. She held Martin Armitage's gaze until she saw it waver and finally wane into defeat. His shoulders slumped. Robin leaned over and put her arm around him. 'It's all right, darling,' she said. 'The police will know what to do. They'll be discreet.' Robin looked at Annie as she spoke, as if daring her to disagree. Annie didn't. Martin ran the backs of his hands across his eyes and nodded.

'I'm sorry about what's happened,' Annie said, 'but Mrs Armitage is right.'

'Robin. Please. As we're involved in such an intimate matter, at least you can call me by my first name. My husband, too.'

'Okay. Robin. Look, I have to tell you that I'm not a negotiator. This isn't my area of expertise. We have people specially trained to deal with kidnappers and their demands.'

'But he said no police,' Martin repeated. 'He said if we brought in the police he'd kill Luke.'

'What did you say?'

'I told him I'd already reported Luke missing.'

'And what did he say to that?'

'He was quiet for a moment, as if he was thinking, like.'

'Or consulting with someone else?'

'He could have been, but I didn't hear anyone. Anyway, when he came back on he said that was fine, but to make sure I told you Luke had rung and said that he was coming home. Which I did.'

'It was a man who made the call, then?'

'Yes.'

'What time?'

'About half-past nine. Just before Robin rang you.'

'How much did he ask for?'

'Ten thousand.'

'Accent?'

'None, really.'

'He didn't sound local?'

'He could've been, but he didn't have a strong accent. Sort of bland.'

'And his voice?'

'What do you mean?'

'High or low? Husky, reedy, whatever?'

'Just ordinary. I'm sorry, I'm not good at this sort of thing, especially recognizing voices on the telephone.'

Annie favoured him with a smile. 'Not many people are. Think about it, though. It could be important if there's anything at all you remember about the voice.'

'Yes. I'll think about it.'

'Did he let you speak to Luke?'

'No.'

'Did you ask?'

'Yes, but he said Luke was being kept somewhere else.'

'And he called you on your mobile?'

'Yes.'

'Who knows the number?'

'Family. Close friends. Business colleagues. I suppose it would be easy enough to find out. Luke, of course. He has it programmed into the electronic phone book of his own mobile. At first, I thought it was him because his name was displayed when the call came.'

'So the kidnapper used Luke's mobile to call you?'

'I suppose so. Why does it matter?'

'At least it tells us he's in an area where there's a signal. Or he was when he made the call. Also, if he's used it at other times, we'll be able to get the information from the phone company. It might help us pinpoint him. Of course, it would be better if he left it switched on, but he's not going to make things that easy for us.'

'Tell me,' said Robin, 'in your experience, in how many cases do they . . . how many times do the victims . . .'

'I don't have any statistics offhand,' Annie admitted. 'But if it makes you feel any better, kidnappers are essentially business people. They're in it for the money, not to hurt anyone. There's every chance that this will be resolved and that you'll see Luke back here safe and sound.' Annie could feel her nose growing as she talked. Too much time had passed, she suspected, for a happy ending, though she hoped she was wrong. 'In the meantime, while appearing to go along with his demands and not alarming him in any way, we want to make sure that in addition to getting Luke home safely we take every opportunity to discover the kidnapper's identity and bring him to justice.'

'How can we help?' asked Robin.

'You don't have to do anything,' said Annie. 'You've already played your part. Just leave the rest to us.'

'Maybe you've scared him off,' Martin said. 'Luke should be back by now. It's been hours.'

'Sometimes they wait a long time just to make sure nobody's watching. He's probably waiting till dark.'

'But you can't be certain, can you?' Robin said.

'Nothing's certain in this world, Mrs Armitage.'

'Robin. I told you. Oh, how rude of me!' She got to her feet. 'All this time and I haven't offered you anything to drink.' She was wearing denim shorts, Annie noticed, cut high on her long, smooth legs. There weren't many women who could get away with the bare midriff look at her age, either, Annie thought. She wouldn't even think of it herself, though she was only thirty-four, but what she could see of Robin's stomach looked flat and taut, with a ring of some sort glinting in her navel.

'No,' she said. 'Really. I'm not stopping long.' There wasn't much else Annie could do for Luke except wait, and she had promised herself a nice pint of bitter at the Black Sheep in Relton, where she could sit in peace and mull things over before calling it a day. 'I just want to make certain that you'll report any future communications, if there are any, straight to me. You've got the numbers where I can be reached?'

Both Martin and Robin nodded.

'And, of course, you'll let me know the second Luke turns up.'

'We will,' said Robin. 'I just hope and pray that he does come home soon.'

'Me, too,' said Annie, getting up. 'There's one more thing that puzzles me.'

'What?' asked Robin.

'Last night, when you rang to tell me you'd heard from Luke, you said he would be back tonight.'

'That's what he told Martin. The kidnapper. He said that if we left the money this morning, then Luke would be home unharmed by tonight.'

'And you knew that I wanted to see Luke as soon as he got back, to talk to him?'

'Yes.'

'So how were you going to explain everything?' asked Annie. 'I'm curious.'

Robin looked over at her husband, who answered, 'We were going to persuade Luke to tell you what we said happened in the first place, that he'd run away and phoned us the night before to say he was coming back.'

'Who thought of this?'

'The kidnapper suggested it.'

'Sounds like the perfect crime,' said Annie. 'Only you two, Luke and the kidnapper would ever know that it had been committed, and none of you would be likely to talk.'

Martin looked down at his drink.

'He would have done that?' Annie went on. 'Luke would have lied to the police?'

'He would have done it for me,' said Robin.

Annie looked at her, nodded and left.

●

The Krays, Banks thought as he lay in his narrow bed that night. Reggie and Ronnie. He didn't remember the exact dates, of course, but he had an idea that they were flying high in the mid-sixties, part of the swinging London scene, mixing with celebrities, pop stars and politicians.

It had always intrigued him the way gangsters became celebrities: Al Capone, Lucky Luciano, John Dillinger, Dutch Schultz, Bugsy Malone. Figures of legend. He had known a few of the lesser ones in his time, and they almost always rubbed shoulders with the rich and famous, as if celebrity recognized only itself and was blind to all else – morality, decency, honour – and they never lacked for beautiful women to run around with, the kind who were attracted by danger and the aura of violence. There seemed to be a glamour and mystique attached to making your money out of running prostitutes, supplying drugs and threatening to destroy people's livelihoods if they didn't pay protection, and it was more than likely that most film stars, sports personalities and pop stars were addle-brained enough to fall for it – the glamour of violence. Or was it the violence of glamour?

The Krays were no exception. They knew how to manipulate the media and being photographed with a famous actress, an MP, or a peer of the realm made it less likely that the truth about their real activities would come out. There was a trial in 1965, Banks remembered, and they came out of that more fireproof than they went in.

It was hard to believe that Graham Marshall's dad had anything to do with them, though, and Banks had to admit that his father was probably right; it had just been the beer talking.

Why, though? Why even hint at something like that if there wasn't a scrap of truth in it? Maybe Bill Marshall was a pathological liar. But over his years as a copper Banks had learned that the old cliché 'There's no smoke without fire' had a great deal to recommend it. And there were two other things: the Marshalls came from the East End of London, Kray territory in the mid-sixties, and Banks now remembered feeling afraid around Mr Marshall.

He already knew a bit about the Krays, most of it picked up when he was on the Met years ago, but he could dig deeper. There were plenty of books about them, though he doubted that any mentioned Bill Marshall. If he had done anything for them, it had obviously been low level, going round the customers and exuding physical menace, maybe clobbering the occasional informer or double-dealer in a dark alley.

He would have to tell DI Hart. Michelle. She had left a message with Banks's mother while he was out asking him to drop by Thorpe Wood at nine a.m. the following morning. It was her case, after all. If there was a connection, though, he was surprised that it hadn't come out in the investigation. Usually the parents come under very close scrutiny in missing-child cases, no matter how grief-stricken they appear. Banks had once come across a young couple he had believed to be genuinely grieving the loss of their child, only to find the poor kid strangled for crying too loud and stuffed in the downstairs freezer. No, you couldn't trust surfaces in police work; you had to dig, if only to make certain you weren't having the wool pulled over your eyes.

Banks picked up his old transistor radio. He had bought a battery earlier and wondered if it would still work after all these years. Probably not, but it was worth the price of a battery to find out. He unclipped the back, connected the battery and put the earpiece in his ear. It was just a single unit, like an old hearing aid. No stereo radio back then. When he turned it on, he was thrilled to find that the old trannie actually worked. Banks could hardly believe it. As he tuned the dial, though, he soon began to feel disappointed. The sound quality was poor, but it wasn't only that. The radio received all the local stations, Classic FM and Radios 1, 2, 3, 4 and 5, just like any modern radio, but Banks realized he had been half-expecting to go back in time. The idea that this was a magic radio that still received the Light Programme, Radio Luxembourg and the pirates, Radio Caroline and Radio London, was lodged somewhere in his mind. He had expected to be listening to John Peel's *The Perfumed Garden*, to relive those magical few months in the spring of 1967, when he should have been studying for his O levels but spent half the night with the radio plugged in his ear, hearing Captain Beefheart, the Incredible String Band and Tyrannosaurus Rex for the first time.

Banks switched off the radio and turned to his *Photoplay* diary. At least he had a bedside light in his room now and didn't have to hide under the sheets with a torch. Beside each week was a full-page photograph of an actor or actress popular at the time, usually an actress, or starlet, chosen because of pulchritude rather than acting ability, and more often than not appearing in a risqué pose, bra and panties, the carefully placed bed sheet, the off-the-shoulder strap. He flipped through the pages and there they all were: Natalie Wood, Catherine Deneuve, Martine Beswick, Ursula Andress. Cleavage abounded. 15–21 August were accompanied by a photo of Shirley Eaton in a low-cut dress.

As he flipped through the diary, Banks discovered that he had hardly been voluminous or the least bit analytical; he had simply noted events, adventures and excursions, often in a very cryptic manner. In a way, it was a perfect model for the policeman's notebook he was to keep later. Still, the pages were small, divided into seven sections, with room for a little fact or piece of cinema history at the bottom. If any of the dates happened to be a star's birthday, as many did, a portion of the available space was taken up with that, too. Given the restrictions, he had done a decent enough job, he thought, deciphering the miniature scrawl. He had certainly been to see a lot of films, listing all of them in his diary, along with his terse opinions, which varied from 'Crap' and 'Boring' through 'Okay' to 'Fantastic!' A typical entry might read, 'Went to the Odeon with Dave and Graham to see *Dr Who and the Daleks*. Okay,' 'Played cricket on the rec. Scored 32 not out,' or, 'Rained. Stopped in and read *Casino Royale*. Fantastic!'

He flipped to the Saturday before Graham disappeared, the 21st. 'Went into town with Graham. Bought *Help!* with Uncle Ken's record token.' It was the same LP they had listened to at Paul's the next day. That was all he had written, nothing unusual about Graham's state of mind. On Friday he had watched the Animals, one of his favourite groups, on *Ready, Steady, Go!*

On Sunday he had written, probably while in bed that night, 'Played records at Paul's place. New Bob Dylan LP. Saw police car go to Graham's house.' On Monday, 'Graham's run away from home. Police came. Joey flew away.'

Interesting he should assume that Graham had run away from home. But of course he would at that age. What else? The alternatives would have been too horrific for a fourteen-year-old boy to contemplate. He flipped back to late June, around the time he thought the event on the riverbank had occurred. It was a Tuesday, he noticed. He hadn't written much about it, simply, 'Skived off school and played by river this afternoon. A strange man tried to push me in.'

Tired, Banks put the diary aside, rubbed his eyes and turned out the light. It felt odd to be back in the same bed he had slept in during his teenage years, the same bed where he had had his first sexual experience, with Kay Summerville, while his parents were out visiting his grandparents one Saturday. It hadn't been very good for either Banks or Kay, but they had persevered and got a lot better with practice.

Kay Summerville. He wondered where she was, what she was doing now. Probably married with kids, the same way he had been until recently. She'd been a beauty, though, had Kay: long blonde hair, slender waist, long legs, a mouth like Marianne Faithfull's, firm tits with hard little nipples and hair like spun gold between her legs. Christ, Banks, he told himself, enough with the adolescent fantasies.

He put on his headphones and turned on his portable CD player, listening to Vaughan Williams's second string quartet, and settled back to more pleasant thoughts of Kay

Summerville. But as he approached the edge of sleep his thoughts jumbled, mixing memory with dream. It was cold and dark, and Banks and Graham were walking across a rugby field, goalposts silhouetted by the moon, cracking spider-web patterns in the ice as they walked, their breath misting the air. Banks must have said something about the Krays being arrested – was he interested in criminals, even then? – and Graham just laughed, saying the law could never touch people like them. Banks asked him how he knew, and Graham said he used to live near them. 'They were kings,' he said.

Puzzled by the memory, or dream, Banks turned the bedside light on again and picked up the diary. If what he had just imagined had any basis in reality, then it had happened in winter. He glanced through his entries for January and February 1965: Samantha Eggar, Yvonne Romain, Elke Sommer . . . But no mention of the Krays until 9 March, when he had written, 'Krays went to trial today. Graham laughed and said they'd get off easy.' So Graham *had* mentioned them. It was flimsy, but a start.

He turned off the light again, and this time he drifted off to sleep without further thoughts of either Graham or Kay Summerville.

8

When Banks arrived at Thorpe Wood the following
morning and asked to see Detective Inspector Hart, he
was surprised when a man came down to greet him. The
telephone call that his mother had told him about when
he got back from the pub had been from Michelle.

'Mr Banks, or should I say DCI Banks? Come with me
please, if you would.' He stood aside and gestured for
Banks to enter.

'And you are?'

'Detective Superintendent Shaw. We'll talk in my
office.'

Shaw looked familiar, but Banks couldn't place him. It
was possible they had met on a course, or even on a case,
years ago, and he had forgotten, but he usually had a good
memory for faces.

They didn't speak on their way to Shaw's office, and as
soon as they got there, Shaw disappeared, saying he'd be
back in a couple of minutes. Old copper's trick, Banks
knew. And Shaw knew he knew.

There wasn't likely to be anything of interest in the office
if Shaw was willing to leave Banks there alone, but he had
a poke around nonetheless. Second nature. He wasn't looking for anything in particular, but just looking for the sake
of it. The filing cabinets were locked, as were the desk
drawers, and the computer required a password. It began to
seem very much as if Shaw *expected* Banks to nose about.

There was an interesting framed photograph on the wall, quite a few years old by the look of it, showing a younger Shaw and Jet Harris standing by an unmarked Rover looking for all the world like John Thaw and Dennis Waterman in *The Sweeney*. Or was it Morse and Lewis? Is that how Shaw saw himself, as Sergeant Lewis to Harris's Chief Inspector Morse?

The bookcase held mostly binders and back issues of the *Police Review*. Mixed in were a few legal texts and an American textbook called *Practical Homicide Investigation*. Banks was browsing through this and trying not to look at the gruesome colour illustrations when, after half an hour, Shaw came back, followed by a rather embarrassed-looking DI Michelle Hart.

'Sorry about that,' said Shaw, sitting down opposite Banks. 'Something came up. You know how it is.' Michelle sat to one side looking uncomfortable.

'I know.' Banks put the book aside and reached for a cigarette.

'There's no smoking in here,' said Shaw. 'Not any-where in the building, not for any of us, these days. Maybe you're a bit behind the times in Yorkshire?'

Banks had known that he probably couldn't smoke, though Shaw had the nicotine-stained fingers of a heavy smoker, and he thought it at least worth a try. Obviously, though, this was going to be played the hard way, even though they had done him the courtesy of conducting the interview in the superintendent's office rather than in a dingy interview room. He didn't feel nervous, just puzzled and pissed off. What was going on?

'So, what can I do for you, Superintendent Shaw?'

'You don't remember me, do you?'

Shaw stared at Banks, and Banks searched through his

store of faces for a match. The ginger hair was thin on top, one long side strand combed over to hide the bald patch, but not fooling anyone, hardly any eyebrows, freckles, pale blue eyes, the face filled out and jowly, the fleshy, red-veined nose of a seasoned drinker. He was familiar, but there was something different about him. Then Banks knew.

'You've had your ears fixed,' he said. 'The wonders of modern medicine.'

Shaw reddened. 'So you *do* remember me.'

'You were the baby DC who came to our house after Graham disappeared.' It was hard to believe, but Shaw would have been about twenty-one at the time, only seven years older than Banks, yet he had seemed an adult, someone from another world.

'Tell me,' said Shaw, leaning forward across the table so Banks could smell the minty breath of a man who drinks his breakfast, 'I've always wondered. Did you ever get your budgie back?'

Banks leaned back in his chair. 'Well, now we've got all the pleasantries out of the way, why don't we get on with it?'

Shaw jerked his head at Michelle, who slid a photograph across the desk to Banks. She looked serious with her reading glasses on. Sexy, too, Banks thought. 'Is this the man?' she asked.

Banks stared at the black and white photo and felt a rush of blood to his brain, ears buzzing and vision clouding. It all flooded back, those few moments of claustrophobia and terror in the stranger's grip, the moments he had thought were his last.

'Are you all right?'

It was Michelle who spoke, a concerned look on her face.

'I'm fine,' he said.

'You look pale. Would you like a drink of water?'

'No, thank you,' said Banks. 'It's him.'

'Are you certain?'

'After all this time I can't be a hundred per cent positive, but I'm as certain as I'll ever be.'

Shaw nodded, and Michelle took the picture back.

'Why?' Banks asked, looking from one to the other. 'Who is it?'

'James Francis McCallum,' Michelle said. 'He went missing from a mental institution near Wisbech on Thursday, the seventeenth of June 1965.'

'That would be about right,' said Banks.

'McCallum hadn't been involved in any violent activity, but the doctors told us that the possibility always existed, and that he might be dangerous.'

'When was he caught?' Banks asked.

Michelle glanced at Shaw before answering. He gave her a curt nod. 'That's just it,' she went on. 'He wasn't. McCallum's body was fished out of the River Nene near Oundle on the first of July.'

Banks felt his mouth open and shut without any sound coming out. 'Dead?' he managed.

'Dead,' echoed Shaw. He tapped his pen on the desk. 'Nearly two months before your friend disappeared. So you see, DCI Banks, you've been labouring under an illusion for all these years. Now, what I'm really interested in is why you lied to me and DI Proctor in the first place.'

Banks felt numb from the shock he had just received. *Dead.* All these years. The guilt. And all for nothing. The man who assaulted him on the riverbank *couldn't* have abducted and killed Graham. He should have felt relieved, but he only felt confused. 'I didn't lie,' he muttered.

'Call it a sin of omission, then. You didn't tell us about McCallum.'

'Doesn't seem as if it would have mattered, does it?'

'Why didn't you tell us?'

'Look, I was just a kid. I hadn't told my parents because I was scared how they'd react. I was upset and ashamed by what happened. Don't ask me why, I don't know, but that's how I felt. Dirty and ashamed, as if it was somehow *my* fault for inviting it.'

'You should have told us. It could have been a lead.'

Banks knew that Shaw was right; he had told reluctant witnesses the same thing himself, time after time. 'Well, I didn't, and it wasn't,' he snapped. 'I'm sorry. Okay?'

But Shaw wasn't going to be so easily put off, Banks could tell. He was enjoying himself, throwing his weight around. It was the bully mentality. To him, Banks was still the fourteen-year-old kid whose budgie had just flown out the door. 'What really happened to your friend?' he asked.

'What do you mean?'

Shaw scratched his chin. 'I remember thinking at the time that you knew something, that you were holding something back. I'd like to have taken you to the station, had you down in the cells for an hour or so, but you were a minor, and Reg Proctor was a bit of a softie, when it came right down to it. What really happened?'

'I don't know. Graham just disappeared.'

'Are you sure you and your mates didn't set on him? Maybe it was an accident, things just went too far?'

'What the hell are you talking about?'

'I'm suggesting that maybe the three of you ganged up on Graham Marshall for some reason and killed him.

These things happen. Then you had to get rid of the body.'

Banks folded his arms. 'And tell me how we did that.'

'I don't know,' Shaw admitted. 'But I don't have to. Maybe you stole a car.'

'None of us could drive.'

'So you say.'

'It wasn't the way it is today, with ten-year-olds behind the wheel.'

'Is that how it happened? A fight broke out and Graham got killed? Maybe fell and smashed his skull, or broke his neck? I'm not saying you *intended* to kill him, but it happened, didn't it? Why don't you come clean with me, Banks? It'll do you good to get it off your chest after all these years.'

'Sir?'

'Shut up, DI Hart. Well, Banks? I'm waiting.'

Banks stood up. 'You'll have a bloody long wait, then. Goodbye.' He walked towards the door. Shaw didn't try to stop him. Just as Banks had turned the handle, he heard the superintendent speak again and turned to face him. Shaw was grinning. 'Only teasing, Banks,' he said. Then his expression became serious. 'My, but you're sensitive. The point I want to make is that you're on *my* turf, and it turns out you can't help us any more now than you could all those years ago. So my advice to you, laddie, is to bugger off back up to Yorkshire, go shag a sheep or two, and forget about Graham Marshall. Leave it to the pros.'

'Bloody good job the pros did last time,' said Banks, leaving and slamming the door behind him, annoyed at himself for losing his temper, but unable to prevent it. Outside the station he kicked a tyre, lit a cigarette and got in his car. Maybe Shaw was right and he should just head back up north. He still had over a week's holiday left and plenty to do around the cottage, whereas there was nothing more he could do down here. Before driving off, he sat for a moment trying to digest what Michelle and Shaw had told him. His guilt over the years had been misplaced, then; McCallum was in no way responsible for Graham's abduction and, by extension, neither was Banks. On the other hand, if he *had* reported the incident, there was a chance that McCallum might have been apprehended and hospitalized instead of drowning. *More guilt, then?*

Banks cast his mind back to that hot June afternoon by the river and asked himself if McCallum would have killed him. The answer, he decided, was yes. So sod the bastard, and sod guilt. McCallum was a dangerous loony and it wasn't Banks's fault he'd fallen in the fucking river and drowned. Good riddance.

Turning up the volume on Cream's 'Crossroads', he sped out of the police car park, daring one of the patrol cars to chase him. Nobody did.

•

They all looked tired, Annie thought, as the Armitage team gathered in the boardroom of Western Area Headquarters late that morning. The boardroom was so called because of its long polished table, high-backed chairs and paintings of nineteenth-century cotton magnates on the walls, red-faced, eyes popping, probably because of the tight collars they were wearing, Annie thought. As works of art, the paintings were negligible, if not execrable, but they lent authority to the room.

Detective Superintendent Gristhorpe sat at the head of the table and poured himself a glass of water. Also present were DCs Templeton, Rickerd and Jackman, and

Detective Sergeant Jim Hatchley, still clearly uneasy with Annie's promotion over him. But as Banks had told Annie more than once, Jim Hatchley was born to be a sergeant, and a damn good one, too. There wasn't much Hatchley didn't know about the shady side of Eastvale. He had a network of informers second only to his network of pub managers and landlords, who all kept an eye on criminal comings and goings for him, and his tiredness was probably due to the fact that his wife had just given birth to their second child a couple of weeks ago. It was the three DCs who had borne the brunt of the previous night's surveillance.

'So we're not much further ahead,' Gristhorpe opened.

'No, sir,' said Annie, who at least had managed her quick pint in Relton, then gone home for a bath and a few hours' sleep before arriving back at the station shortly after dawn. 'Except we've checked with the phone company and got Luke's records. We'll be tracking down all the people he phoned over the last month, though there aren't many. The ransom call to Martin Armitage was the only call made after Luke's disappearance, the only call made that day, and it was local. Wherever Luke is, he's not far away, or he wasn't on Tuesday evening.'

'Anything else?'

'We've got a fair idea of Luke's movements until five-thirty the day he disappeared.'

'Go ahead.'

Annie walked over to the whiteboard and listed the times and places as she mentioned them. She knew the details by heart and didn't need to consult her notebook. 'He arrived at the bus station by the Swainsdale Centre at a quarter to three. The bus driver and several of the passengers remember him. We've been looking at some of the CCTV footage, and he walked around the centre for a while, went into W.H. Smith's, then into HMV, but he didn't appear to buy anything. That takes us up until half-past three. He appeared in that small computer shop on North Market Street at a quarter to four, which is about right, as he was on foot. He stayed there half an hour, trying out some games, then he visited the music shop at the corner of York Road and Barton Place.'

'Did anyone notice anything unusual about his state of mind?' Gristhorpe asked.

'No. Everyone said he just seemed normal. Which, I guess, was pretty weird to start with. I mean, he wasn't exactly a barrel of laughs.'

'And next?'

'The used book shop on the market square.' Annie walked over to the window and pointed. 'That one down there. Norman's.'

'I know it,' said Gristhorpe. 'What did he buy?'

'*Crime and Punishment* and *Portrait of the Artist as a Young Man.*' Right up Gristhorpe's alley, Annie thought.

Gristhorpe whistled. 'Pretty heavy going for a fifteen-year-old. What next?'

'That was it. He walked out of the market square CCTV range at half-past five, and we haven't found anyone who admits to seeing him since. Oh, and he was also seen talking to a group of lads in the square after coming out of the bookshop. It looked as if they were ragging him. One of them took the parcel of books from his hand and they tossed it around to one another while he flailed around trying to get it back.'

'What happened in the end?'

'One of them threw it to him and they went off laughing.'

'Classmates?'

'Yes. We've had a chat with them. At least DC Templeton has.'

'Nothing there, sir,' said Templeton. 'They've all got alibis.'

'Which direction did he walk off in?' Gristhorpe asked.

'Down Market Street. South.'

Gristhorpe scratched his chin and frowned. 'What do you make of it all, Annie?' he asked.

'I don't know, sir. He's been gone three nights now and nobody's seen hide nor hair.'

'What about the Armitages?'

'Nothing.'

'Sure they're telling you the truth?'

'They've no reason to lie now,' Annie said. 'And the kidnapper knows we're treating Luke as a misper. Remember, it was him who suggested that the Armitages get Luke to back up their story.'

'Too late for that, now, isn't it?' said DC Kevin Templeton. 'I mean, wasn't he supposed to come home yesterday?'

'Yes.'

'So what happened?' Gristhorpe asked.

'He's probably dead, sir,' cut in DC Winsome Jackman.

'But why hasn't the kidnapper gone for the money?'

'Because he knows we're watching,' Annie answered. 'It's the only explanation. He must have seen me when I went up to the shelter to check the briefcase.'

Nobody said anything; there was nothing they *could* say. Annie knew they agreed with her and could all sense what she was feeling herself, that gut-wrenching fear that *she* might be responsible for the boy's death, that if she had stuck to rules and procedure, then things might have gone according to plan. To give him his due, though, whatever he thought, Gristhorpe didn't say anything.

'Unless . . .' Annie went on.

'Aye, lass?'

'Well, a couple of things have puzzled me about all this right from the start.'

'I agree that, as kidnappings go, it's hardly conventional,' said Gristhorpe, 'but go on.'

Annie took a sip of water. 'In the first place,' she said, 'why did the kidnapper wait so long before getting in touch with the Armitages and making his demand? Luke disappeared sometime late Monday afternoon or evening, according to what we've managed to find out so far, yet the demand didn't come until after dark on *Tuesday*.'

'Maybe the kidnapper didn't get hold of him until Tuesday,' DC Templeton suggested.

'You mean he really did run away and just happened to get picked up by a kidnapper before he could go back?'

'It's possible, isn't it?'

'Too much of a coincidence, I'd say.'

'Coincidences do happen.'

'Sometimes, maybe.'

'Or the kidnapper might have been keeping an eye on Luke for a while, watching his movements, biding his time.'

'I'll grant you that's more likely,' said Gristhorpe. 'Annie?'

'It still doesn't explain the time delay between Luke not turning up at home Monday night and the ransom demand on Tuesday evening, sir. These people don't usually like to waste time. If they snatched him on Monday, then they'd have rung the Armitages on Monday. Besides, that's only the first thing that bothered me.'

'What's next?' Gristhorpe asked.

'Well, Martin Armitage told me that when he asked to speak to Luke, the kidnapper wouldn't let him, said Luke was somewhere else.'

'So?' said DC Templeton. 'That's perfectly likely, isn't it?'

'But he was calling from Luke's mobile,' Annie pointed out.

'I still don't see your point,' said Templeton. 'Mobiles are mobile. You can take them anywhere. That's what they're for.'

Annie sighed. 'Think about it, Kev. If Luke's being kept somewhere where there isn't a phone, then the kidnapper might have to go to a phone box, and he'd be unlikely to take Luke with him. But the kidnapper was using Luke's mobile, so why isn't he with Luke?'

'Could be where they're keeping the lad is out of cell range,' suggested DC Rickerd.

'Possible,' Annie agreed, remembering her time out of range. 'But isn't it usual for kidnappers to let the people they want the money from speak to their loved ones? Isn't it an incentive to pay? Proof of life?'

'Good point, Annie,' said Gristhorpe. 'So we've got two unusual variations on the formula. First, the time delay, and second, no proof of life. Anything else?'

'Yes,' said Annie. 'The ransom demand.'

'What about it?' asked Gristhorpe.

'It's nowhere near enough.'

'But the Armitages aren't as rich as people think they are,' argued Templeton.

'My point exactly, Kev. So they're struggling to maintain Swainsdale Hall and whatever lifestyle they've become accustomed to. We know that now, since I talked to them, but it wasn't common knowledge. As police, we're privy to a lot of inside information. It's our life-blood. But if you kidnapped the son of a famous ex-model and a famous ex-footballer living in a place like Swains-dale Hall, how much would you *think* they were worth? How much would you ask them for the life of their son? Ten thousand? Twenty thousand? Fifty? I'd go to a hundred, myself, or maybe a quarter of a million. Let them negotiate down a few thousand from there. I certainly wouldn't start at ten.'

'So maybe the kidnapper knew they were on their uppers?' Templeton suggested. 'Maybe it's someone who knows the family?'

'Then why kidnap Luke at all? Why not go for someone who had more money?'

'Maybe that's all they needed. Maybe it's enough.'

'You're clutching at straws, Kev.'

Templeton smiled. 'Just playing devil's advocate, Ma'am, that's all. But if you're right, then perhaps they don't have quite the intelligence we're crediting them with.'

'Okay. Point taken.' Annie looked at Gristhorpe. 'But don't you think it's all a bit puzzling when you add it up, sir?'

Gristhorpe paused and made a steeple of his thick fingers on the desk before answering. 'I do,' he said. 'I can't say I've had to deal with many kidnappings over the course of my career – and for that I thank the Lord, because it's a cowardly crime – but I've dealt with a few, and none of them have been as riddled with anomalies as this one. What are your conclusions, Annie?'

'Either it's an amateur job,' Annie answered. '*Very* amateur, like some junkie who saw the chance to get enough money for his next few fixes and now he's too scared to go through with it.'

'Or?'

'Or it's something else entirely. A set-up, a diversion, the ransom demand merely to deflect us, confuse us, and something else is going on.'

'Like what?' Gristhorpe asked.

'I don't know, sir,' Annie answered. 'All I know is that in either scenario the outcome looks bad for Luke.'

•

It wasn't fair, thought Andrew Naylor, the man from the Ministry, as he drove his government Range Rover over the disinfectant pad at the entrance to the unfenced road above Gratly. He had nothing to do with foot-and-mouth control, yet in the eyes of the locals, all government employees were tarred with the same brush. Everyone knew him in the area, and before the outbreak no one had paid him much mind. Now, though, he was getting sick of the resentful looks he got when he walked into a shop or a pub, the way conversations stopped and whispers began, and the way people sometimes even expressed their anger to his face. In one pub they had been so hostile towards him he thought they were going to beat him up.

It didn't do the slightest bit of good to tell them that he worked for the Department for Environment, Food and Rural Affairs, DEFRA, in the Water and Land Directorate, and that his job was water, because that only made them think of Yorkshire Water – of droughts, leakages, shortages and restrictions on washing their bloody cars and watering their lawns – and then they got even angrier.

It was part of Andrew's job to collect water samples from local lakes, ponds, tarns and reservoirs, and these were later tested for contaminants at the Central Science Laboratory. Because some of these bodies of water were surrounded by open country, Andrew was one of the few with a special dispensation to visit them, after taking all the proper precautions, of course.

That day, his last call was Hallam Tarn, a godforsaken, hollowed-out bowl of water on the very top of the moor, beyond Tetchley Fell. Legend had it that the place used to be a village once, but the villagers took to Satanic practices, so God smote them with his fist and the tarn was created in place of the village. It was said that on certain days of the year you could see the old houses and streets beneath the water's surface and hear the cries of the villagers. Sometimes, when the light was right and the curlew's cry piped across the desolate moor, Andrew could almost believe it.

Today, though, the sun was shining, and the honeyed air was still and sweet. Summer seemed to have arrived at last, and Andrew couldn't imagine any hint of evil taking place.

The deepest part of the tarn ran closest to the road, and a tall, solid, drystone wall separated it from children and drunks and anyone else foolish enough to wander around up there in the dark. To get access to the water, you had to drive a few yards further on, cross the stile and take a footpath that led to its shallow shore. In the days before the government restrictions it was a popular spot for ramblers and picnickers, but these days it was off-limits, except to people such as Andrew. A government poster nailed to the stile warned people to stay out on penalty of a steep fine.

Before heading out with his dinghy and his sample jar, Andrew sprayed his wellington boots with disinfectant and donned his plastic outerwear. He felt like a spaceman preparing for a walk on the moon. He also felt hot inside the protective clothing, and all he wanted to do was get this over with as soon as possible then head home for a nice long bath and an evening out in Northallerton with Nancy, maybe the pictures, a spot of dinner and a drink after.

Feeling the sweat drip down the back of his neck, he walked along the narrow dirt path the hundred yards or so to the edge of the tarn and squatted by the waterside to fill his sample jar. It was so quiet up there, he could imagine himself the only man left in the world. Because he had to take samples from various depths, he got in the small dinghy and began to row. The tarn wasn't much bigger than a large pond, maybe a couple of hundred yards long and a hundred wide, but it was quite deep in places. Andrew felt a little disquiet at being out there all alone, not another soul in sight, and whenever he looked down into the water, he fancied he could see a roof or a street below. It was an optical illusion, of course, most likely caused by the sun on the water, but it unnerved him nonetheless.

When he neared the wall, he noticed some dark material snagged on the roots of an old tree. The tree was gone, but gnarled roots still jutted out of the bank like arms reaching out of a grave, and there was something about their arched, sinewy shapes that upset Andrew even more. Curious about the material, however, he put his fears aside and rowed closer. Legends and myths couldn't harm him.

When he got near enough, he stretched out his arm and tried to free the material from the root. It was heavier than he thought, and as it jerked free, the dinghy tipped and Andrew, off-balance, fell into the tarn. He was a strong swimmer, so drowning didn't worry him, but what chilled his blood was that the thing he was holding as tightly as a lover in a slow dance was a dead body, and from its ashen face, open dead eyes looked directly into his.

Andrew let go of the burden, mouth full of bile. He struggled back into the dinghy, salvaged his oars and rowed back to shore, where he stopped only long enough to be sick, before squelching back to his van, hoping to God his mobile worked up here. It didn't. Cursing, he threw it on the floor and started the van with shaking hands. As he drove back towards Helmthorpe, he glanced frequently in his rear-view mirror to make sure that no misshapen, supernatural beasts from the depths of the tarn were following him.

•

Banks still felt angry when he pulled up outside his parents' house, brakes squealing, but before he went inside he took several deep breaths and reined in his anger, determined not to let it show. His parents didn't need it; they had problems enough of their own. He found his father in front of the television watching horse racing and his mother in the kitchen fussing over a cake.

'I'm heading home this afternoon,' he said, popping his head around the kitchen door. 'Thanks for letting me stay.'

'There's always a bed for you here,' his mother said. 'You know that, son. Have you finished what you came for?'

'Not really,' said Banks, 'but there's not a lot more I can do.'

'You're a policeman. Surely you can do something to help?'

The way Banks's mother said 'policeman' wasn't quite as vehement as the way his father said it, nor was it as tinged with distaste as the way she used to say it, but it wasn't far off, which was why it had surprised Banks when Mrs Marshall told him his mother was proud of him. Banks's mother had always made it clear that she thought he had sold himself short, that he should have gone into commerce and worked himself up to be managing director of some big international company. It didn't seem to matter how well he did in his job, or how often he was promoted; to his mother, his career choice was undignified, and his achievements always seemed to pale beside those of his stockbroker brother, Roy. Banks had always suspected that Roy was a bit of a shady dealer, a frequent enough occurrence in the world of financial speculation, in his experience, though he would never voice such suspicions to his mother, or indeed to Roy himself. Still, he lived in dread of that telephone call coming from his brother one day: 'Alan, can you help me? I'm in a bit of a fix with the law.'

'It's not my case, Mum,' he said. 'The locals are good. They'll do the best they can.'

'Will you have something to eat with us before you go?'

'Of course. Know what I'd like?'

'What?'

'Fish and chips from over the road,' said Banks. 'I'll get them. My treat.'

'Well, maybe I'll have a fishcake,' said his mother. 'Your dad hasn't eaten from there since it went Chinese, though.'

'Go on, Dad,' said Banks, turning to the living room. 'Or maybe you should stick to your low-fat diet?'

'Bugger low fat,' said Arthur Banks. 'I'll have the

special and chips. Just make sure there's no bloody chop suey or sweet and sour sauce gone anywhere near it.' Banks winked at his mother and walked over to the shop.

The strip of shops across the main road, set back by a stretch of tarmac for customer parking, had gone through dozens of changes over the years. When Banks first moved to the estate, he remembered, there had been the fish and chip shop, a ladies' hairdresser, a butcher's, a greengrocer's and a launderette. Now there was a video rental shop, a takeaway pizza and tandoori place called Caesar's Taj Mahal, a mini-mart and a unisex hair salon. The only constants were the fish and chip shop, which now also sold takeaway Chinese food, too, and the news-agent's, which, according to the signs, was still run by the Walkers, who had taken over from Donald Bradford all those years ago, in 1966. Banks wondered what had become of Bradford. He was said to have been devastated over what had happened to Graham. Had the local police ever followed up on him?

Banks waited to cross the busy road. To the left of the shops stood the remains of the old ball-bearing factory, still untouched for some reason. It could hardly be for historical preservation, as it was a real eyesore. The gates were chained and padlocked shut, and it was surrounded by high wire-mesh fencing with barbed wire on top, the windows beyond covered by rusty grilles. Despite these security precautions, most of the windows were broken anyway, and the front of the blackened brick building was covered in colourful graffiti. Banks remembered when the place was in full production, lorries coming and going, factory whistle blowing and crowds of workers waiting at the bus stop. A lot of them were young women, or girls scarcely out of school – a rough lot, his mother called them – and Banks often used to time his visits to the shops to coincide with the whistle going and the factory gates opening because he lusted after some of the girls.

There was one girl in particular, he remembered, who used to stand at the bus stop smoking, a faraway look in her eyes, scarf done up like a turban on her head. Even her serviceable work clothes couldn't disguise the curves, and she had pale smooth skin and looked a bit like Julie Christie in *Billy Liar*. When Banks used to walk as casually as possible past the bus stop, he remembered as he stood in the fish and chip shop queue, the other girls used to tease him with lewd comments and make him blush.

'Hey, Mandy,' one of them would call out. 'Here comes that lad again. I think he fancies you.'

They would all howl with laughter, Mandy would tell them to shut up and Banks would blush. Once, Mandy tousled his hair and gave him a cigarette. He smoked it over a week, taking a few drags at a time, then nicking it to save for later. In the end it tasted like something he might have picked up from the gutter, but he finished it anyway. After that, Mandy would sometimes smile when he passed by. She had a nice smile. Sometimes strands of hair escaped from under her turban and curled over her cheek, and other times she might have a smudge of oil or dirt on her face. She must have been about eighteen. Four years' age difference. Far from an impossible gap when you get older, but wider than the Grand Canyon at that age.

Then, one day, he noticed that she had started wearing an engagement ring, and a few weeks later she no longer stood at the bus stop with the others, and he never saw her again.

Where was Mandy now? he wondered. She'd be in her fifties if she was still alive, older than Kay Summerville. Had she put on a lot of weight? Had her hair turned grey? Did she look old and worn after years of struggle and poverty? Had she stayed married to the same man? Had she won the Lottery and gone to live on the Costa del Sol? Did she ever think of that love-struck adolescent who used to time his visits to the shops so he could see her waiting at the bus stop? He doubted it very much. The lives we leave behind. So many people. Our paths cross for a while, even as fleetingly as his had crossed Mandy's, and we move on. Some encounters are impressed indelibly on our memories; others slip away into the void. Of course Mandy never thought of him; he was a mere passing amusement to her, whereas she fed deeper into his adolescent dreams of sex, and in his memory she would always be standing there with her hip against the bus stop smoking in her turban with a far-away look in her eyes, a loose lock of hair resting softly against her pale cheek, always beautiful and always eighteen.

'Two specials and chips and one fishcake.'

Banks paid for the fish and chips and set off back home carrying the paper bag. No newspaper-wrapped fish and chips any more. Dirty. Not healthy.

'There was a telephone call for you while you were out, Alan,' his mother said when he got back.

'Who was it?'

'Same woman as called last night. Have you got a new girlfriend already?'

Already. Sandra had been gone nearly two years, was pregnant with another man's child and about to marry him. Had Banks got a new girlfriend *already*?

'No, Mum,' he said. 'It's one of the local coppers. You already know that from last night. They let women on the force these days.'

'No need to be cheeky. Eat your fish and chips before they go cold.'

'What did she say?'

'To ring her back when you had a moment. I wrote down the number just in case you'd forgotten it.'

Banks's mother rolled her eyes when he left the table and headed towards the telephone. His father didn't notice; he had his fish and chips on the paper on his lap and was eating them with his fingers, engrossed in the one-thirty from Newmarket, glass of beer balanced precariously on the arm of the chair.

The number scribbled on the pad by the hall telephone wasn't familiar. It certainly wasn't Thorpe Wood. Curious, Banks dialled.

'DI Hart here. Who's speaking?'

'Michelle? It's me. Alan Banks.'

'Ah, DCI Banks.'

'You left a message for me to call. Is this your mobile number?'

'That's right. Look, first off, I'm sorry about Detective Superintendent Shaw this morning.'

'That's all right. Not your fault.'

'I just felt . . . well, anyway, I'm surprised he's taking such an interest. It's not even his case. I had him marked down as just putting in time till his retirement, now he's all over me like a dirty shirt.'

'What did you want to talk to me about?'

'Are you going home?'

'Yes.'

'When?'

'I don't know. This afternoon. This evening. No point hanging around where I'm not wanted.'

'Don't feel sorry for yourself. It doesn't suit you. Only I was wondering if you'd like to meet up for a chat before you go, if you're not in a hurry.'

'Any particular reason?'

'Perhaps because I *didn't* treat you like an undesirable alien, despite your less than polite introduction.'

'Yes, okay. Why not?'

'Shall we say half-past five in Starbucks, Cathedral Square?'

'There's a Starbucks? In Peterborough?'

'Don't sound so surprised. We're very with it these days. There's a McDonald's, too, if you'd prefer?'

'No. Starbucks will do fine. Half-five it is. That'll give me plenty of time to pack and say my goodbyes. See you there.'

●

Annie and Gristhorpe arrived at Hallam Tarn in time to see two police frogmen haul up the body and pull it back to shore with them. Peter Darby, crime scene photographer, sat in a dinghy nearby and videotaped everything. He had already taken several stills and Polaroids of the spot where the body had been first seen by Andrew Naylor. One of the lads at Helmthorpe had found a dry set of clothes for Naylor, and he stood with the small group, chewing his fingernails as the frogmen edged closer to shore.

Once on shore, they laid the body on the grass at the feet of Dr Burns, the police surgeon. Dr Glendenning, the Home Office pathologist, was unavailable that day, as he had been called in to help a colleague with a difficult case in Scarborough. Detective Sergeant Stefan Nowak, crime scene co-ordinator, and his scene of crime officers were on their way.

Well, Annie thought with some relief, at least it wasn't a floater. She had been at the scene of more than one bloated, misshapen lump pulled from the water, and she didn't relish another. But when she saw the face, she would gladly have accepted an anonymous floater any day. The body was Luke Armitage's. No doubt about it. He was wearing the black T-shirt and jeans that Robin had said he had on when he went to Eastvale, and he hadn't been in the water long enough for his features to become unrecognizable, though the skin was white and there were signs of *cutis anserina*, more commonly known as 'gooseflesh'. The once dark curls were straight now and stuck to his head and face like seaweed.

Annie stood aside and let Dr Burns perform his in situ examination. 'This is going to be difficult,' he told Annie. 'In general, bodies decompose twice as fast in air as in water, but there are so many variables to take into account.'

'Any chance he drowned?'

The doctor examined Luke's mouth for signs of foam and his eyes for the telltale petechial haemorrhages associated with asphyxia, of which drowning is a form. He shook his head and turned back to Annie. 'Hard to be certain. We'll have a better idea when Dr Glendenning checks the lungs and runs a diatomic analysis.'

Diatoms, Annie knew from her basic courses in forensic science, were micro-organisms that lived in the water. If you drowned, you breathed in a lot of them with the water and they spread to every nook and cranny of your body, even your bone marrow; if you hadn't drowned but were found dead in water, then a few diatoms might be found, but they would be nowhere near as abundant or widely spread.

Dr Burns turned the body over and pointed to the back of Luke's head. Annie could see the signs of a blow. 'Would that have been enough to cause death?' she asked.

'Hard blow to the cerebellum?' said Dr Burns. 'Certainly.' He began to examine the body in more detail. 'He's cold,' he said, 'and there's no rigor.'

'What does that tell you?'

'Usually a body is cold after eight to ten hours in the water. I'll have to take his temperature to substantiate this, of course, and we'll need to know the temperature of the water, too. As for the rigor, given the obvious effects of water on his skin, it must have come and gone.'

'How long does that take?'

'In water? Anything from two to four days.'

'Not sooner?'

'Not usually, no. Again, though, I'll have to make some temperature checks. It might be summer but we've hardly been enjoying seasonal temperatures of late.'

Two days, Annie thought. It was Thursday afternoon now, and the ransom demand had come two days ago, on Tuesday evening. Was Luke already dead by then? If so, his death was nothing to do with her rash actions. She began to feel a glimmer of hope. If that were the case, then the kidnapper was trying to cash in on Luke's death, which could have come about for other reasons. Curious. She would have to begin casting about for a motive now.

The sound of an approaching van interrupted Annie's stream of thought, and she looked across to the wall to see DS Nowak and his SOCO team jumping the stile one after another, looking like sheep in their white protective clothing. Well, she thought, maybe the experts would be able to tell her a bit more.

•

Banks arrived half an hour early for his meeting with Michelle, parked in the short-stay round the back of the town hall and cut through the arcade to Bridge Street, where he nipped into Waterstone's and bought a book called *The Profession of Violence*, the story of the Kray twins. As he walked up the busy street towards the square, he marvelled at how much the city centre had changed since his day. For a start, it was all pedestrian precinct now, not busy roads the way it had been when he lived there. And it seemed cleaner, the buildings less shabby and grime-coated. It was a sunny afternoon, and tourists wandered in and out of the cathedral grounds into the square to spend a while browsing through the shops. Banks found it all quite pleasant, which didn't square with his memory of being stuck in a dirty, small-minded provincial backwater. Maybe it was he who had changed the most.

He found Starbucks on the corner by the cathedral entrance and sipped a latte grande while he flipped through the book.

Michelle arrived five minutes late, cool and collected, wearing black slacks and a slate-grey jacket over a cream blouse. She went to the counter for a cappuccino then sat down opposite Banks.

'Bit of a shock for you, wasn't it, this morning?' she said.

'I suppose so,' Banks said. 'After all these years . . . I don't know, I suppose I'd allowed myself to believe there had to be a connection. Conned myself.'

'We all do, one way or another.'

'You're too young to be so cynical.'

'And you should be old and wise enough to realize that flattery will get you nowhere. You've got a bit of froth on your lip.'

Before Banks could wipe it away, Michelle reached out her finger and did it for him, her fingertip brushing his lip.

'Thanks,' he said.

Michelle blushed, turned her head away and let out a little giggle. 'I don't know why I did that,' she said. 'My mother used to do it when I drank milkshakes.'

'Haven't had a milkshake in years,' said Banks.

'Me neither. What next?'

'Home. And you?'

'Dunno. The leads are hardly jumping out at me left, right and centre.'

Banks thought for a moment. He hadn't told Shaw about the possible Kray connection because Shaw had behaved like a bastard. Besides, it wasn't his case. There was no reason to keep it from Michelle, though. It probably meant nothing, but at least it would give her something to do, the illusion of progress.

'I've heard rumours that Graham Marshall's dad was connected with the Krays in London just before the family moved up here.'

'Connected? In what way?'

'Strong-arm man. Enforcer. I don't know how true it is – you know how these things can be exaggerated – but it might be worth a bit of delving into.'

'How do you know this?'

Banks touched the side of his nose. 'I've got my sources.'

'And how long have you known?'

'Just found out before I came here.'

'Yeah, and the Pope's Jewish.'

'The point is, what are you going to do about it?'

Michelle moved the froth in her cup around with a spoon. 'I don't suppose it'd do any harm to set a few enquiries in motion. Might even get a trip to London out of it. You sure I won't come out looking like a complete moron?'

'I can't guarantee that. It's always a risk. Better than being the moron who missed the vital clue, though.'

'Thanks. That's *really* encouraging. I don't know very much about the Krays – before my time. I haven't even seen the film. I do remember the big funeral they gave one of them in the East End not so long ago, though.'

'That'd be Reggie. Couple of years ago. The whole East End came out for him. It was the same when Ronnie died in 1995. Very popular among East Enders, the Krays were. Loved their mother. There were three of them, an older brother called Charlie, but Ronnie and Reggie, the twins, are the ones people focus on. They pretty much ran the East End during the fifties and sixties, and a fair bit of the West End, too, till they got put away. Ronnie was the crazy one. Paranoid schizophrenic. He ended up in Broadmoor. Reggie was Category "A" in Parkhurst. I suppose you could say that he was led astray by his more dominant twin brother, if you wanted to be charitable.'

'But what could they have to do with Graham Marshall's disappearance and murder?'

'Probably nothing,' Banks said. 'They didn't operate outside London much, except for maybe a few clubs in cities like Birmingham or Leicester. But if Bill Marshall did work for them, then there's always the chance he left them reason to bear a grudge, and the twins had a long reach.'

'And for that they'd kill his son?'

'I don't know, Michelle. These people have a very warped sense of justice. And, don't forget, Ronnie was crazy. He was a sexual sadist, a serious pervert, among other things. He was the one who walked into the Blind Beggar and shot George Cornell right between the eyes in front of a room full of witnesses. Know what was playing on the jukebox?'

'Tell me.'

'It was the Walker Brothers, "The Sun Ain't Gonna Shine Anymore". And they say the needle got stuck on "anymore" when he was shot.'

'How melodramatic. I don't remember the Walker Brothers.'

'Not many people do. Want me to sing you a couple of verses?'

'I thought you said you never sing to women you've just met?'

'I did?'

'Don't you remember?'

'Nothing slips past you, does it?'

'Not much. I know you read Philip Larkin, too.'

'How?'

'You quoted him.'

'I'm impressed. Anyway, who knows how someone like Ronnie Kray thinks, if "think" is even the right word? He was seeing enemies all around him by then and coming up with more and more dramatic ways of hurting people. He loved to inspire fear and trembling, even in his own men. He was also a homosexual with a taste for teenage boys. They wouldn't have done Graham themselves, of course – they'd have got agoraphobia if they came this far north of London – but they could have sent someone to do it. Anyway, it's not only that.'

'What, then?'

'If Bill Marshall did work as a strong-arm man for the Krays, what was he doing up here? You know as well as I do that people don't just walk away from that line of work. Maybe he got himself fixed up with someone local, a branch manager.'

'So you're saying he might have been up to the same tricks here and that might have had something to do with Graham's death?'

'I'm just saying it's possible, that's all. Worth investigating.'

'There was a reference to a protection racket in the old crime logs,' Michelle said. 'Someone called Carlo Fiorino. Ring any bells?'

'Vaguely,' said Banks. 'Maybe his name was in the papers when I was a kid. Anyway, it's something to think about.'

'So why didn't it come up in the original investigation?'

'Didn't it?' said Banks. 'Dunno. Want another coffee?'

Michelle looked into her empty cup. 'Sure.'

Banks went and got two more coffees, and when he came back Michelle was leafing through the book.

'Borrow it if you want,' he said. 'I just picked it up to see if I could fill in a bit more background.'

'Thanks. I'd like to read it. Did Graham ever mention the Krays to you?'

'Yes, but I'm not sure that he ever said he or his dad knew them. I've also been thinking about the time frame. Graham and his parents came up here around July or August 1964. In July there was a big brouhaha in the press over Ronnie's alleged homosexual relationship with Lord

Boothby, who denied everything and sued the *Sunday Mirror* for libel. Ronnie followed suit, but all he got was an apology. Still, there was an upside in that the press had to lay off the Krays for a while after that. Nobody wanted any more libel suits. One day Ronnie was a thug and a gangster, the next a sporting gentleman. It set the police investigation back, too. Everyone had to walk on eggs around them. Even so, they were arrested the next January for demanding money with menaces. There was no bail and they were tried at the Old Bailey.'

'What happened?'

'They got off. It was a flimsy enough case to start with. There was talk of jury tampering. See, back then, there was no majority verdict like we have today. All twelve had to agree, or there'd be a retrial, which would give the accused even more time to fix things. They dug up some dirt on one of the main prosecution witnesses and that was it, they were free.'

'But how does any of this relate to Graham?'

'I'm not saying it does, only that that was what was happening around 1964 and 1965, the period we're concerned with. The Krays were in the public eye a lot. The libel case and the trial were both big news, and after they got off they were fireproof for a long time. It was the start of their ascendancy as celebrities, the dark side of Swinging London, you might say. Soon they were being photographed with film stars, sporting figures and pop singers: Barbara Windsor, Sonny Liston, Judy Garland, Victor Spinetti – who was in *A Hard Day's Night*, *Help!* and *Magical Mystery Tour*, if you can handle another piece of trivia. In the summer of 1965 they had a fiddle involving selling stolen American securities and bonds for the Mafia, and they were squaring up for a big fight with their rivals, the Richardson gang.' Banks tapped the book. 'It's all in there. I don't know if it means anything. But as your boss made clear this morning, it's none of my business.'

Michelle frowned. 'Yeah, I know. I keep thinking he's looking over my shoulder, even now, in here.'

'I don't want you to get into trouble for talking to me.'

'Don't worry. I wasn't followed. I'm only being paranoid.'

'It doesn't mean you're *not* being followed. Will you keep in touch, let me know if you come up with anything?'

'I shouldn't, but I will.'

'And if there's any way I can help . . .'

'Of course. If you remember anything Graham said or did that might be useful, I'd appreciate knowing.'

'You will. Look, Graham's mother mentioned a funeral, when the remains have been released. Any idea how long that might be?'

'I'm not sure. It shouldn't be long. I'll see how Dr Cooper's doing tomorrow.'

'Would you? Good. I think I'd like to come down for it. Even Shaw can't complain about *that*. Will you let me know?'

'Of course. Can I ask you something?'

'Go ahead.'

'That remark Shaw made about the budgie. What did he mean?'

Banks related the sad story of Joey's flight to freedom and certain death. By the end, Michelle was smiling. 'That's so sad,' she said. 'You must have been heartbroken.'

'I got over it. He wasn't exactly a wonder-budgie. He couldn't even talk. As everyone told me at the time, he wasn't Goldie the Eagle.'

'Goldie the Eagle?'

'Yes. Earlier the same year, 1965, Goldie the Eagle escaped from London Zoo. They got her back a couple of weeks later. It was a big story at the time.'

'But your Joey was never found?'

'No. He had no defences. He must have thought he was home free, but he couldn't survive all the predators out there. He was in way over his plumage. Look,' Banks went on, 'will you answer a question for me?'

Michelle nodded but looked wary and shuffled in her seat.

'Are you married?' Banks asked.

'No,' she said. 'No, I'm not.' And she got up and walked out without even saying goodbye.

Banks was about to go after her when his mobile rang. Cursing, and feeling like a bit of a pillock, the way he always did when it went off in a public place, Banks answered the call.

'Alan? It's Annie. Hope I haven't called at a bad time.'

'No, not at all.'

'Only we could use a bit of extra help, if you've finished your business down there.'

'Pretty much,' said Banks, thinking that his partings with both members of the local constabulary he had met left a lot to be desired. 'What's up?'

'Know that missing kid I told you about?'

'Luke Armitage?'

'That's the one.'

'What about him?'

'It looks as if it's just turned into a murder case.'

'Shit,' said Banks. 'I'm on my way.'

9

'**Strictly speaking**, you know,' said Banks, 'this is your case. It has been from the start. Are you sure you want me muscling in?'

'I wouldn't have rung you if I didn't, would I?' said Annie. 'Besides, you know I'm not that kind of copper.'

'What kind of copper?'

'All territorial and bureaucratic. I don't go in for pissing matches. I'm all for cooperation, me, not competition.'

'Fair enough. Let's chalk my comment down to recent experience.'

'What do you mean?'

Banks told her about Detective Superintendent Shaw.

'Well,' Annie said. 'Don't say I didn't warn you they wouldn't exactly welcome you with open arms.'

'Thanks.'

'My pleasure. Anyway, you can help me just as long as you give me the respect I deserve and don't treat me like a skivvy.'

'Have I ever?'

'This is a pretty good start.'

Banks's car was in the garage for servicing and wouldn't be ready until after lunch, so they had signed out a department car that morning, and Annie was driving, something Banks usually liked to do himself.

'I was thinking I could sort of get to like it,' said Banks. 'There's a lot to be said for having a *chauffeuse*.'

Annie shot him a look. 'Feel like getting out and walking the rest of the way?'

'No thanks.'

'Well, behave yourself. Anyway,' she went on, 'if you want to be all official about it, it's the Big Man's case. He's the SIO, and he's the one who suggested if I asked you nicely you might come back from leave early and give us the benefit of your considerable expertise.'

'The Big Man?'

'Detective Superintendent Gristhorpe.'

'Does he know you call him that?'

Annie grinned. 'You should hear what we call *you* in the squad room.'

'I must say it's great to be home,' said Banks.

Annie glanced sideways at him. 'How did things go, other than your run-in with the local constabulary?'

'All a bit embarrassing, really.' Banks told her about McCallum turning out to be an escaped mental patient who drowned before Graham disappeared.

'I'm so sorry, Alan,' she said, touching his knee. 'After all those years feeling guilty and responsible . . . But you must be relieved, in a way . . . I mean, knowing it couldn't have been him, so it wasn't your fault?'

'I suppose I must. You know, apart from the police down there, you're the only other person I've ever told about what happened by the river that day.'

'You never told Sandra?'

'No.'

'Why?'

'I don't know.'

Banks felt Annie retreat into silence beside him and knew he'd done again exactly the sort of thing that caused her to end their romantic relationship. It was as if she offered him something warm, soft and sensitive, yet the moment he reached out and touched it, she shot back into her hard, impenetrable shell.

Before either of them could think of anything else to say, they arrived at the end of the Armitages' drive, where reporters clamoured around them with pens, microphones and cameras. The officer on duty lifted the tape and let them through.

'Impressive,' said Banks, when the building's solid, symmetrical architecture came into view. 'I've only seen the place from the riverside walk before.'

'Just wait until you meet the beautiful people inside.'

'Go easy, Annie, they've just lost their son.'

Annie sighed. 'I know that. And I will. Okay?'

'Okay.'

'I'm just not looking forward to this.'

'Who dealt with the identification?'

'Winsome did. Last night.'

'So you haven't seen the family since the boy's body was found?'

'No.'

'If you don't think I'm being patronizing, why don't you let me deal with them?'

'Be my guest. Honest. Given my track record with Martin Armitage, I'd be grateful to be an observer this time. Fresh approach and all that.'

'Okay.'

Josie answered the front door almost the moment they rang the bell and led the two of them into the living room, where Banks introduced himself.

'What is it now?' Martin Armitage asked, glaring at Annie. Neither he nor his wife looked as if they had had much sleep, and they probably hadn't.

'A murder investigation,' said Banks. 'Or so it seems. And we need your help.'

'I don't see how we can help any more than we have done already. We cooperated with you, against the kidnapper's wishes, and look what happened.' He glanced towards Annie again, voice rising. 'I hope you realize this is your fault, that Luke's death is *your* responsibility. If you hadn't followed me to the shelter and then come nosing around here, the kidnapper would have picked up the money and Luke would be home safe and sound.'

'Martin,' said Robin Armitage. 'We've been over this again and again. Don't make a scene.'

'Don't make a scene! Good God, woman, this is your son we're talking about. She as good as killed him.'

'Calm down, Mr Armitage,' said Banks. Martin Armitage wasn't quite as tall as Banks had imagined, but he was fit and bursting with energy. Not the kind of man to sit around waiting for results, but one who went out and made the result happen. That was the way he'd played football, too, Banks remembered. Armitage hadn't been content to hang around the goal mouth waiting for a midfielder to feed him the ball; he had created scoring opportunities himself, and the main criticism levelled at him was that he was greedy for the ball, more apt to shoot and miss than pass to someone in a better scoring position. He had also lacked self-control and attracted a high number of red and yellow cards. Banks remembered once seeing him lash out at a member of the other team who had taken the ball from him fairly in the penalty area. He'd given away a penalty over that, and it lost his side the game.

'This is a difficult enough job as it is,' said Banks, 'without you making it worse. I'm sorry for your loss, but it's no good flinging blame about. We don't know how or why Luke died yet. We don't even know where or when. So until we've been able to answer some of those basic questions we're not in a position to jump to conclusions. I suggest you exercise the same restraint.'

'What else would you say?' said Martin. 'You always stick together, you lot.'

'Can we get down to business?'

'Yes, of course,' said Robin, sitting on the sofa in jeans and a pale green blouse, long legs crossed, hands folded on her lap. Without make-up and with her famous gold-blonde hair tied back in a ponytail, she still looked gorgeous, Banks thought, and the crow's feet only enhanced her beauty. She had the classic model's face, high cheekbones, small nose, pointed chin, perfect proportions, but she also had character and individuality in her features.

Banks had once worked on a case for the Met involving a modelling agency and he had been surprised that so many of these women who looked beautiful in magazines and on television lacked something in real life, their features perfect but bland, unformed and unfinished, like a blank canvas or an actor without a role. But Robin Armitage had presence.

'I'm sure you know,' said Banks, 'that Luke's death changes everything. It changes the way we proceed in the investigation, and we're going to have to go over much of the same ground again. This may seem tedious and pointless to you but, believe me, it's necessary. I'm new to the case, but I took the time this morning to familiarize myself with the investigation so far, and I have to say that I've found nothing out of order, nothing I wouldn't have done had I been in charge myself.'

'Like I said,' Martin chipped in, 'you lot stick together. I'll be complaining to the chief constable. He's a personal friend of mine.'

'That's your privilege, but he'll only tell you the same as I'm telling you. If everyone gave in to a kidnapper's demands without informing the police, it would be the most popular crime in the country.'

'But look what happened when we *did* inform the police. Our son is dead.'

'Something went wrong. This was an unusual case from the start; there are a number of inconsistencies.'

'What are you suggesting? That it *wasn't* a straight-forward kidnapping?'

'There was nothing straightforward about it at all, Mr Armitage.'

'I don't understand,' said Robin. 'The phone call . . . the ransom demand . . . they were genuine, surely?'

'Yes,' said Annie, taking a cue from Banks, 'but the ransom demand came an unusually long time after Luke disappeared, the kidnapper didn't let you speak to your son, and the sum he asked for was ridiculously low.'

'I don't know what you're talking about,' said Martin. 'We're not made of money.'

'I know that,' Annie said. 'But how would the kidnapper know? To all intents and purposes footballers and models make millions, and you're living in a mansion.'

Martin frowned. 'I suppose you've got a point. Unless . . .'

'Yes?' Banks picked up the questioning again.

'Unless it was someone close to us.'

'Can you think of anyone?'

'Of course not. I can't imagine any of our friends doing something like this. Are you insane?'

'Mrs Armitage?'

Robin shook her head. 'No.'

'We'll still need a list of people to talk to.'

'I'm not having you going around bullying our friends,' said Martin.

'Don't worry, we'll be discreet. And, don't forget, you're the one who suggested it might be someone close to you. Anyone have a grudge against either of you?'

'A few goalies, I suppose,' said Martin, 'but nothing serious, no.'

'Mrs Armitage?'

'I don't think so. Modelling can be a brutally competitive career, and I'm sure I stood on my share of toes on the catwalk, but nothing so . . . terrible . . . I mean, nothing to make anyone do something like this, especially so long after.'

'If you'd both like to think about it for a while, it would be a great help.'

'You said it was odd that he wouldn't let us talk to Luke,' Robin said.

'It's unusual, yes,' Annie answered.

'Do you think it was because . . . because Luke was already dead?'

'That's possible,' said Annie, 'but we won't know until the pathologist has finished his job.'

'When will that be?'

'Perhaps by this evening or early tomorrow.' Dr Burns, the police surgeon, had been unable to give an accurate estimate of time of death at the scene, so they would have to wait until Dr Glendenning had finished his post-mortem examination of Luke's body. Even then, they had learned not to expect miracles from medical science.

'Can you remember anything else about the caller?' Banks asked Martin Armitage.

'I've told you everything I know. I can't remember any more.'

'The voice definitely wasn't familiar?'

'No one I recognized.'

'And there was only the one call?'

'Yes.'

'Is there anything else you can tell us that might be of help?'

Both Martin and Robin Armitage shook their heads. Banks and Annie got up. 'We'll need to have a look at Luke's room next,' said Banks, 'and then we'd like to talk to your housekeeper and her husband.'

'Josie and Calvin?' said Martin. 'But why?'

'They might be able to help.'

'I can't see how.'

'Were they close to Luke?'

'Not especially. If truth be told, I always got the impression that they thought him a bit of a weirdo. They're wonderful people, salt of the earth, but sort of traditional in their views of people and behaviour.'

'And Luke didn't fit the mould?'

'No. He might as well have come from outer space as far as they're concerned.'

'Was there any animosity?'

'Of course not. They are our employees, after all. What are you suggesting, that they had something to do with this?'

'I'm not suggesting anything, merely asking. Look, Mr Armitage, I can understand your feelings, honestly I can, but you must let us do our jobs the way we see fit. It's not going to help at all if you start challenging every move we make. I promise you we'll be as discreet as we can with all our enquiries. No matter what you think, we don't go around bullying people. But we also don't accept everything at face value. People lie for a variety of reasons, many of them irrelevant to the investigation, but sometimes it's because they did it, and it's for us to sort out the lies from the truth. You've already lied to us once yourself that we know of, when you rang DI Cabbot and told her you'd heard from Luke.'

'I did that to protect Luke.'

'I understand *why* you did it, but it was still a lie. Maybe you can see how complicated our job becomes when you take all the lies into account. The lies of the innocent, especially. As I said, we don't take things, or people, at face value and, like it or not, every murder investigation begins close to home then moves outwards. Now, if you don't mind, we'll take a look at Luke's room.'

•

Michelle had been joking when she told Banks she was getting paranoid, but she was beginning to think that every time she visited the archives, Mrs Metcalfe rang Detective Superintendent Shaw. Here he was again, preceded by the dark chill of his shadow, on the threshold of the tiny room.

'Any progress?' he asked, leaning against the door.

'I'm not sure,' said Michelle. 'I've been going over the old crime reports for 1965 looking for some sort of connection with Graham's disappearance.'

'And have you found any?'

'Not directly, no.'

'I told you you were wasting your time.'

'Maybe not entirely.'

'What do you mean?'

Michelle paused. She had to be careful what she said because she didn't want Shaw to know that Banks had tipped her off to the Kray connection. That would send him into a tantrum she could well do without. 'I was reading over the reports and statements on a protection racket investigation in July 1965, and Graham's dad's name came up.'

'So? Where's the connection?'

'A club on Church Street called Le Phonographe.'

'I remember that place. It was a discotheque.'

Michelle frowned. 'I thought disco was in the seventies, not the sixties.'

'I'm not talking about the music, but the establishment itself. Clubs like Le Phonographe offered memberships and served meals, usually an inedible beefburger, if my memory serves me well, so they could sell alcohol legally after regular closing time. They'd stay open till three in the morning, or so. There'd be music and dancing, too, but it was usually Motown or soul.'

'You sound familiar with the place, sir.'

'I was young once, DI Hart. Besides, Le Phonographe was the sort of place you kept an eye on. It was a villains' club. Owned by a nasty piece of work called Carlo Fiorino. Used to like to pretend he was Mafia, wore the striped, wide-lapel suits, pencil-thin moustache, spats and everything – very Untouchables – but his father was a POW who ended up staying on after the war and marrying a local farm girl out Huntingdon way. Plenty of local villains hung out there, and you could often pick up a tip or two. And I don't mean for the three-thirty at Kempton Park.'

'So it was a criminal hangout?'

'Back then, yes. But petty. People who liked to think they were big players.'

'Including Bill Marshall?'

'Yes.'

'So you knew about Bill Marshall's activities?'

'Of course we did. He was strictly a minor presence. We kept an eye on him. It was routine.'

'What was this Carlo Fiorino's game?'

'Bit of everything. Soon as the new town expansion was well under way he turned Le Phonographe into a more upmarket club, with decent grub, a better dance floor and a casino. He also owned an escort agency. We think he also got into drugs, prostitution and pornography, but he was always clever enough to stay one step ahead, and he played both sides against the middle. Most of the time.'

'What do you mean, sir?'

'Got himself shot in a drug war with the Jamaicans in 1982.'

'But he never did time?'

'Never got charged with anything, far as I remember.'

'Doesn't that strike you as odd, sir?'

'Odd?' Shaw seemed to snap out of his reminiscing mood and become his grumpy old self again. He stuck his face so close to hers that she could smell his tobacco, mint and whisky breath and see the lattice of purple veins throbbing in his bulbous nose. 'I'll tell you what's bloody odd, DI Hart. It's you asking these questions. That's what's odd. None of this can possibly have anything to do with what happened to Graham Marshall, and that's a fact. You're muck-raking. I don't know why, but that's what you're doing.'

'Sir, all I'm doing is trying to get a handle on the circumstances of the boy's disappearance. Looking over the investigation and over other investigations around the same time seems a reasonable way of doing it to me.'

'It's not your brief to look into the Marshall investigation, DI Hart, or any other for that matter. Who do you think you are, Complaints and Discipline? Stick to your job.'

'But, sir, Bill Marshall was one of the men interviewed in connection with this protection racket, all involved with Carlo Fiorino and Le Phonographe. Some of the city centre shopkeepers filed a complaint, and Marshall was one of the people they named.'

'Was he charged?'

'No, sir. Only questioned. One of the original complainants ended up in hospital and the other witnesses backed off, retracted their statements. No further action.'

Shaw smirked. 'Then it's hardly relevant, is it?'

'But doesn't it seem odd to you that no further action was taken? And that when Graham Marshall disappeared, his father never came under close scrutiny, even though he had recently been implicated in a criminal ring?'

'Why should he? Maybe he didn't do it. Did that thought ever enter your head? And even if he was involved in some petty protection racket, it doesn't make him a child killer, does it? Even by your standards that's a long stretch of the imagination.'

'Was Bill Marshall a police informer?'

'He might have let slip the odd snippet of information. That's how we played the game back then. Tit for tat.'

'Is that why he was protected from prosecution?'

'How the hell should I know? If you've read your paperwork, you'll know I wasn't on that case.' He took a deep breath, then seemed to relax and soften his tone.

'Look,' he said, 'policing was different back then. There was more give and take.'

Plenty of *take*, Michelle thought. She'd heard stories of the old days, of departments, of stations and even of whole counties run wild. But she didn't say anything.

'So we bent the rules every now and then,' Shaw continued. 'Grow up. Welcome to the real world.'

Michelle made a mental note about Bill Marshall's possible role as a police informer. If he had informed on criminals here in Peterborough, she could only imagine what the Krays might have done if he'd tried anything like that with them and then disappeared. The South Pole wouldn't have been far enough, let alone Peterborough. 'From what I can piece together,' she went on, 'the Graham Marshall investigation followed one line of enquiry and one only when it became clear that he hadn't run away from home: a sex killing by a passing pervert.'

'Well? What's so odd about that? It's what the evidence pointed to.'

'Just seems a bit of a coincidence, that's all, that some pervert should happen to be driving by a quiet street at that hour in the morning, just as Graham's doing his paper rounds.'

'Wrong place at the wrong time. Happens often enough. Besides, do you think perverts don't know about paper rounds? Don't you think someone could have been watching, studying, stalking the Marshall kid, the way such perverts often do? Or didn't they teach you that at Bramshill?'

'It's possible, sir.'

'You think you can do better than us, do you?' said Shaw, his face turning red again. 'Think you can out-detect Jet Harris?'

'I didn't say that, sir. It's just the advantage of hindsight, that's all. A long perspective.'

'Look, we worked our bollocks off on that case, Jet Harris, Reg Proctor and me, not to mention dozens more DCs and uniforms. Have you any idea what that sort of investigation is like? The scope of it. How wide a net we cast. We were getting a hundred sightings a day from as far afield as Penzance and the Mull of fucking Kintyre. Now you come along with your fancy education and your Bramshill courses and you have the gall to tell me we were wrong.'

Michelle took a deep breath. 'I'm not saying you were wrong, sir. Only you didn't *solve* the case, did you? You didn't even find a body. Look, I know you came up the hard way, and I respect that, but there are advantages to an education.'

'Yes. Accelerated promotion. They let you buggers run before you can toddle.'

'Policing has changed, sir, as you pointed out not so long ago. And crime has changed, too.'

'Sod that for a theory. Don't spout your book learning at me. A criminal's a criminal. Only the coppers have got softer. Especially the ones at the top.'

Michelle sighed. Time to change tack. 'You were a DC on the Graham Marshall investigation, sir. Can *you* tell me anything at all?'

'Look, if I'd known anything we'd have solved the bloody case, wouldn't we, instead of having you point out how stupid we were?'

'I'm not trying to make anyone look stupid.'

'Aren't you? That's how it sounds to me. It's easy to second-guess, given twenty-twenty hindsight. If Bill Marshall had anything to do with his son's disappearance, believe me, we'd have had him. In the first place, he had an alibi—'

'Who, sir?'

'His wife.'

'Not the most reliable of alibis, is it?'

'She'd hardly give him an alibi for doing in her own son now, would she? Tell me even you aren't so twisted as to think Mrs Marshall was involved.'

'We don't know, sir, do we?' But Michelle remembered Mrs Marshall, her sincerity and dignity, the need to bury her son after all these years. Certainly it was possible she was lying. Some criminals are very good actors. But Michelle didn't think so. And she wouldn't be getting any answers out of Bill Marshall. 'Did the Marshalls own a car?'

'Yes, they did. But don't expect me to remember the make and number. Look, Bill Marshall might have been a bit of a Jack the Lad, but he wasn't a child molester.'

'How do you know that was the motive behind Graham's abduction?'

'Have some brains, woman. Why else does a fourteen-year-old boy go missing without a trace? If you ask me, I'd still say he might have been one of Brady and Hindley's, though we could never prove it.'

'But it's way out of their area. A geographical pro-filer—'

'More benefits of a university education. Profilers? Don't make me laugh. I've had enough of this. It's about time you stopped nosing about down here and got back on the bloody job.' And he turned and stalked out.

Michelle noticed that her hand was shaking when he left, and she felt her breath held tight in her chest. She didn't like confrontation with authority; she had always respected her bosses and the police hierarchy in general; an organization like the police couldn't run efficiently without a quasi-military structure, she believed, orders given and obeyed, sometimes without question, if it came right down to it. But Shaw's rage seemed out of proportion to the situation.

She got up and returned the files to their boxes and gathered together her notes. It was well after lunchtime and time for some fresh air, anyway. Perhaps she would make a few phone calls, find someone who'd been on the job during the Kray era and head down to London the next day.

Back in her office, she found a message slip on her desk informing her that Dr Cooper had rung and wanted to know if she would drop by the mortuary sometime that afternoon. No time like the present, she thought, telling DC Collins where she was going and heading out to her car.

●

The search of Luke's room didn't reveal much except a cassette tape marked 'Songs from a Black Room', which Banks, with Robin's permission, slipped in his pocket to listen to later. Luke's desktop computer contained nothing of interest. There was hardly any email, which was only to be expected, and most of the web sites he visited were connected with music. He also did a fair bit of online purchasing, mostly CDs, also to be expected from someone living in so remote a spot.

Banks was surprised at the range of Luke's musical tastes. There was the usual stuff, of course, the CDs Annie had told him about, but also among the grunge, metal, hip-hop and gothic, he had found other oddities, such as Britten's setting of Rimbaud's 'Les Illuminations' and

Miles Davis's *In a Silent Way*. There were also several indie CDs, including, Banks was thrilled to see, his son Brian's band's first recording, *Blue Rain*. Not your usual listening for a fifteen year old. But Banks was coming to believe that Luke Armitage had been a far from typical fifteen year old.

He had also read some of the stories and poems Annie had collected from her previous visit, and in his humble opinion they showed real promise. They didn't tell him anything about what might have happened to Luke, or his feelings about his father or stepfather, but they revealed a young mind preoccupied with death, war, global destruction and social alienation.

Unlike Annie, Banks wasn't surprised by the room's decor. Brian hadn't painted his room black, but he had stuck posters on the walls and surrounded himself with his favourite music. And the guitar, of course, always the guitar. Annie had no children, so Banks could imagine how the black room would seem more outlandish to her. The only thing that disturbed him was Luke's apparent obsession with dead rock stars, and with the absence of anything to do with his famous father, Neil Byrd. Something was definitely out of kilter there.

Brian had gone on to make a career of music, and now his band was on the verge of recording its first CD for a major label. After getting over the initial shock that Brian wasn't going to follow any safe paths in life, Banks had come to feel very proud of him, a leap of faith that his own parents hadn't seemed able to make yet. Banks wondered if Luke had been any good. Maybe the tape would tell him. From what Annie had told him, and from his own first impressions, he doubted that Martin Armitage would have been thrilled by any signs of musical ability in his stepson: physical fitness and sports seemed to be his measures of success.

Josie and Calvin Batty lived in their own small apartment upstairs at the far eastern end of Swainsdale House. There they had a sitting room, bedroom and a small kitchen, in addition to WC and bathroom with a power shower, all modernized by the Armitages, Josie told them as they stood with her in the kitchen while she boiled the kettle for tea. The whole place was brightly decorated in light colours, creams and pale blues, and made the best of the available light.

Josie looked as if she could be quite an attractive young woman if she made the effort, Banks thought. But as it was, her hair seemed lifeless and ill-cut, her clothes rather plain, shapeless and old-fashioned, and her complexion pale and dry. Her husband was short and thickset with dark, gypsyish colouring and heavy eyebrows that met in the middle.

'What exactly are your duties here?' Banks asked the two of them when they were settled in the living room opposite an enormous TV and VCR combination with a tray of tea and chocolate digestives in front of them.

'General, really. I do most of the washing, ironing, cleaning and cooking. Calvin does odd jobs, takes care of the cars and any heavy work, building repairs, garden, that sort of thing.'

'I imagine there must be a lot of that sort of thing,' Banks said, glancing at Calvin. 'A big old house like this.'

'Aye,' Calvin grunted, dunking a biscuit in his tea.

'What about Luke?'

'What about him?' asked Josie.

'Did any of your duties involve taking care of him?'

'Calvin'd give him a lift to school sometimes, or bring

him back if he happened to be in town. I'd make sure he was well fed if sir and madam had to go away for a few days.'

'Did they do that often?'

'Not often, no.'

'When was the last time he was left alone here?'

'Last month. They both went down to London for some fancy gala charity do.'

'What did Luke do when he was left alone in the house?'

'We didn't spy on him,' said Calvin, 'if that's what you're getting at.'

'Not at all,' said Banks. 'But did you ever hear anything? TV? Stereo? Did he ever have his friends over? That sort of thing.'

'Music were loud enough, but he didn't have no friends to ask over, did he?' said Calvin.

'You know that's not true,' said his wife.

'So he did entertain friends?'

'I didn't say that.'

'Did he, Mrs Batty?'

'Not here.'

Banks took a deep breath. 'Where, then?'

She hugged her grey cardie closer to her. 'I shouldn't be telling tales out of school.'

Annie leaned forward and spoke for the first time. 'Mrs Batty, this is a murder investigation. We need your help. We're in the dark here. If you can help throw any light at all on what happened to Luke, please do so. This is way beyond telling tales or keeping promises.'

Josie looked at Banks, uncertain.

'DI Cabbot's right,' he said. 'All bets are off when it's murder. Who was this friend?'

'Just someone I saw him with, that's all.'

'Where?'

'In Eastvale. Swainsdale Centre.'

'When?'

'Recently.'

'Past week or two?'

'A bit longer.'

'A month?'

'Aye, about that.'

'How old? His age? Older? Younger?'

'Older. She wasn't no fifteen year old, I can tell you that.'

'How old?'

'Hard to say when they're that age.'

'What age?'

'Young woman.'

'How young? Late teens, early twenties?'

'Aye, around that.'

'Taller or shorter than him?'

'Shorter. Luke were a big lad for his age. Tall and skinny.'

'What did she look like?'

'Dark.'

'You mean she was black?'

'No, her skin was pale. She just dressed dark, like him. And her hair was dyed black. She had red lipstick on and them studs and chains all over t'place. And she had a tattoo,' she added in a hushed tone, as if saving the greatest sin for last.

Banks glanced at Annie, who, he happened to know from experience, had a butterfly tattoo just above her right breast. Annie gave him a look. 'Where?' she asked Josie.

Josie touched her upper left arm, just below the shoulder. 'There,' she said. 'She was wearing one of them leather waistcoats over a T-shirt.'

'What was the tattoo?' Annie asked her.

'Couldn't tell,' said Josie. 'Too far away. I could just see there was a mark, like.'

This woman shouldn't be too difficult to find if she lived in or near Eastvale, Banks thought. It was hardly Leeds or Manchester when it came to girls in black with studs, chains and tattoos. There was only one club, the Bar None, which catered for such a crowd, and then only two nights a week, the rest of the time being reserved for the techno-dance set. It was possible she was a student at the college, too, he thought. 'Would you mind if we sent a sketch artist over to work on an impression with you this afternoon?' he asked.

'I suppose not,' said Josie. 'If sir and madam don't mind, like. Only I'm supposed to be doing t'upstairs.'

Banks looked at her. 'I don't think Mr and Mrs Armitage will mind,' he said.

'All right, then. But I can't promise owt. Like I said, I didn't get a close look.'

'Can you tell us anything more about her?' Banks asked.

'No. It was just a quick look. I were having a coffee and a KitKat at the food court when I saw them walk by and go into that there big music shop.'

'HMV?'

'That's the one.'

'Did they see you?'

'No.'

'Did you tell anyone you'd seen them?'

'Not my place, is it. Besides . . .'

'Besides what?'

'It was a school day. He should have been in school.'

'What were they doing?'

'Just walking.'

'Close together?'

'They weren't holding hands, if that's what you mean.'

'Were they talking, laughing, arguing?'

'Just walking. I didn't see them so much as look at one another.'

'But you knew they were together? How?'

'You just know, don't you?'

'Had you seen them together before?'

'No. Only the once.'

'And you, Mr Batty?'

'No. Never.'

'Not even when you picked him up from school?'

'She weren't no schoolgirl,' said Josie. 'Not like I ever saw.'

'No,' said Mr Batty.

'What did you talk about when you gave Luke a lift?'

'Nowt, really. He wasn't much of a one for small talk, and we'd nowt in common. I mean, he weren't interested in sport or anything like that. I don't think he watched telly much, either. He'd nothing to talk about.'

Only death and poetry and music, thought Banks. 'So these journeys passed in silence?'

'I usually put the news on the radio.'

'How did he get on with his parents?'

'Wouldn't know,' answered Josie.

'Hear any rows or anything?'

'There's always rows between parents and kids, isn't there?'

'So you did?'

'Nothing out of the ordinary.'

'Who between? Luke and his mother?'

'Nay. Butter wouldn't melt in his mouth as far as she were concerned. Spoiled him rotten.'

'His stepfather, then?'

'Like I said, it were nowt out of t'ordinary.'

'Did you ever hear what was said, what they were arguing about?'

'Walls is too thick around here.'

Banks could believe that. 'Did anything unusual happen lately?'

'What do you mean?' Josie asked.

'Something out of the routine.'

'No.'

'Seen any strangers hanging about?'

'Fewer than normal, since they can't go for their country walks.'

'So you haven't seen anyone?'

'Hanging about? No.'

'Mr Batty?'

'Nobody.'

They were getting no further with the Battys. Banks wasn't certain whether they were holding anything back or not, but he decided he might have another chat with them a little later on. Just as they were leaving, he turned around to Mr Batty and said, 'Ever been arrested, Mr Batty?'

'No.'

'We can easily find out, you know.'

Batty glared at him. 'All right. Once. It were a long time ago.'

'How long?'

'Twelve years. Public nuisance. I were drunk, all right?

I used to drink a lot in those days. Then I met Josie. I don't drink any more.'

'What was all that about?' Annie asked when they were back in the car.

'What?'

'Asking him if he'd been arrested. You know an offence like that is hardly still going to be in the records.'

'Oh, that,' said Banks, buckling up and settling back in the passenger seat while Annie started the ignition. 'I just wanted to see whether he's a good liar or not. People usually lie the first time when you ask them if they've ever been arrested.'

'And?'

'Well, there was a slightly different inflection on that last "no", the lie, but not different enough to convince me he's not a good liar.'

'Bloody hell,' said Annie, heading off down the drive and spraying gravel. 'A proper Sherlock Holmes I've got beside me.'

•

It was only a short drive down Longthorpe Parkway from police headquarters to the District Hospital, and early that Friday afternoon the traffic was light. Instinctively, Michelle found herself checking her rear-view mirror to see if she was being followed. She wasn't.

She parked in the official visitors' area and made her way to pathology. The forensic anthropology department was small, just a couple of offices and one lab, and none of the staff was permanent. Dr Cooper herself lectured in nearby Cambridge, in addition to her practical duties at the hospital. There certainly weren't enough skeletons to justify a full-time forensic anthropology department –

most counties didn't have one at all and had to hire the services of an expert when circumstances demanded – but there had been enough Anglo-Saxon and Viking remains found in East Anglia for a small, part-time department to be thought justified. For the most part, that was Wendy Cooper's main area of interest, too, ancient remains, not skeletons of boys buried in 1965.

'Ah, DI Hart,' Dr Cooper greeted her in her office, standing up and shaking hands. 'Good of you to come.'

'Not at all. You said you had something to tell me?'

'Show you, actually. It's not much, but it might help. Follow me.'

Curious, Michelle followed her into the lab, where Graham Marshall's bones were still laid out on the table and Tammy Wynette was singing 'Stand by Your Man' on Dr Cooper's portable cassette player. Though still a dirty brownish-yellow, like bad teeth, the bones were a hell of a lot cleaner than they had been a few days ago, Michelle noticed. Dr Cooper and her assistant, nowhere in sight at the moment, had clearly been working hard. The body looked asymmetrical, though, Michelle noticed, and wondered what was missing. When she looked more closely, she could see it was the bottom rib on the left side. Hadn't they been able to find it? But no, there it was on the bench Dr Cooper led her towards.

'We couldn't see it before because of the accumulated dirt,' Dr Cooper explained, 'but once we'd cleaned it up, it was plain as daylight. Look.'

Michelle bent closer and looked. She could see a deep, narrow notch in the bone. It was something she had come across before. She looked at Dr Cooper. 'Knife wound?'

'Very good. That's what I'd say.'

'Pre- or post-mortem?'

'Oh, pre. Cuts in green bone are different from cuts made in bones after death, when they're more brittle. This is a clean, smooth cut. Definitely pre-mortem.'

'Cause of death?'

Dr Cooper frowned. 'I can't say that for certain,' she said. 'I mean, there could have been lethal poison in the system, or the victim might have drowned first, but what I can say is that, in my opinion, the wound would have been sufficient to cause death. If you follow the trajectory of the blade to its natural destination, it pierces the heart.'

Michelle paused a moment, looking at the rib in question, to take it all in. 'Front or behind?' she asked.

'Does it matter?'

'If it was done from behind,' Michelle explained, 'it could have been a stranger. If it happened from the front, someone had to get close enough to the boy to do it without his knowing what was going to happen.'

'Yes, I see,' said Dr Cooper. 'Good point. I never have managed to get the hang of thinking the way you police do.'

'Different training.'

'I suppose so.' Dr Cooper picked up the rib. 'Judging from the position of the cut on the bone – see, it's almost on the *inside* – and by the straightness I'd say that it was done from in front, the classic upthrust though the ribcage and into the heart. Harder to be that accurate from behind. Much more awkward, far more likely to be at an angle.'

'So it had to be someone he would let get that close to him without being suspicious.'

'Close enough to pat him on the shoulder, yes. And whoever did it was right handed.'

'What kind of knife?'

'That I can't tell you, except that it was very sharp and the blade wasn't serrated. It's quite a deep cut, as you can see, so there's plenty of scope for analysis and measurement. There's someone I know who can probably tell you the date it was made and the company who made it, an expert. His name's Dr Hilary Wendell. If you like I can try to track him down, get him to have a look.'

'Could you?'

Dr Cooper laughed. 'I said I'd *try*. Hilary's all over the place. And I mean all over. Including the United States, and Eastern Europe. He's very well known. He even spent some time with the forensic teams in Bosnia and Kosovo.'

'You were there, too, weren't you?'

Dr Cooper gave a little shudder. 'Yes. Kosovo.'

'Any idea when the coroner can release the bones for burial?'

'He can release them now as far as I'm concerned. I'd specify burial rather than cremation, though, just in case we need to exhume.'

'I think that's what they have in mind. And some sort of memorial service. It's just that I know the Marshalls are anxious for some sense of closure. I'll give them a ring and say it's okay to go ahead and make arrangements.'

'Funny thing, that, isn't it?' said Dr Cooper. 'Closure. As if burying someone's remains or sending a criminal to jail actually marks the end of the pain.'

'It's very human, though, don't you think?' said Michelle, for whom closure had simply refused to come, despite all the trappings. 'We need ritual, symbols, ceremonies.'

'I suppose we do. What about this, though?' She pointed to the rib on the lab bench. 'It could even end up being evidence in court.'

'Well,' said Michelle, 'I don't suppose the Marshalls will mind if they know Graham's being buried with a rib missing, will they? Especially if it might help lead us to his killer. I'll get their permission, anyway.'

'Fine,' said Dr Cooper. 'I'll talk to the coroner this afternoon and try to track Hilary down in the meantime.'

'Thanks,' said Michelle. She looked again at the bones on the table, laid out in some sort of semblance of a human skeleton, and then glanced back at the single rib on the bench. Strange, she thought. It didn't matter – they were only old bones – but she couldn't help but feel this odd and deep sense of significance, and the words 'Adam's rib' came to mind. Stupid, she told herself. Nobody's going to create a woman out of Graham Marshall's rib; with a bit of luck, Dr Hilary Wendell is going to tell us something about the knife that killed him.

•

A few dark clouds had blown in on a strong wind from the north, and it looked as if rain was about to spoil yet another fine summer's day when Banks drove out in his own car to the crime scene late that afternoon, listening to Luke Armitage's 'Songs from a Black Room'.

There were only five short songs on the tape, and lyrically they were not sophisticated, about what you'd expect for a fifteen year old with a penchant for reading poetry he couldn't understand. There were no settings of Rimbaud or Baudelaire here, only pure, unadulterated adolescent angst: 'Everybody hates me, but I don't care. / I'm safe in my black room, and the fools are out there.' But at least they were Luke's own songs. When Banks was fourteen, he had got together with Graham, Paul and Steve to form a rudimentary rock band, and all they had managed were rough cover versions of Beatles and Stones songs. Not one of them had had the urge or the talent to write original material.

Luke's music was raw and anguished, as if he were reaching, straining, to find the right voice, his own voice. He backed himself on electric guitar, occasionally using special effects, such as fuzz and wah-wah, but mostly sticking to the simple chord progressions Banks remembered from his own stumbling attempts at guitar. The remarkable thing was how much Luke's voice resembled his father's. He had Neil Byrd's broad range, though his voice hadn't deepened enough to handle the lowest notes yet, and he also had his father's timbre, wistful but bored, and even a little angry, edgy.

Only one song stood out, a quiet ballad with a melody Banks recognized vaguely, perhaps an adaptation of an old folk tune. The last piece on the tape, it was a love song of sorts, or a fifteen year old's version of salvation:

> *He shut me out but you took me in.*
> *He's in the dark but you're a bird on the wing.*
> *I couldn't hold you but you chose to stay.*
> *Why do you care? Please don't go away.*

Was it about his mother, Robin? Or was it the girl Josie had seen him with in the Swainsdale Centre? Along with Winsome Jackman and Kevin Templeton, Annie was out showing the artist's impression around the most likely places. Maybe one of them would get lucky.

The SOCOs were still at Hallam Tarn, the road still taped off, as was a local TV van, along with a gaggle of reporters who barely kept their distance. As he pulled up by the side of the road, Banks even noticed a couple of middle-aged ladies in walking gear; sightseers, no doubt.

Stefan Nowak was in charge, looking suave even in his protective clothing.

'Stefan,' Banks greeted him. 'How's it going?'

'We're trying to get everything done before the rain comes,' Stefan said. 'We've found nothing else in the water so far, but the frogmen are still looking.'

Banks looked around. Christ, but it was wild and lonely up there, an open landscape, hardly a tree in sight, with miles of rolling moorland, a mix of yellow gorse, sandy-coloured tufts of grass and black patches where fires had raged earlier that summer. The heather wouldn't bloom for another month or two, but the dark multi-branched stems spread tough and wiry all around, clinging close to the ground. The view was spectacular, even more dramatic under the louring sky. Over in the west, Banks could see as far as the long flat bulk of the three peaks: Ingleborough, Whernside and Pen-y-ghent.

'Anything interesting?' he asked.

'Maybe,' said Stefan. 'We tried to pin down the exact point on the wall where the body had been dropped over, and it matches the spot where these stones stick out here like steps. Makes climbing easy. Good footholds.'

'I see. It would have taken a bit of strength, though, wouldn't it?'

'Oh, I don't know. He might have been a big lad for his age, but he was still only a kid, and pretty skinny.'

'Could one person have done it?'

'Certainly. Anyway, we've been looking for scuff marks. It's also possible that the killer scratched himself climbing up.'

'You've found blood on the wall?'

'Minute traces. But hold your horses, Alan. We don't even know if it's human blood yet.'

Banks watched the SOCOs taking the wall apart stone by stone and packing it in the back of a van. He wondered what Gristhorpe would think of such destruction. Gristhorpe was building a drystone wall at the back of his house as a hobby. It went nowhere and fenced in nothing. Some of these walls had been standing for centuries without any sort of cement holding them together, but they were far more than mere random piles of rocks. Gristhorpe knew all about the techniques and the patience it took to find just the right stone to fit with the others, and here the men were demolishing it. Still, if it could lead them to Luke's killer, Banks thought, that was worth a drystone wall or two. He knew Gristhorpe would agree.

'Any chance of footprints?'

Stefan shook his head. 'If there was any sort of impression in the grass or the dust you can be sure it's gone now. Don't get your hopes up.'

'Do I ever? Tyre tracks?'

'Again, too many, and it's not a good road surface. But we're looking. We've got a botanist coming up from York, too. There may be some unique plant life by the roadside, especially with it being close to a body of water. You never know. If you find someone with a bit of purple-speckled ragwort sticking to the bottom of his shoe, it just might be your man.'

'Wonderful.' Banks walked back to his car.

'Chief Inspector?' It was one of the reporters, a local man Banks recognized.

'What do you want?' he asked. 'We've just told you lot all we know at the press conference.'

'Is it true what we've been hearing?' the reporter asked.

'What have you been hearing?'

'That it was a botched kidnapping.'

'No comment,' said Banks, muttering, 'shit,' under his breath as he got in his car, turned around in the next lay-by and set off home.

After tracking down a retired detective inspector who had worked out of West End Central and persuading him to talk to her in London the following day, Michelle had left the station and stopped off to rent the video of *The Krays* on her way home. She hoped the film would at least give her a general picture of their life and times.

She had been living in her riverside flat on Viersen Platz for two months now, but it still felt temporary, just another place she was passing through. Partly it was because she hadn't unpacked everything – books, dishes, some clothes and other odds and ends – and partly it was the job, of course. Long hours made it difficult to keep house, and most of her meals were eaten on the run.

The flat itself was cosy and pleasant enough. A modern four-storey building, part of the Rivergate Centre, it faced south, overlooking the river, got plenty of light for the potted plants she liked to keep on her small balcony, and was so close to the city centre as to be practically in the shadow of the cathedral. She didn't know why she hadn't settled in more; it was one of the nicest places she had ever lived in, if a bit pricey. But what else did she have to spend her money on? She particularly liked to sit out on the balcony after dark, look at the lights reflected in the slow-moving river and listen to the trains go by. On weekends she could hear blues music from Charters Bar, an old iron barge moored opposite, by Town Bridge; the customers sometimes made a bit too much noise at closing time, but that was only a minor irritant.

Michelle had no friends to invite for dinner, nor the time or inclination to entertain them, so she hadn't even bothered to unpack her best chinaware. She had even let such basics as laundry, dusting and ironing slip, and as a consequence her flat had the air of someone who used to maintain a certain level of tidiness and cleanliness but had let things go. Even the bed was unmade since that morning.

She glanced at the answering machine, but no light flashed. It never did. She wondered why she even bothered to keep the thing. Work, of course. After a quick blitz on the dishes in the sink and a run around with the Hoover, she felt ready to sit down and watch *The Krays*. But she was hungry. As usual there was nothing in the fridge, at least nothing edible, so she went around the corner to the Indian takeaway and got some prawn curry and rice. Sitting with a tray on her lap and a bottle of South African Merlot beside her, she pressed the remote and the video began.

When it had finished, Michelle didn't feel she knew much more about the Kray twins than before it had begun. Yes, theirs was a violent world and you'd better not cross them. Yes, they seemed to have plenty of money and spend most of their time in ritzy clubs. But what exactly did they do? Apart from vague battles with the Maltese and meetings with American gangsters, the exact nature of their businesses was left unexplained. And, as far as the film was concerned, coppers might as well have not even existed.

She turned to the news, still feeling a little queasy from the violence. Or was it from the curry and wine? She didn't really believe that the Krays had anything to do with Graham Marshall's murder, any more than she believed Brady and Hindley had, and she could imagine how Shaw would laugh if he heard her suggest such a thing.

If Bill Marshall had any serious criminal aspirations, they hadn't done him much good. He never got out of the council house, though the Marshalls had bought it for £4,000 in 1984.

Perhaps he swore off crime. Michelle had checked subsequent police records and found no further mention of him, so he had gone either straight or uncaught. She would guess at the former, given his standard of living. Graham's disappearance must have shaken him, then. Maybe he sensed a connection to the world he had been involved in, so he severed all ties. She would have to find time to have an even closer look at the old crime reports, dig out old action books and the notebooks of the detectives involved. But that could wait until after the weekend.

She turned on her computer and tried to put her thoughts and theories into some kind of order, the way she usually did last thing at night, then she played a couple of games of Freecell and lost.

It got dark. Michelle turned off her computer, cleared away the detritus of her lonely dinner, found there wasn't enough wine left in the bottle to be worth saving, so topped up her glass. As it so often did around bedtime, the depression seemed to close in on her like a dense fog. She sipped her wine and listened to rain tapping against her window. God, how she missed Melissa, even after all this time. She missed Ted, too, sometimes, but mostly she missed Melissa.

Her thoughts went back to the day it happened. It was a movie that ran in her mind, as if on a constant loop. She wasn't there – that was a big part of the problem – but she could picture Melissa outside the school gates, her golden curls, little blue dress with the flowers on it, the other kids milling around, vigilant teachers nearby, then Melissa seeing what she thought was her father's car pulling to a stop across the road, though they always picked her up on *her* side. Then she pictured Melissa waving, smiling, and, before anyone could stop her, running right out in front of the speeding lorry.

Before getting into bed, she took Melissa's dress, the same dress she had died in, from her bedside drawer, lay down, held it to her face and cried herself to sleep.

10

As Annie waited outside ACC McLaughlin's office at county headquarters the following morning, having been 'summoned', she felt the same way she had when her geography teacher sent her to the headmaster's office for defacing a school atlas with her own cartographic designs: fantastic sea creatures and warnings that 'Beyond this point be monsters.'

She had little fear of authority, and a person's rank or status was something she rarely considered in her daily dealings, but somehow this summons made her nervous. Not 'Red Ron' himself – he was known to be stern but fair and had a reputation for standing behind his team – but the situation she might find herself in.

It seemed that since she had decided to pursue her career again, she had made nothing but mistakes. First, sliding arse over tit down the side of Harkside reservoir in full view of several of her colleagues and against the orders of the officer in charge; then the debacle of her excessive force investigation of probationary PC Janet Taylor during her brief (but not brief enough) spell with Complaints and Discipline; and now being blamed for the murder of Luke Armitage. Pretty soon everyone would be calling her Fuck-up Annie, if they didn't already. 'Got a case you want fucking up, mate? Give it to Annie Cabbot, she'll see you right.'

So much for a revitalized career. At least she was

determined to go down with her middle finger high in the air.

It wasn't bloody fair, though, Annie thought, as she paced. She was a damn good detective. Everything she had done in all those instances had been right; it was just the spin, the way it all added up, that made her look bad.

Red Ron's secretary opened the door and ushered Annie into the presence. As befitted his rank, ACC McLaughlin had an even bigger office than Detective Superintendent Gristhorpe's and a carpet with much thicker pile. At least he didn't have the books that intimidated her so in Gristhorpe's office.

Red Ron had done a few things to personalize it since he first came to the job about eight months ago: a framed photo of his wife Carol stood on the desk, and a print of Constable's *The Lock* hung on the wall. The glass cabinet was full of trophies and photos of Red Ron with various police athletics teams, from rowing to archery. He looked fit and was rumoured to be in training for a marathon. He was also rumoured to keep a bottle of fine single malt in his bottom drawer, but Annie didn't expect to see much evidence of that.

'DI Cabbot,' he greeted her, glancing over the top of his wire-rimmed glasses. 'Please sit down. I'll be with you in a moment.'

Annie sat. There was something different about him, she thought. Then she realized. Red Ron had shaved off his moustache since she had last seen him. She was surprised to find that he had an upper lip. She always thought men grew moustaches and beards to hide weak jaws and thin lips. He kept his receding silver hair cut short instead of growing one side long and trying to hide a bald centre by combing it over the top of the skull, the way some men did. Annie didn't understand that. What was so wrong with going bald? She thought some bald men were quite sexy. It was one of those ridiculous macho male things, she guessed, like the obsession with penis length. Were all men so bloody insecure? Well, she would never find out because none of them would ever talk about it. Not even Banks, though he did at least try more than most. Perhaps it was something they really *couldn't* do, something they were genetically incapable of, something going back to the caves and the hunt.

Annie brought herself back to the present. The ACC had just finished signing a stack of papers and after he had buzzed his secretary to come and take them away, he leaned back in his chair and linked his hands behind his head. 'I suppose you know why you're here?' he began.

'Yes, sir.'

'The chief constable got in touch with me last night – just as I was settling down to my dinner, by the way – and said he'd had a complaint about you from Martin Armitage. Would you care to explain what happened?'

Annie told him. As she spoke, she could tell he was listening intently, and every now and then he made a jotting on the pad in front of him. Nice fountain pen, she noticed. A maroon Waterman. Sometimes he frowned, but he didn't interrupt her once. When she had finished, he paused for a while, then said, 'Why did you decide to follow Mr Armitage from his house that morning?'

'Because I thought his behaviour was suspicious, sir. And I was looking for a missing boy.'

'A boy he had already told you was due back that very day.'

'Yes, sir.'

'You didn't believe him?'

'I suppose not, sir.'

'Why not?'

Annie went over the Armitages' behaviour on the morning in question, the tension she had felt, the brusqueness of their response to her, the haste with which they wanted rid of her. 'All I can say, sir,' she said, 'is that I found their behaviour to be out of synch with what I'd expect from parents who'd discovered that their son was all right and was coming home.'

'All very speculative on your part, DI Cabbot.'

Annie gripped the arms of the chair hard. 'I used my judgement, sir. And I stand by it.'

'Hmm.' Red Ron took off his glasses and rubbed his eyes. 'It's a bad business,' he said. 'We've had the press all over us, and needless to say they're hot to trot with this idea of a simple kidnapping gone wrong. Add police cock-up to that, and they'd like nothing better.'

'With all due respect, sir, it wasn't a simple kidnapping.' Annie gave her reasons why, as she had done before with Gristhorpe and Banks.

Red Ron stroked his chin as he listened, plucking at his upper lip as if he still expected to feel the moustache. When she had finished, he asked, as she had hoped he wouldn't, 'Didn't it cross your mind just for one moment that the kidnapper might have been watching Mr Armitage make the drop?'

'I . . . er . . .'

'You didn't think of it, did you?'

'I wanted to know what he'd left there.'

'DI Cabbot. Use your intelligence. A man's stepson is missing. He's edgy and anxious to be somewhere, annoyed that the police are on his doorstep. You follow him and see him enter a disused shepherd's shelter with a briefcase and come out without it. What do you surmise?'

Annie felt herself flush with anger at the rightness of his logic. 'When you put it like that, sir,' she said through gritted teeth, 'I suppose it's clear he's paying a ransom. But things don't always seem so clear-cut in the field.'

'You've no need to tell me what it's like in the field, DI Cabbot. I might be an administrator now, but I wasn't always behind this desk. I've served my time in the field. I've seen things that would make your hair curl.'

'Then I'm sure you'll understand what I'm saying.' Was that a half-smile Annie spotted fleeting across Red Ron's features? Surely not.

He went on, 'The point remains that you must have known the risk of being seen by the kidnapper was extremely high, especially as you were in open country-side, and that for whatever reason you disregarded that risk and went into the shelter anyway. And now the boy's dead.'

'There's some indication that Luke Armitage might have been killed even *before* his stepfather delivered the money.'

'That would be a piece of luck for you, wouldn't it?'

'That's not fair, sir. I needed to know what was in the briefcase.'

'Why?'

'I needed to be sure. That's all. And it turned out to be a clue of sorts.'

'The low amount? Yes. But how did you know that wasn't just the first instalment?'

'With respect, sir, kidnappers don't usually work on the instalment plan. Not like blackmailers.'

'But how did you know?'

'I didn't *know*, but it seemed a reasonable assumption.'

'You assumed.'

'Yes, sir.'

'Look, DI Cabbot. I'm not going to beat about the bush. I don't like it when members of the public make complaints about officers under my command. I like it even less when a self-important citizen such as Martin Armitage complains to his golf-club crony, the chief constable, who then passes the buck down to me. Do you understand?'

'Yes, sir. You don't like it.'

'Now, while your actions weren't exactly by the book, and while you might have lacked judgement in acting so impulsively, I don't see anything serious enough in what you did to justify punishment.'

Annie began to feel relieved. A bollocking, that was all she was going to get.

'On the other hand . . .'

Annie's spirits sank again.

'We don't have all the facts in yet.'

'Sir?'

'We don't know whether you *were* seen by the kidnapper or not, do we?'

'No, sir.'

'And we don't know exactly *when* Luke Armitage died.'

'Dr Glendenning's doing the post-mortem sometime today, sir.'

'Yes, I know. So what I'm saying is that until we have all the facts I'll postpone judgement. Go back to your duties, Detective Inspector.'

Annie stood up before he changed his mind. 'Yes, sir.'

'And DI Cabbot?'

'Sir?'

'If you're going to keep on using your own car on the job, get a bloody police radio fitted, would you?'

Annie blushed. 'Yes, sir,' she mumbled, and left.

•

Michelle got off the Intercity train at King's Cross at about half-past one that afternoon and walked down the steps to the tube, struck, as she always was, by the sheer hustle and bustle of London, the constant noise and motion. Cathedral Square on a summer holiday weekend with a rock band playing in the market place didn't even come close.

Unlike many of her contemporaries, Michelle had never worked on the Met. She had thought of moving there after Greater Manchester, after Melissa had died and Ted had left, but instead she had moved around a lot over the past five years and taken numerous courses, convincing herself that it was all for the good of her career. She suspected, though, that she had just been running. Somewhere a bit more out of the way had seemed the best option, at least for the time being, another low-profile position. And you didn't get anywhere in today's police force without switching back and forth a lot – from uniform to CID, from county to county. Career detectives like Jet Harris were a thing of the past.

A few ragged junkies sat propped against the walls of the busy underpass, several of them young girls, Michelle noticed, and too far gone even to beg for change. As she passed, one of them started to moan and wail. She had a bottle in her hand and she banged it hard against the wall until it smashed, echoing in the tiled passage and scattering broken glass all over the place. Like everyone else, Michelle hurried on.

The tube was crowded and she had to stand all the way to Tottenham Court Road, where retired Detective Inspector Robert Lancaster had agreed to talk to her over a late lunch on Dean Street. It was raining when she walked out on to Oxford Street. Christ, she thought, *not again*! At this rate, summer would be over before it had begun. Michelle unfurled her umbrella and made her way through the tourists and hustlers. She turned off Oxford Street and crossed Soho Square, then followed Lancaster's directions and found the place easily enough.

Though it was a pub, Michelle was pleased to see that it looked rather more upmarket than some establishments, with its hanging baskets of flowers outside, stained glass and shiny dark woodwork. She had dressed about as casually as she was capable of, in a mid-length skirt, a pink V-neck top and a light wool jacket, but she would still have looked overdressed in a lot of London pubs. This one, however, catered to a business luncheon crowd. It even had a separate restaurant section away from the smoke and video machines, with table service, no less.

Lancaster, recognizable by the carnation he told Michelle he would be wearing in his grey suit, was a dapper man with a full head of silver hair and a sparkle in his eye. Perhaps a bit portly, Michelle noticed as he stood up to greet her, but definitely well-preserved for his age, which she guessed at around seventy. His face had a florid complexion, but he didn't otherwise look like a serious drinker. At least he didn't have that telltale calligraphy of broken red and purple veins just under the surface, like Shaw.

'Mr Lancaster,' she said, sitting down. 'Thank you for agreeing to see me.'

'The pleasure's mine entirely,' he said, traces of a cockney accent still in his voice. 'Ever since my kids flew the coop and my wife died, I'll take any opportunity to get out of the house. Besides, it's not every day I get to come down the West End and have lunch with a pretty girl like yourself.'

Michelle smiled and felt herself blush a little. A *girl*, he'd called her, when she had turned forty last September. For some reason, she didn't feel offended by Lancaster's particular brand of male chauvinism; it had such a quaint, old-fashioned feel to it that it seemed only natural on her part to accept the compliment and thank him with as much grace as possible. She'd soon find out if it got more wearing as their conversation continued.

'I hope you don't mind my choice of eatery.'

Michelle looked around at the tables with their white linen cloths and weighty cutlery, the uniformed waitresses dashing around. 'Not at all,' she said.

He chuckled, a throaty sound. 'You wouldn't believe what this place used to be like. Used to be a real villains' pub back in the early sixties. Upstairs, especially. You'd be amazed at the jobs planned up there, the contracts put out.'

'Not any more, I hope?'

'Oh, no. It's quite respectable now.' He spoke with a tinge of regret in his voice.

A waitress appeared with her order book.

'What would you like to drink?' Lancaster asked.

'Just a fruit juice, please.'

'Orange, grapefruit or pineapple?' the waitress asked.

'Orange is fine.'

'And I'll have another pint of Guinness, please,' Lancaster said. 'Sure you don't want something a bit stronger, love?'

'No, that'll be just fine, thanks.' Truth was, Michelle had felt the effects of last night's bottle of wine that morning, and she had decided to lay off the booze for a day or two. It was still manageable. She never drank during the day, anyway, only in the evening, alone in her flat with the curtains closed and the television on. But if she didn't nip it in the bud, she'd be the next one with broken blood vessels in her nose.

'The food's quite good here,' said Lancaster while the waitress was fetching their drinks. 'I'd stay away from the lamb curry if I were you, though. Last time I touched it I ended up with a case of Delhi belly.'

Michelle had eaten a curry the previous evening, and though it hadn't given her 'Delhi belly', it had made its presence felt during the night. She wanted something plain, something unencumbered with fancy sauces, something *British*.

The waitress returned with her Britvic orange and Lancaster's Guinness and asked them for their orders.

'I'll have the Cumberland sausage and mashed potatoes, please,' Michelle said. And diet be damned, she added under her breath. Lancaster ordered the roast beef.

'Bangers and mash,' he said, beaming, when the waitress had wandered off. 'Wonderful. One doesn't often meet people who go for the more traditional food these days. It's all that nasty foreign muck, isn't it?'

'I don't mind a bit of pasta or a curry now and then,' said Michelle, 'but sometimes you can't beat the traditional English.'

Lancaster paused for a few moments, drumming his

fingers on the table. Michelle could sense him changing gear, from old-fashioned gallant to seasoned street copper, wondering what she was after and whether it could harm him. She could see it in his eyes, their gaze sharpening, becoming more watchful. She wanted to set him at ease but decided it was best to let him lead, see where it went. At first.

'The bloke that put you on to me said you wanted to know about Reggie and Ronnie.'

There, they were out. The dreaded words. Reggie and Ronnie: *the Krays*.

'Sort of,' Michelle said. 'But let me explain.'

Lancaster listened, taking the occasional sip of Guinness, nodding here and there, as Michelle told him about the Marshalls and what had happened to Graham.

'So, you see,' she finished, 'it's not really the twins, or not *just* them, anyway, that I'm interested in.'

'Yes, I see,' said Lancaster, drumming his fingers again. Their food arrived and they both took a few bites before he spoke again. 'How's your sausage?' he asked.

'Fine,' said Michelle, wondering if he was going to be any use at all or if it was going to be one of those pleasant but pointless sessions.

'Good. Good. I knew Billy Marshall and his family,' said Lancaster. Then he stuffed his mouth full of roast beef and mashed potato and looked at Michelle, eyes wide and expressionless as he chewed, watching for her reaction. She was surprised, and she was also pleased that the information Banks had given her led somewhere, although she still had no idea where.

'Billy and I grew up just around the corner from one another. We went to the same schools, played on the same streets. We even used to drink in the same pub,' he went on when he'd washed his food down with Guinness. 'Does that surprise you?'

'A bit, I suppose. Though, I must say, not much about those days surprises me any more.'

Lancaster laughed. 'You're right there, love. Another world. See, you've got to understand where detectives came from, Michelle. Can I call you Michelle?'

'Of course.'

'The first detectives came from the criminal classes. They were equally at home on either side of the law. Jonathan Wild, the famous thief-taker, for example. Half the time he set up the blokes he fingered. Did you know that? They hanged him in the end. And Vidocq, the Froggie? Thief, police informer, master of disguise. Criminal. And back then, the days you're asking about, I think we were a bit closer to our prototypes than the office boys we seem to have in the force today, if you'll pardon my criticism. Now, I'm not saying I was ever a criminal myself, but I lived close enough to the line at times to know what a thin line it is, and I was also close enough to know how they thought. And do you imagine for a moment those on the other side didn't know that, too?'

'You turned a blind eye sometimes?'

'I told you. I went to school with Billy Marshall, grew up the next street over. Only difference was, he was thick as two short planks, but he could fight, and me, well I had the smarts and the stealth, but I wasn't much of a scrapper. Enough to survive. And believe me you had to have that much or you were a goner. Any trouble and I'd talk my way out of it, and if that didn't work I'd leg it. Mostly I'd talk my way out. Is it any wonder we went our different ways? Thing is, it could've gone either way for me. I ran a bit wild when I was kid, got into a scrape or two. I knew exactly where people like Reggie and Ronnie were coming from. We lived in the same poor neighbourhood, in the shadow of the war. I could think like them. I could've easily used my street-smarts for criminal purposes like Reggie and Ronnie or . . .' He let the sentence trail and ate some more roast beef.

'You're saying morality doesn't come into it?' Michelle asked. 'The law? Justice? Honesty?'

'Words, love,' Lancaster said when he'd finished eating. 'Nice words, I'll grant you, but words nonetheless.'

'So how did you choose? Toss a coin?'

Lancaster laughed. '"Toss a coin." Good one, that. I'll have to remember it.' Then his expression turned more serious. 'No, love. I probably joined for the same reasons you did, same as most people. There wasn't much pay then, but it seemed a decent enough job, maybe even a bit glamorous and exciting. Fabian of the Yard, and all that stuff. I didn't want to be a plod walking the beat – oh, I did it, of course, we all did, had to – but I knew I wanted CID right from the start, and I got it. What I'm saying, love, is that when it came right down to it, when you stood at the bar of your local, or took your usual table in the corner, the one your father had sat at all his life, and when someone like Billy came in, someone you knew was a bit dodgy, well, then it was just a job you did. Everybody knew it. Nothing personal. We mixed, tolerated one another, hoped our paths never crossed in a serious way, a professional way. And remember I was working out of West End Central then. The East End wasn't my manor. I just grew up there, lived there. Of course, we were all aware there was a barrier between us, at least one we'd better not breech in public, so it was all, "Hello, Billy. How's it going? How's the wife and kid? Oh, fine Bob, can't complain. How's things down the nick? Thriving, Billy boy, thriving. Glad to hear it, mate." That sort of thing.'

'I can understand that,' said Michelle, who thought she took policing a bit more seriously and wouldn't be caught dead in the same pub as known villains, unless she was meeting an informant. It was the same thing that Shaw had said. The lines between them and us weren't so clearly drawn as they are today, mostly because many cops and criminals came from the same backgrounds, went to the same schools and drank in the same pubs, as Lancaster had just pointed out, and as long as no innocent bystanders got hurt . . . no harm done. Nothing personal. Different times.

'Just wanted to get it clear,' said Lancaster, 'so you wouldn't go away thinking I was bent or anything.'

'Why would I think that?'

He winked. 'Oh, there were plenty that were. Vice, Obscene Publications, the Sweeney. Oh, yes. It was all just getting going then, sixty-three, sixty-four, sixty-five. There are some naive buggers who look at it as the beginnings of some new age of enlightenment or something. Aquarius, call it what you will. Fucking hippies, with their peace and love and beads and long hair.' He sneered. 'Know what it really was? It was the beginnings of the rise of organized crime in this country. Oh, I'm not saying we hadn't had gangsters before that, but back in the mid-sixties, when Reggie and Ronnie were at their peak, you could have written what your average British copper knew about organized crime on the back of a postage stamp. I kid you not. We knew bugger all. Even "Nipper" Read, the bloke in charge of nailing the twins. Porn was coming in by the lorryload from Denmark, Germany,

Sweden, the Netherlands. Someone had to control distribution, wholesale, resale. Same with drugs. Opening of the floodgates, the mid-sixties. Licence to print money. Maybe the hippies saw a revolution of peace and love in the future, but people like Reggie and Ronnie only saw even more opportunities to make cash, and ultimately all your hippies were just consumers, just another market. Sex, drugs, rock and roll. Your real criminals were rubbing their hands in glee when flower power came along, like kids given the free run of the sweet shop.'

This was all very well, Michelle thought, but a man with a bee in his bonnet, the way Lancaster seemed to have, could be difficult to get information from. Lancaster ordered another Guinness – Michelle asked for coffee – and sat back in his chair. He took a pill from a small silver container and washed it down with stout.

'Blood pressure,' he explained. 'Anyway, I'm sorry, love,' he went on, as if reading her mind. 'I do go on a bit, don't I? One of the few benefits of getting old. You can go on and on and nobody tells you to shut up.'

'Bill Marshall.'

'Yes, Billy Marshall, as he was called back then. I haven't forgotten. Haven't seen or heard of him for years, by the way. Is he still alive?'

'Barely,' said Michelle. 'He's suffered a serious stroke.'

'Poor sod. And the Missis?'

'Coping.'

He nodded. 'Good. She always was a good coper, was Maggie Marshall.'

Maggie. Michelle just realized that she hadn't known Mrs Marshall's first name. 'Did Bill Marshall work for Reggie and Ronnie?' she asked.

'Yes. In a way.'

'What do you mean?'

'A lot of people in the East End worked for Reggie and Ronnie at one time or another. Fit young geezer like Billy, I'd've been surprised if he hadn't. He was a boxer. Amateur, mind you. And so were the Krays. They were into boxing in a big way. They met up at one of the local gyms. Billy did a few odd jobs with them. It paid to have the twins on your side back then, even if you weren't in deep with them. They made very nasty enemies.'

'So I've read.'

Lancaster laughed. 'You don't know the half of it, love.'

'But he wasn't regularly employed, not on their payroll?'

'That's about it. An occasional encouragement to pay up, or deterrent against talking. You know the sort of thing.'

'He told you this?'

Lancaster laughed. 'Come off it, love. It wasn't something you discussed over a game of darts at the local.'

'But you knew?'

'It was my job to know. Keeping tabs. I liked to think I knew what was going on, even outside my manor, and that those who counted knew that I knew.'

'What do you remember about him?'

'Nice enough bloke, if you didn't cross him. Bit of a temper, especially after a jar or two. Like I said, he was strictly low-level muscle, a boxer.'

'He used to boast that he knew Reggie and Ronnie when he was in his cups, after he'd moved up to Peterborough.'

'Typical Billy, that. Didn't have two brain cells to rub together. I'll tell you one thing, though.'

'What's that?'

'You said the kid was stabbed?'

'That's what the pathologist tells me.'

'Billy never went tooled up. He was strictly a fist man. Maybe a cosh or knuckledusters, depending who he was up against, but never a knife or a gun.'

'I didn't really regard Bill Marshall as a serious suspect,' Michelle said, 'but thanks for letting me know. I'm just wondering if or how all this could have had any connection with Graham's death.'

'I can't honestly say I can see one, love.'

'If Billy did something to upset his masters, then surely—'

'If Billy Marshall had done anything to upset Reggie or Ronnie, love, he'd have been the one pushing up daisies, not the kid.'

'They wouldn't have harmed the boy to make a point?'

'Not their way, no. Direct, not subtle. They had their faults, and there wasn't much they wouldn't do if it came right down to it. But if you crossed them, it wasn't your wife or your kid got hurt, it was you.'

'I understand Ronnie was—'

'Yes, he was. And he liked them young. But not that young.'

'Then—'

'They didn't hurt kids. It was a man's world. There was a code. Unwritten. But it was there. And another thing you've got to understand, love, is that Reggie and Ronnie were like Robin Hood, Dick Turpin and Billy the Kid all rolled into one as far as most East Enders were concerned. Even later, you only have to look at their funerals to see that. Fucking royalty. Pardon my French. Folk heroes.'

'And you were the sheriff of Nottingham?'

Lancaster laughed. 'Hardly. I was only a DC, a mere foot soldier. But you get the picture.'

'I think so. And after the day's battles you'd all adjourn to the local and have a jolly old drink together and talk about football.'

Lancaster laughed. 'Something like that. You know, maybe you're right. Maybe it was a bit of a game. When you nicked someone fair and square, there were no hard feelings. When they put one over on you, you just filed it away till next time. If the courts let them off, then you bought them a pint next time they came in the pub.'

'I think Billy Marshall took the game to Peterborough with him. Ever hear of a bloke called Carlo Fiorino?'

Lancaster's bushy eyebrows knitted in a frown. 'Can't say as I have, no. But that's way off my manor. Besides, I've already told you, Billy didn't have the brains to set up an operation. He didn't have the authority, the command, charisma, call it what you will. Billy Marshall was born to follow orders, not give them, let alone decide what they ought to be. Now that lad of his, he was another matter entirely.'

Michelle pricked up her ears. 'Graham? What about him?'

'Young lad with the Beatle cut, right?'

'Sounds like him.'

'If anyone in that family was destined to go far, I'd have said it would've been him.'

'What do you mean? *Graham* was a criminal?'

'No. Well, not apart from a bit of shoplifting, but they all got into that. Me, too, when I was his age. We figured the shops factored the losses into their prices, see, so we were only taking what was rightfully ours anyway. No, it was just that he had brains – though God knows who he got them from – *and* he also was what they call street-smart these days. Never said much, but you could tell he was taking it all in, looking for the main chance.'

'You're saying that *Graham* might have been involved with the Krays?'

'Nah. Oh, he might have run an errand or two for them, but they didn't mess around with twelve-year-old kids. Too much of a liability. Only that he watched and learned. There wasn't much got by him. Sharp as a tack. Billy used to leave him outside the local, sitting in the street playing marbles with the other kids. It was common enough, then. And some pretty shady customers went in there. Believe me, I know. More than once the young lad would get half a crown and a watching brief. "Keep an eye on that car for me, kid," like. Or, "If you see a couple of blokes in suits coming this way, stick your head around the door and give me a shout." No flies on young Graham Marshall, that's for sure. I'm just sorry to hear he came to such an early end, though I can't say as it surprises me that much.'

•

Dr Glendenning was delayed in Scarborough, so the post-mortem had been put off until late in the afternoon. In the meantime, Banks thought his time would be well spent talking to some of Luke's teachers, starting with Gavin Barlow, the head teacher of Eastvale Comprehensive.

Despite the threatening sky and earth damp from an earlier shower, Barlow was weeding the garden of his north Eastvale semi, dressed in torn jeans and a dirty old shirt. A collie with a sleek coat jumped up at Banks as he entered through the garden gate, but Barlow soon brought the dog to heel, and it curled in a corner under the lilac bush and seemed to go to sleep.

'He's old,' Gavin Barlow said, taking off a glove, wiping his hand on his jeans and offering it. Banks shook and introduced himself.

'Yes, I've been expecting a visit,' said Barlow. 'Terrible business. Let's go inside. No, stay, Tristram. Stay!'

Tristram stayed and Banks followed Barlow into the bright, ordered interior of the house. He was clearly interested in antiques, and by the looks of the gleaming sideboard and drinks cabinet, into restoring them, too. 'Can I offer you a beer, or a lager perhaps? Or aren't you supposed to drink on duty? One never knows, watching Morse and the like on telly.'

Banks smiled. 'We're not supposed to,' he said, not that it had ever stopped him. But it was far too early in the day, and he didn't have weeding the garden as an excuse. 'I'd love a coffee, if you've got some.'

'Only instant, I'm afraid.'

'That's fine.'

'Come on through.'

They went into a small but well-arranged kitchen. Whoever had designed the maple cabinets over the slate-grey countertops had decided on following a pattern of horizontal grain rather than vertical, which made the room seem much more spacious. Banks sat at a breakfast nook with a red-and-white checked tablecloth while Barlow made the coffee.

'Daddy, who's this?'

A girl of about sixteen appeared in the doorway, all long blonde hair and bare leg. She reminded Banks a bit of Kay Summerville.

'It's a policeman come to talk about Luke Armitage, Rose. Off you go.'

Rose pouted, then made a theatrical about-turn and sashayed away, wiggling her hips. 'Daughters,' said Barlow. 'Have you any of your own?'

Banks told him about Tracy.

'Tracy Banks. Of course, now I remember her. I just didn't put two and two together when I saw your identification. Tracy. Very bright girl. How is she doing?'

'Fine. She's just finished her second year at Leeds. History.'

'Do give her my best regards when you see her. I can't say I knew her well . . . so many pupils and so little time . . . but I do remember talking to her.'

Gavin Barlow looked a bit like Tony Blair, Banks thought. Definitely more of an educational unit manager than an old-style school headmaster, the way his predecessor Mr Buxton had been. Banks remembered the old fellow who'd been in charge during the Gallows View case, when Banks had first moved up north. Buxton was the last of a dying breed, with his bat-like cape and a well-thumbed copy of Cicero on his desk. Gavin Barlow probably thought 'Latin' referred to a type of dance music, though maybe that was being a bit unfair. At least the radio station he was tuned into was playing Thelonious Monk's 'Epistrophy' at eleven o'clock in the morning – a good sign.

'I'm not sure I can tell you very much about Luke,' said Gavin Barlow, bringing over two mugs of instant coffee and sitting opposite Banks. 'It's usually only the persistent trouble-makers who come to my attention.'

'And Luke wasn't a trouble-maker?'

'Good heavens, no! You'd hardly know he was there if he didn't move once in a while.'

'Any trouble at all?'

'Not really trouble. Nothing his form-tutor couldn't deal with.'

'Tell me.'

'Luke didn't like games, and he once forged a note from his mother excusing him on the grounds of a stomach upset. It was a note the PE teacher remembered seeing a few months earlier, and Luke had traced it out with a new date. Quite a good forgery, really.'

'What happened?'

'Nothing much. Detention, a warning to his mother. Odd, as he wasn't bad at all.'

'Wasn't bad at what?'

'Rugby. Luke was a decent wing three-quarters. Fast and slippery. When he could be bothered playing.'

'But he didn't like games?'

'He had no interest in sports. He'd far rather read, or just sit in a corner and stare out of the window. God only knows what was going on in that head of his half the time.'

'Did Luke have any close friends at school, any other pupils he might have confided in?'

'I really can't say. He always seemed to be a bit of a loner. We encourage group activities, of course, but you can't always . . . I mean you can't *force* people to be sociable, can you?'

Banks opened his briefcase and slipped out the artist's impression of the girl Josie Batty had seen going into HMV with Luke. 'Do you recognize this girl?' he asked, not sure how close a likeness it was.

Barlow squinted at it, then shook his head. 'No,' he said. 'I can't say as I do. I'm not saying we don't have pupils who affect that general look, but not very many, and nobody quite like this.'

'So you've never seen her or anyone like her with Luke?'

'No.'

Banks returned the sketch to his briefcase. 'What about his schoolwork? Did he show any promise?'

'Enormous promise. His work in maths left a lot to be desired, but when it came to English and music he was remarkably gifted.'

'What about the other subjects?'

'Good enough for university, if that's what you mean. Especially languages and social studies. You could tell that even at his early age. Unless . . .'

'What?'

'Well, unless he went off the rails. I've seen it happen before with bright and sensitive pupils. They fall in with the wrong crowd, neglect their work . . . You can guess the rest.'

Banks, who had gone off the rails a bit himself after Graham's disappearance, could. 'Were there any teachers Luke was particularly close to?' he asked. 'Anyone who might be able to tell me a bit more about him?'

'Yes. You might try Ms Anderson. Lauren Anderson. She teaches English and art history. Luke was way ahead of his classmates in his appreciation of literature, and in its composition, and I believe Ms Anderson gave him extra tuition.'

Lauren Anderson's name had come up in the company's records of Luke's cell-phone calls, Banks remembered. 'Is that something the school does often?'

'If the student seems likely to benefit from it, then yes, certainly. You have to understand that we get such a broad range of abilities and interests, and we have to pitch our teaching level just a little above the middle. Too high and you lose most of the class, too low and the brighter students become bored and distracted. But it's not all as bad as they say it is in the newspapers. We're lucky in that we have a lot of passionate and committed teachers at Eastvale Comprehensive. Ms Anderson is one of them. Luke was also taking violin lessons after school.'

'Yes, he had a violin in his bedroom.'

'I told you, he's not your common-or-garden pupil.' Barlow paused for a moment, staring out the window. '*Wasn't*. We'll miss him.'

'Even if you hardly knew he was there?'

'I was probably overstating the case,' Barlow said with a frown. 'Luke had a certain presence. What I meant was that he just didn't make a lot of noise or demand a lot of attention.'

'Who was giving him violin lessons?'

'Our music teacher, Alastair Ford. He's quite a skilled player himself. Plays with a local string quartet. Strictly amateur, of course. You might have heard of them; they're called the Aeolian Quartet. I understand they're very good, though I must admit that my tastes edge more towards Miles than Mahler.'

The Aeolian. Banks had, indeed heard of them. Not only that, but he had *heard* them. The last time was shortly after Christmas, at the community centre with Annie Cabbot. They had played Schubert's 'Death and the Maiden' quartet and made a very good job of it, Banks remembered.

'Is there anything else you can tell me?' he asked, standing to leave.

'I don't think there is,' said Barlow. 'All in all, Luke Armitage was a bit of a dark horse.'

As they walked through to the hall, Banks felt certain

he caught a flurry of blonde hair and long leg ducking through a doorway, but he could have been mistaken. Why would Rose Barlow want to listen in on their conversation, anyway?

•

The rain seemed to have settled in for the day after a short afternoon respite, a constant drizzle from a sky the colour of dirty dishwater, when Annie did the rounds of Luke's final ports of call. She found out nothing from the HMV staff, perhaps because they had such a high turnover and it was a large shop, hard to keep an eye on everyone. No one recognized the sketch. Besides, as one salesperson told her, many of the kids who shopped there looked pretty much the same. Black clothing wasn't exactly unusual as far as HMV's customers were concerned, nor were body piercing or tattoos.

She fared little better at the computer shop on North Market Street. Gerald Kelly, the sole proprietor and staff member, remembered just about all his customers, but he had seen no one resembling the girl in black with Luke, who had always been alone on his visits to the shop.

Annie had just one last call. Norman's Used Books was a dank, cramped space down a flight of stone steps under a bakery, one of several shops that seemed to be set right into the church walls in the market square. The books all smelled of mildew, but you could find the most obscure things sometimes. Annie herself had shopped there once or twice, looking for old art books, and had even found some decent prints among the boxes the owner kept at the back of the shop, though they were sometimes warped and discoloured because of the damp.

The roof was so low and the small room so full of

books – not only in cases against the walls, but piled up haphazardly on tables, ready to teeter over if you so much as breathed on them – that you had to stoop and make your way around the place very carefully. It must have been even harder for Luke, Annie thought, as he was taller and more gangly than her.

The owner himself, Norman Wells, was just a little over five feet, with thin brown hair, a bulbous sort of face and rheumy eyes. Because it was so cold and damp down there, no matter what the weather was like up above, he always wore a moth-eaten grey cardigan, woolly gloves with the fingers cut off and an old Leeds United scarf. He couldn't make much of a living out of the little shop, Annie thought, though she doubted the overheads were very high. Even in the depths of winter a one-element electric fire was the only source of heat.

Norman Wells glanced up from the paperback he was reading and nodded in Annie's direction. He seemed surprised when she showed her warrant card and spoke to him.

'I've seen you before, haven't I?' he said, taking off his reading glasses, which hung on a piece of string around his neck.

'I've been here once or twice.'

'Thought so. I never forget a face. Art, isn't it?'

'Pardon?'

'Your interest. Art.'

'Oh, yes.' Annie showed him a photograph of Luke. 'Remember him?'

Wells looked alarmed. 'Course I do. He's the lad who disappeared, isn't he? One of your lot was around the other day asking about him. I told him all I know.'

'I'm sure you did, Mr Wells,' said Annie, 'but things

have changed. It's a murder investigation now and we have to go over the ground afresh.'

'Murder? That lad?'

'I'm afraid so.'

'Bloody hell. I hadn't heard. Who'd . . . ? He wouldn't say boo to a goose.'

'Did you know him well, then?'

'Well? No, I wouldn't say that. But we talked.'

'What about?'

'Books. He knew a lot more than most kids his age. His reading level was way beyond that of his contemporaries.'

'How do you know?'

'I . . . never mind.'

'Mr Wells?'

'Let's just say I used to be a teacher, that's all. I know about these things, and that lad was bordering on genius.'

'I understand he bought two books from you on his last visit.'

'Yes, like I told the other copper. *Crime and Punishment* and *Portrait of the Artist as a Young Man*.'

'They sound a bit advanced, even for him.'

'Don't you believe it,' Wells protested. 'If I hadn't thought him ready I wouldn't have sold him them. He'd already been through *The Waste Land*, most of Camus and *Dubliners*. I didn't think he was quite ready for *Ulysses* or Pound's *Cantos*, but he could handle the *Portrait*, no problem.'

Annie, who had heard of these books but had read only the Eliot and a few of Joyce's short stories at school, was impressed. So the books she had seen in Luke's room weren't just for show; he really did read and probably even understand them. At fifteen, she'd been reading historical sagas and sword and sorcery series, not literature with a capital 'L'. That was reserved for school and was tedious in the extreme, thanks to Mr Bolton, the English teacher, who made the stuff sound about as exciting as a wet Sunday in Cleethorpes.

'How often did Luke call by?' she asked.

'About once a month. Or whenever he was out of something to read.'

'He had the money. Why didn't he go to Waterstone's and buy them new?'

'Don't ask me. We got chatting the first time he dropped in—'

'When was that?'

'Maybe eighteen months or so ago. Anyway, as I say, we got chatting and he came back.' He looked around at the stained ceilings, flaking plaster and tottering piles of books and smiled at Annie, showing crooked teeth. 'I suppose there must have been something he liked about the place.'

'Must be the service,' Annie said.

Wells laughed. 'I can tell you one thing. He liked those old Penguin Modern Classics. The ones with the grey spines, not these modern pale green things. Real paperbacks, not your trade size. And you can't buy those at Waterstone's. Same with the old Pan covers.'

Something moved in the back of the shop and a pile of books fell over. Annie thought she glimpsed a tabby cat slinking away into the deeper shadows.

Wells sighed. 'Familiar's gone and done it again.'

'Familiar?'

'My cat. No bookshop's complete without a cat. After *witch's familiar*. See?'

'I suppose so. Did Luke ever come in here with anyone else?'

'No.'

Annie took her copy of the artist's impression out and set it on the table in front of him. 'What about her?'

Wells leaned forward, put his glasses on again and examined the sketch. 'It *looks* like her,' he said. 'I told you I never forget a face.'

'But you told me Luke never came in with anyone else,' Annie said, feeling a tingle of excitement rise up her spine.

Wells looked at her. 'Who said she was with him? No, she came in with another bloke, same sort of clothing and body piercing.'

'Who are they?'

'I don't know. They must have been a bit short of money, though.'

'Why do you say that?'

'Because they came in with an armful of brand-new books to sell. Stolen, I thought. Plain as day. Stolen books. I don't have any truck with that sort of thing, so I sent them packing.'

11

Before he cut into Luke Armitage's flesh, Dr Glendenning made a thorough examination of the body's exterior. Banks watched as the doctor examined and measured the head wound. Luke's skin was white and showed some wrinkling from exposure to the water, and there was a slight discoloration around the neck.

'Back of the skull splintered into the cerebellum,' the doctor said.

'Enough to kill him?'

'At a guess.' Glendenning bent over and squinted at the wound. 'And it would have bled quite a bit, if that's any use.'

'Could be,' said Banks. 'Blood's a lot harder to clean up than most people think. What about the weapon?'

'Looks like some sort of round-edged object,' the doctor said. 'Smooth sided.'

'Like what?'

'Well, it's not got a very large circumference, so I'd rule out something like a baseball bat. I can't see any traces – wood splinters or anything – so it could have been metal or ceramic. Hard, anyway.'

'A poker, perhaps?'

'Possible. That would fit the dimensions. It's the angle that puzzles me.'

'What about it?'

'See for yourself.'

Banks bent over the wound, which Dr Glendenning's assistant had shaved and cleaned. There was no blood. A few days in the water would see to that. He could see the indentation clearly enough, about the right size for a poker, but the wound was oblique, almost horizontal.

'You'd expect someone swinging a poker to swing downwards from behind, or at least at a forty-five degree angle, so we'd get a more vertical pattern,' Dr Glendenning said. 'But this was inflicted from sideways on, not from in front or behind, by someone a little shorter than the victim, if the angle's to be believed. That means whoever did it was probably standing *beside* him. Unusual angle, as I said.' He lit a cigarette, strictly forbidden in the hospital, but usually overlooked in Glendenning's case. Everyone knew that when you were dealing with the smells of a post-mortem, a ciggie now and then was a great distraction. And Glendenning was more careful these days; he rarely dropped ash in open incisions.

'Maybe the victim was already bent double from a previous blow?' Banks suggested. 'To the stomach, say. Or on his knees, head bent forward.'

'Praying?'

'It wouldn't be the first time,' Banks said, remembering that more than one executed villain had died on his knees praying for his life. But Luke Armitage wasn't a villain, as far as Banks knew.

'Which side did the blow come from?' Banks asked.

'Right side. You can tell by the pattern of indentation.'

'So that would indicate a left-handed attacker?'

'Likely so. But I'm not happy with this, Banks.'

'What do you mean?'

'Well, in the first place, it's hardly a surefire way to kill somebody. Head blows are tricky. You can't count on them, especially just one.'

Banks knew that well enough. On his last case a man had taken seven or eight blows from a side-handled baton and still survived for a couple of days. In a coma, but alive. 'So our killer's an amateur who got lucky.'

'Could be,' said Glendenning. 'We'll know more when I get a look at the brain tissue.'

'But could this blow have been the cause of death?'

'Can't say for certain. It *could* have killed him, but he might have been dead already. You'll have to wait for the full toxicology report to know whether that might have been the case.'

'Not drowned?'

'I don't think so, but let's wait until we get to the lungs.'

Banks watched patiently, if rather queasily, as Dr Glendenning's assistant made the customary Y-shaped incision and peeled back the skin and muscle from the chest wall with a scalpel. The smell of human muscle, rather like raw lamb, Banks had always thought, emanated from the body. Next the assistant pulled the chest flap up over Luke's face and took a bone-cutter to the ribcage, finally peeling off the chest plate and exposing the inner organs. When he had removed these en bloc, he placed them on the dissecting table and reached for his electric saw. Banks knew what was coming next, that unforgettable sound and burnt-bone smell of the skull, so he turned his attention to Dr Glendenning, who was dissecting the organs, paying particular attention to the lungs.

'No water,' he announced. 'Or minimal.'

'Meaning Luke was dead when he went in the water?'

'I'll send the tissues for diatomic analysis, but I don't expect they'll find much.'

The electric saw stopped, and seconds later Banks heard something rather like a combination grating and sucking sound, and he knew it was the top of the skull coming off. The assistant then cut the spinal cord and the tentorium and lifted the brain out. As he carried it to the jar of formalin in which it would hang suspended for a couple of weeks, making it firmer and easier to handle, Dr Glendenning had a quick look.

'Aha,' he said. 'I thought so. Look, Banks, do you see that damage there, to the frontal lobes?'

Banks saw it. And he knew what it meant. '*Contre coup*?'

'Exactly. Which might explain the unusual angle.'

If a blow is delivered while the victim's head is stationary, then the damage is limited to the point of impact – bones splintered into the brain – but if the victim's head is in motion, then the result is a *contre coup* injury: additional damage *opposite* the point of impact. *Contre coup* injuries are almost always the result of a fall.

'Luke *fell*?'

'Or he was pushed,' said Glendenning. 'But as far as I can tell, there are no other injuries, no broken bones. And as I said, if there was bruising, if someone hit him, say, knocked him over, then unless there are any small bones in the cheek broken, we won't be able to tell. We'll be checking, of course.'

'Can you give me any idea about time of death? It's important.'

'Aye, well . . . I've looked over Dr Burns's measurements at the scene. Very meticulous. He'll go far. Rigor's been and gone, which indicates over two days at the temperatures noted.'

'What about the wrinkling and whitening?'

'*Cutis anserina*? Three to five hours. Water preserves, delays putrefaction, so it makes our job a little harder. There's no lividity, and I'm afraid it'll be almost impossible to tell whether there was any other bruising. The water takes care of that.' He paused and frowned. 'But there's the discoloration around the neck.'

'What about it?'

'That indicates the beginnings of putrefaction. In bodies found in water, it always starts at the root of the neck.'

'After how long?'

'That's just it,' Dr Glendenning said, looking at Banks. 'You understand I can't be more specific, I can't give you less than a twelve-hour margin of error, but not until at least three or four days, not at the temperatures Dr Burns recorded.'

Banks made a mental calculation. 'Bloody hell,' he said. 'Even at the outside, that means Luke had to have been killed just after he went missing.'

'Sometime that very night, by my calculations. Taking everything into account, between about eight p.m. and eight a.m.'

And Dr Glendenning's calculations, perhaps because of his insufferable habit of being unwilling to commit himself to a specific time, were usually not far from the truth. In which case, Banks thought, Luke had died before Annie had even paid her *first* visit to Swainsdale Hall, let alone before she had followed Martin Armitage to the site of the drop.

•

Before she went off duty – though such a thing was somewhat of an illusion in the thick of a major murder investigation – Annie had made a few enquiries around the bookshops, asking after the couple who had tried to sell Norman Wells books he believed were stolen, but she drew a blank. Before meeting Banks for a drink at the Queen's Arms, she had also checked recent shoplifting reports but turned up nothing there either. The artist's impression would be in the evening paper, so she would see what happened after that. There was something else she had intended to do, but it was like that name you can't quite remember, the one on the tip of your tongue. If she put it out of her mind, it would come to her eventually.

Banks was already waiting for her at a corner table, and she saw him before he saw her. He looked tired, Annie thought, and distracted, smoking and staring into the distance. She tapped him on the shoulder and asked him if he wanted a refill. He came back from a long way and shook his head. She bought herself a pint of Theakston's bitter and walked over to join him. 'So what was that mysterious message about your wanting to see me?' she asked.

'Nothing mysterious about it at all,' Banks said, brightening up a little. 'I just wanted to deliver a message myself, in person.'

'I'm all ears.'

'It looks as if you're off the hook as far as Luke Armitage's death is concerned.'

Annie felt her eyes open wide. 'I am? How?'

'Dr Glendenning pegs time of death at least three or four days ago.'

'Before—'

'Yes. Before the first kidnap call even came in.'

Annie raised her eyes to the ceiling and clapped her hands. 'Yes!'

Banks smiled at her. 'Thought you'd be pleased.'

'How? He didn't drown, did he?'

Banks sipped some beer. 'No,' he said. 'Pending tox results, it looks as if cause of death was a blow to the cerebellum, quite possibly the result of a fall.'

'A struggle of some sort, then?'

'Exactly what I thought. Perhaps with the kidnapper, very early on. Or whoever he was with.'

'And that person decided to try and collect anyway?'

'Yes. But that's pure speculation.'

'So Luke died somewhere else and was dumped in the tarn?'

'Yes. Probably wherever he was being held – *if* he was being held. Anyway, there'd have been a fair bit of blood, the doc says, so there's every chance of our still finding evidence at the original scene.'

'If we can find the scene.'

'Exactly.'

'So we *are* making progress?'

'Slowly. What about the girl?'

'Nothing yet.' Annie told him about her meeting with Norman Wells.

She noticed Banks was watching her as she spoke. She could almost see his mind moving, making the connections, taking a shortcut here and filing this or that piece of information away for later. 'Whoever they are,' he said when she'd finished, 'if Wells is right and they had been shoplifting, then that tells us they're short of money. Which gives them a motive for demanding a ransom if they were somehow responsible for Luke's death.'

'More speculation?'

'Yes,' Banks admitted. 'Let's assume they got into a fight over something or other and Luke ended up dead. Maybe not intentionally, but dead is dead. They panicked, thought of a suitable spot and drove out and dumped him into Hallam Tarn later that night, under cover of darkness.'

'They'd need a motor, remember, which might be a bit of a problem if they were broke.'

'Maybe they "borrowed" one?'

'We can check car-theft reports for the night in question. No matter how much they covered up the body, there might still be traces of Luke's blood.'

'Good idea. Anyway, they know who Luke's parents are, think they might be able to make a few bob out of them.'

'Which would explain the low demand.'

'Yes. They're not pros. They've no idea how much to ask. And ten grand is a bloody fortune to them.'

'But they were watching Martin Armitage make the drop and they saw me.'

'More than likely. Sorry, Annie. They might not be pros, but they're not stupid. They knew the money was tainted then. They'd already dumped Luke's body, remember, so they must have known it was just a matter of time before someone found it. They could expect the footpath restrictions to work in their favour for a while, but someone was bound to venture over Hallam Tarn eventually.'

Annie paused to digest what Banks had said. She *had* made a mistake, had scared the kidnappers off, but Luke had already been dead by then, so his death wasn't down to her. What else could she have done, anyway? Stayed away from the shepherd's shelter, perhaps. Red Ron was right about that. She had guessed that the briefcase contained money. Did she need to know exactly how much? So she had behaved impulsively, and not for the first time, but it was all salvageable, the case, her career, everything. It could all be redeemed. 'Have you ever thought,' she said, 'that they *might* have planned on kidnapping Luke right from the start? Maybe that was why they befriended him in the first place, and why they had to kill him. Because he knew who they were.'

'Yes,' said Banks. 'But too many things about this seem hurried, spontaneous, ill thought out. No, Annie, I think they just took advantage of an existing situation.'

'So why kill Luke, then?'

'No idea. We'll have to ask them.'

'If we find them.'

'Oh, we'll find them, all right.'

'When the girl sees her picture in the paper she might go to ground, change her appearance.'

'We'll find them. The only thing is . . .' Banks said, letting the words trail off as he reached for another cigarette.

'Yes?'

'That we need to keep an open mind as regards other lines of enquiry.'

'Such as?'

'I'm not sure yet. There might be something even closer to home. I want to talk to a couple of teachers who knew Luke fairly well. Someone should talk to the Battys again, too. Then there's all the people we know he came into contact with the day he disappeared. Put a list together and get DCs Jackman and Templeton to help with it. We've still got a long way to go.'

'Shit,' said Annie, getting to her feet. She had

remembered the task that had been eluding her all evening.

'What?'

'Just something I should have checked out before.' She looked at her watch and waved goodbye. 'Maybe it's not too late. See you later.'

•

Michelle sat back in her seat and watched the fields drift by under a grey sky, rain streaking the dirty window. Every time she took a train she felt as if she was on holiday. This evening the train was full. Sometimes she forgot just how close Peterborough was to London – only eighty miles or so, about a fifty-minute train ride – and how many people made the journey every day. That was, after all, what the new town expansion had been about. Basildon, Bracknell, Hemel Hempstead, Hatfield, Stevenage, Harlow, Crawley, Welwyn Garden City, Milton Keynes, all in a belt around London, even closer than Peterborough, catchment areas for an overflowing capital, where it was fast becoming too expensive for many to live. She hadn't been around back then, of course, but she knew that the population of Peterborough had risen from about 62,000 in 1961 to 134,000 in 1981.

Unable to concentrate on *The Profession of Violence*, which she had to remember to post back to Banks, she thought back to her lunch with ex-Detective Inspector Robert Lancaster. He had quite a few years on Ben Shaw, but they were both very much cut from the same cloth. Oh, no doubt about it, Shaw was ruder, more sarcastic, a far more unpleasant personality, but underneath they were the *same kind of copper*. Not necessarily bent – Michelle took Lancaster's word on that – but not above turning a blind eye if it was to their advantage, and not above fraternizing with villains. As Lancaster had also pointed out, he had grown up shoulder to shoulder with criminals like the Krays and smaller fry like Billy Marshall, and when it came to future career choices it was often very much a matter of there but for the grace of God go I.

It was interesting what he had said about Graham Marshall, she thought. Interesting that he should even remember the boy at all. She had never considered that it might have been Graham's *own* criminal activities that got him killed, and even now she found it hard to swallow. Not that fourteen year olds were immune to criminal activity. Far from it, especially these days. But if Graham Marshall had been involved in something that was likely to get him killed, wouldn't somebody have known and come forward? Surely Jet Harris or Reg Proctor would have picked up the scent?

The real problem, though, was how she could gather any more information about Graham. She could go through the statements again, read the investigating detectives' notebooks and check all the actions allocated, but if none of them focused on Graham himself as a possible line of enquiry, then she would get no further.

The train slowed down for no apparent reason. It was an Intercity, not a local train, so Michelle went to the buffet car and bought herself a coffee. The paper cup was far too hot, even when she used three or four serviettes to hold it. If she took the top off, it would spill when the train started moving again, so she tore a small hole in the plastic top and decided to wait a little while it cooled.

Michelle looked at her watch. After eight o'clock. Getting dark outside. She had spent a couple of hours shopping on Oxford Street after parting with Lancaster, and she felt a little guilty that she had spent over a hundred pounds on a dress. Perhaps she was turning into a shopaholic. Like the drinking, the spending had to stop. She'd never get a chance to wear the damn thing anyway, as it was a party dress, elegant, strapless and stylish, and she never went to any parties. What could she have been thinking of?

When the train started up again half an hour later, with no explanation for the delay, Michelle realized that if Graham had been involved in anything untoward, there was one person who might know something, even if he didn't know he did: *Banks*. And thinking of him made her once again regret the way she had left him at Starbucks the other day. True, she had resented his intrusion into what she regarded as her private life, a life she kept very guarded indeed, but she had perhaps overreacted a tad. After all, he had only asked her if she was married: a perfectly innocent question in its way, and one you might ask a stranger over a coffee. It didn't have to mean anything, but it was such a raw-nerve point with her, such a no-go area, that she had behaved rudely, and now she regretted it. Well, she wasn't married; that was certainly the truth. Melissa had died because she and Ted got their wires crossed. She was on surveillance and thought *he* was picking up their daughter after school; he had an afternoon meeting and thought *she* was going to do it. Possibly no marriage could survive that amount of trauma – the guilt, blame, grief and anger – and theirs hadn't. Almost six months to the day after Melissa's funeral they had agreed to separate, and Michelle had begun her years of wandering from county to county trying to put the past behind her. Succeeding to a large extent, but still haunted, still in some ways maimed by what had happened.

She hadn't had either the time or the inclination for men, and that was another thing about Banks that bothered her. He was the only man, beyond her immediate colleagues on the Job, with whom she had spent any time in years, and she liked him, found him attractive. Michelle knew that she had been nicknamed the 'Ice Queen' at more than one station over the past five years, but it had only amused her because it couldn't be further from the truth. She was, she knew, deep down, a warm and sensual person, as she had been with Ted, though that was a part of her nature she had neglected for a long time, perhaps even suppressed, out of punishment, being more preoccupied with self-blame. She didn't know if Banks was married or not, though she had noticed that he didn't wear a ring. And he *had* asked her if she were married. In addition to being an intrusion, that had seemed like a come-on line at the time, and maybe it was. The problem was that part of her wanted him, against all her common sense and all the barriers she had built inside, and the result flustered and confused her almost beyond bearing. Banks might be one of the few people who could help her reconstruct Graham Marshall's past, but could she bear to face Banks again in the flesh?

She would have no choice, she realized as the train pulled up and she reached for her briefcase. Graham Marshall's memorial service would be taking place in a matter of days, and she had promised to call and let him know about it.

•

It was almost dark when Banks turned into the lane that ran in front of his small cottage, and he was tired. Annie had left by the time he got back to headquarters after finishing his beer, so he stuck around for an hour or so picking away at the pile of paperwork, then decided to call it a day. Whatever it was she was after, she'd tell him after the weekend.

Memories of Luke's post-mortem hovered unpleasantly close to the surface of his consciousness, the way past cases also haunted him. Over the past few months he had dreamed more than once of Emily Riddle and of the partially buried bodies he had seen in a cellar in Leeds, toes poking through the dirt. Was he going to have to add Luke Armitage to his list of nightmare images now? Was there never any end to it?

Someone had parked a car, an ancient clapped-out Fiesta by the looks of it, in front of the cottage. Unable to get past the obstacle, Banks parked behind it and took out his house keys. There was no one inside the car, so it wasn't a pair of lovers seeking seclusion. Maybe someone had dumped it there, he thought, with a flash of irritation. The dirt lane was little more than a cul-de-sac. It dwindled to a riverside footpath when it reached the woods about twenty feet beyond Banks's cottage, and there was no way for a car to get through. Not everyone knew that, of course, and sometimes cars turned down it by mistake. He ought to consider putting up a sign, he thought, though he had always thought it obvious enough that the track was a private drive.

Then he noticed that the living-room light was on and the curtains closed. He knew he hadn't left the light on that morning. It *could* be burglars, he thought, moving carefully, though if it was, they were very incompetent ones, not only parking in a cul-de-sac but not even bothering to turn their car around for a quick getaway. Still, he'd known far stupider criminals, like the would-be bank robber who had filled out the withdrawal slip with his real name before writing on the back: 'Giv me yor munny, I've got a ~~gun~~ nife' and handing it to the teller. He didn't get far.

The car was definitely a Fiesta, with rusted wheel arches. It would be lucky to pass its next MOT without major and expensive work, Banks thought as he gave it the once-over and memorized the number plate. This was no burglar. He tried to remember to whom he had given a key. Not Annie, at least not any more. Certainly not Sandra. And just as he opened the door, it came to him. There was his son Brian stretched out on the sofa with Tim Buckley playing low on the stereo: 'I Never Asked to Be Your Mountain'. When he heard Banks come in, he uncoiled his long length, sat up and rubbed his eyes.

'Oh. Hi, Dad, it's you.'

'Hello, son. Who else were you expecting?'

'Nobody. I was just half-asleep I suppose. Dreaming.'

'Don't you believe in telephones?'

'Sorry. It's been a bit hectic lately. We're doing some gigs around Teesside starting tomorrow night, so I thought I'd, you know, just drop in and say hello. I had a long drive. All the way from south London.'

'It's good to see you.' Banks gestured with his thumb. 'I'm surprised you made it in one piece. Is that pile of junk out there the car you borrowed two hundred quid off me for?'

'Yeah. Why?'

'I hope you didn't pay any more than that for it, that's all.' Banks put his car keys down on the low table, took off his jacket and hung it on a hook behind the door. 'I didn't know you were a Tim Buckley fan,' he said, sitting down in the armchair.

'You'd be surprised. Actually, I'm not, really. Haven't heard him much. Hell of a voice, though. You can hear it in his son's. Jeff's. He did a great version of this song at a memorial concert for his dad. Most of the time he refused to acknowledge Tim, though.'

'How do you know all this?'

'Read a book about them. *Dream Brother*. It's pretty good. I'll lend it you if I can find it.'

'Thanks.' Mention of Tim and Jeff Buckley's relationship reminded Banks of Luke Armitage and the tape he still had in his pocket. Maybe he'd get Brian's opinion. For the moment, though, a stiff drink was in order. A Laphroaig. 'Can I get you anything to drink?' he asked Brian. 'Drop of single malt, perhaps?'

Brian made a face. 'Can't stand the stuff. If you've got any lager, though . . .'

'I think I can manage that.' Banks poured himself the whisky and found a Carlsberg in the back of the fridge. 'Glass?' he called from the kitchen.

'Can's fine,' Brian called back.

If anything, Brian seemed even taller than the last time Banks had seen him, at least five or six inches taller than his own five-foot nine. He had inherited Banks's constitutional thinness, by the looks of him, and wore the usual uniform of torn jeans and a plain T-shirt. He'd had his hair cut. Not just cut, but massacred, even shorter than Banks's own close crop.

'What's with the haircut?' Banks asked him.

'Kept getting in my eyes. So what are you up to these days, Dad? Still solving crime and keeping the world safe for democracy?'

'Less of your lip.' Banks lit a cigarette. Brian gave him a disgusted look. 'I'm trying to stop,' Banks said. 'It's only my fifth all day.' Brian said nothing, merely raised his eye-brows. 'Anyway,' Banks went on. 'Yes, I'm working.'

'Neil Byrd's son, Luke, right? I heard it on the news while I was driving up. Poor sod.'

'Right. Luke Armitage. You're the musician in the family. What do you think of Neil Byrd?'

'He was pretty cool,' said Brian, 'but maybe just a bit too folksy for me. Too much of a romantic, I guess. Like Dylan, he was a lot better when he went electric. Why?'

'I'm just trying to understand Luke's relationship with him, that's all.'

'He didn't have one. Neil Byrd committed suicide when Luke was only three. He was a dreamer, an idealist. The world could never match up to his expectations.'

'If that were a reason for suicide, Brian, there'd be nobody left alive. But it had to have a powerful effect on the boy. Luke had a bunch of posters in his room. Dead rock stars. Seemed obsessed with them. Not his dad, though.'

'Like who?'

'Jim Morrison, Kurt Cobain, Ian Curtis, Nick Drake. You know. The usual suspects.'

'Covers quite a range,' said Brian. 'I'll bet you thought your generation had cornered the market in dying young, didn't you? Jimi, Janis, Jim.' He nodded towards the stereo. 'Present company.'

'I know some of these were more recent.'

'Well, Nick Drake was another one of your lot. And do you know how old I was when Ian Curtis was with Joy Division? I can't have been more than six or seven.'

'But you have *listened* to Joy Division?'

'I've listened, yeah. Too depressing for me. Kurt Cobain and Jeff Buckley are a lot closer to home. But where's all this going?'

'I honestly don't know,' said Banks. 'I'm just trying to get some sort of grip on Luke's life, his state of mind. He was into some very weird stuff for a fifteen year old. And there was nothing in his room connected with his father.'

'Well, he'd feel pissed off, wouldn't he? Wouldn't you? Only stands to reason. Your old man does a bunk when you're just a baby and then offs himself before you can get to know him at all. Hardly makes you feel wanted, does it?'

'Want to listen to some of his songs?'

'Who? Neil Byrd?'

'No. Luke.'

'Sure.'

Banks paused the Tim Buckley CD, put the tape in, and they both sat in silence sipping their drinks and listening.

'He's good,' said Brian, when the tape had finished. 'Very good. I wish I'd been that good at his age. Still raw, but with a bit of hard work and a lot of practice . . .'

'Do you think he had a future in music, then?'

'It's possible. On the other hand, you see plenty of bands with no talent get to the top and some really terrific musicians struggle just to make a living, so who can say? He's got what it takes in its raw form, though. In my humble opinion. Was he with a band?'

'Not that I know of.'

'He'd be a steal for some up-and-coming group. He's got talent, for a start, and they could milk the Neil Byrd connection for all it was worth. Did you notice the voice? The similarities. Like Tim and Jeff.'

'Yes,' said Banks. 'I did.' He started the Tim Buckley

CD again. It was 'Song to the Siren', which always sent shivers up his spine. 'How's the CD going?' he asked.

'Haven't bloody started it yet, have we? Our manager's still haggling over the contracts. Hence that crappy pile of junk you saw outside.'

'I was expecting a Jag or a red sports car.'

'Soon, Dad, soon. By the way, we've changed our name.'

'Why?'

'The manager thought Jimson Weed was a bit too sixties.'

'He's right.'

'Yeah, well, we're the Blue Lamps now.'

'The police.'

'No, that's another band. The Blue Lamps.'

'I was thinking of *Dixon of Dock Green*.'

'Come again?'

'*The Blue Lamp*. It was a film. Fifties. It's where George Dixon made his debut before it became a TV series. A blue lamp used to be a sign of a police station. Still is in some places. I'm not sure you want to be going around associating yourself with that.'

'The stuff you know. Anyway, our manager thinks it's okay, more modern – you know, White Stripes, Blue Lamps – but I'll tell him what you said. Our sound's hardened up a bit too, got a bit more grungy and less slick. I get to play some real down and dirty guitar solos. You must come and hear us again. We've come a long way since that last gig you were at.'

'I'd love to, but I thought you sounded just fine then.'

'Thanks.'

'I saw your grandparents the other day.'

'Yeah? How are they?'

'Same as ever. You should visit them more often.'

'Oh, you know how it is.'

'No. I don't know.'

'They don't like me, Dad. Not since I screwed up my degree and joined the band. Whenever I see them, it's always Tracy's doing this and Tracy's doing that. They don't care how well *I* do.'

'You know that's not true,' said Banks, who suspected it probably was. After all, weren't they the same way with him? It was all Roy, Roy, Roy, no matter what Banks achieved. He'd had a hard enough time reconciling himself to his son's chosen career, just the same way his mother and father had with him. The only difference was that he had come to terms with Brian's choice, whereas his own parents hadn't even come to terms with *his* career, let alone their grandson's. 'Anyway, I'm sure they'd love to see you.'

'Yeah. Okay. I'll try go and see them when I've got time.'

'How's your mother?'

'Fine, I suppose.'

'Seen her lately?'

'Not for a few weeks.'

'How's she doing with the . . . you know . . . It must be due soon.'

'Yeah, I guess so. Look, Dad, is there anything to eat? I haven't had any dinner yet, and I'm starving.'

Banks thought. He'd eaten a prawn sandwich earlier in the Queen's Arms and wasn't particularly hungry. He knew there was nothing substantial in the fridge or the freezer. He looked at his watch. 'There's a Chinese take-away down in Helmthorpe. They should still be open, if you like.'

'Cool,' said Brian, finishing off his lager. 'What are we waiting for?'

Banks sighed and reached for his jacket again. So much for quality time.

•

Michelle could have walked to Rivergate, it wasn't that far, but it wasn't a particularly pleasant walk and the rain was still pouring down, so she decided to treat herself to a taxi from the station.

The first inkling she got that something was wrong in the flat was when she heard the creaking door of her 'Mystery' screen-saver and saw the lights going on and off in the creepy-looking mansion as the full moon slowly crossed the starlit sky. She knew she had turned her computer off after she'd checked her e-mail that morning. She always did; she was compulsive about it. Also, someone had pulled some of the books out of one of the boxes that she hadn't got round to unpacking. They weren't damaged or anything, just piled up on the floor beside the box.

Michelle jogged the mouse and the computer returned to its regular display. Only it was open at Michelle's file of notes about the Marshall case, and she knew she hadn't opened that since the previous night. There was nothing secret about her speculations, nothing she had thought would even interest anyone else, so she hadn't bothered with password protection. In future she would know better.

With the hairs prickling at the back of her neck, Michelle stood still and strained her ears for any odd sounds in the flat. Nothing except the clock ticking and the humming of the refrigerator. She took her old side-handled baton from her uniform days out of the closet by the door. Gripping that made her feel a little more courageous as she went to explore the rest of the flat.

The kitchen light was on, and a couple of items that she knew she had put back in the fridge that morning – milk, butter, eggs – lay on the countertop. The butter had melted into a shapeless lump and it oozed over her fingers when she picked it up.

Her bathroom cabinet stood open, and the various pills and potions she kept there were not in their usual order. Her bottle of aspirins sat on the edge of the sink, top off and cotton wool missing. Even as the chills went up her spine, Michelle wondered what the hell all this was about. If someone had searched the place, though she couldn't imagine why anyone would want to, then why not just leave it in a mess? Clearly, whoever had done this had done it to scare her – and they were succeeding.

She went into the bedroom cautiously, gripping the side-handled baton more tightly, expecting the worst. Nobody jumped out of the wardrobe at her, but what she saw there made her drop her baton and put her hands to her mouth.

There was no mess. Perhaps some of her drawers weren't completely closed, the way she had left them, but there was no mess. It was much, much worse.

Spread out neatly on the centre of the bed lay Melissa's dress. When Michelle reached out to pick it up, she found it had been cut cleanly into two halves.

Michelle staggered back against the wall, half the dress clutched to her chest, hardly able to believe what was happening. As she did so, her eye caught the writing on the dressing-table mirror: FORGET GRAHAM

MARSHALL, BITCH. REMEMBER MELISSA. YOU COULD JOIN HER.

Michelle cried out, covered her face with the dress and slid down the wall to the floor.

12

Norman Wells sat in the interview room with his folded arms resting on the top of his paunch and his lips pressed tight together. If he was scared, he wasn't showing it. But then, he didn't know how much the police already knew about him.

Banks and Annie sat opposite him, files spread out in front of them. Banks felt well rested after a day off. He had stayed up late Saturday night, eating Chinese food and talking with Brian, but on Sunday, after Brian left, he had done nothing but read the papers, go for a walk from Helmthorpe to Rawley Force and back by himself, stopping for a pub lunch and fiddling with the *Sunday Times* crossword on the way. In the evening, he had thought of ringing Michelle Hart in Peterborough but decided against it. They hadn't parted on the best of terms, so let her contact him first, if she wanted to. After a small Laphroaig and a cigarette outside, enjoying the mild evening air around sunset, he had listened to Ian Bostridge's *English Songbook* CD, gone to bed before half-past ten, and slept as soundly as he could remember in a long time.

'Norman,' said Banks. 'You don't mind if I call you Norman, do you?'

'It's my name.'

'Detective Inspector Cabbot here has been doing a bit of digging around in your background, and it turns out you've been a naughty boy, haven't you?'

Wells said nothing. Annie pushed a file towards Banks, and he opened it. 'You used to be a schoolteacher, am I right?'

'You know I did, or you wouldn't have dragged me in here away from my business.'

Banks raised his eyebrows. 'It's my understanding that you came here of your own free will when asked to help us with our enquiries. Am I wrong?'

'Do you think I'm an idiot?'

'I don't follow.'

'And there's no need to play the thickie with me. You know what I mean. If I hadn't come willingly, you'd have found some way to bring me here, whether I wanted to come or not. So just get on with it. It might not seem much to you, but I have a business to run, customers who rely on me.'

'We'll try to see that you get back to your shop as soon as possible, Norman, but first I'd like you to answer a few questions for me. You taught at a private school in Cheltenham, right?'

'Yes.'

'How long ago?'

'I left seven years ago.'

'Why did you leave?'

'I grew tired of teaching.'

Banks glanced at Annie, who frowned, leaned over and pointed at some lines on the typed sheet of paper in front of Banks. 'Norman,' Banks went on, 'I think I ought to inform you that Detective Inspector Cabbot spoke to your old headmaster, Mr Fulwell, earlier this morning. He was reticent to discuss school business at first, but when she informed him that we were conducting a possible murder investigation, he was a little more forthcoming. We know all about you, Norman.'

The moment of truth. Wells seemed to deflate and shrink in his chair. His plump lower lip pushed up and all but obscured the upper, his chin disappeared into his neck and his arms seemed to wrap more tightly around his lower chest. 'What do you want from me?' he whispered.

'The truth.'

'I had a nervous breakdown.'

'What caused it?'

'The pressures of the job. You've no idea what teaching's like.'

'I don't imagine I have,' Banks admitted, thinking that the last thing he'd want to do was stand up in front of thirty or forty scruffy, hormonally challenged teenagers and try to get them interested in Shakespeare or the War of Jenkins's Ear. Anyone with that skill deserved his admiration. And a medal, too, for that matter. 'What particular pressures led you to decide to leave?'

'It was nothing specific. Just a general sort of breakdown.'

'Stop beating about the bush, Norman,' Annie cut in. 'Does the name Steven Farrow mean anything to you?'

Wells paled. 'Nothing happened. I never touched him. False accusations.'

'According to the headmaster, Norman, you were infatuated with this thirteen-year-old boy. So much so that you neglected your duties, became an embarrassment to the school, and on one occasion—'

'Enough!' Wells slammed his fist down on the metal table. 'You're just like everyone else. You poison the truth with your lies. You can't stare beauty in the eye, so you have to destroy it, poison it for everyone else.'

'Steven Farrow, Norman,' Annie repeated. 'Thirteen years old.'

'It was pure. A pure love.' Wells rubbed his teary eyes with his forearm. 'But you wouldn't understand that, would you? To people like you, anything other than a man and a woman is dirty, abnormal, *perverted*.'

'Try us, Norman,' said Banks. 'Give us a chance. You loved him?'

'Steven was beautiful. An angel. All I wanted was to be close to him, to be with him. What could be wrong with that?'

'But you touched him, Norman,' said Annie. 'He told—'

'I never touched him! He was lying. He turned on me. He wanted money. Can you believe it? My little angel wanted *money*. I would have done anything for him, made any sacrifice. But something so vulgar as *money* . . . I blame them, of course, not Steven. They poisoned him against me. They made him turn on me.' Wells wiped his eyes again.

'Who did, Norman?'

'The others. The other boys.'

'What happened?' Banks asked.

'I refused, of course. Steven went to the headmaster and . . . I was asked to leave, no questions asked, no scandal. All for the good of the school, you see. But word got around. On the scrapheap at thirty-eight. One foolish mistake.' He shook his head. 'That boy broke my heart.'

'Surely you couldn't expect them to keep you on?' Banks said. 'In fact, you're bloody lucky they didn't bring in the police. And you know how we feel about paedophiles.'

'I am not a child molester! I would have been content

just . . . just to be with him. Have you ever been in love, Chief Inspector?'

Banks said nothing. He sensed Annie glance at him.

Wells leaned forward and rested his forearms on the table. 'You can't choose the object of your desire. You know you can't. It may be a cliché to say that love is blind, but like many clichés it's not without a grain of truth. I didn't *choose* to love Steven. I simply couldn't help myself.'

Banks had heard this argument before from paedophiles – that they weren't responsible for their desires, that they didn't *choose* to love little boys – and he had at least a modicum of sympathy for their predicament. After all, it wasn't only paedophiles who fell in love with the wrong people. But he didn't feel enough sympathy to condone their actions. 'I'm sure you are aware,' he said, 'that it's illegal for a thirty-eight-year-old man to initiate a sexual relationship with a thirteen-year-old boy, and that it's inappropriate for a teacher to be involved in any way with a pupil, even if that pupil happened to be over the age of consent, which Steven wasn't.'

'There was no sexual relationship. Steven lied. They made him do it. I never touched him.'

'That's as may be,' said Banks. 'You might not have been able to help your feelings, but you could have controlled your actions. I think you know right from wrong.'

'It's all so hypocritical,' Wells said.

'What do you mean?'

'Who says there can be no real love between youth and age? The Greeks didn't think so.'

'Society,' said Banks. 'The law. And it's not the *love* we legislate against. The law's there to protect the innocent and the vulnerable from those predators who should know better.'

'Ha! It shows how little you know. Who do you think was the vulnerable one here, the innocent one? Steven Farrow? Do you think just because a boy is of a certain tender age that he is incapable of manipulating his elders, incapable of blackmail? That's very naive of you, if you don't mind my saying so.'

'Luke Armitage,' Annie cut in.

Wells leaned back and licked his lips. He was sweating profusely, Banks noticed, and starting to smell sour and rank. 'I wondered when we'd be getting around to him.'

'That's why you're here, Norman. Did you think it was about Steven Farrow?'

'I'd no idea what it would be about. I haven't done anything wrong.'

'The Farrow affair's all water under the bridge. Hushed up. No charges, no serious damage done.'

'Except to me.'

'You were among the last people to see Luke Armitage on the day he disappeared, Norman,' Annie went on. 'When we found out about your past, wasn't it only natural that we should want to talk to you about him?'

'I know nothing about what happened to him.'

'But you were friends with him, weren't you?'

'Acquaintances. He was a customer. We talked about books sometimes. That's all.'

'He was an attractive boy, wasn't he, Norman? Like Steven Farrow. Did he remind you of Steven?'

Wells sighed. 'The boy left my shop. I never saw him again.'

'Are you certain?' Banks asked. 'Are you sure he didn't come back, or you didn't meet him somewhere else? Your house, perhaps?'

'I never saw him again. Why would he come to my house?'

'I don't know,' said Banks. 'You tell me.'

'He didn't.'

'Never?'

'Never.'

'Did he come back to the shop? Did something happen there? Something bad. Did you kill him and then move him after dark? Maybe it was a terrible accident. I can't believe you meant to kill him. Not if you loved him.'

'I didn't *love* him. Society has seen to it that I'm quite incapable of loving anyone ever again. No matter what you think of me, I am not a fool. I *do* know wrong from right, Chief Inspector, whether I agree with the definition or not. I am capable of self-control. I am an emotional eunuch. I know that society regards my urges as evil and sinful, and I have no desire to spend the rest of my days in jail. Believe me, the prison of my own making is bad enough.'

'I suppose the money was an afterthought, was it?' Banks went on. 'But why not? Why not make a little money out of what you'd done? I mean, you could do with it, couldn't you? Look at the dump you spend your days in. A crappy used-book business in a dank, cold dungeon can't be making much money, can it? An extra ten thousand quid would have set you up nicely. Not too greedy. Just enough.'

Wells had tears in his eyes again, and he was shaking his head slowly from side to side. 'It's all I've got,' he said, his voice catching in his throat, his whole body starting to shake now. 'My books. My cat. They're all I've got. Can't you see that, man?' He pushed his florid, bulbous face towards Banks and banged his fist to his heart. 'There's nothing else left here for me. Have you no humanity?'

'But it's still not very much, is it?' Banks pressed on.

Wells looked him in the eye and regained some of his composure. 'Who are you to say that? Who are you to pronounce judgement on a man's life? Do you think I don't know I'm ugly? Do you think I don't notice the way people look at me? Do you think I don't know I'm the object of laughter and derision? Do you think I have no feelings? Every day I sit down there in my dank, cold dungeon, as you so cruelly refer to it, like some sort of pariah, some deformed monster in his lair, some . . . some *Quasimodo*, and I contemplate my sins, my desires, my dreams of love and beauty and purity deemed ugly and evil by a hypocritical world. All I have is my books, and the unconditional love of one of God's creatures. How *dare* you judge me?'

'No matter what you feel,' said Banks, 'society has to protect its children, and for that we need laws. They may seem arbitrary to you. Sometimes they seem arbitrary to me. I mean, fifteen, sixteen, seventeen, eighteen? Fourteen? Where do you draw the line? Who knows, Norman, maybe one day we'll be as enlightened as you'd like us to be and lower the age of consent to thirteen, but until then we have to have those lines, or all becomes chaos.' He was thinking of Graham Marshall as well as Luke Armitage as he spoke. Society hadn't done a very good job of protecting either of them.

'I have done nothing wrong,' said Wells, crossing his arms again.

The problem was, as Banks and Annie had already discussed, that the closed-circuit television cameras corroborated Wells's story. Luke Armitage had entered Norman's Used Books at two minutes to five and left – alone – at five twenty-four.

'What time did you close that day?' Banks asked.

'Half-past five, as usual.'

'And what did you do?'

'I went home.'

'Number 57 Arden Terrace?'

'Yes.'

'That's off Market Street, isn't it?'

'Close, yes.'

'Do you live alone?'

'Yes.'

'Do you own a car?'

'A second-hand Renault.'

'Good enough to get you out to Hallam Tarn and back?'

Wells hung his head in his hands. 'I've told you. I did nothing. I haven't been near Hallam Tarn in months. Certainly not since the foot-and-mouth outbreak.'

Banks could smell his sweat even more strongly now, sharp and acrid, like an animal secretion. 'What did you do after you went home?'

'Had my tea. Leftover chicken casserole, if you're interested. Watched television. Read for a while, then went to sleep.'

'What time?'

'I'd say I was in bed by half-past ten.'

'Alone?'

Wells just glared at Banks.

'You didn't go out again that evening?'

'Where would I go?'

'Pub? Pictures?'

'I don't drink and I don't socialize. I prefer my own

company. And I happen to believe that there hasn't been a decent picture made in the last forty years.'

'Did Luke Armitage visit your house at any time that evening?'

'No.'

'Has Luke Armitage ever visited your house?'

'No.'

'He's never even stepped inside your front door, not just for a moment?'

'I talk to him in the shop sometimes. That's all. He doesn't even know where I live.'

'Did you ever give him a lift anywhere?'

'No. How could I do that? I walk to and from the shop every day. It's not far, and it's good exercise. Besides, you know what parking's like around the market square.'

'So Luke has never been in your car?'

'Never.'

'In that case,' said Banks, 'I'm sure you won't mind if our forensic experts have a close look at your house and your car. We'd also like to take a DNA sample, just for comparison.'

Wells stuck his chin out. 'What if I *do* mind?'

'We'll keep you here until we get a search warrant. Remember, Norman, I wouldn't like to say judges are swayed by such things, but Luke Armitage came from a wealthy and well-respected family, while you're a disgraced schoolteacher eking out a living in a dingy used bookshop. And that shop was the last place we know Luke visited before he disappeared.'

Wells hung his head. 'Fine,' he said. 'Go ahead. Do what you will. I don't care any more.'

•

After a sleepless night on Saturday, Michelle had spent Sunday getting over the shock of what had happened in her flat and trying to rein in her emotional response in favour of more analytical thought.

She hadn't got very far.

That someone had gained entry and arranged things in order to frighten her was obvious enough. Why was another matter entirely. That the interloper knew about Melissa surprised her, though she supposed people could find out anything about her if they really wanted to. But, given that he knew, it would have been evident when he searched her bedside drawers that the little dress was Melissa's, and that its desecration would cause her a great deal of anguish. In other words, it had been a cold, calculated assault.

The flats were supposed to be secure, but Michelle had been a copper long enough to know that a talented burglar could get around almost anything. Though it went against every grain in Michelle's nature not to report the break-in to the police, in the end she decided against it. Mostly this was because Graham Marshall's name had been written in her own red lipstick on the dressing-table mirror. The intrusion was meant to frighten her off the case, and the only people who knew she was working on it, apart from the Marshalls themselves, were other police officers, or people connected with them, like Dr Cooper. True, Michelle's name had been in the papers once or twice when the bones had first been found, so technically everyone in the entire country could know she was on the case, but she felt the answers lay a lot closer to home.

The question was, 'Was she going to be frightened off the case?' The answer was, 'No.'

At least there hadn't been much cleaning up to do.

Michelle had, however, dumped the entire contents of her bathroom cabinet and would have to contact her doctor for new prescriptions. She had also dumped the contents of the fridge, which hadn't been a big job at all. More important, she had found a locksmith in the *Yellow Pages* and arranged to have a chain and an extra deadbolt lock put on her door.

As a result of her weekend experience, Michelle felt drained and edgy on Monday morning and found herself looking at everyone in Divisional Headquarters differently, as if they knew something she didn't, as if they were pointing at her and talking about her. It was a frightening feeling, and every time she caught someone's eye she looked away. Creeping paranoia, she told herself, and tried to shake it off.

First, she had a brief meeting with DC Collins, who told her he was getting nowhere checking the old perv reports. Most of the people the police had interviewed at the time were either dead or in jail, and those who weren't had nothing new to add. She phoned Dr Cooper, who still hadn't located her knife expert, Hilary Wendell, yet, then she went down to the archives to check out the old notebooks and action allocations.

These days, since the Police and Criminal Evidence Act, there were very strict rules regarding police notebooks. You couldn't leave blank pages, for example. Each page was numbered, and if you missed one by mistake you had to draw a line through it and write 'omitted in error'. Entries had to be preceded by date and time, underlined, and at the end of each day the officer had to draw a continuous line below the final entry. Most of this was to prevent officers from 'verballing' suspects – attributing to them words they hadn't used, confessions they hadn't made – and to avoid any sort of revisions after the fact. Notes were made on the spot, often quickly, and accuracy was important because the notebooks might need to be used in court.

An officer's notebooks could be invaluable when trying to reconstruct the pattern of an investigation, as could the action allocations, records made of all the instructions issued to investigating officers by the senior investigating officer. For example, if DC Higginbottom was asked to go and interview Joe Smith's neighbour, that order, or 'action', would be recorded in the actions allocation book, and his record of the interview would be in his notebook. By looking at the actions, you could determine which areas of enquiry had been pursued and which had not, and by reading the notebooks, you could unearth impressions that might not have made it into final statements and formal reports.

Completed notebooks were first handed to a detective inspector, who would look them over and, if everything was acceptable, send them to the records clerk for filing. That meant they piled up over the years. Whoever said we were heading for a paperless world, Michelle thought, as she walked along the rows of shelving stacked to the ceiling with boxes, obviously wasn't a copper.

Mrs Metcalfe showed her where the notebooks were filed, and Michelle went first, by instinct, to Ben Shaw's. But no matter how many times she flipped through the boxes, checked and rechecked the dates, in the end she had to admit that if there had been notebooks covering the period of major activity in the Graham Marshall case, on the day of his disappearance, 22 August 1965, and over the next month or two, then they had vanished.

Michelle found it difficult to decipher Shaw's

handwriting in the notebooks she did find, but she could just about make out that his last entry was on 15 August 1965, when he had been questioning a witness to a post office robbery, and the next one was a new notebook started on 6 October of the same year.

Michelle asked for Mrs Metcalfe's help, but after half an hour even the poor records clerk had to admit defeat. 'I can't imagine where they've got to, love,' she said. 'Except they might have got misfiled by my predecessor, or been lost in one of the moves.'

'Could someone have taken them?' Michelle asked.

'I don't see who. Or why. I mean, it's only people like you who come down here. Other police.'

Exactly what Michelle had been thinking. She could have taken out anything she wanted during her visits and Mrs Metcalfe would have been none the wiser. Which meant that anyone else could too. Someone had gained entry to her flat and tried to scare her off the case, and now she found that nearly two months' worth, a crucial two months' worth, of notebooks had somehow disappeared. Coincidence? Michelle didn't think so.

Half an hour later, when they had run into the same problem with the action allocation book for the Graham Marshall case, Michelle knew in her bones that the actions and the notebooks were gone for ever, destroyed most likely. But why? And by whom? The discovery didn't help her paranoia one bit. She was beginning to feel way out of her depth. What the hell should she do now?

•

After the interview, Banks felt the urge to get out of the station, away from the acrid stink of Norman Wells's sweat, so he decided to head out Lyndgarth way and talk to Luke Armitage's music teacher, Alastair Ford, while Annie continued to supervise the search for Luke's mystery woman.

In Banks's experience, music teachers were an odd lot indeed, partly, no doubt, because of the frustration of trying to instil the beauties of Beethoven and Bach into minds addled with Radiohead and Mercury Rev. Not that Banks had anything against pop music. In his day, the class had kept pestering their music teacher, Mr Watson, to play the Beatles. He relented once, but looked glum the whole time. His feet didn't tap, and his heart wasn't in it. When he played Dvorak's 'New World Symphony' or Tchaikovsky's 'Pathétique', however, it was another matter. He closed his eyes, swayed and conducted, hummed along as the main themes swelled. All the time the kids in the class were laughing at him and reading comics under their desks, but he was oblivious, in a world of his own. One day Mr Watson failed to turn up for class. Rumour had it that he'd suffered a nervous breakdown and was 'resting' in a sanatorium. He never returned to teaching as far as Banks knew.

Yesterday's rain had rinsed the landscape clean and brought out the bright greens of the lower daleside, dotted with purple clover, yellow buttercups and celandines. The limestone scar of Fremlington Edge glowed in the sunlight, and below it the village of Lyndgarth, with its small church and lopsided village green, like a handkerchief flapping in the wind, seemed asleep. Banks consulted his map, found the minor road he was looking for and turned right.

Ford's cottage was about as isolated as Banks's own, and when he parked behind the dark blue Honda, he understood why. It wasn't the 'New World Symphony' but the beautiful 'Recordare' for soprano and mezzo-soprano from Verdi's *Requiem* blasting out of the open windows at full volume. If Banks hadn't been playing the Stones' *Aftermath* CD in the car, he would have heard it a mile away.

It took a bit of hammering at the door, but eventually the music quietened down and it was answered by the man Banks recognized from the Aeolian String Quartet concert. Alastair Ford had a five o'clock shadow, a long, hooked nose and a bright gleam in his eyes. If he had any, his hair would probably have been sticking out in all directions, but he was quite bald. What was it about Luke Armitage? Banks wondered. This was the second person he'd met that day who had spent time with the boy and looked as mad as a hatter. Maybe Luke attracted weirdos. Maybe it was because he was more than a little weird himself. However, Banks determined to keep an open mind. Whether Alastair Ford's eccentricity had a dangerous edge remained to be seen.

'I'm as fond of Verdi as the next man,' said Banks, showing his warrant card, 'but don't you think it's a bit too loud?'

'Oh, don't tell me old Farmer Jones has complained about the music again. He says it curdles his cows' milk. Philistine!'

'I'm not here about the noise, Mr Ford. Might I come in and have a word?'

'Now I'm curious,' said Ford, leading the way inside. His house was clean but lived in, with little piles of sheet music here and there, a violin on a table, and the massive stereo system dominating the living room. 'A policeman who knows his Verdi.'

'I'm no expert,' Banks said, 'but I've recently bought a new recording, so I've listened to it a few times lately.'

'Ah, yes. Renée Fleming and the Kirov. Very nice, but I must admit I'm still rather attached to the von Otter and Gardiner. Anyway, I can't imagine you've come here to discuss old Joe Green with me. What can I do for you?' Ford was birdlike in many ways, especially in his sudden, jerky movements, but when he sat down in the over-stuffed armchair he fell still, fingers linked in his lap. He wasn't relaxed, though. Banks could sense the man's tension and unease, and he wondered what its cause was. Maybe he just didn't like being questioned by the police.

'It's about Luke Armitage,' said Banks. 'I understand you knew him?'

'Ah, poor Luke. A remarkably talented boy. Such a great loss.'

'When did you last see him?'

'Around the end of term.'

'Are you sure you haven't seen him since?'

'I've barely left the cottage since then, except to drive into Lyndgarth for groceries. Alone with my music after a term of teaching those philistines. What bliss!'

'I gather Luke Armitage wasn't a philistine, though?'

'Far from it.'

'You were giving him violin lessons, am I right?'

'Yes.'

'Here or at school?'

'At school. Tuesday evenings. We have a reasonably well-equipped music room there. Mind you, we ought to be grateful for anything these days. They'll spend a fortune on sports equipment, but when it comes to music . . . '

'Did Luke ever talk to you about anything that was on his mind?'

'He didn't talk a lot. Mostly he concentrated on his playing. He had remarkable powers of concentration, unlike so many of today's youth. He wasn't much of a one for small talk. We did chat about music, argued once or twice about pop music, which I gathered he was rather fond of.'

'Never about anything else?'

'Like what?'

'Anything that might have been bothering him, worrying him, anyone he might have been afraid of. That sort of thing.'

'I'm afraid not. Luke was a very private person, and I'm not the prying kind. Truth be told, I'm not very good at helping people with their emotional problems.' He ran his hand over his smooth head and smiled. 'That's why I prefer to live alone.'

'Not married?'

'Was. Many moons ago.'

'What happened.'

'Search me. What usually happens?'

Banks thought of Sandra. *What usually happens?* 'So you just taught him the violin, that's all?'

'Mainly, yes. I mean, he was in my class, too, at school. But I wouldn't say I *knew* him or that we were friends or anything like that. I respected his talent, even if he did dabble in pop music, but that's as far as it went.'

'Did he ever mention his parents?'

'Not to me.'

'What about his biological father? Neil Byrd?'

'Never heard of him.'

Banks looked around the room. 'It's a very isolated cottage you have here, Mr Ford.'

'Is it? Yes, I suppose it is.'

'Isolation suits you?'

'It must do, mustn't it?' Ford's foot started tapping on

the floor, his knee jerking, and not to the rhythm of the now barely audible *Requiem*.

'Do you ever have company?'

'Rarely. I play in a string quartet, and sometimes the other members come out here to rehearse. Other than that, I'm rather given to solitary pursuits. Look, I—'

'No girlfriends?'

'I told you, I'm not good at relationships.'

'Boyfriends?'

Ford raised an eyebrow. 'I'm not good at relationships.'

'Yet you manage the teacher–student relationship.'

'I have a talent for teaching.'

'Do you enjoy it?'

'In a way. Sometimes.'

Banks got up and walked over to the window. There was a fine view of the dale, looking back towards Eastvale in the distance. Banks thought he could just make out the castle on its hill.

'Did Luke Armitage ever come here?' he asked, turning to face Ford.

'No.'

'You're certain?'

'Very few people come here. I would remember. Look, if you want to know about Luke, ask Lauren.'

'Lauren Anderson?'

'Yes. She knew him far better than I did. She's a . . . well, you know, she's the sort of person people talk to, about their problems and stuff.'

'Emotions.'

'Yes.'

'Do you know if Luke was close to anyone else?'

'You could try our headmaster's daughter.'

Banks had a quick flash of that sudden flurry of blonde hair and long leg he had noticed after his conversation with Gavin Barlow. 'Rose Barlow?'

'That's the one. Little minx.'

'Were she and Luke friends?'

'Thick as thieves.'

'When was this?'

'Earlier this year. February or March.'

'Where did you see them together?'

'At school.'

'Nowhere else?'

'I don't go anywhere else. Except here. All I can say is I saw them talking sometimes in the corridors and playground, and they seemed close.'

Banks made a mental note to follow up on Rose Barlow. 'Do you have a mobile phone?' he asked.

'Good Lord, what an odd question!'

'Do you?'

'No. I see no use for one, personally. I barely use the telephone I do have.'

'Where were you last Monday?'

'Here.'

'Were you in Eastvale at all last week?'

'I've already told you. I've hardly left the cottage.'

'What have you been doing?'

'What do you mean?'

'Here. In the cottage. Alone. All this time.'

Ford got to his feet and the birdlike motions started up again. 'Playing music. Listening. Reading. Dabbling in a little composition. Look, really it's none of your business, you know, even if you *are* a policeman. The last time I noticed, we were still living in a free country.'

'It was just a simple question, Mr Ford. No need to get upset.'

Ford's voice took on a piercing edge. 'I'm not getting upset. But you're prying. I hate people prying. I can't tell you anything. Go and talk to Lauren. Leave me alone.'

Banks stared at him for a moment. Ford wouldn't meet his gaze. 'If I find out you've been lying to me, Mr Ford, I'll be back. Do you understand?'

'I'm not lying. I haven't done anything. Leave me alone.'

Before leaving, Banks showed him the artist's impression of the girl Josie Batty had seen with Luke. Ford hardly glanced at the sketch and said he didn't recognize her. He was weird, without a doubt, Banks thought as he started his car, but you couldn't arrest people just for being weird. The volume went way up again, and Banks could hear Verdi's 'Lacrimosa' chasing him all the way to Lyndgarth.

•

'Thank you for seeing to the release, love,' Mrs Marshall said. 'We'll be holding the funeral service at St Peter's the day after tomorrow. Joan's coming back up for it, of course. I must say the vicar's been very good considering none of us were what you'd call regular church-goers. You'll be there?'

'Yes, of course,' said Michelle. 'There's just one thing.'

'What's that, love?'

Michelle told her about the rib they needed for evidence.

Mrs Marshall frowned and thought for a moment. 'I don't think we need worry about a little thing like a missing rib, need we? Especially if it might help you.'

'Thank you,' said Michelle.

'You look tired, love. Is everything all right?'

'Yes. Fine.' Michelle managed to dredge up a weak smile.

'Is there any more news?'

'No, I'm afraid not. Only more questions.'

'I can't understand what else I have to tell you, but please go ahead.'

Michelle leaned back in her chair. This was going to be difficult, she knew. To find out about any mischief Graham might have been up to without suggesting that he got up to mischief – which his mother would never accept – was almost to do the impossible. Still, she could but try. 'Was Graham ever away from home for any periods of time?'

'What do you mean? Did we send him away?'

'No. But you know what kids are like. Sometimes they just like to take off and not tell you where they've been. They worry you sick, but they don't seem to realize it at the time.'

'Oh, I know what you mean. I'm not saying our Graham was any different from other kids that way. He missed his tea from time to time, and once or twice he missed his nine o'clock curfew. And many's the occasion we didn't see hide nor hair of him from dawn till dusk. Not during term-time, mind you. Just weekends and school holidays he could be a bit unreliable.'

'Did you have any idea where he'd been when he turned up late?'

'Playing with his pals. Sometimes he'd have his guitar with him, too. They were practising, see. The group.'

'Where did they do that?'

'David Grenfell's house.'

'Other than group practice, did he ever stay out late on other occasions?'

'Once in a while. He was just a normal boy.'

'How much pocket money did you give him?'

'Five shillings a week. It was all we could afford. But he had his paper round and that made him a bit extra.'

'And you bought all his clothes?'

'Sometimes he'd save up if there was something he really wanted. Like a Beatles jumper. You know, like the one he's wearing in the photo there.'

'So he didn't go short of anything?'

'No. Not so's you'd notice. Why? What are you trying to get at?'

'I'm just trying to get a picture of his activities, Mrs Marshall. It'll help me try to work out what might have happened to him, who might have stopped and picked him up.'

'You think it was somebody he knew?'

'I didn't say that, but it's possible.'

Mrs Marshall fiddled with her necklace. The idea clearly upset her. Whether it was the idea of an acquaintance being responsible, or whether she had suspected such a thing deep down, was impossible to say. 'But we didn't know anybody like that,' she said.

'Like what?'

'A pervert,' she whispered.

'We don't know that it *was* a pervert.'

'I don't understand. That's what the police said. Who else could it be?'

'Jet Harris told you that?'

'Yes.'

'Did anyone ever suggest, at any time, that Graham might have been abducted by someone he knew?'

'Heavens, no! Why would anyone do that?'

'Why indeed?' said Michelle. 'And you know nothing about any unsavoury company Graham might have been keeping – perhaps on the occasions when he stayed out late or was gone all day?'

'No. He was with his friends. I don't understand what you're trying to say.'

'It's all right,' said Michelle. 'I'm not sure that I under-stand it myself. I suppose all I really want to ask is whether Graham had any friends you disliked, or spent time with anyone you didn't approve of.'

'Oh. No. They were all just regular lads. We knew their mums and dads. They were just like us.'

'No older boys? No one you thought was a bad influence?'

'No.'

'And Graham never seemed to have more money than you expected him to have?'

Mrs Marshall's expression sharpened and Michelle knew she'd gone too far. She also knew that she had touched a raw nerve.

'Are you suggesting our Graham was a thief?'

'Of course not,' Michelle backtracked. 'I just wondered if he maybe did other odd jobs he didn't tell you about, other than the paper round, perhaps when he should have been at school.'

Mrs Marshall still eyed her suspiciously. Bill Marshall seemed to be taking everything in, his beady eyes moving from one to the other as they spoke, but they were the only things moving in his face. If only he could talk, Michelle thought. And then she realized that would be no use. He wouldn't tell her anything.

'I suppose it's just a mark of my frustration with the case,' Michelle admitted. 'After all, it was so long ago.'

'Jet Harris always said it was them Moors Murderers, the ones who were tried the year after. He said we'd all probably have nightmares for the rest of our lives if we ever knew how many young lives they'd taken and where the bodies were buried.'

'He told you that, did he?' said Michelle. How very convenient. She was fast coming to the conclusion – or reaffirming what she had suspected earlier – that Detective Superintendent Harris had run the case with blinkers on, and Mrs Marshall, like so many mothers, hadn't a clue what her son was up to most of the time. She wondered if his father knew. Bill Marshall's lopsided face gave away nothing, but Michelle fancied she could see wariness in his eyes. And something else. She couldn't say with any certainty that it was guilt, but it looked like that to her. Michelle took a deep breath and plunged in.

'I understand your husband used to work for the Kray twins back in London.'

There was a short silence, then Mrs Marshall said, 'Bill didn't *work* for them, as such. He did used to spar with them down the gym. We knew them. Of course we did. We grew up in the same neighbourhood. Everybody knew Reggie and Ronnie. Always polite to me, they were, no matter what anybody says about them, and I've heard some stories as would make your hair curl. But they were basically good lads. People don't like it when others get a bit above their station, you know.'

Michelle could feel her jaw dropping. There was nothing more to be gained here, she realized, and if she was going to solve this case she was going to do so without the family's help, and without Ben Shaw's. And perhaps in peril of her life. '*Remember Melissa. You could join her . . .*' Promising again that she would be at the funeral, Michelle excused herself and hurried off.

•

That evening at home, Banks glanced through the evening paper over a Madras curry he'd bought earlier at Marks & Spencer, slipped Bill Evans's *Paris Concert* into the CD player, poured himself a couple of fingers of Laphroaig and flopped down on the sofa with his 1965 *Photoplay* diary. He thought it was Oscar Wilde who had said, 'I never travel without my diary. One should always have something sensational to read on the train,' but he could have been wrong. It was easy to attribute just about any witty saying to Oscar Wilde or Groucho Marx. Curious, though, he stirred himself and checked *The Oxford Dictionary of Quotations* and found that he was right this time.

Banks's diary was far from sensational. As he flipped the pages once again, glancing at the pretty actresses he hardly remembered – Carol Lynley, Jill St John, Yvette Mimieux – he was struck by how many records he had bought and films he had seen. Until, just a couple of weeks from Graham's disappearance, Banks saw that his diary did, in fact, have its moments, and as he read the trivial or cryptic entries, he was able to fill in the rest with his memory and imagination.

In the first week of August 1965 the Banks family had set off for their annual holidays. There was nothing unusual in that; they went every year at the same time, his father's annual factory shut-down fortnight. What *was* unusual that year was that they went to Blackpool – much further afield than their usual trip to Great Yarmouth or

Skegness – and that they took Graham Marshall with them.

At fourteen, Banks was of an age when he found wandering around a seaside resort with his parents embarrassing, and riding the donkey on the beach or playing with a bucket and spade no longer held any appeal. As Graham's dad had just started on a large building project – his work being far more seasonal than Arthur Banks's – and it didn't look as if the Marshalls would get a holiday that year, financial arrangements were made and Graham was allowed to accompany them.

Visit Blackpool! See the Famous Tower! Hear Reginald Dixon at the Mighty Organ! See the glorious Golden Mile! Go to a star-studded Variety Show on one of the Three Piers! Have hours of Family Fun at the Pleasure Beach!

It might as well have been the moon.

At some ridiculously early hour in the morning, because that was when they always set off on holiday, they would have piled their cases into the back of Arthur Banks's Morris Traveller, a popular sort of estate car with a wood-frame rear, and headed north on their long journey, no doubt arriving tired and cranky, but in good time for tea at Mrs Barraclough's boarding house. Bed, breakfast and evening meal at six o'clock on the dot, and woe betide you if you were late. Mrs Barraclough was a large, forbidding presence, whom Banks remembered even now as dressed in a pinny, standing with her thick legs apart and her arms folded under her massive bosom.

Banks saw that he had recorded the weather every day at the top of his entry, and as holidays went they had done quite well: nine days of at least partial sunshine out of fourteen, and only two and a half complete washouts. On the rainy days Banks and Graham had hung about the amusement arcades on the Golden Mile, he noted, or on one of the piers, and played the one-armed bandits and pinball machines. One rainy Sunday afternoon they spent watching the old war films that always seemed to be showing on rainy Sunday afternoons, patriotic films with titles such as *The Day Will Dawn*, *In Which We Serve* and *Went the Day Well?*

On overcast days they would wander along the prom eating fish and chips from newspapers or boiled shrimps from paper bags and go hunting through the town's few second-hand bookshops, Banks looking for Sexton Blake novelettes (he had bought one called *The Mind Killers*) or Ian Fleming novels, while Graham went after *Famous Monsters* magazines and Isaac Asimov stories.

One night they all went to the Tower Circus, and Banks noted in his diary that he found Charlie Cairoli's act 'very funny'. They also took in a variety show on the North Pier, with Morecambe and Wise providing the comedy and the Hollies the music.

But most evenings after tea they spent watching television in the guests' lounge. The TV was an old model, even for then, with a small screen, Banks remembered, and you turned it on by opening a sprung flap on the top, under which were the volume and contrast controls. Banks hadn't recorded it in his diary, but no doubt there would have been some adult wanting to watch *Sunday Night at the London Palladium* instead of *Perry Mason*, which was only to be expected of adults. Luckily, Roy was sleeping on a camp bed in his parents' room, so Banks and Graham would just go up to their room and read, listen to Radio Luxembourg on their transistors, or pore over the dirty magazines Graham seemed to get hold of in abundance.

Of course, they didn't spend every minute of every day together. Graham had been moody at times, unusually quiet, and looking back Banks suspected he had been preoccupied with some problem or other. At the time, though, he hadn't given it a second thought, had simply gone his own way on occasion.

On his third day, wandering the streets alone looking for somewhere to sit down and have a cigarette, Banks discovered a coffee bar down a flight of stairs off the beaten track. He hadn't thought of this in years, but the stark diary entry brought it back in all its rich detail. He could even hear the hissing of the espresso machine and smell the dark-roasted coffee.

The place had a tropical ambience, with rough stucco walls, potted palms and soft calypso music playing in the background, but it was the girl behind the counter who drew him back there time after time. She was far too old for him, even if he did look older when he smoked and could pass for sixteen and get into 'X' films. Probably over twenty, she would have an older boyfriend with a car and lots of money, a pretty girl like her, but Banks fell for her the way he had fallen for the factory girl, Mandy. Linda was her name.

That Linda was beautiful went without saying. She had long dark hair, sparkling blue eyes, an easy smile and lips he yearned to kiss. What he could see of the rest of her body when she came out from behind the counter was also the stuff that fantasies were made on: like Ursula Andress walking out of the sea in *Dr No*. She was nice to him, too. She talked to him, smiled at him, and one day she even gave him a second cup of espresso for nothing. He loved to watch her working the machines behind the counter, nibbling her lower lip as she frothed the milk.

Once or twice she caught him looking and smiled. He could feel himself blush to the roots of his being and he knew that she knew he was in love with her. This was one secret, and one place, he didn't share with Graham.

As the holiday progressed, Banks and Graham did all the usual things, some with the rest of the family, and some by themselves. When it was warm enough, they spent time lounging with Banks's mother and father on the beach in their swimming trunks among crowds of rough northerners with knotted hankies on their heads. They even went in the sea once or twice, but it was cold, so they didn't stay long. Mostly they just lay there plugged into their radios hoping to hear the Animals singing 'We've Gotta Get Out of This Place' or the Byrds doing 'Mr Tambourine Man', and surreptitiously eyeing the girls in their bathing costumes.

In fact, reading over his diary, not only of the holiday but of the entire year, Banks was amazed at how much of his time was taken up with girls, with thoughts and dreams of sex. His hormones were running his life that year, no doubt about it.

The highlight of the week, though, was the two girls, and that was where Banks's diary approached the sensational. One fine evening Banks and Graham headed down to the Pleasure Beach opposite the South Pier. They took one of the open trams, sitting on the upper deck and thrilling at the lights with the wind in their hair.

The Pleasure Beach was a bustle of colour and sound, from the rattling of the rides to the shrieks and screams of the passengers. As they were walking around trying to decide which ride to go on first, they noticed two girls about their own age who kept looking at them, whispering to one another and giggling, the way girls did. They weren't mods, but wore blouses and skirts of the more conservative length some parents still insisted on.

Eventually, Banks and Graham approached them and, Graham being the silent, moody type, Banks offered them cigarettes and started chatting them up. He couldn't remember what he said, just something to make the girls laugh and think these boys were cool. The way it turned out, this time he linked up with the one he fancied most, though to be honest they were both all right, not like the usual pairing of the good-looking one with the ugly friend.

Tina was short with rather large breasts, a dark complexion and long wavy brown hair. Her friend, Sharon, was a slender blonde. The only flaws Banks noticed were a couple of spots under her make-up and the bubblegum she was chewing. But there was nothing she could do about the spots – he knew, he had a couple of embarrassing ones himself – and she soon took out the gum and threw it away.

They went on the Ghost Train first, and the girls got scared when phosphorescent skeletons jumped out and hung in front of the slow-moving cars. But what made them scream and lean closer into the chests of their companions were the cobwebs that occasionally brushed across their faces in the dark.

After the Ghost Train they were holding hands, and Graham suggested they ride on the Big Dipper, a huge roller-coaster, next. Tina was scared, but the others assured her it would be okay. Graham paid.

That was something Banks remembered as he read through his diary. He lit a cigarette, sipped some Laphroaig and thought about it for a moment as Bill Evans played on. Graham often paid. He always seemed to have plenty of money, always enough, even back in Peterborough, for ten Gold Leaf and a double bill at the Gaumont. Maybe even some Kia-Ora and a choc ice from the woman who came around with the tray during the intermission. Banks never wondered or asked where he got it from at the time; he just assumed that Graham got plenty of pocket money from his dad in addition to his paper-round money. Looking back now, though, it seemed odd that a working-class kid, a bricklayer's son, should always have so much ready cash to spend.

If the Ghost Train had set things up nicely, Banks thought, going back to the memory, the Big Dipper had the girls throwing their arms around Banks and Graham and burying their faces in their shoulders. Banks even stole a quick kiss from Sharon as they rose up towards one of the steepest descents, and she clung to him all the way down, hair streaming, shrieking blue murder.

Flushed and exhilarated, they walked out of the Pleasure Beach on to the prom. The Illuminations didn't start until later in the year, but there were still bracelets and necklaces of lights all over the front, like Christmas decorations, Banks had written in a strangely rare poetic moment, and the trams themselves were lit with bulbs so you could see their outlines coming from miles away.

After only token resistance, the girls agreed to a walk on the beach and the four of them inevitably settled under the South Pier, a well-established 'courting' spot. Banks remembered as he read his vague and brief descriptions, how he lay with Sharon and kissed her, gently at first, then the two of them working their lips harder, trying a little tongue, feeling her body stir under him. He let his imagination go to work on the scanty details he had recorded in his bed back at Mrs Barraclough's that night: 'G and me went with Tina and Sharon under south pier!'

Somehow, he had worked his hand under her blouse and felt her firm little breast. She didn't complain when after a while of that he wriggled under her bra and felt the warm, soft flesh itself, squeezing the nipple between his thumb and forefinger. She took a sharp breath and went back to kissing him with her tongue. He got some of her hair in his mouth. He could smell bubblegum on her breath, mingled with the seaweed and brine of the beach. Trams rolled by above them and waves crashed on the shore. Sometime later, getting brave, he slid his hand down her thigh and put it up inside her skirt. She would only let him touch her over the cloth of her knickers, freezing or firmly pulling his hand away when he tried to go further, but that was the furthest he had ever been before, so it was all right with him. Graham said later that Tina let him go all the way with her, but Banks didn't believe him.

And that was as sensational as it got.

They went out with Sharon and Tina twice more, once to the pictures to see *Help!* and once to the amusement arcades, Graham as usual supplying most of the cash, and their evenings ended the same way. No matter how much Banks tried and hinted, Sharon wouldn't relinquish her treasure. She always stopped him at the threshold. It was a tease balanced only later with the delicious ritual of self-administered relief.

When it was time to leave, they exchanged names and addresses and said they'd write, but Banks never heard from Sharon again. As far as he knew, Graham hadn't heard from Tina before he disappeared, either. Now, looking back, Banks hoped she really *had* let him go all the way with her.

Remembering their holiday had made him also

remember other things, and some of them started to ring alarm bells in his policeman's mind. Quiet at first, then getting louder and louder.

But soon, it wasn't an inner alarm bell, it was the telephone that was ringing. Banks picked it up.

'DCI Banks?' A woman's voice, familiar, strained.

'Yes.'

'It's DI Hart. Michelle.'

'I haven't forgotten your name yet,' Banks said. 'What can I do for you? Any news?'

'Are you busy?'

'Just after you left me in Starbucks a missing persons case turned into a murder, so yes, I am.'

'Look, I'm sorry about that. I mean . . . This is so difficult.'

'Just tell me.'

Michelle paused for so long that Banks was beginning to think she would just hang up. She seemed to be good at putting an abrupt end to conversations. But she didn't. After an eternity she said, 'Today I discovered that Ben Shaw's notebooks and the Graham Marshall actions allocations are missing.'

'Missing?'

'I looked all over the files. I couldn't find them. I got the records clerk to help, too, but even she couldn't find them. There's a gap in the notebooks from 15 August to 6 October 1965.'

Banks whistled between his teeth. 'And the actions?'

'Just for that case. Gone. I don't know . . . I mean, I've never . . . There's something else, too. Something that happened over the weekend. But I don't want to talk about it over the phone.' She gave a nervous laugh. 'I suppose I'm asking you for advice. I don't know what to do.'

'You should tell someone.'

'I'm telling you.'

'I mean someone in your station.'

'That's the problem,' she said. 'I just don't know who I can trust down here. That's why I thought of you. I know you have a personal interest in the case, and it would be helpful for me to have another professional around. One I know I can trust.'

Banks thought it over for a moment. Michelle was right; he did have an interest in the case. And the way it sounded, she was out on a limb by herself down there. 'I'm not sure what I can do to help,' he said, 'but I'll see if I can get away.' As he spoke the words, an image of himself charging down to Peterborough and Michelle on a white steed, wearing armour and carrying a lance, mocked him. 'Any news on the funeral service?'

'Day after tomorrow.'

'I'll get away as soon as I can,' he said. 'Maybe tomorrow. In the meantime, don't say or do anything. Just carry on as normal. Okay?'

'Okay. And Alan?'

'Yes?'

'Thanks. I mean it. I'm in a jam.' She paused, then added, 'And I'm scared.'

'I'll be there.'

After Banks hung up, he refilled his glass, put the second Bill Evans set on and settled down to think over the repercussions of what he had realized earlier that evening, reading his diary, and of what he had just heard from Michelle.

13

Lauren Anderson lived in a small semi not too far from where Banks used to live with Sandra before their separation. He hadn't passed the end of his old street in a long time, and it brought back memories he would rather forget. He felt cheated, somehow. The memories should have been good – he and Sandra *had* had good times together, had been in love for many years – but everything seemed tainted by her betrayal and now by her forthcoming marriage to Sean. And the baby, of course. The baby hurt a lot.

He spoke nothing of his thoughts to Annie, who sat beside him. She didn't even know he used to live there, as he had only met her after he moved to the Gratly cottage. Besides, she had made it clear that she wasn't interested in his old life with Sandra and the kids; that was one of the main things that had come between them and broken up their brief and edgy romance.

It was as fine a summer's day as they had seen in a while. They were in Banks's car this time, the way he preferred it, with the windows open listening to Marianne Faithfull singing 'Summer Nights' on a greatest hits CD. That was back when her voice was rich and smooth, before the booze, drugs and cigarettes had taken their toll, the same way it had happened with Billie Holiday. It was also a hit around the time Graham disappeared and it captured the mood of that sex-preoccupied adolescent summer.

'I can't believe you still listen to this stuff,' said Annie.

'Why not?'

'I don't know. It's just so . . . old.'

'So is Beethoven.'

'Clever clogs. You know what I mean.'

'I used to fancy her like crazy.'

Annie shot him a sidelong glance. 'Marianne Faithfull?'

'Yes. Why not? She used to come on *Ready, Steady, Go!* and *Top of the Pops* every time she had a new record out, and she'd sit on a high stool with her guitar looking just like a schoolgirl. But she'd be wearing a low-cut dress, legs crossed, and that sweet voice would come out, and you'd just want to . . .'

'Go on.'

Banks stopped at a traffic light and smiled at Annie. 'I'm sure you get the picture,' he said. 'She just looked so innocent, so virginal.'

'But if the stories are true, she put herself about quite a bit, didn't she? Far from virginal, I'd say.'

'Maybe that was part of it, too,' Banks agreed. 'You just knew she . . . *did* it. There were stories. Gene Pitney. Mick Jagger. The parties and all that.'

'Saint and Sinner all in one package,' said Annie. 'How perfect for you.'

'Christ, Annie, I was only a kid.'

'Quite a randy one, too, it seems.'

'Well, what did you think about at fourteen?'

'I don't know. Boys, maybe, but not in a sexual way. Having fun. Romance. Clothes. Make-up.'

'Maybe that's why I always fancied older women,' said Banks.

Annie nudged him hard in the ribs.

'Ouch! What did you do that for?'

'You know. Park here. Men,' she said, as Banks parked and they got out of the car. 'When you're young you want older women, and when you're old you want younger women.'

'These days,' said Banks, 'I take whatever I can get.'

'Charming.' Annie pressed the doorbell and a few seconds later saw the shape coming towards them through the frosted glass.

Lauren Anderson was dressed in jeans and a thin V-neck jumper, and she wore no make-up. Younger than Banks had expected, she was willowy, with full lips, a pale oval face and heavy-lidded pale blue eyes, all framed by long auburn hair spilling down over her shoulders. As she stood in the doorway, she wrapped her arms around herself as if she were cold.

'Police,' Banks said, holding out his warrant card. 'May we come in?'

'Of course.' Lauren stood aside.

'In here?' Banks asked, pointing towards what looked like the living room.

'If you like. I'll make some tea, shall I?'

'Lovely,' said Annie, following her into the kitchen.

Banks could hear them talking as he had a quick look around the living room. He was impressed by the two walls of bookshelves groaning under the weight of classics he had meant to read but never got around to. All the Victorians, along with the major Russians and French. A few recent novels: Ian McEwan, Graham Swift, A.S. Byatt. Quite a lot of poetry, too, from Heaney's *Beowulf* translation to the latest issue of *Poetry Review* lying on the low coffee table. There were plays, too: Tennessee Williams, Edward Albee, Tom Stoppard, the Elizabethans and Jacobeans. There was also a section devoted to art and one to classical mythology. Not to mention the rows of literary criticism, from Aristotle's *Poetics* to David Lodge on the vagaries of post-structuralism. Most of the music in the CD rack was classical, favouring Bach, Mozart and Handel.

Banks found a comfortable chair and sat down. In a short while Annie and Lauren came in with the tea. Noting an ashtray on the table and getting a distinct whiff of stale smoke in the air, Banks asked if he might light up. Lauren said sure and accepted one of his Silk Cut. Annie turned up her nose the way only an ex-smoker can do.

'It's a nice place,' Banks said.

'Thank you.'

'Do you live here alone?'

'I do now. I used to share it with one of the other teachers, but she got her own flat a few months ago. I'm not sure, but I think I like it better by myself.'

'I don't blame you,' said Banks. 'Look, the reason we're here is that we heard you used to give Luke Armitage extra tuition in English, and we wondered if you could tell us anything about him.'

'I'm not sure I can tell you anything about him, but, yes, I used to tutor Luke.' Lauren sat on the small sofa with her legs tucked under her, cup held in both hands. She blew on the tea. 'He was so far ahead of the rest of his class he must have been bored silly at school. He was far ahead of me most of the time.' She raised her hand and flicked some troublesome locks of hair out of her face.

'That good?'

'Well, his enthusiasm made up for what he lacked in formal training.'

'I gather he was a talented writer, too.'

'Very. Again, he needed discipline, but he was young, raw. He'd have gone far if . . . if . . .' She held her cup in one hand and rubbed her sleeve across her eyes. 'I'm sorry,' she said. 'I just can't get over it. Luke. Dead. Such a waste.'

Annie passed her a tissue from the box on one of the bookshelves. 'Thank you,' she said, then blew her nose. She shifted on the sofa and Banks noticed her feet were bare and her toenails painted red.

'I know it's hard to accept,' said Banks, 'but I'm sure you can understand why we need to know as much about him as possible.'

'Yes, of course. Though, as I said, I don't see how I can tell you much.'

'Alastair Ford said you're the kind who listens to people's problems.'

She snorted. 'Alastair! He was probably trying to say I'm a prying bitch. Alastair runs a mile if anyone comes within vague hailing distance of whatever warped emotions he might possess.'

Banks had got the same impression himself, though he wouldn't have put it in quite those words. On early impressions, Lauren Anderson was turning out to be perhaps the most *normal* friend Luke had had. But the competition – Ford and Wells – wasn't very stiff.

'Did Luke ever talk about himself?'

'Not much,' said Lauren. 'He could be very closed, could Luke.'

'Sometimes?'

'Sometimes he might let his guard drop a little, yes.'

'And what did he talk about then?'

'Oh, the usual. School. His parents.'

'What did he say about them?'

'He hated school. Not only were most things boring for him, but he didn't like the discipline, the formality.'

Banks thought of the boys who had tormented Luke in the market square. 'What about bullying?'

'Yes, that too. But it wasn't serious. I mean, Luke was never beaten up or anything.'

'What was it, then?'

'Mostly teasing. Name-calling. A bit of jostling. Oh, I'm not saying he wasn't hurt by it. He was very sensitive. But he could handle it, in a way.'

'What do you mean?'

'It didn't really bother him. I mean, he knew the boys who were doing it were morons, that they couldn't help themselves. And he knew they were doing it because he was different.'

'Superior?'

'No, I don't think Luke ever believed himself to be superior to anyone else. He just knew he was different.'

'What did he have to say about his parents?'

Lauren paused for a moment before answering. 'It was very private,' she said.

Annie leaned forward. 'Ms Anderson,' she said. 'Luke's dead.'

'Yes. Yes, I know.'

'And we need to know everything.'

'But you surely can't think his parents had anything to do with his death?'

'What did he say about them?'

Lauren paused, then went on. 'Not much. It was clear he wasn't very happy at home. He said he loved his mother, but he gave the impression that he didn't get along with his stepfather.'

Banks could well imagine it. Martin Armitage was a physical, dominating presence, used to getting his own way, and his interests seemed worlds away from those of his stepson. 'Did you get the impression that his step-father abused him in any way?' he asked.

'Good Lord, no,' said Lauren. 'Nobody ever beat him or abused him in any way. It was just . . . they were so different. They'd nothing in common. I mean, Luke couldn't care less about football, for a start.'

'What was he going to do about his problems?'

'Nothing. What could he do? He was only fifteen. Maybe he'd have left home in a year or so, but we'll never know now, will we? For the time being he had to put up with it.'

'Kids put up with a lot worse,' said Banks.

'Indeed they do. The family was well off and Luke never lacked for material comforts. I'm sure that both his mother and his stepfather loved him very much. He was a sensitive, creative boy with a boorish stepfather and an empty-headed mother.'

Banks wouldn't have said Robin Armitage was empty-headed, but perhaps Lauren was making the sort of assumption people often make about models. 'What about Neil Byrd?' Banks went on. 'Did Luke ever talk about him?'

'Hardly ever. He got very emotional when the subject came up. Angry, even. Luke had a lot of unresolved issues. You just knew to back away.'

'Can you explain?'

Lauren's brow furrowed. 'I think he was angry because he never knew his father. Angry because Neil Byrd abandoned him when he was just a baby and then went and committed suicide. Can you imagine how that would make you feel? You don't even mean enough to your father for him to stay alive and watch you grow up.'

'Was there anything in particular that might have been bothering him recently, anything he might have mentioned to you?'

'No. The last time I saw him, at the end of term, he was excited about the summer holidays. I assigned him some reading.'

'*A Portrait of the Artist as a Young Man* and *Crime and Punishment*?'

Her eyes widened. 'Those were two of the books. How do you know that?'

'It doesn't matter,' said Banks. 'How did you go about tutoring him?'

'Usually I'd assign him some reading, maybe a novel or some poetry, and then we'd meet here and discuss it. Often we'd move out from there and discuss painting, history, Greek and Roman mythology. He was very advanced when it came to understanding literature. And he had an insatiable appetite for it.'

'Advanced enough for Rimbaud, Baudelaire. Verlaine?'

'Rimbaud was a mere boy himself. And young teens are often attracted to Baudelaire.'

'Le Poëte se fait voyant par un long, immense et raisonné dérèglement de tous les sens,' Banks quoted, in an accent he hoped wasn't too incomprehensible. 'Does that mean anything to you?'

'Why, of course. It's Rimbaud's description of the method he used to make himself a *seer*. "A total disordering of all the senses."'

'It was written on Luke's bedroom wall. Did it involve taking drugs?'

'Not that I know of. Not in Luke's case, anyway. It was

about opening oneself to experience of all kinds. To be quite honest, I didn't approve of Luke's fascination with Rimbaud. In so many cases like that it's a fascination with the romantic ideal of the tortured boy-poet, not with the work itself.'

Not wanting to get lost in the realms of literary criticism, Banks moved on. 'You felt very close to Luke, am I right?'

'In a way, I suppose. If you really *could* be close to him. He was slippery, chameleon-like, often moody, quiet and withdrawn. But I liked him and I believed in his talent, if that's what you mean.'

'If Luke had come to you for help, would you have given it?'

'That depends on the circumstances.'

'If he was running away from home, for example.'

'I'd do all I could to discourage him.'

'That sounds like the official line.'

'It's the one I'd follow.'

'You wouldn't harbour him?'

'Of course not.'

'Because we don't know where he went the day he disappeared. Not after about five-thirty, anyway. But he was last seen walking north on Market Street. That would eventually have brought him to your neighbourhood, wouldn't it?'

'Yes, but . . . I mean . . . why would he come here?'

'Maybe he trusted you, needed your help with something.'

'I can't imagine what.'

'When were the two of you next due to meet?'

'Not until next term. I'm going home next week for the rest of the holidays. My father's not been well lately and my mother's finding it hard to cope.'

'I'm sorry to hear that. Where's home?'

'South Wales. Tenby. A sleepy little place, but it's by the sea, lots of cliffs to walk on and think.'

'Are you sure Luke never came to see you the Monday before last?'

'Of course I'm sure. He had no reason to.'

'You were only his tutor, right?'

Lauren stood up and anger flashed in her eyes. 'What do you mean? What are you trying to insinuate?'

Banks held his hand up. 'Whoa. Wait a minute. I was only thinking that he might have considered you as a friend and mentor, someone he could go to if he was in trouble.'

'Well, he didn't. Look, as it happens, I wasn't even home the Monday before last.'

'Where were you?'

'Visiting my brother, Vernon.'

'And where does Vernon live?'

'Harrogate.'

'What time did you leave?'

'About five. Shortly after.'

'And what time did you get back?'

'I didn't. As a matter of fact, I had a bit too much to drink. Too much to risk driving, at any rate. So I slept on Vernon's sofa. I didn't come back here until about lunchtime on Tuesday.'

Banks glanced at Annie, who put her notebook aside and pulled the artist's impression out of her briefcase. 'Have you ever seen this girl, Ms Anderson?' she asked. 'Think carefully.'

Lauren studied the drawing and shook her head. 'No. I've seen the look, but the face isn't familiar.'

'Not someone from school?'

'If she is, I don't recognize her.'

'We think she might have been Luke's girlfriend,' Banks said. 'And we're trying to find her.'

Lauren shot Banks a glance. '*Girlfriend?* But Luke didn't have a girlfriend.'

'How do you know? You said he didn't tell you everything.'

She fingered the collar of her V-neck. 'But . . . but I'd have *known*.'

'I can't see how,' said Banks. 'What about Rose Barlow?'

'What about her?'

'I've heard she and Luke were pretty friendly.'

'Who told you that?'

'Were they?'

'I believe they went out once or twice earlier this year. Rose Barlow isn't anywhere near Luke's league. She's strictly a plodder.'

'So it didn't last.'

'Not to my knowledge. Though, as you pointed out, I wouldn't necessarily be the one to know.'

Banks and Annie stood up to leave. Lauren walked to the door with them.

'Thanks for your time,' Banks said. 'And if you do remember anything else, you'll let us know, won't you?'

'Yes, of course. Anything I can do,' Lauren said. 'I do hope you catch whoever did this. Luke had such a promising future ahead of him.'

'Don't worry,' said Banks, with more confidence than he felt. 'We will.'

●

Ever since she had rung Banks, Michelle had thought of confronting Shaw with what she had discovered. It would have been easy enough for any authorized person to remove the notebooks and actions from their file boxes. Michelle could have done it herself, so who would think to question an officer of Shaw's rank? Certainly not Mrs Metcalfe.

But still she resisted a direct approach. The thing was, she *had* to be certain. Once something like that was out in the open, there was no taking it back. She had been down in the archives again first thing that morning on another fruitless search, which had at least convinced her that the objects she was looking for were missing. And they *should* have been there.

What she needed to do now was think. Think about what it all meant. She couldn't do that in the station with Shaw wandering around the place, so she decided to drive over to the Hazels estate and walk Graham's route again.

She parked in front of the row of shops opposite the estate and stood for a moment enjoying the feel of the sun on her hair. She looked at the newsagent's shop, now run by Mrs Walker. That was where it had all begun. On a whim, Michelle entered the shop and found the sturdy, grey-haired old lady arranging newspapers on the counter.

'Yes, love,' the woman said with a smile. 'What can I do for you?'

'Are you Mrs Walker?'

'Indeed I am.'

'I don't know if you can do anything,' said Michelle, presenting her warrant card, 'but you might have heard we found some bones not long ago and—'

'The lad who used to work here?'

'Yes, that's right.'

'I read about it. Terrible business.'

'It is.'

'But I don't see how I can help you. It was before my time.'

'When did you come here?'

'My husband and I bought the shop in the autumn of 1966.'

'Did you buy it from Mr Bradford, the previous owner?'

'As far as I know we did. The estate agent handled all the details, along with my husband, of course, bless his soul.'

'Mr Walker is deceased?'

'A good ten years now.'

'I'm sorry.'

'No need to be. He went just like that. Never felt a thing. Brain aneurysm. We had a good life together, and I'm well provided for.' She looked around the shop. 'I can't say it's exactly a goldmine, but it's a living. Hard work, too. People say I should retire, sell up, but what would I do with my time?'

'Did you know Graham Marshall at all?'

'No. We moved here from Spalding, so we didn't know anyone at first. We'd been looking for a nice little news-agent's shop and this one came on the market at the right price. Good timing, too, what with the new town development starting in 1967, shortly after we got here.'

'But you did meet Mr Bradford?'

'Oh, yes. He was very helpful during the transition. Showed us the ropes and everything.'

'What was he like?'

'I can't say I knew him well. My husband had most dealings with him. But he seemed all right. Pleasant enough. A bit abrupt, maybe. A bit stiff and military in his bearing. I remember he was something important during the war, a member of some special unit or other in Burma. But he was helpful.'

'Did you hear from him after you took over?'

'No.'

'Did he ever mention Graham?'

'Oh, yes. That's why he left. Partly, at any rate. He said his heart hadn't been in the business since the boy disappeared, so he wanted to move away and try to forget.'

'Do you know where he moved to?'

'The north, or so he said. Carlisle.'

'That's certainly far enough away.'

'Yes.'

'I don't suppose you had a forwarding address, did you?'

'Didn't you know? Mr Bradford died. Killed in a burglary not weeks after he moved. Tragic, it was. In all the local papers at the time.'

'Indeed?' said Michelle, curious. 'No, I didn't know.' It probably wasn't relevant to her enquiry, but it was suspicious. One of the last people to see Graham alive had, himself, been killed.

Michelle thanked Mrs Walker and went back outside. She crossed the road and started walking along Hazel Crescent, the same route Graham would have taken all those years ago. It was an early morning in August 1965, she remembered; the sun was just up, but an overcast sky made it still fairly dark. Everybody was sleeping off Saturday night, and the church-goers were not even up yet. Lights would have been on in one or two windows, perhaps – the insomniacs and chronic early risers – but nobody had seen anything.

She reached Wilmer Road at the far end of the estate. Even now, years later and in mid-morning, there wasn't much traffic, and most of it was for the DIY centre, which hadn't existed back in 1965. Michelle was almost certain that Graham *knew* his attacker and that he got in the car willingly, taking his canvas bag of papers with him. If someone had tried to force him into a car, he would have dropped the papers and struggled, and the abductor was unlikely to stick around and pick them up.

But how could Graham be persuaded to go somewhere without finishing his paper round? A family emergency, perhaps? Michelle didn't think so. His family only lived a few yards away, back on the estate; he could have walked there in less than a minute. There was no doubt that fourteen-year-old kids could act irresponsibly, so maybe he did just that and skived off somewhere for some reason.

As Michelle stood in the street watching the people come and go from the DIY centre, she thought again about the missing notebooks and actions and was struck by a notion so obvious she could have kicked herself for not seeing it earlier.

That the missing notebooks were Detective Superintendent Shaw's disturbed her for a different reason now she realized what she should have seen the moment she discovered they were missing. Shaw was a mere DC, a junior, on the case, so what on earth could he have had to hide? He had no power; he wasn't in charge, and he certainly hadn't assigned the actions. He had simply been along taking notes of Detective Inspector Reg Proctor's interviews; that was all.

Michelle had focused on Shaw mostly because she disliked him and resented the way he had been treating her, but when it came right down to it, the person in charge of the case, the one who might possibly have had the most to hide in the event of a future investigation was not Shaw but that legend of the local constabulary: Detective Superintendent John Harris.

Thinking about Jet Harris, and what he might possibly have had to hide, Michelle walked back to where she had left her car parked in front of the shops. Perhaps she was a little distracted by her thoughts, and perhaps she didn't pay as much attention as she usually did to crossing the road, but on the other hand, perhaps the beige van with the tinted windows really *did* start up as she approached, and perhaps the driver really *did* put his foot on the accelerator when she stepped into the road.

Either way, she saw it coming – fast – and just had time to jump out of the way. The side of the van brushed against her hip as she stumbled and fell face forward onto the warm tarmac, putting out her arms to break her fall. Another car honked and swerved around her and a woman across the street came over to help her to her feet. By the time Michelle realized what was happening, the van was out of sight. One thing she did remember, though: the number plate was so covered in mud it was impossible to read.

'Honestly,' the woman said, helping Michelle to the other side. 'Some drivers. I don't know what the place is coming to, I really don't. Are you all right, love?'

'Yes,' said Michelle, dusting herself off. 'Yes, I'm fine, thanks very much. Just a bit shaken up.' And she was still trembling when she got in her own car. She gripped the steering wheel tightly to steady herself, took several deep breaths and waited until her heart rate slowed to normal before she set off back to the station.

•

'Can you manage by yourself for a day or so?' Banks asked Annie over a lunchtime pint in the Queen's Arms. Like most of the pubs in the area since the outbreak of foot and mouth it was half-empty, and even the jukebox and video machines were mercifully silent. One of the local farmers, who had already had too much to drink, stood at the bar fulminating against the government's mishandling of the outbreak to the landlord, Cyril, who gave a polite grunt of agreement every now and then. Everybody was suffering: not only the farmers, but the pub landlords, bed-and-breakfast owners, local trades-men, butcher, baker and candlestick-maker, old Uncle Tom Cobbleigh and all. And, unlike the farmers, they didn't get any compensation from the government. Only a week or so ago the owner of a walking-gear shop in Helmthorpe had committed suicide because his business had gone down the tubes.

Annie put her glass down. 'Course I can,' she said. 'What's up?'

'It's Graham Marshall's funeral tomorrow. There'll likely be some old friends around. I'd like to go down this evening.'

'No problem. Have you asked the boss?'

'Detective Superintendent Gristhorpe has given me permission to be absent from school for two days. I just wanted to clear it with you before taking off.'

'I've got plenty to keep me occupied. Talking about school, you told me you weren't satisfied with your Alastair Ford interview yesterday.'

Banks lit a cigarette. 'No,' he said. 'No, I'm not. Not at all.'

'So is he a suspect?'

'I don't know. Maybe his coming hot on the heels of

Norman Wells was just a bit too much for me. His house is very isolated, which makes it a good place to keep someone prisoner, or kill someone and dump the body in the middle of the night without any neighbours noticing. But then you could probably get away with murder in the town centre, too, given most people's powers of observation and unwillingness to get involved.'

'Except for the CCTV.'

'And a damn lot of good that's done us. Anyway, Ford is a solitary. He jealously protects his privacy, probably feels superior to people who are content to make small talk and share their opinions. He *may* be homosexual – there was something distinctly odd about the way he responded to my question about boyfriends – but even that doesn't make him a suspect. We don't know the motive for Luke's murder, and according to Dr Glendenning there was no evidence of sexual assault, although a few days in the water might have taken care of any traces of that. You know, Annie, the more I think about it, the more the kidnapping *seems* as if it was just a smokescreen, but oddly enough it might turn out to be the most important thing.'

Annie frowned. 'What do you mean?'

'I mean, why? If somebody just wanted Luke dead, whatever the reason, then why come up with this elaborate and iffy kidnapping scheme and increase the risk of getting caught?'

'Money?'

'Well, yes, but you told me yourself whoever it was set his sights remarkably low. It wasn't a professional job.'

'That did bother me. It's what made me think he *knew* about the Armitages' finances. I mean, they could certainly manage ten grand to get Luke back, but hardly more, at least not at such short notice.'

'But Luke was already dead.'

'Yes. Perhaps he tried to escape.'

'Perhaps. Or maybe we need to look a lot closer to home.'

'The parents?'

'It's possible, isn't it?' Banks said. 'Maybe we've been looking at this all wrong. Maybe Martin Armitage killed Luke and set up the elaborate hoax of a kidnapping just to put us off the scent.'

'Martin?'

'Why not? He was gone for two hours the evening Luke disappeared, according to his statement, just driving around, or so he says. Maybe he found Luke and they had an argument and Luke ended up dead. An accident, even. Excessive roughness. That wouldn't be unusual for Martin Armitage. According to Lauren Anderson and everything you've told me, Luke had a difficult relationship with his stepfather. Armitage is the antithesis of Neil Byrd in many ways. Byrd was sensitive, creative, artistic, and he also had many of the problems that seem to come with that territory: drugs, drink, an addictive personality, need for oblivion, experimentation, self-absorption, mood swings, depression. It can't have been easy being Neil Byrd, as his songs tell us so many times, but he was aiming at some kind of exalted spiritual state, some sort of transcendence, and he believed he caught glimpses of it from time to time. They gave him enough faith to keep going, for a while, at least. I often thought some of the songs were also a cry for help, and Luke's songs echo that in a weird way.'

'And Martin Armitage?'

'Physical, rational, powerful, clean living. Football was his life. It got him out of the slums and made him a national figure. It also made him rich. I dare say he's had his share of ale, but I doubt he tried anything more experimental. I don't think he has the capability to understand or tolerate the artistic temperament his stepson seems to have inherited. Probably the kind who associates artistic interests with homosexuality. I'm sure he tried to be a loving father, treated the lad as his own, but Luke had Neil Byrd's genes.'

'And Robin?'

'Now, there's an interesting one,' Banks said. 'You tell me. You've seen more of her than I have.'

'She clearly had a wild youth. Sex, drugs, rock and roll. Early fame and fortune often seem to send people over the top. But, however she did it, she came through, and with a son. I'd say she's tougher than she looks, and no doubt she loved Luke but had no more idea how to deal with his problems than her husband had. I think boys like Luke invent secret worlds to exclude adults and protect themselves, even from their contemporaries. He probably spent most of his time in his room reading, writing or recording his songs. That black room.'

'Do you think he had ambitions to follow in his father's footsteps?'

'Musically, perhaps. But I think his attitude towards his father was very complex and ambiguous. A mix of admiration and anger at abandonment.'

'None of this seems to transform into a motive, though, does it?' said Banks. He stubbed out his cigarette. 'What about Josie and Calvin Batty?'

'As suspects?'

'In general.'

'Josie is the only person we've talked to so far who says she saw Luke with the tattooed girl.'

'Norman Wells recognized the description.'

'Yes,' Annie pointed out. 'But not in connection with Luke. I'm not saying we stop looking for her, just that we mustn't pin all our hopes on her. We still have to keep an open mind on this one.'

'Agreed.'

'By the way, Winsome ran a check on all cars reported stolen in the Eastvale area the night Luke disappeared. There are two possibilities, one abandoned near Hawes, in Wensleydale, and the other in Richmond.'

'Then we'd better have Stefan's team check them both for any signs of blood.'

Annie made a note. 'Okay.'

The server brought their lunches over: a salad sandwich for Annie and lasagne and chips for Banks. He didn't usually like pub lasagne – it was too soupy – but Cyril's wife Glenys made a good one.

'Talking about cars,' Banks said, after pausing for a few mouthfuls, 'how are forensics coming on with Norman Wells's?'

'Stefan called in a couple of hours ago. Nothing yet. Do you really expect anything?'

'Maybe not. But it's got to be done.'

'Do you think we should have detained him?'

Banks took a sip of beer before answering. 'We've nothing to hold him on,' he said. 'And he does have his business to run. Besides, I don't think Mr Wells is going anywhere.'

'What about Lauren Anderson?'

'Methinks the lady did protest too much.'

'What do you mean?'

'I don't know. Just that her reaction to a simple question seemed extreme.'

'She did sound awfully close to Luke. Emotionally, I mean.'

'But she does have an alibi. Ask Winsome to check with the brother, Vernon, just to be certain, but I can't imagine she'd risk lying about that. And it was a man's voice on the ransom call.'

'I'm not suggesting she *did* it – she certainly seemed genuine in her regard for him – just that she might know more than she's letting on about what Luke was up to.'

'You're right,' said Banks. 'We shouldn't rule her out. Maybe you could get Winsome and young Kevin to run background checks on everyone we know who was connected with Luke, and that includes the Battys, Alastair Ford, Lauren Anderson and the mystery girl, if we ever find her.'

'What about Rose Barlow?'

'I don't know,' Banks said. 'We should have a word with her, though it seems that whatever went on between her and Luke ended months ago.'

'What about forensic checks on Ford's house and the Anderson woman's?'

Banks shook his head. 'We can't afford to be sending expensive forensic teams to everyone's house. With Wells we had good reason – his history, for a start. Besides, we know Luke has been in Lauren Anderson's house.'

'But if there's blood . . .?'

'We still can't justify the expense at this point.'

'And Alastair Ford?'

'Check into his background first. We'll keep that one up our sleeves in case we need it.'

'You'll stay in touch?'

'I'll leave my mobile on all the time. I'm not deserting you, Annie.' Banks still couldn't help feeling a little guilty – and it wasn't because he was leaving the case to Annie, but because he would be seeing Michelle again, and the idea appealed to him.

Annie touched his sleeve. 'I know you're not. Don't think I'm so insensitive as not to know how hard it is for you, them finding Graham Marshall's bones and all.' She grinned. 'You go and pay your respects and have a piss-up with your old mates. You'll have a lot to catch up on. When did you last see them?'

'Not since I went to London, when I was eighteen. We just sort of lost touch.'

'I know what you mean. It happens. I don't know anyone I went to school with any more.'

Banks considered telling Annie about Michelle's phone call but decided against it. Why complicate matters? Annie had enough on her plate. Besides, he wasn't sure there was much he could do about Michelle's concerns. If there had been some sort of cover-up, then it would have to be investigated by an outside force, not some maverick from North Yorkshire. Yet a part of him wanted to get involved, wanted to get to the bottom of Graham's death, as well as Luke's. They were linked in his mind in some odd way. Not technically, of course, but two very different boys from very different times had ended up dead before their time, and both had died violently. Banks wanted to know why, what it was about these two children that had attracted such cruel fates.

14

Early in the afternoon Annie showed the artist's impression of the mystery girl around the Swainsdale Centre and the bus station again. At the end of an hour she was beginning to wonder whether the girl existed, or whether she was just a figment of Josie Batty's puritan imagination.

She walked along York Road enjoying the sunshine, glancing in the shop windows as she walked. A stylish red leather jacket caught her eye in one of the more exclusive clothes shops, but she knew it would be way out of her price range. Even so, she went in and enquired. It was.

The market square was clogged with wandering tourists and cars trying to find parking space. A large group of Japanese, along with their tour guide and translator, stood gazing up at the front of the Norman church, where several sculpted figures of saints were carved in a row high over the doors. Some of the tourists were catching the moment on videotape, though Annie didn't remember the stone saints ever doing the can-can or anything that even remotely involved movement.

One of the cars, she noticed – partly because it screeched straight into a disabled parking space and almost hit a young woman – was Martin Armitage's BMW. What the hell was he doing here? And what the hell was he doing in a disabled parking spot? Maybe she should arrange for him to get towed? But when she saw him jump out of the car, slam the door and head for the shops built into the side of the church, she knew what was going on.

Annie pushed her way through the tourist crowd by the church and got there just in time to see Armitage disappearing down the stairs into Norman's Used Books. *Shit*. She dashed down right behind him, but he already had Wells by the throat and judging by the blood pouring from the little man's nose had punched him at least once. Wells was whimpering and trying to wriggle free. The bookshop was as dank as ever, but the day's heat had permeated enough to make the air humid. Annie felt clammy the moment she entered. Familiar, the cat, was screeching and hissing somewhere in the dark recesses of the cavern.

'Mr Armitage!' Annie called out as she grabbed his arm. 'Martin! Stop it. This won't get you anywhere.'

Armitage shook her off as if she were a troublesome insect. 'This pervert killed my son,' he said. 'If you lot can't do it, I'll get a bloody confession, even if I have to shake it out of him.' As if to prove his point, he started to shake Wells again and slap him back and forth across the face. Blood and saliva dribbled from Wells's slack jaw.

Annie tried to wedge herself between them, knocking over a teetering pile of books as she did so. A cloud of dust rose up and the cat screeched even louder. Armitage was strong. He pushed Annie and she staggered back into a table. It broke and more books slid to the floor. She almost joined them there.

Gathering all her strength, Annie made one more attempt, launching herself towards the struggling men in the cramped space, but Armitage saw her coming and swung his fist beyond Wells's head, connecting directly with Annie's mouth. The blow stunned her and she fell back again, in pain this time, and put her hand to her mouth. It came away covered in blood.

Armitage was still shaking Wells and Annie feared the bookseller was going to choke to death, if he didn't have a heart attack first. Armitage was paying her no mind now, and she managed to edge behind him to the door and dash up the steps. The police station was only yards away, across Market Street, and nobody asked her any questions when she rushed in the front door, blood streaming from her mouth.

Two burly PCs followed her back to the shop, and it took both of them to subdue Armitage, wrecking most of the place in the process. There were old books all over the floor, broken tables and clouds of dust in the air by the time they got the handcuffs on him and marched him outside up the stairs. Wells was bleeding, clutching his chest and looking distinctly unwell. Annie got his arm around her shoulder and helped him stumble up into the fresh air. Hearing the fracas, the Japanese tourists turned away from the church facade and pointed their camcorders at the five of them. Well, Annie thought, digging for a handkerchief deep in her purse, at least we're bloody *moving*.

•

It had been a while since Banks had spent much time in his office, and the *Dalesman* calendar was still open at July's photo of Skidby Windmill on the edge of the Yorkshire Wolds. He had the radio tuned in to Radio 3 and was listening to an orchestral concert of music by Holst, Haydn and Vaughan Williams as he whittled away at the pile of paperwork on his desk. He had just settled into the *Lento Moderato* of Vaughan Williams's 'Pastoral' Symphony and yet another memo on cost-effectiveness, when his phone rang.

'Alan, it's Stefan.'

'Good news, I hope?'

'Depends on how you look at it. Your man Norman Wells is clean, as far as we can tell. We were pretty thorough, and I'm sure if there'd been any traces of Luke Armitage in his car or house we'd have found something.'

'You didn't?'

'Nada.'

'Okay, well I suppose that shows us where *not* to concentrate our attention. Anything positive?'

'The blood on the drystone wall.'

'I remember.'

'There was enough for DNA analysis. It's definitely human, and it doesn't match the victim's.'

Banks whistled. 'So there's a good chance it could belong to whoever dropped Luke over the wall?'

'A pretty good chance, yes. But don't get your hopes up too high. It *could* belong to anyone.'

'But you'll be able to match it with any samples we can get?'

'Of course.'

'Okay. Thanks, Stefan.'

'My pleasure.'

Banks wondered whom he should ask to provide DNA samples. Norman Wells, of course, even though the forensic search of his house had turned up nothing incriminating. Alastair Ford, perhaps, just because he lived in a remote cottage and was connected to Luke though the violin lessons. And because he was weird. Lauren Anderson, because she gave Luke English tuition after school hours and seemed to be close to him. Who else? Josie and Calvin Batty, perhaps. And the parents, Martin and Robin. They'd no doubt kick up a holy fuss and run crying to the chief constable, but that couldn't be helped. DNA could be processed in two or three days now, but it was a very expensive proposition. Banks would just have to see how much he could get away with.

Then there was the mystery girl, of course. They would definitely need a sample from her if they ever found her, if she existed.

No sooner had the *Moderato Pesante* begun than his phone rang again. This time it was the duty constable. Someone to see him in connection with Luke Armitage. A young woman.

'Send her up,' said Banks, wondering if *this* could be the mystery woman. She must know that she was wanted by now, and if she did, then her failure to show up was suspicious in itself.

A minute or so later a uniformed constable tapped on Banks's office door and ushered in the girl. Banks recognized Rose Barlow immediately. She strutted into his office all blue-jeaned leg, blonde hair and attitude. Her visit would save him or Annie the trouble of seeking her out.

'I'm Rose,' she said. 'Rose Barlow. You don't remember me, do you?'

'I know who you are,' said Banks. 'What can I do for you?'

Rose carried on snooping around the office, taking books off the shelf and rifling through the pages, putting them back, adjusting the calendar so it was square with the filing cabinet. She wore a short, sleeveless top so that, Banks presumed, the rose tattoo on her upper left arm and the collection of jewellery dangling from her navel showed to best advantage.

'It's more a matter of what *I* can do for *you*,' she said, sitting down and giving him what he was sure she thought of as an enigmatic look. It came across as vacant. She must be a handful for her father, he thought. It seemed so often the case that the daughters of authority figures – vicars, headmasters, chief constables – were the first to rebel, and he could only think himself lucky that Tracy, a mere chief inspector's daughter, seemed to have a good head on her shoulders. She must have got it from her mother, Banks thought, then veered away from thoughts of Sandra, showing now, no doubt, glowing with the joys of coming motherhood. Well, good luck to her and Sean; they'd need it.

'And what can you do for me?' Banks asked, deciding to let her get to her reason for coming before asking questions of his own.

She turned her nose up at the radio. 'What's that?'

'Vaughan Williams.'

'It's boring.'

'Sorry you don't like it. What can you do for me?'

'Do you know who killed Luke?'

'I thought you could do something for me?'

'Spoilsport. Why won't you tell me?'

Banks sighed. 'Rose. Miss Barlow. If we'd found Luke's killer you'd have read about it in the papers by now. Now, tell me what you came to say. I'm busy.'

Rose didn't like that, and Banks realized that letting his impatience show was a mistake. She probably got that sort of response from her father all the time, the way Tracy and Brian had often heard the same thing from Banks. Rose craved attention because she didn't feel she got enough. Banks wondered if his children felt the same way. Did Tracy try so hard and do so well academically because she wanted attention? Did Brian stand up on stage in front of an audience night after night and bare his soul because he craved it, too? And had Luke Armitage craved the same thing? Perhaps. In his children's cases, though, the response to the need was a pretty healthy, creative one. Banks wasn't sure to what lengths Rose Barlow might go to get the attention *she* felt she deserved.

'I'm sorry,' he went on, 'but I'm sure you understand that we're in a hurry to find out who killed Luke, and if you know anything that might help us . . . '

Rose leaned forward, her eyes wide. 'Why? Do you think he's going to kill someone else? Do you think it's a serial killer?'

'We've no reason to think anything of the sort.'

'Then relax, why don't you?'

Banks felt his back teeth grinding as he tried to smile.

'Anyway,' Rose went on, 'I was going to tell you. Have you talked to Miss Anderson yet?'

'Lauren Anderson? Yes.'

A mischievous glint lit Rose's eyes. 'And did she tell you about her and Luke?'

'She told us she gave him extra tuition in English because he was ahead of the rest of the class.'

Rose laughed. '*Extra tuition.* That's a good one. And did she tell you where she gave this tuition?'

'At her house.'

Rose leaned back and folded her arms. 'Exactly.'

'So?'

'Oh, come on. Surely you can't be *that* naive? Do I have to spell it out for you?'

'I'm not sure what you're getting at,' said Banks,

who was perfectly sure but wanted her to get there by herself.

'They were having it off, weren't they?'

'You know that for a fact?'

'Stands to reason.'

'Why?'

'She's nothing but a slut, that Miss Anderson, and a cradle-snatcher.'

'What makes you say that?'

'Well, she didn't give anybody *else* private tuition in her home, did she?'

'I don't know,' said Banks.

'Well she *didn't*.'

'Tell me, Rose,' Banks said, wishing he could have a cigarette, 'what did you think of Luke? You knew him, didn't you?'

'We were in the same class, yes.'

'Did you like him?'

Rose twirled some strands of hair. 'He was all right, I suppose.'

'Pretty cool, huh?'

'*Cool!* More like sad, if you ask me.'

'Why?'

'He never talked to anybody – except high and mighty Miss Anderson, of course. It's like he was better than the rest of us.'

'Maybe he was shy.'

'Just because he had a famous father. Well, I think his father's music sucks, and he couldn't have been much of a father if he went and killed himself, could he? He was nothing but a drug addict.'

Nice line in compassion, Rose, Banks thought, but he didn't bother voicing his opinion. 'So you didn't like Luke?'

'I told you. He was all right. Just a bit weird.'

'But he was pretty good-looking, wasn't he?'

Rose made a face. 'Ugh! I wouldn't have gone out with him if he was the last boy on earth.'

'I don't think you're telling me the truth, Rose, are you?'

'What do you mean?'

'You know very well what I mean. You and Luke. Earlier this year.'

'Who told you that?'

'Never you mind. How far did it go?'

'Go? That's a laugh. It didn't go anywhere.'

'But you wanted it to, didn't you?'

Rose twisted in her chair. 'He thought he was better than the rest of us.'

'So why did you spend time talking to him?'

'I don't know. Just . . . I mean, he was different. The other boys, they only want one thing.'

'And Luke didn't?'

'I never got to find out, did I? We just talked.'

'What about?'

'Music and stuff.'

'You never actually went out together?'

'No. I mean, we went to McDonald's a couple of times after school, but that's all.'

'Rose, do you have any evidence at all to support your accusation that Luke and Lauren Anderson were having an affair?'

'If you mean was I watching at her window, then no. But it's obvious, isn't it? Why else would she spend her spare time with someone like him?'

'But *you* spent time with him.'

'Yeah. Well . . . that was different.'

'Didn't you try to be nice to him, to befriend him, when you talked to him in the hallways and the playground, and when you went to McDonald's with him?'

Rose looked away and continued twirling her hair around her fingers. 'Of course I did.'

'And what happened?'

'Nothing. He just sort of . . . like he got *bored* with me or something. Like I didn't read all those stupid books he was always carrying around, and I didn't listen to the same lousy music. I wasn't good enough for him. He was a snob. Above the rest of us.'

'And because of this you assumed he was having sexual relations with a teacher. That's a bit of a far stretch, isn't it?'

'*You* didn't see them together.'

'Did you see them kissing, touching, holding hands?'

'Of course not. They were too careful to do anything like that in public, weren't they?'

'What then?'

'The way they looked at each other. The way she always left him alone in class. The way they talked. The way he made her laugh.'

'You were just jealous, weren't you, Rose? That's why you're saying all this. Because you couldn't get along with Luke, but Miss Anderson could.'

'I was *not* jealous! Certainly not of that ugly old bitch.'

For a moment, Banks wondered if there was anything in what Rose Barlow was telling him other than sour grapes. It may have been innocent, a true teacher–pupil relationship, but Banks had enough experience to know that anything involving two people of the opposite sex – or the same sex for that matter – in close proximity could turn into something sexual, no matter what the difference in their ages. He had also read about such things in the newspapers. He would keep an open mind and have another talk with Lauren Anderson when he got back from Peterborough, push her a little harder and see if any cracks showed.

'What do you think of Miss Anderson?' he asked Rose.

'She's all right, I suppose.'

'You just called her an ugly old bitch.'

'Well . . . I didn't mean . . . I was angry . . . I mean she's okay as a teacher. All right?'

'Do you get on well with her in class?'

'Okay.'

'So if I ask any of the other pupils in the class they'd tell me that you and Miss Anderson get along just fine?'

Rose reddened. 'She picks on me sometimes. She put me in detention once.'

'What for?'

'Not reading some stupid Shakespeare play. So I was reading a magazine under the desk. So what? I can't be bothered with all that boring *English* stuff.'

'So you had a few run-ins with her?'

'Yes. But that's not why I'm here. That's not why I'm telling you what I know.'

'I'm sure it's not, Rose, but you have to admit it does give you a bit of a motive to cause trouble for Miss Anderson, especially if you also tried to get Luke to be *your* boyfriend.'

Rose jumped to her feet. 'Why are you being so horrible to me? I come here to help you and give you important information and you treat *me* like a criminal. I'm going to tell my *father* about you.'

Banks couldn't help smiling. 'It wouldn't be the first time I've been reported to the head teacher,' he said.

Before Rose could respond, two things happened in quick succession. First, there came an urgent tap at his door and Annie Cabbot walked in, a handkerchief to her mouth covered with what looked like blood. But before Annie could speak, Kevin Templeton poked his head around the door behind her, his gaze resting on Rose for a few seconds too long for her comfort, and said to Banks, 'Sorry to interrupt you, sir, but we think we've got a positive ID on you know who.'

Banks knew who he meant. The mystery girl. So she *did* exist.

'Better than that,' Templeton went on, 'we've got an address.'

•

Michelle discovered from DC Collins that Shaw had gone home after lunch, complaining of a stomach upset. Collins's tone was such as to suggest it might be more a matter of the number of whiskies Shaw had downed at lunch. He had been taking quite a lot of time off lately. At least that left the coast clear for Michelle. She didn't want to see Shaw, especially after what had happened in her flat on Saturday. Sometimes, when she let her guard down, it was him she saw in her imagination, going through her bedside drawers, cutting Melissa's dress in half. It wasn't such a stretch to imagine him driving the beige van that bore down on her as she crossed the road earlier, either; he had been out of the station at the time. And the whiskies? Dutch courage?

It was time to stop idle speculation and follow up on what she had discovered from Mrs Walker. Michelle picked up the telephone and an hour or so later, after a lot of false trails and time wasted on hold, she managed to reach one of the retired Carlisle police officers who had looked into Donald Bradford's death: ex-Detective Sergeant Raymond Scholes, now living out his retirement on the Cumbrian coast.

'I don't know what I can tell you after all this time,' Scholes said. 'Donald Bradford was just unlucky.'

'What happened?'

'Surprised a burglar. Someone broke into his house, and before Bradford could do anything he got beaten so badly he died of his injuries.'

Michelle felt a chill. The same thing might have happened to her on Saturday if she'd been home earlier. 'Ever catch the burglar?' she asked.

'No. He must have taken Bradford by surprise, though.'

'Why do you say that?'

'Because he was a pretty tough customer, himself. *I* wouldn't have fancied tackling him. Way it looks is the burglar must have heard him coming and hid behind the door, then bashed the back of Bradford's head in with a cosh of some kind.'

'You never found a weapon?'

'No.'

'No clues? No prints?'

'Nothing usable.'

'No witnesses?'

'None that we could find.'

'What was taken?'

'Wallet, a few knick-knacks, by the looks of it. Place was a bit of a mess.'

'Did it appear as if someone had been *looking* for something?'

'I never really thought about that. As I say, though, it

was a mess. Turned upside down. Why the sudden interest?'

Michelle told him a little bit about Graham Marshall.

'Yes, I've read about that. Terrible business. I hadn't realized there was a connection.'

'Was Bradford married?'

'No. He lived alone.'

Michelle could sense him pause, as if he was going to add something. 'What?' she asked.

'Oh, it's nothing. Bit of a laugh, really.'

'Tell me anyway.'

'Well, afterwards, you know, we had to have a look around the house and we found . . . well . . . at the time it seemed quite risqué, though by today's standards . . .'

Out with it, man, Michelle found herself thinking. What are you talking about?

'What was it?' she asked.

'Pornographic magazines. A bundle of them. And some blue films. I won't go into detail, but they covered quite a range of perversions.'

Michelle found herself gripping the receiver tighter. 'Including paedophilia?'

'Well, there were some pretty young-looking models involved, I can tell you that. Male and female. Not kiddy porn, though, if that's what you're thinking.'

Michelle supposed there was a distinction to be made. In some ways, once you had pubic hair, breasts and all the rest, you didn't qualify as 'kiddy porn', but you still might only be fourteen years old. Grey area.

'What happened to all this stuff?'

'Destroyed.'

But not before you and your lads had a good look at it, I'll bet, Michelle thought.

'We didn't let anything slip at the time,' he went on, 'because it didn't seem . . . well, the bloke *had* just been killed, after all. There seemed no point in blackening his name with that sort of thing.'

'Understandable,' said Michelle. 'Who claimed the body?'

'Nobody. Mr Bradford had no immediate family. The local authorities took care of everything.'

'Thank you, Mr Scholes,' she said. 'You've been a great help.'

'Think nothing of it.'

Michelle hung up and nibbled the end of her pencil as she thought about what she'd heard. She hadn't come to any conclusions yet, but she had a lot to discuss with Banks when he arrived.

•

PC Flaherty, who had tracked down the mystery girl's address, had been asking around Eastvale College, thinking that a girl who looked like she did must be a student. As it turned out, she wasn't, but her boyfriend was, and one of the people he spoke to remembered seeing her at a college dance. The boyfriend's name was Ryan Milne and the girl was known as Elizabeth Palmer. They lived together in a flat above a hat shop on South Market Street, the direction in which Luke Armitage had been walking when he was last seen.

Annie insisted that she felt well enough to make the call. She was damned, she told Banks, if she was going to be excluded after all the footwork she'd done just because some over-testosteroned lout had punched her in the mouth. It was her pride that hurt more than anything. After she'd cleaned up the wound, it didn't look too bad anyway. Some women, she went on to say, paid a fortune for collagen shots to make themselves look like she did. Banks decided he would make the call with her before setting off for Peterborough. He phoned and arranged to meet Michelle in a city-centre pub at nine o'clock, just to be on the safe side.

Martin Armitage was cooling off in the custody suite and Norman Wells was in Eastvale General Infirmary. No doubt there would be recriminations from Armitage's pal the chief constable, but for the moment he could stay where he was. They could also charge him with assaulting a police officer. After they had visited the mystery girl.

Within twenty minutes of getting the address, Banks and Annie climbed the lino-covered stairs and knocked on the door. The building seemed so silent that Banks couldn't imagine anyone being at home, but only seconds later a young woman opened the door. *The* young woman.

'DCI Banks and DI Cabbot,' Banks said, flashing his card. 'We'd like a word.'

'You'd better come in then.' She stood aside.

One reason why it had taken so long to locate her was obvious to Banks: she didn't look anywhere near as *weird* as the description Josie Batty had given of her, which was hardly surprising when you imagined that most young people probably looked weird to Josie Batty.

The pixyish facial features were right enough, the heart-shaped face, large eyes and small mouth, but that was about all. She was far prettier than Josie Batty had indicated to the police artist, and she had a pale, flawless complexion. She also had the sort of breasts adolescent boys, and many grown men, dream about, and her smooth cleavage was shown to advantage by the laced-up leather waistcoat she wore. The small tattoo on her upper arm was a simple double helix, and there was no sign of body piercing anywhere except the silver spider-web earrings dangling from her ears. Her short black hair was dyed and gelled, but there was nothing weird about that.

The flat was clean and tidy, not a filthy crack house full of sprawled drug-addled kids. It was an old room with a fireplace complete with poker and tongs, which must only have been for show, as a gas fire filled the hearth. Sunlight shone through the half-open window and the sounds and smells of South Market Street drifted up: car exhaust and horns, warm tar, fresh-baked bread, take-away curry and pigeons on the rooftops. Banks and Annie walked around the small room, checking it out, while the girl arranged beanbag cushions for them.

'Elizabeth, is it?' asked Banks.

'I prefer Liz.'

'Okay. Ryan not here?'

'He's got classes.'

'When will he be back?'

'Not till after teatime.'

'What do you do, Liz?'

'I'm a musician.'

'Make a living at it?'

'You know what it's like . . .'

Banks did, having a son in the business. But Brian's success was unusual, and even that hadn't brought in heaps of money. Not even enough for a new car. He moved on. 'You know why we're here, don't you?'

Liz nodded. 'About Luke.'

'You could have come forward and saved us a lot of trouble.'

Liz sat down. 'But I don't know anything.'

'Let us be the judge of that,' said Banks, pausing in his examination of her CD collection. He had noticed a cassette labelled 'Songs from a Black Room' mixed in with a lot of other tapes.

'How was I to know you were looking for me?'

'Don't you read the papers or watch television?' Annie asked.

'Not much. They're boring. Life's too short. Mostly I practise, listen to music or read.'

'What instrument?' Banks asked.

'Keyboards, some woodwinds. Flute, clarinet.'

'Did you study music professionally?'

'No. Just lessons at school.'

'How old are you, Liz?'

'Twenty-one.'

'And Ryan?'

'The same. He's in his last year at college.'

'He a musician, too?'

'Yes.'

'Do you live together?'

'Yes.'

Annie sat down on one of the beanbags, but Banks went to stand by the window, leaning the backs of his thighs against the sill. The room was small and hot and seemed too crowded with three people in it.

'What was your relationship with Luke Armitage?' Annie asked.

'He's . . . he *was* in our band.'

'Along with?'

'Me and Ryan. We don't have a drummer yet.'

'How long have you been together?'

She chewed on her lip and thought for a moment. 'We've only been practising together since earlier this year, after we met Luke. But Ryan and me had been talking about doing something like this for ages.'

'How did you meet Luke?'

'At a concert at the college.'

'What concert?'

'Just a couple of local bands. Back in March.'

'How did Luke get into a college concert?' Banks asked. 'He was only fifteen.'

Liz smiled. 'Not to look at. Or to talk to. Luke was far more mature than his years. You didn't know him.'

'Who was he with?'

'No one. He was by himself, checking out the band.'

'And you just started talking to him?'

'Ryan did, first.'

'And then?'

'Well, we found out he was interested in music, too, looking to get a band together. He had some songs.'

Banks pointed towards the tape. 'Those? "Songs from a Black Room"?'

'No. Those are more recent.'

'How recent?'

'Past month or so.'

'Did you know he was only fifteen?'

'We didn't find out until later.'

'How?'

'He told us.'

'He told you? Just like that?'

'No, not just like that. He had to explain why he couldn't just do what he wanted, you know. He was living with his parents and going to school. He said he was sixteen at first, but then told us later he'd lied because he was worried we'd think he was too young to be in the band.'

'And did you?'

'No way. Not someone with his talent. We might have had a few problems down the line, if things had got that far. Playing licensed premises, you know, stuff like that, but we figured we'd just deal with all that when we got there.'

'What about who his real father was? Did you know that?'

Liz looked away. 'He didn't tell us that until later, either. He didn't seem to want anything to do with Neil Byrd and his legacy.'

'How did you find out?' Banks asked. 'I mean, did Luke just come right out and tell you who his father was?'

'No. No. He didn't like to talk about him. It was something on the radio while he was over here, a review of that new compilation. He got upset about it and then it just sort of slipped out. It made a lot of sense.'

'What do you mean?' Annie asked.

'That voice. His talent. There was *something* about it all that rang a bell.'

'What happened after you knew?'

'What do you mean?'

'Did it make a difference?'

'Not really.'

'Oh, come on, Liz,' said Banks. 'You had Neil Byrd's *son* in your band. You can't expect us to believe that you weren't aware that would make a big difference commercially.'

'Okay,' said Liz. 'Sure, we were all aware of that. But the point is that we weren't *anywhere* commercially at that time. We're still not. We haven't even played in public yet, for crying out loud. And now, without Luke . . . I don't know.'

PETER ROBINSON

Banks moved away from the window and sat on a hard-backed chair against the wall. Annie shifted on her beanbag, as if trying to get comfortable. It was the first time he'd seen her look ill at ease in any sort of seat, then he realized she might have hurt herself falling over in the bookshop. She should be at the hospital getting checked out, especially the way on-the-job injury insurance worked these days, but there was no telling her. He didn't blame her; he'd be doing the same himself.

'Who did the singing?' Banks asked.

'Mostly me and Luke.'

'What kind of music do you play?'

'What does it matter?'

'Let's just say I'm interested. Humour me.'

'It's hard to describe,' Liz answered.

'Try.'

She looked at him, as if trying to size up his musical knowledge. 'Well, it's all about the songs, really. We're not trendy and we don't go in for long solos and stuff. It's more . . . have you heard of David Gray?'

'Yes.'

'Beth Orton?'

'Yes.'

If Liz was surprised by Banks's familiarity with contemporary music, she didn't show it. 'Well, we're not *like* them, but that's sort of what we're interested in. Having something to say, and maybe a bit jazzy and bluesy. I play quite a bit of flute as well as organ.'

'Did you know that Luke was taking violin lessons?'

'Yes. That would have been wonderful. We were looking to expand, bring in more musicians, but we were being very careful about it.' She looked Banks in the eye. 'We were serious about making a real go of this, you

344

know,' she said. 'But without selling out or being commercial. We're absolutely gutted by what's happened. Not just as a band, I mean, but personally, too.'

'I understand, and I appreciate that,' said Banks. 'Did you have any other sort of relationship with Luke? Other than musical?'

'What do you mean?'

'Did you sleep with him?'

'With Luke?'

'Why not? He was a good-looking kid.'

'But that's all he was. A kid.'

'You said he was wise beyond his years.'

'I know that, but I'm not a bloody cradle-snatcher. Besides, I'm perfectly happy with Ryan, thank you very much.' Liz's face was red.

'So you were never Luke's girlfriend?'

'No way. I told you. I was with Ryan when we met. It was all about the music.'

'So there's no chance that Ryan caught the two of you in bed together and ended up killing Luke, then deciding he might as well cash in on it?'

'I don't know how you can even suggest something as horrible as that.' Liz seemed close to tears and Banks was starting to feel like a shit. She seemed a good kid. But *seemed* wasn't good enough. He remembered Rose Barlow's visit, as well as her angry exit. Liz was younger than Lauren Anderson, and a far more likely candidate for Luke's bedfellow, in Banks's opinion. He didn't know how strong Liz's relationship with Ryan was, or how open.

'It happens,' Banks said. 'You'd be surprised. Maybe it was an accident, you just couldn't see any other way out.'

'I told you. Nothing like that happened. Luke was in the band, that's all.'

'Did Luke ever confide in you?' Annie asked, easing off the pressure a little. 'You know, tell you what was on his mind, what was worrying him.'

Liz paused, regaining her composure. She seemed to be looking at Annie's swollen red lips, but she didn't ask about them. 'He complained about school a lot,' she said finally.

'Ever say anything about his stepfather?'

'The rugby player?'

'Ex-footballer.'

'Whatever. No, not a lot. I don't think Luke liked him very much.'

'Why do you say that?'

'Nothing in particular. Just the way he talked.'

'Did you ever meet Luke's parents?'

'No. I don't think he even told them about us, about the band.'

'How do you know?'

'Just my impression.'

It was probably true, Banks realized. According to Annie and to his own observations, the Armitages didn't seem to have a clue what Luke was up to half the time. 'Did he seem worried about anything?'

'Like what?'

'Anything at all,' Annie went on. 'Did he mention if any threats had been made against him, for example, or if he thought someone was following him? Anything unusual, out of the ordinary?'

'No, nothing like that. Like I said, he didn't like school and couldn't wait to leave home. I'd say that's pretty normal, wouldn't you?'

Banks smiled. He'd been the same at that age. Later, too. And he had also left home at the first opportunity.

'When did you last see Luke?' Annie asked.

'About a week before he disappeared. Band practice.'

Annie looked around the small room and struggled to her feet. 'Where do you practise?'

'Church basement, down the street. The vicar's pretty broad-minded, a young bloke, and he lets us use their space if we don't make too much noise.'

'And you haven't seen Luke since?'

'No.'

'Has he ever been here?' Banks asked. 'In this flat?'

'Sure. Plenty of times.' Liz stood up, as if she sensed they were leaving.

'Did he ever leave anything here?'

'Like what?'

'Any of his stuff. You know, notebooks, poems, stories, clothes, that sort of thing. We're looking for anything that might help us understand what happened to him.'

'He never left any clothes here,' Liz said coldly, 'but he sometimes left tapes of songs for us, if that's what you mean. And some lyrics, maybe. But . . .'

'Could you collect them all together for us?'

'I suppose so. I mean, I don't know what's here or where everything is. Do you mean right now? Can't you come back later?'

'Now would be best,' said Banks. 'We'll help you look, if you like.'

'No! I mean, no. It's all right. I'll find them.'

'Is there something here you don't want us to see, Liz?'

'No, nothing. There's only a few tapes and some poems, notes for songs. I don't see how they can help you. Look . . . will I get these tapes and things back?'

'Why would you get them back?' Annie asked. 'They were Luke's property, weren't they?'

'Technically, I suppose. But he brought them for us. The band. To share.'

'They'll still most likely go to the family,' Banks told her.

'Luke's family! But they don't care. They can't . . .'

'Can't what, Liz?'

'I was going to say they can't appreciate his talent. They'll just throw them away. How could you let something like that happen?'

'Can't be helped. It's the law.'

Liz shifted from foot to foot, arms folded, as if she needed to go to the toilet. 'Look, couldn't you go away and come back, just for a while, give me just a bit of time to get everything together?'

'We can't do that, Liz. I'm sorry.'

'So you'll just take everything and give it to Luke's parents, just like that? You won't even give me time to make copies.'

'This is a murder investigation,' Annie reminded her.

'But still . . .' Liz sat down, close to tears again. 'It doesn't seem fair. It seems such a waste . . . I don't know. His parents don't care. We were so close.'

'So close to what?'

'To *making* something of ourselves.'

Banks felt sorry for her. He suspected that she wanted to hang on to Luke's tapes and writings for selfish reasons, so that the band could one day ride on Luke's and his father's coat-tails to success. If they couldn't do it with Luke's voice and talent, at least they could try to do it with some of his material. That Luke had been murdered would also, no doubt, help boost the public interest. Banks didn't think particularly ill of Liz for this. He'd probably have wanted the same if he were in her situation and felt passionate about a career in music. He didn't think it lessened her genuine feelings for Luke. But there was something else that bothered him; the way she had reacted when he had offered to help look around. He glanced at Annie. It was one of those rare moments when each knew what the other was thinking.

'Mind if we have a little look around?' Annie asked.

'What? Why? I've told you. I'll give you everything you want.' She got up and went over to the tapes, picking out three. 'These for a start. The writings are in—'

'Why are you so jumpy, Liz?'

'I'm not jumpy.'

'Yes, you are. I think we should have a look around the place.'

'You can't do that. You need a search warrant.'

Banks sighed. *Again*. 'Are you certain you want that?' he asked. 'Because we can get one.'

'Go do it then. Get one.'

Banks looked at Annie. 'DI Cabbot, will you please go—'

Liz looked from one to the other, puzzled. 'Not just *her*. Both of you go.'

'It doesn't work like that,' said Banks. 'One of us has to stay here to make sure you don't interfere with anything. We'd hardly be doing our jobs if we disappeared and let drug dealers flush their stuff down the toilet, would we?'

'I'm not a drug dealer.'

'I'm sure you're not. But there's something you don't want us to find. I'll stay here while DI Cabbot gets the warrant, then she'll come back with four or five constables and we'll tear the place apart.'

Liz turned so pale Banks worried she might faint. He

could tell she was sensitive and he didn't like bullying her, but he didn't like what had happened to Luke, either. 'What's it to be, Liz? Will you give us consent to look around now, or do we do it the hard way?'

Liz looked up at him, big eyes brimming with tears. 'I don't have much choice, do I?'

'There's always a choice.'

'You'd find it anyway. I told Ryan he was stupid to keep it.'

'Find what, Liz?'

'It's in the cupboard by the door, under the sleeping bag.'

Banks and Annie opened the cupboard by the door and moved aside the sleeping bag. Underneath it was a battered leather shoulder bag, exactly the kind that Luke Armitage had been carrying when the bullies taunted him in the market square.

'I think you and Ryan have got quite a bit of explaining to do, don't you?' said Banks.

15

The Bridge Fair came every March. As a young boy, Banks would go with his parents. He remembered sitting on his father's knee in the dodgem car, clinging on for dear life, remembered the feel of the rough nap and the raw-wool smell of his dad's jacket, the sparks flashing off the high poles. He remembered strolling around holding his mother's hand, eating candyfloss or toffee apples while she nibbled at a brandysnap and his father ate a hot dog smothered in fried onions. He would hear his father curse as he tried to throw biased darts at playing cards and his mother laugh as she tried to toss ping-pong balls into goldfish bowls.

But when Banks was fourteen, he wouldn't be seen dead at the fair with his parents; he went with his mates, and Saturday night was the big night.

Why was it, he thought, as he drove past the small roadside fair which had sparked his memory, that they always seemed to be playing old rock-and-roll music at fairgrounds, even in the sixties? Whenever he thought of nights at the fair with Paul, Graham, Steve and Dave, it was always Freddy Cannon's 'Palisades Park' that played in his mind, or Eddie Cochran's 'Summertime Blues' as the waltzers spun and the bright lights blazed in the dark, not the Beatles or the Rolling Stones.

His favourite ride was the caterpillar, but you had to go on that one with a girl. As the train went faster and faster in undulating circles, the canvas cover, like a shop's awning, would slowly unfurl until it covered up the whole ride – hence the name caterpillar – and you were in the dark, riding fast with your girl. On his own, he liked the waltzers and the speedway best, but all rides were better shared with girls when you were fourteen.

For Banks and his friends, the fair began days before it opened. He remembered passing the stretch of common ground with Graham one wet afternoon – it must have been 1965 because that was the only year Graham was around for the spring fair – and watching the brightly coloured lorries roll in, watching the suspicious and unsmiling fairground workers unload sections of track and cars and begin the magical process of fitting the whole thing together. Banks would come back to check the progress, watch the men put the last section of the carousel in place, set up the booths, the stalls and the shies, and sure enough, everything was ready on opening night.

You had to go after dark. There was no point if the brightly coloured lights didn't flash and spin and if the music wasn't loud, if the smell of fried onions and spun sugar didn't waft through the night air to mingle with the discernible whiff of violence. For the fairs were where you went to pick a fight or settle your scores, and you could always see trouble brewing a mile off. First the looks, the whispers, the casual bumps, then someone running, others in pursuit, a scuffle and muffled cries, the fairground workers always somehow outside or beyond it all, stepping between the spokes as the waltzers got faster and faster, collecting money, impressing the girls with their dare-devil nonchalance.

And the girls . . . Well, the girls were all on parade at the fair, all bubblegum, miniskirts and eyeshadow. *If you didn't get shagged on Saturday night, you didn't get shagged at all*, as the old rugby song went. Well, Banks didn't get shagged, but he sometimes got kissed. That night it was Sylvia Nixon, a pretty little blonde from the girls' school down the street. They'd been eyeing one another shyly all night, standing up on the boards right beside the rides, watching the riders scream and yell and cling on tight. She was with her quiet friend, June, that was the problem. Which Graham, bless his soul, helped solve. Soon they were off on the caterpillar, and Banks felt that delicious anticipation as the cover started to close over them.

But something odd happened later.

Banks was persuading the girls to come with them to the park the next day if the weather was fine. There were plenty of sheltered, well-hidden areas where you could lie in the grass or stand up against a tree and snog. He was almost there, just overcoming the last, perfunctory shreds of resistance, when Graham said, 'Sorry, I can't go tomorrow.' When Banks asked him why, he just smiled vaguely and answered with his characteristic evasiveness, 'I've got something else to do, that's all.' The girls weren't too thrilled with that, and Banks never got to go out with Sylvia Nixon again.

A fight broke out somewhere near the dodgems, Banks remembered, and a couple of older men broke it up. But his chief memory, apart from kissing Sylvia on the caterpillar and Graham's weak reason for missing the next day's rendezvous, was that Graham paid. Again. He had Benson & Hedges, too: ten of them, king size, in the golden packet.

As Banks turned off the A1 to Peterborough, he racked his brains, trying to remember if he had ever asked Graham where he got his money, but he didn't think he had. Maybe he didn't want to know. Kids are selfish, and as long as they're having a good time they don't feel the need to question where it's coming from, or at whose expense it might be. But there weren't many places a kid Graham's age could get his hands on so much ready cash. The paper round wouldn't cover it, but an occasional dip in the till might. Or perhaps he stole it from his mother's purse?

The trouble was that it didn't seem to matter so much, just as long as Graham had the money. That he was generous went without saying. But what had he done to get it, and where, and *whom*, had he got it from?

Now, Banks also found himself wondering what it was that Graham had to do that Sunday that was so much more important than snogging with Sylvia Nixon's friend June in the park. And he remembered other occasions, too, right up until the day of his disappearance, when Graham simply wasn't there. No reason, no excuse, no explanation.

•

Annie's face was starting to ache when she went to interview Liz Palmer. She'd taken a couple of paracetamol earlier, but the effect was wearing off. She took another two and probed a loose tooth with her tongue. Wonderful. The last thing she needed was a trip to the dentist's. That bastard Armitage. His high-priced lawyer had been down the station like a shot, and as soon as the custody officer had drawn up the papers charging Armitage with criminal assault, he'd been bound over to appear in front of the magistrate the following day and sent off home. Annie would have liked to see him cooling his heels in the custody suite at least overnight, but no such luck. He'd probably walk on the charges, too. People like him usually did.

Because the Luke Armitage murder was a high-profile case, Gristhorpe and DC Winsome Jackman were interviewing Ryan Milne at the same time next door. So far, since they had picked him up at the college, Milne had been about as forthcoming as Liz.

Annie took DC Kevin Templeton with her into Interview Room 2, made sure Liz was clear about her rights and started the tape recorders. As yet, Annie explained, no charges had been brought and nobody was under arrest. She simply wanted an explanation as to how Luke Armitage's shoulder bag had got into Liz's hall cupboard. The bag and its contents were already with forensics.

'You told me you last saw Luke at band practice in the church basement about a week before he disappeared, right?' Annie began.

Liz nodded. She slumped in her chair and worked at a fingernail, looking a lot younger than her twenty-one years.

'Did he have the shoulder bag with him?'

'He always had it with him.'

'Then what was it doing in your cupboard?'

'I've no idea.'

'How long has it been there?'

'Must've been since band practice.'

'He came to the flat first?'

'Yes.'

Annie glanced at Kevin Templeton and sighed. 'Problem is, Liz,' she went on, 'that the market square CCTV cameras caught Luke before he disappeared a week ago last Monday, and he had the bag with him then.'

'It must've been a new one.'

'No,' Annie said. 'It was the same one.' She couldn't be

certain of that, of course – perhaps Luke *had* left his bag at Liz's and bought a new one – but she thought it unlikely Luke would have left all his things there, too. After all, it wasn't the bag itself that counted, but the possessions it contained: his notebook, his laptop computer, portable CD player, tapes and CDs.

Liz frowned. 'Well, I don't see how . . .'

'Me, neither. Unless you're not telling us the truth.'

'Why would I lie?'

'Oh, come off it,' Kevin Templeton butted in. 'Luke's dead. I'd say that's a pretty good reason to lie, wouldn't you?'

Liz jerked forward. '*I* didn't kill him! You can't think I killed him.'

'I don't know what we're supposed to think,' said Annie, spreading her hands. 'But I'm sure you can see our problem. Luke and his bag go missing, then Luke turns up dead, and we find his bag in your cupboard. Bit of a coincidence, don't you think?'

'I've told you, I don't know when he put it there.'

'Where were you that afternoon?'

'What afternoon?'

'The Monday Luke disappeared.'

'I don't know. Home, I suppose.'

'Are you sure he didn't call at the flat, then perhaps forget his bag when he went off somewhere else?' Annie knew she was giving Liz an out, but it seemed the only way to get her talking.

'I didn't see him.'

'Did he have a key?'

'No.'

'So you couldn't have gone out for a minute and he let himself in?'

'I don't see how.'

So much for that line of questioning. 'Liz, you're not making our job any easier. I'll ask you again: how did Luke's bag find its way into your hall cupboard?'

'I told you, I don't know.'

'And I don't believe you.'

'Well, that's your problem.'

'No, Liz. It's *your* problem. And it's going to be a very big one if you don't tell us the truth soon.'

'Maybe it was Ryan,' Kevin Templeton suggested.

Liz looked confused. 'Ryan? What do you mean?'

'Well,' Templeton went on, 'let me tell you what I think happened.' Annie gave him the nod. 'I think Luke went to your flat after he'd been in the market square—'

'No. I told you. He didn't come that day.'

'Let me finish.'

'But it's not true! You're making it up.'

'Be quiet,' Annie said. 'Listen to what DC Templeton has to say.'

Liz flopped back in her chair. 'Whatever.'

'Luke came to your place after he'd been in the market square. It was late afternoon. Ryan was out and the two of you thought you had time for a roll on the bed. He was a good-looking kid, fit, looked older than his age—'

'No! That didn't happen. It wasn't like that!'

'But Ryan came home and caught you at it. The two of them got in a scuffle and one way or another Luke ended up dead. I'm sure Ryan didn't mean to kill him, but you had a body on your hands. What could you do? You waited until dark and then you loaded Luke's body into the car and took it to Hallam Tarn, where Ryan hoisted him up the wall and dropped him over. He should have sunk the way dead bodies do, at least for a while, until they start to decompose and the gases build up and carry them to the surface, but he didn't. His T-shirt snagged on an old tree root. Bad luck. Ryan wasn't to know that. And nobody should have been in a position to find Luke because the whole area was quarantined due to foot-and-mouth restrictions. But a man from the Ministry had to take water samples. Bad luck, again. Ryan wasn't to know that, either.' Templeton smiled, showing his white teeth, and folded his arms. 'How am I doing so far, Liz?'

'It's all lies. Nothing like that happened. You're just making it up to get us in trouble. I've heard about the police doing things like this before.'

'You're already in trouble,' Annie said. 'We're trying to help you out, find an explanation for what happened. Maybe it did happen the way DC Templeton suggested. Maybe it *was* an accident. If it was, we can help. But you *have to tell us the truth.*'

'Look, I don't know how that bag got there,' Liz said. 'We hadn't seen Luke since the last band practice.'

'You're not making it easy for us,' Annie said.

'I can't help it! What do you want me to do? Make something up just to satisfy you?'

'I want the truth.'

'I've told you the truth.'

'You've told us nothing, Liz.'

'Look,' said Templeton, 'we can check, you know. Our forensics people are very good.'

'What do you mean?'

'I mean they'll go through your flat with the proverbial fine-tooth comb, and if there's any evidence of wrong-doing, even a drop of Luke's blood, they'll find it.'

'He's right,' Annie said. 'There's the poker, for a start. I noticed it when we were talking to you. You don't see them very often these days. If there's any trace of Luke's blood or hair on it, we'll find it. And if there are any traces on the carpet, between the floorboards, down the sink, we'll find them.'

Liz crossed her arms and bit her lip. Annie could tell she'd touched a nerve. What was it? The mention of blood? Did Liz know they'd find traces of Luke's blood in the flat? 'What is it, Liz?' she asked. 'Something to tell me?'

Liz shook her head.

'Ryan's being interviewed just next door,' Templeton said. 'I'll bet he's telling them it was all your fault, that you killed Luke and he had to get rid of the body for you.'

'Ryan wouldn't do that.'

'Even if it were true?' Annie asked.

'But it's *not* true. We didn't kill anyone. How many times do I have to tell you?'

'Until we believe you,' Annie said. 'And until you come up with a satisfactory explanation of how Luke's bag got into your cupboard.'

'I don't know.'

'What about the ransom demands?'

'What about them?'

'Whose idea was that? Was it Ryan's? Did he see it as an easy opportunity to make some money now that Luke was dead anyway? Or did he do it to confuse us?'

'I don't know what you're talking about.'

Annie stood up and Templeton followed suit. 'Right,' Annie said, switching off the tapes. 'I'm fed up with this. Have her taken to the custody suite, Kev, and arrange for the taking of intimate samples. Maybe we'll be lucky and get a DNA match with the blood on the wall. And get a search warrant. We'll have forensics in her flat within an hour. Then we'll talk to the super and find out what Ryan had to say for himself.'

'Right, Ma'am,' said Templeton.

And don't bloody call me Ma'am, Annie added under her breath.

Liz stood up. 'You can't do this! You can't keep me here.'

'Just watch us,' said Annie.

•

Banks tapped on his parents' front door and walked in. It was early evening, and he had plenty of time to spare before his nine o'clock meeting with Michelle. His parents had finished washing the dishes and were settling down to watch *Coronation Street*, just as they had all those years ago, the night the police came to call about Graham, the night Joey flew away.

'It's all right, don't get up,' Banks said to his mother. 'I'm not stopping long. I have to go out. I just came by to drop off my overnight bag first.'

'You'll have a cup of tea, though, won't you, dear?' his mother insisted.

'Maybe he wants something stronger,' his father suggested.

'No thanks, Dad,' said Banks. 'Tea will be fine.'

'Up to you,' said Arthur Banks. 'The sun's well over the yardarm. I'll have that bottle of ale while you're up, love.'

Ida Banks disappeared into the kitchen, leaving Banks and his father to their uneasy silence.

'Any progress?' Banks senior finally asked.

'On what?'

'Your old pal. Graham Marshall.'

'Not much,' said Banks.

'That why you're here again?'

'No,' Banks lied. 'It's not my case. It's the funeral tomorrow.'

Arthur Banks nodded.

Banks's mother popped her head around the kitchen door. 'I knew I had something to tell you, Alan. I've got a head like a sieve these days. I was talking to Elsie Grenfell yesterday, and she said her David's coming down for the service tomorrow. And that Major lad's supposed to be here as well. Won't it be exciting, seeing all your old pals again?'

'Yes,' said Banks, smiling to himself. Some things, like the *Coronation Street* ritual – and thank the Lord there was still ten minutes to go before the programme started – never changed. Paul Major had always been 'that Major lad' to Ida Banks, even though she knew full well that his name was Paul. It was meant to indicate that she didn't quite approve of him. Banks couldn't imagine why. Of all of them, Paul Major had been the most goody-goody, the one most likely to become a chartered accountant or a banker.

'What about Steve?' Banks asked. 'Steve Hill?'

'I haven't heard anything about him for years,' Ida Banks said, then disappeared back into the kitchen.

It wasn't surprising. The Hills had moved off the estate many years ago when Steve's dad got transferred to Northumberland. Banks had lost track of them and didn't know where they lived now. He wondered if Steve had even heard about the finding of Graham's bones.

'I don't suppose it came to anything, what we were talking about in the Coach last time you were here?' Arthur Banks said.

'About the Krays and Mr Marshall? Probably not. But it was useful background.'

Arthur Banks coughed. 'Had over half the Metropolitan Police in their pockets, the Krays did, in their time.'

'So I've heard.'

Mrs Banks came through with the tea and her husband's beer on a rose-patterned tray. 'Our Roy phoned this afternoon,' she said, beaming. 'He said to say hello.'

'How is he?' Banks asked.

'Thriving, he said. He's jetting off to America for some business meetings, so he just wanted us to know he'd be away for a few days in case we were worried or anything.'

'Oh, good,' said Banks, who much to his mother's chagrin, he imagined, never jetted anywhere – unless Greece counted. Just like brother Roy to let his mother know what a high-powered life he was leading. He wondered what kind of shady dealings Roy was up to in America. None of his business.

'There was a programme on telly the other night about that police corruption scandal a few years back,' Banks's father said. 'Interesting, some of the things your lot get up to.'

Banks sighed. The defining event of Arthur Banks's life was not the Second World War, which he had missed fighting in by about a year, but the miners' strike of 1984, when Maggie Thatcher broke the unions and brought the workers to their knees. Every night he had been glued to the news and filled with the justified outrage of the working man. Over the years, Banks knew, his father had never been able to dispel the image of policemen in riot gear waving rolls of overtime fivers to taunt the starving miners. Banks had been working undercover in London then, mostly on drugs cases, but he knew that in his father's mind he was one of them. The enemy. Would it never end? He said nothing.

'So where are you going tonight, love?' Ida Banks asked. 'Are you seeing that policewoman again?'

She made it sound like a date. Banks felt a brief wave of guilt for thinking of it that way himself, then he said, 'It's police business.'

'To do with Graham?'

'Yes.'

'I thought you said that wasn't your case,' his father chipped in.

'It's not, but I might be able to help a bit.'

'Helping police with their enquiries?' Arthur Banks chuckled. It turned into a coughing fit until he spat into a handkerchief.

Fortunately, before anyone could say another word, the *Coronation Street* theme music started up and all conversation ceased.

•

It wasn't often that Detective Superintendent Gristhorpe visited the Queen's Arms, but after they had finished the interviews and put Ryan Milne and Liz Palmer under lock and key for the night, he suggested to Annie that they discuss the results over a bite to eat. Hungry and thirsty, Annie thought it a good idea.

Gristhorpe, like a true gentleman, insisted on going to the bar to get their drinks, though Annie would have been happy to go herself. Instead she sat down and made herself comfortable. Gristhorpe still intimidated her a little, though she didn't know why, but she felt easier with him in an environment like the Queen's Arms than in his book-lined office, so she was doubly glad he had suggested the pub. She definitely had a loose tooth, though, so she would have to be careful how she ate.

PETER ROBINSON

Gristhorpe returned with a pint of bitter for her and a half of shandy for himself. They glanced over the menu chalked on the blackboard, and Annie went for a vegetarian lasagne, which ought to be easy on her tooth, while Gristhorpe settled on fish and chips. The old man was looking healthier than he had in quite a while, Annie thought. The first few times she had seen him after his accident, he had seemed pale, gaunt and drawn, but now he had a bit more flesh on his bones and a warm glow to his pock-marked face. She supposed that accidents and illness took a lot more out of you the older you got, and that recovery took longer. But how old was he? He couldn't be all that much over sixty.

'How's your mouth feeling?' he asked.

'The pain seems to have gone for now, sir, thanks for asking.'

'You should have gone to the hospital.'

'It was nothing. Just a glancing blow.'

'Even so . . . these things can have complications. How's Wells?'

'Last I heard still in the infirmary. Armitage gave him a real going over.'

'He always was a hot-head, that one. Even as a football player. Now what about the Palmer girl? Anything interesting there?'

Annie recounted what little she had got from Liz Palmer, then Gristhorpe sipped some shandy and told her about Ryan Milne's interview. 'He said he knew nothing about the bag, just like his girlfriend. He told me he was out that day and didn't see Luke at all.'

'Did you believe him, sir?'

'No. Winsome went at him a bit – she's very good in

364

interviews, that lass, a real tigress – but neither of us could shake him.'

'So what are they hiding?'

'Dunno. Maybe a night in the cells will soften them up a bit.'

'Do you think they did it, sir?'

'Did it?'

'Killed Luke and dumped the body.'

Gristhorpe pursed his lips, then said, 'I don't know, Annie. Milne's got an old banger, so they had the means of transport. Like you, I suggested some sort of romantic angle, something going on between Luke and Liz, but Milne didn't bite, and to be quite honest I didn't notice any signs I'd hit the nail on the head.'

'So you don't think there was any romantic angle?'

'Luke was only fifteen, and Liz Palmer is what?'

'Twenty-one.'

'As I remember, the last thing a twenty-one-year-old woman would want is a fifteen-year-old boyfriend. Now maybe if she were forty-one . . .'

Annie smiled. 'A toyboy?'

'I've heard it called that. But I still think fifteen's too young.'

'I don't know,' said Annie. 'The head teacher's daughter told DCI Banks she thought Luke was having it off with his English teacher, and she's pushing thirty.'

'Lauren Anderson?'

'That's the one.'

'Stranger things have happened. What does Alan think?'

'That little Miss Barlow had reasons of her own for causing trouble for Miss Anderson.' Annie sipped some beer. Nectar. 'But I wouldn't say it's out of the question that

Luke was having relations with someone older than himself. Everything I've heard about him indicates he seemed much older than his age, both physically and mentally.'

'How about emotionally?'

'That I don't know.'

'Well, that's the one that counts,' Gristhorpe mused. 'That's what causes people to get out of their depth. They can understand something intellectually, accomplish something physically, but the emotional aspect can hit them like a sledgehammer if they're not mature enough. Teenagers are particularly vulnerable.'

Annie agreed. She'd had enough experience with troubled teens in her job to know it was true, and Luke Armitage had been a complex personality, a mass of conflicting desires and unresolved problems. Add to that his creativity, his sensitivity, and Luke was probably as volatile to handle as nitroglycerine.

'Does the Anderson woman have a jealous boyfriend?' Gristhorpe asked.

'Not according to Winsome. She did a bit of digging. Only bit of dirt on Ms Anderson is that her brother Vernon's got a record.'

Gristhorpe raised his bushy eyebrows. 'Oh?'

'Nothing really nasty. Just dodgy cheques.'

'I've written a few of those in my time, according to my bank manager. What about the other teacher, Alastair Ford?'

'Kevin Templeton says there are rumours he's gay, but only rumours. As far as anyone *knows* he has no sex life at all.'

'Any evidence that Luke Armitage was gay, too?'

'None. But there's no evidence he was straight, either. Ford has a temper, though, like Armitage, and he's been seeing a psychiatrist for several years now. Definitely the unstable kind.'

'Not to be ruled out, then?'

'No.'

'And Norman Wells?'

'Looking less likely, isn't he?'

When their food arrived, both were hungry enough to stop talking for a while and eat, then Gristhorpe slowed down. 'Any ideas of your own about how Luke's bag ended up where it did, Annie?' he asked.

Annie finished her mouthful of lasagne, then said, 'I think Luke went there after his run-in with the three bullies in the market square. What happened after that, I don't know, but either he died there or something happened that made him run off without his bag, which I don't think he'd do under any normal circumstances.'

'So *something* happened there?'

'Yes. Certainly.'

'What about his mobile?'

'One of those tiny models you can just flip open and shut. Probably couldn't find it among all the stuff if he kept it in his bag, so he carried it in his pocket. Anyway, it hasn't been found yet.'

'Has it been used?'

'Not since the ransom call. Hasn't even been switched on. I checked again with the company.'

'Anything valuable in the bag?'

'Stefan's going through it. From what I saw, though, I don't think so. I mean, the laptop was worth a bob or two, but I don't think theft was the motive here. That is . . .'

'Yes, Annie?'

'Well, there was nothing valuable to you or me, nothing of any real material value, but I got the impression that Liz, at least, is ambitious, and there's a chance they could ride a lot further and a lot faster on Luke Armitage's coat-tails – or rather Neil Byrd's coat-tails.'

'I think I must be a bit of an old fogey,' said Gristhorpe, scratching the side of his hooked nose, 'but I can't say I've ever heard of Neil Byrd. I know who he was to Luke and what happened to him, of course, but that's about as far as it goes.'

'Alan – DCI Banks – knows a lot more about it than I do, sir, but Byrd was quite famous in his time. The record company is still bringing out CDs of previously unreleased stuff, greatest hits and live concerts, so there's still a thriving Neil Byrd industry out there, a dozen years after his death. Luke inherited some of his father's talent, and if Liz and Ryan wanted to milk the connection, I'm sure there are plenty of song ideas and fragments on the laptop and in his notebooks.'

'But he was only a kid, Annie. Surely he can't have had *that* much to say?'

'It's not what you say, sir, it's how you say it. Teenage angst, mostly, from what I've heard. But it's the *name* that's the point. And, not to be too ghoulish about it, the circumstances. Dead son of famous rock suicide. With a promotion like that, the songs wouldn't *need* to be that good. It'd get Liz's band known, get them a name, and that's more than half the battle in the music business.'

'But legally all Luke's stuff belongs to his family now. Wouldn't they sue if these people got as far as making a record of Luke's songs?'

'Maybe, but it'd be too late then, wouldn't it? And you know what they say: no publicity's bad publicity. A lawsuit would only further Liz's and Ryan's career. It's just a thought, sir.'

Gristhorpe finished his last chip and pushed his plate aside, taking a sip of shandy. 'So what you're saying is that, whether the two of them killed Luke or not, they somehow found themselves with a goldmine of material, and they thought they might as well hang on to it until they could use it?'

'As I said, sir, it's only an idea. If they'd been a bit more cautious, they'd have got rid of the bag and we'd be none the wiser.'

'But they never thought we'd search their flat.'

'Why would they? They didn't even know that anyone had seen Luke with Liz.'

'What about the vicar at that church where they practised?'

Annie rolled her eyes. 'Winsome talked to him. Said he's so otherworldly he hadn't a clue who Luke Armitage was or that he'd disappeared.'

'Would Liz and Ryan have killed Luke for his stuff?' he asked.

'I don't think so, sir. That's the problem. Whichever way you look at it, they'd be far better off with Luke alive. *He* would have been the real draw. Without him, well . . . they're simply doing the best they can.'

'So they had nothing to gain by killing him?'

'No. Not unless he was intending to walk out on them, for example, and take all his works with him. One of them could have lost it with him then. Or, as I suggested earlier, unless there was some sort of romantic relationship and Ryan found out.'

'A *crime passionel*? I suppose so. Wouldn't be the first time. We can't discount anything yet. Let's just give them a bit of time, hope forensics turn up something, and have at them again in the morning.'

'Good idea, sir.' Annie finished her pint.

'Annie, before you go . . . ?'

'Sir?'

'I don't mean to pry, but you and Alan . . . ?'

'Just colleagues, sir. And friends.'

Gristhorpe seemed pleased with her answer. 'Aye,' he said. 'Good. Good. Get some sleep, lass. I'll see you bright and early in the morning.'

•

The pub was closer to the riverside than the city centre, though even that wasn't very far. Banks parked by the Rivergate Centre and walked the rest of the way. It was a pleasant evening, not a leaf stirring in the warm air. The sunset painted the sky bright orange and crimson. Banks could see Venus low on the horizon, and the constellations were slowly taking shape overhead. He wished he could recognize them all, but he could only make out Hercules. That made him think of those dreadful spaghetti spectacles he used to love in the early sixties with cheap special effects, Steve Reeves, and a scantily clad Sylva Koscina.

Michelle was five minutes late, and Banks had already settled at a small corner table with a pint of bitter. The lounge was small and smoky, but most of the people stood at the bar, and the video machines were mercifully silent. Piped music played softly, some sort of modern pop stuff Banks didn't recognize. Michelle was wearing tight black trousers and a green blouse tucked in at the waist. She carried a tan suede jacket slung over her shoulder. Banks had never seen her dressed so casually before. Hadn't seen her looking as good, either. She'd had her hair done, he noticed: nothing drastic, just tidied up a bit, the fringe trimmed, highlights renewed. And she wore a little make-up, just enough to accentuate her green eyes and high cheekbones.

She seemed self-conscious about her appearance because she wouldn't meet his eyes at first. Only when he had offered her a drink and she asked for a dry white wine, did she favour him with a look and a shy smile.

'Thanks for coming,' Michelle said, when Banks placed the drink in front of her and sat down.

'My pleasure,' said Banks. 'I'd have come tomorrow for the service, anyway, so another evening doesn't make much difference.'

'I know you're busy.'

'I'm covered. Besides, we had a lucky break just before I set off.' Banks told her about finding Luke Armitage's bag at Liz Palmer's flat.

'Poor kid,' said Michelle. 'He wasn't much older than Graham Marshall, was he?'

'A year or so.'

'Why would anyone want to kill a boy that age? What could he possibly have done?'

'I don't know. I suppose that's why we assume it's a paedophile when the victim's so young. We can easily imagine older people being killed for other motives, for greed or to cover up something, but it's hard with kids. Anyway, it looked like a kidnapping, but I have my doubts. What about you? Any more news?'

Michelle gave him the gist of her conversation with retired DI Robert Lancaster in London, especially his remarks about Graham seeming streetwise beyond his years.

'So your ex-copper thought Graham had a future in crime, did he?' Banks said. 'Interesting, that.'

'Why? Have you remembered something?'

'Nothing, really. Just that Graham never seemed short of money, and I'd no idea where he got it from.'

'There's something else,' Michelle said. She seemed hesitant, Banks thought, unwilling to meet his eyes.

'Yes?'

'Someone was in my flat on Saturday, while I was down in London.'

'Anything taken?'

'Not as far as I can tell, just a few things out of place. But whoever it was had also been having a good look at my computer files.'

Banks got the impression that she wasn't telling him everything, but he didn't pursue it. If there was something she was omitting, it was probably for a good reason, such as personal embarrassment. She'd hardly want to tell him if someone had been going through her undies, would she? 'Anything there?'

'Not much. Personal notes. Speculations.'

'About the case?'

'Some of it.'

'Did you report the break-in?'

'Of course not. Under the circumstances.'

'How did he get in?'

'Finessed the lock somehow.' Michelle smiled. 'Don't worry, I've had it changed. The locksmith assures me the place is as impregnable as a fortress now.'

'Anything else?'

'Maybe.'

'What does that mean?'

'Yesterday, as I was crossing the road near the Hazels estate, I was almost hit by a small van.'

'Almost?'

'Yes, no damage. I couldn't be certain, but I thought it was deliberate.'

'Any idea who?'

'The number plate was obscured.'

'A guess?'

'Well, I hesitate to say it, but after the missing notebooks and actions, my mind can't help but wander towards Shaw. Thing is, I can't bring myself to believe it, that he would do something like that.'

Banks didn't have much of a problem believing it. He'd known bent coppers before, and known them well enough to realize that they were capable of anything when cornered. Many coppers were also as skilled at picking locks as burglars were. But why did Shaw feel cornered? And what was it he'd done? Banks remembered the quiet young man with the freckles, ginger hair and sticking-out ears, rather than the bloated, red-nosed bully Shaw had become. 'Shaw was teamed up with DI Proctor, right?'

'Reg Proctor, yes. He took early retirement in 1975 and then died of liver cancer in 1978. He was only forty-seven.'

'Any rumours, hints of scandal?'

Michelle sipped some wine and shook her head. 'Not that I could uncover. Seems to have had an exemplary career.'

Banks asked Michelle's permission and lit a cigarette. 'Shaw and Proctor were the detectives who came to our house,' he said. 'They were obviously interviewing friends of Graham's and people on the estate. There would no doubt have been other teams assigned other tasks, but for some reason someone wanted rid of *Shaw*'s notes. Shaw himself?'

'He was only a DC at the time,' said Michelle.

'Right. What could he have to hide? There must have been something in his notebooks that incriminated someone else. Maybe Harris or Proctor.'

'The notebooks *could* have been missing since Harris retired in 1985,' Michelle said. 'They could also have been taken before Proctor's death in 1978, I suppose.'

'But why? Nobody's had reason to look at them for years. Graham had been missing since 1965. Why mess with the paperwork unless there was some compelling reason? And what could that be except that his body's been found and the case is open again?'

'True enough,' said Michelle.

'The actions would show us how the investigation was managed,' Banks mused. 'Most of them probably came from Jet Harris himself. They'd show the direction the investigation took, or didn't take, the shape of it.'

'We keep getting back to this blinkered approach,' Michelle said. 'DS Shaw even hinted they all knew Brady and Hindley did it.'

'That's a load of bollocks,' said Banks.

'The timing's right.'

'But that's all that's right. You might just as well say Reggie and Ronnie did it.'

'Maybe they did.'

Banks laughed. 'It makes more sense than Brady and Hindley. They operated miles away. No, there's something else going on. Something we can't figure out because there are still too many missing pieces. Another?'

'I'll go.'

Michelle walked to the bar and Banks sat wondering what the hell it was all about. So far, all they had was an investigation that had concentrated on only one possibility – the passing paedophile. Now they had Bill

Marshall's relationship with the Krays and with Carlo Fiorino and Le Phonographe, and the fact that Banks remembered Graham often had money enough to pay for their entertainment. And now the missing records. There were links – Graham, Bill Marshall, Carlo Fiorino – but where did it go after that? And how did Jet Harris fit in? It was possible that he'd been on the take, paid by Fiorino to head off trouble. Jet Harris, bent copper. That would go down well at headquarters. But how did it relate to Graham and his murder?

Michelle came back with the drinks and told him about Donald Bradford's death and the pornography that had been found in his flat. 'There might be no connection,' she said. 'I mean, Bradford could have been the victim of a random break-in, and plenty of people have collections of pornography.'

'True,' Banks said. 'But it's a bit of a coincidence, isn't it?'

'It is indeed.'

'What if Bradford was using the newsagent's shop as an outlet for distributing porn?' Banks suggested.

'And Graham delivered it?'

'Why not? He always seemed to be able to get his hands on it. That's another thing I remember. A bit of Danish submission with your *Sunday Times*, sir? Or how about some Swedish sodomy with your *News of the World*, madam? Gives a whole new meaning to the term Sunday supplement, doesn't it?'

Michelle laughed. 'Maybe he just found out about it.'

'Is that worth killing someone for?'

'Who knows? People have killed for less.'

'But all we're assuming is that Bradford was a minor porn dealer.'

'He had to get it from a wholesaler, didn't he? Maybe Bradford was working for someone with even more at stake?'

'Someone like Carlo Fiorino?' suggested Banks. 'And Harris was on Fiorino's payroll? It's possible, but still speculation. And it doesn't get us a lot further with the missing notebooks.'

'Unless Proctor and Shaw inadvertently hit on the truth during their interviews, and it was recorded in Shaw's notebooks. I don't know how we'd find out, though. It's not as if we can talk to Harris or Proctor.'

'Maybe not,' said Banks. 'But we might be able to do the next best thing. Were they married?'

'Harris was. Not Proctor.'

'Is his wife still alive?'

'As far as I know.'

'Maybe she'll be able to tell us something. Think you can find her?'

'Piece of cake,' said Michelle.

'And let's delve a little deeper into Donald Bradford's domain, including the circumstances of his death.'

'Okay. But what about DS Shaw?'

'Avoid him as best you can.'

'That shouldn't be too difficult these days,' Michelle said. 'He's off sick half the time.'

'The booze?'

'That's what I'd put my money on.'

'Are you going to the funeral tomorrow?'

'Yes.'

'Good.' Banks finished his drink. 'Another?'

Michelle looked at her watch. 'No. Really. I'd better go.'

'Okay. I suppose I should go, too.' Banks smiled. 'I'm sure my mum'll be waiting up for me.'

Michelle laughed. It was a nice sound. Soft, warm, musical. Banks realized he hadn't heard her laugh before. 'Can I give you a lift?' he asked.

'Oh, no. Thank you,' said Michelle, standing up. 'I'm just around the corner.'

'I'll walk with you, then.'

'You don't need to. It's quite safe.'

'I insist. Especially after what you've just told me.'

Michelle said nothing. They walked out into the mild darkness, crossed the road and neared the riverside flats, close to where Banks had parked his car. Michelle had been right; it really was within spitting distance.

'This is right across the river from where they used to have the fair when I was a kid,' he said. 'Funny, but I was just thinking about it as I was driving down.'

'Before my time,' said Michelle.

'Yes.' Banks walked her up to her door.

'Well,' she said, fumbling for her key, giving him a brief smile over her shoulder. 'Goodnight, then.'

'I'll just wait and make sure everything's okay.'

'You mean until you're sure there are no bogeymen waiting for me?'

'Something like that.'

Michelle opened her door, put on the lights and did a quick check while Banks stood in the doorway and glanced around the living room. It seemed a bit barren, no real character, as if Michelle hadn't put her stamp on it yet.

'All clear,' she said, emerging from the bedroom.

'Goodnight, then,' said Banks, trying to hide his disappointment that she didn't even invite him in for a coffee. 'And take care. See you tomorrow.'

'Yes.' She gave him a smile. 'Tomorrow.' Then she closed the door gently behind him, and the sound of the bolt slipping home seemed far louder than it probably was.

•

It was all very well for Gristhorpe to tell Annie to get a good night's sleep, but she couldn't. She had taken more paracetamol and gone to bed early, but the pain had returned to her mouth with a vengeance. Every tooth ached and now two of them felt loose.

The blow from Armitage had shaken her more than she had cared to admit to either Banks or Gristhorpe because it had made her feel the same way she had felt when she was raped nearly three years ago: a powerless victim. She had sworn afterwards that she would never allow herself to feel that way again, but down in the cramped, dank space of Norman Wells's book cellar, she had felt it, the deep, gut-wrenching fear of female powerlessness against male strength and sheer brute force.

Annie got up, went downstairs and poured herself a glass of milk with shaking hands, sitting at the kitchen table in the dark as she sipped it. She remembered the very first time Banks had been to her house. They had sat in the kitchen and eaten dinner together while the light faded. All the while Annie had been wondering what she would do if he made a move. She had impulsively invited him into her home, after all, offering to cook dinner instead of going to a restaurant or a pub, as he had suggested. Had she known right then, when she did that, what was going to happen? She didn't think so.

As the evening wore on, their mood had got more and more mellow, thanks partly to liberal quantities of Chianti. When she had gone outside into the backyard with Banks, who wanted a cigarette, and when he had put his arm around her, she'd felt herself tremble like a teenager as she had blurted out all the reasons about why they *shouldn't* do what they were about to do.

Well, they had done it. And now she had ended the affair. Sometimes she regretted that and wondered why she had done it. Partly it was because of her career, of course. Working in the same station as the DCI you were screwing was bad policy. But maybe that was just an excuse. Besides, it didn't have to be that way. She could have worked in another station, somewhere where the opportunities were just as good, if not better, than at Western Area Headquarters.

It was true that Banks still seemed tied to his past, to his marriage, but she could have handled that. It was also something that would have waned in time. Everyone had emotional baggage, including Annie herself. No, she thought, the reasons for what she did were within herself, not the job, not Banks's past. Intimacy had felt like a threat to her, and the closer she had got to Banks, the more she had felt suffocated and tried to pull away.

Would it be like that with every man she met? Was it to do with the rape? Possibly, she thought. Or at least partly. She wasn't sure she would *ever* completely get over that. What happened that night had certainly damaged her deeply. She didn't think she was beyond repair, just that she had a long way to go. She still had occasional nightmares, and though she had never told Banks this, sex had sometimes been an effort for her, had even hurt at times. Sometimes the simple act of penetration, however consensual and gentle, had brought back the surge of panic and the feeling of sheer *powerlessness* she had first experienced that night. Sex certainly had its dark side, Annie knew. It could be demonic, close to violence, pushing you into dangerous and vaguely imagined desires and dark areas, beyond taboo. It was no wonder, then, she thought, that the idea of sex was so often mentioned in the same breath as violence. Or that sex and death were so intimately linked in the words and works of so many writers and artists.

Annie finished her milk and tried to laugh off her morbid thoughts. Still, they seemed to be the only kind she had at night, alone and unable to sleep. She put the kettle on for tea and went into the living room to browse through her small video collection. In the end she settled on *Doctor Zhivago*, which had always been one of her favourite films, and when the tea was ready she lounged on the sofa in the dark with her steaming mug, legs tucked under her and gave herself up to the haunting theme music and the epic story of love in a time of revolution.

•

Banks walked down the stairs and tried to shake off his sense of disappointment. It was just as well, he told himself; the last thing he needed right now was to make a fool of himself over yet another woman. And Michelle had her own demons, whatever they were. Everyone did, it seemed. You couldn't get to a certain age without attracting a lot of clutter. But why did it always have to get in the way? Why couldn't you just shrug it off and get on with life? Why was misery so easy to embrace and joy so bloody elusive?

Just around the corner from the flats, he stopped to light a cigarette. Before he got his lighter out of his pocket, he felt something thud into him from behind. He staggered forward and turned to face whoever had hit him. He got only a quick glimpse of a pug nose and piggy eyes before a blow to the face upset both his vision and his balance. Another blow knocked him to the ground. Next he felt a sharp pain in his ribs and a kick to his stomach made him retch.

Then he heard a dog barking and a man's voice shouting beyond the walls of pain, felt rather than saw his attacker hesitate and heard him whisper, 'Go back where you came from, or there'll be more of that,' before he ran off into the night.

Banks got to his knees and felt sick, head hanging on his chest. Christ, he was getting too old for this kind of thing. He tried to stand, but his legs still felt too wobbly. Then a hand grasped his elbow and he managed to get to his feet.

'Are you all right, Mister?' Banks swayed and took a couple of deep breaths. That felt a little better. His head was still spinning, but his vision had cleared. A young man stood beside him, Jack Russell terrier on a leash. 'Only I was just taking Pugwash here for a walk and I saw two blokes setting on you.'

'Two? Are you certain?'

'Yes. They ran off towards the city centre.'

'Thank you,' said Banks. 'That was very brave of you. You saved my bacon.'

'Is there anything else I can do? Call you a taxi or something?'

Banks paused to get his thoughts in some sort of order, then he looked towards the flats. 'No,' he said. 'No thanks. I've a friend lives just over there. I'll be fine.'

'If you're certain.'

'Yes. And thanks again. Not many people bother to get involved these days.'

The young man shrugged. 'No problem. Come on,

Pugwash.' And they wandered off, the man casting a couple of backward glances as he went.

Still a bit wobbly, Banks made his way back to Michelle's flat and pressed the intercom. A few moments later her voice crackled into the night air. 'Yes? Who is it?'

'It's me, Alan,' said Banks.

'What is it?'

'I've had a little accident. I wonder if . . .'

But before he could finish Michelle buzzed him in, and he made his way up to her door. She was already standing there, looking concerned, and came forward to help him towards the sofa. Not that it was necessary, but he thought it was a nice gesture.

'What happened?' she asked.

'Someone jumped me. Thank God for dog walkers or I'd probably be in the river by now. Funny, isn't it? I thought I was going to end up in the Nene all those years ago and I almost ended up there tonight.'

'You're rambling,' Michelle said. 'Sit down.'

Banks still felt a bit dizzy and nauseated when he sat down. 'Just give me a few minutes,' he said. 'I'll be fine.'

Michelle handed him a glass. 'Drink,' she said.

He drank. Cognac. A good one, too. As the fiery liquor spread through his limbs he started to feel even better. His mind came into sharper focus, and he was able to assess the damage. Not much, really. His ribs felt tender, but he didn't feel as if anything was broken. He looked up and saw Michelle standing over him.

'How do you feel now?'

'Much better, thank you.' Banks sipped some more cognac. 'Look,' he said, 'I'd better call a taxi. I don't feel very much like driving in this condition, especially not after this.' He held up the glass. Michelle tipped in more from the Courvoisier VSOP bottle, and poured herself a generous measure, too.

'Okay,' she said. 'But you must let me see to your nose first.'

'Nose?' Banks realized his nose and upper lip felt numb. He put his hand up and it came away bloody.

'I don't think it's broken,' Michelle said, leading him towards the bathroom, 'but I'd better clean you up and put something on it before you go. There's a small cut on your lip, too. Whoever hit you must have been wearing a ring or something.'

The bathroom was small, almost too small for two people to stand without touching. Banks stood with the backs of his legs against the toilet bowl as Michelle used a damp facecloth to wipe away the blood then looked in the cabinet and came up with some TCP liquid antiseptic. She put a small swab of cotton wool over the top of the bottle and tipped it up, then carefully applied it to his lip. It stung, and the acrid smell made him gasp. Michelle took the cotton wool away.

'It's all right,' he said.

She dropped one bloodstained swab into the waste bin and prepared another. Banks watched her face close to his, the look of concentration as she applied the cotton wool, tip of her tongue nipped between her teeth. She caught his eye, blushed and looked away. 'What?'

'Nothing,' he said. She was so close he could feel the warmth of her body, smell the cognac on her breath.

'Go on,' she said. 'You were going to say something.'

'It's just like *Chinatown*,' Banks said.

'What do you mean?'

'The film, *Chinatown*. Haven't you seen it?'

'What happens?'

'Jack Nicholson gets his nose cut by Roman Polanski, and Faye Dunaway, well . . . she does what you're doing now.'

'Puts TCP on it?'

'Well, I don't think it was TCP – I don't think they have that in America – but the idea's the same. Anyway, it's a very sexy scene.'

'Sexy?' Michelle paused. Banks could see her flushed skin, feel the heat from her cheeks. The bathroom seemed to be getting smaller.

'Yes,' said Banks.

She dabbed at him again. Her hand was trembling. 'I don't see how putting TCP on a cut could be sexy,' she said. 'I mean, what happens?'

She was so close to him now that he could feel her breast touching ever so lightly against his arm. He could have leaned the top half of his body further back, bent at the knees, but he stood his ground. 'First, they kiss,' he said.

'But wouldn't it hurt?'

'It was just his nose that got cut. Remember?'

'Of course. How silly of me.'

'Michelle?'

'What? What is it?'

Banks took her trembling hand by the wrist and moved it away from his mouth, then he put his other hand under her chin and cupped it gently so she was looking at him, her brilliant green eyes questioning but holding his gaze, not looking away now. He could feel his heart thudding in his chest and his knees wobbling as he pulled her closer to him and felt her yield.

16

'**You were late back last night**,' Banks's mother said, without turning from the kitchen sink. 'Tea's fresh.'

Banks poured himself a cup of tea and added a splash of milk. He had expected this sort of reaction. His mother had probably lain awake until two in the morning listening for him the way she did when he was a teenager. He and Michelle had decided that, for many reasons, it was not a good idea for him to stay with her overnight, but even so Michelle had laughed at the idea of his having to go home to his mother.

Ida Banks turned. 'Alan! What *have* you done to your face?'

'It's nothing,' said Banks.

'But it's all bruised. And your lip's cut. What have you been up to?'

Banks turned away. 'I told you, it's nothing.'

'Were you fighting? Was it some criminal you were arresting? Is that why you were so late? You could have rung.' She gave him a look that spoke volumes about what she thought of his chosen career.

'Something like that,' Banks said. 'I had a bit of business to take care of. Look, I'm sorry I didn't ring, but it was so late. I didn't want to wake you.'

His mother gave him the reproving look she was so good at. 'Son,' she said, 'you ought to know by now that I can't get to sleep until you're home safe and sound.'

'Well, you can't have slept much these past thirty years or so,' Banks said, and immediately regretted it when he saw the other look she was so good at, the suffering martyr, lower lip trembling. He went over and gave her a hug. 'Sorry, Mum,' he said, 'but I'm all right. Really I am.'

His mother sniffed and nodded. 'Well,' she said. 'I suppose you'll be hungry. Bacon and eggs?'

Banks knew from experience that feeding him would help his mother get over her bad night. He wasn't all that hungry, but he couldn't deal with the protests he knew he'd get if all he asked for was cereal. He was also in a hurry. Michelle had suggested he come down to headquarters to search through the mugshots for his attacker. He wasn't certain he could identify the man, though the piggy eyes and pug nose were distinctive enough. Still, Mother comes first; bacon and eggs it had to be. 'If it's no trouble,' he said.

His mother walked over to the fridge. 'It's no trouble.'

'Where's Dad?' he asked, as his mother turned on the cooker.

'Down at the allotment.'

'I didn't know he still went there.'

'It's more of a social thing. He doesn't do much digging or anything these days. Mostly he sits and passes the time of day with his mates. And he has a cigarette or two. He thinks I don't know, but I can smell it on him when he comes home.'

'Well, don't be too hard on him, Mum.'

'I'm not. But it's not only *his* health, is it? What am I supposed to do if he goes and drops dead?'

'He's not going to drop dead.'

'Doctor says he's not supposed to smoke. And you should stop, too, while you're still young.'

Young? It was a long time since Banks had been called young. Or felt young, for that matter. Except perhaps last night, with Michelle. Once she had made her decision, dropped her defences a little, she was a different person, Banks marvelled. It had clearly been a long time since she had been with anyone, so their love-making was slow and tentative at first, but none the worse for that. And once she threw aside her inhibitions she proved to be a warm and generous lover. Michelle had also been gentle because of Banks's cut lip and bruised ribs. He cursed his bad luck, that he had to be injured in combat the first night he got to sleep with her. He also thought it was ironic that such physical injuries were so rare in his line of work, yet both he and Annie had been hurt within hours of one another. Some malevolent force working against them, no doubt.

Banks remembered Michelle's sleepy late-night kiss at the door as he left, her warm body pressed against him. He sipped some tea. 'Is the paper around?' he asked his mother.

'Your dad took it with him.'

'I'll just nip over the road, then.' His father took the *Daily Mail*, anyway, and Banks preferred the *Independent* or the *Guardian*.

'Your bacon and eggs will be ready.'

'Don't worry. I'll be back before they're done.'

Banks's mother sighed, and he headed out. It was warm but cloudy outside, and looking like rain again. That close, sticky muggy weather he hated. As he entered the newsagent's shop, he remembered the way it used to be laid out, the counter in a different place, racks arranged differently. Different magazines and covers back then, too: *Film Show*, *Fabulous*, *Jackie*, *Honey*, *Tit-Bits*, *Annabelle*.

Banks remembered his conversation with Michelle in the pub about Donald Bradford and his collection of porn, and wondered if he really had acted as a distributor. While Banks couldn't imagine Graham slipping a magazine of French *fellatio* between the pages of the *People* and putting it through Number 42's letterbox, he *could* imagine Bradford keeping his stock under the counter or hidden in the back. And maybe Graham had stumbled upon it.

He could remember the first time he had ever seen a pornographic magazine. Not just the ones with naked women in them, like *Playboy*, *Swank* and *Mayfair,* but true porn, magazines that showed people *doing* things.

It was in their den inside the tree and, interestingly enough, the magazines were Graham's. At least, he brought them. Had Banks never wondered at the time where Graham got them from? He didn't know. And if Graham had mentioned it, Banks didn't remember.

It was a warm day, and there were only three of them there, but he wasn't sure whether the third was Dave, Paul or Steve. The branches and leaves came right down to the ground, hard, shiny green leaves with thorns on them, he remembered now, and he could feel himself slipping through the concealed entrance, where the foliage wasn't too dense, the thorns pricking his skin. Once you got inside, the space seemed bigger than it could possibly be, just the way the inside of Dr Who's TARDIS was bigger than the outside. They had plenty of space to sit around and smoke, and enough light got through for them to look at dirty magazines. The smell of the place came back, too, so real he could smell it as he stood waiting to cross the road. Pine needles. Or something similar. And there was a soft beige carpet of them on the ground.

That day Graham had the two magazines stuffed down the front of his shirt and he brought them out with a flourish. He probably said, 'Feast your eyes on this, lads,' but Banks couldn't remember the actual words, and he didn't have time to settle down and try to reconstruct the memory in full. It wasn't important anyway.

What *was* important was that for the next hour or so the three teenagers looked in awe on some of the most amazing, exciting, unbelievable images they had ever seen in their lives, people doing things they had never even dreamed could or *should* be done.

By today's standards, Banks realized, it was pretty mild, but for a fourteen-year-old provincial kid in the summer of 1965 to see colour photos of a woman sucking a man's penis or a man sticking his penis up a woman's arse was shocking in the extreme. There were no animals, Banks remembered, and certainly no children. Mostly he remembered images of impossibly large-breasted women, some of them with semen spurting all over their breasts and faces, and well-endowed men usually on top of them or being ridden by them. Graham wouldn't lend the magazines out, Banks remembered, so the only time they had to look at them was then and there, inside the tree. The titles and text, or what he remembered of them, were in a foreign language. He knew it wasn't German or French because he took those languages at school.

While this didn't become a regular occurrence, Banks did remember a couple of other occasions that summer when Graham brought magazines to the tree. Different ones each time. And then, of course, Graham disappeared and Banks didn't see that kind of porn again until he became a policeman.

So was it a clue or not? As Michelle had said last night,

it hardly seemed something worth murdering over, even back then, but if it was a part of something bigger – the Kray empire, for example – and if Graham had got involved in it way beyond his depth, beyond borrowing a few magazines, then there might be a link to his murder. It was worth looking into, at any rate, if Banks could figure out where to start.

Tapping the newspaper against his thigh, Banks crossed the busy road and hurried back home before his bacon and eggs turned cold. The last thing he needed was to upset his mother again this morning.

•

Despite her late night, Michelle was at her desk long before Detective Superintendent Shaw was likely to see the light of day. If he bothered coming in at all. Maybe he would take another sick day. At any rate, the last thing she wanted was him breathing over her shoulder while Banks was in an interview room looking through the mugshots. There were people around the office, so she and Banks hadn't had a chance to do much more than say a quick hello before they got down to business. She had given him a choice of the computer version or the plain, old-fashioned photo albums, and he had chosen the albums.

She had felt a little shy when he walked in and could still hardly believe that she had gone ahead and slept with him like that, even though she knew she had wanted to. It wasn't as if she had been saving herself or anything, or that she was afraid, or had lost interest in sex, only that she had been far too preoccupied by the aftermath of Melissa's death and the end of her marriage to Ted. You don't get over something like that overnight.

Still, she was surprised at her new-found boldness and blushed even now as she thought about the way it had made her feel. She didn't know what Banks's personal situation was, except that he was going through a divorce. He hadn't talked about his wife, or his children, if he had any. Michelle found herself curious. She hadn't told him about Melissa and Ted either, and she didn't know if she would. Not for a while, anyway. It was just too painful.

The only real drawback was that he was on the Job. But where else was she likely to meet someone? People who form relationships often meet at their places of work. Besides, North Yorkshire was a fair distance from Cambridgeshire, and after they'd got the Graham Marshall case sorted, she doubted they would ever have to work together again. But would they even *see* each other? That was the question. It was a long way to travel. Or perhaps it was foolish of her even to imagine a relationship, or to want one. Maybe it had just been a one-night stand and Banks already had a lover up in Eastvale.

Putting aside her thoughts, and her memories of the previous night, Michelle got down to work. She had a couple of things to do before Graham Marshall's funeral service that afternoon, including tracking down Jet Harris's wife and ringing Dr Cooper. But before she could pick up the telephone, Dr Cooper rang *her*.

'Dr Cooper. I was going to ring you this morning,' said Michelle. 'Any news?'

'Sorry it took me so long to get the information you wanted, but I told you Hilary Wendell's a tough man to track down.'

'You've got something?'

'Hilary has. He won't commit himself to this abso-

lutely, so he'd be very unwilling to testify if it ever came
to a court case.'

'It probably won't,' said Michelle, 'but the information
might be useful to me.'

'Well, from careful measurement of the nick on the
underside of the rib, he's made a few projections and he's
pretty certain it's a military knife of some kind. His
money's on a Fairbairn–Sykes.'

'What's that?'

'British commando knife. Introduced in 1940. Seven-
inch, double-edged blade. Stiletto point.'

'A commando knife?'

'Yes. Is that of any use?'

'It might be,' said Michelle. 'Thanks a lot.'

'You're welcome.'

'And please thank Dr Wendell from me.'

'Will do.'

A *commando knife*. In 1965 the war had only been over
for twenty years and plenty of men in their early forties
would have fought in it, and had access to such a knife.
What worried Michelle most of all, though, was that the
only person she *knew* had served as a Royal Marines
Commando was Jet Harris; she remembered it from the
brief biography she had read when she first came to
Thorpe Wood. He had also been awarded a Distinguished
Conduct Medal.

The thought of it sent shivers up her spine: Jet Harris,
himself, as killer, misdirecting the investigation at every
turn, away from Bradford, perhaps because of Fiorino, as
Banks had suggested, and away from himself. This was
one theory she certainly couldn't go to Shaw with, or to
anyone else in the division either. Harris was a local hero
and she'd need a hell of a lot of hard evidence if she

expected anyone to entertain even the remotest suspicion that Jet Harris was a murderer.

After he'd been in about an hour, Banks poked his head out of the interview-room door, no doubt looking to see if Shaw was around, then carried one of the books over to Michelle.

'I think that's him,' he said.

Michelle looked at the photo. The man was in his late twenties, with medium-length brown hair, badly cut, a stocky build, piggy eyes, and a pug nose. His name was Des Wayman, and according to his record he had been in and out of the courts ever since his days as juvenile car thief, progressing from that to public disorder offences and GBH. His most recent incarceration, a lenient nine months, was for receiving stolen goods, and he had been out just over a year and a half.

'What next?' Banks asked.

'I'll go and have a word with him.'

'Want me to come along?'

'No. I think it would work better if I could question him without you there. After all, it might come to an identity parade. If any charges are brought, I want to make sure this is done right.'

'Fair enough,' said Banks. 'But he looks like a tough customer.' He rubbed his jaw. 'Feels like one, too.'

Michelle tapped her pen against her lips and looked across the office, where DC Collins sat talking on the phone, shirtsleeves rolled up, scribbling on the pad in front of him. She hadn't let him in on her suspicions about Shaw and Harris. Could she trust him? He was almost as new as she was, for a start, and that went in his favour. She had never seen him hanging around with Shaw or with any of the other old brigade, either, another plus. In the end, she decided she *had* to trust someone, and Collins was it.

'I'll take DC Collins,' she said, then lowered her voice. 'Look, there's a couple of things I need to talk to you about, but not here.'

'After the funeral this afternoon?'

'Okay,' said Michelle, jotting Des Wayman's address down in her notebook. 'I should know a bit more about Mr Wayman's activities by then. Oh, and guess where he lives?'

'Where?'

'The Hazels.'

•

Annie pored over Luke Armitage's notebooks and computer files in her office that morning. At least she felt a bit better, despite a poor night's sleep. Eventually, the painkillers had kicked in and she woke up at half-past seven in the morning, not even having got around to putting in the second *Doctor Zhivago* tape. This morning, though her jaw was still throbbing a bit, it didn't hurt anywhere near as much as it had.

The one thing that intrigued her about Luke's jottings was the increasing eroticism mixed in with the vague classical references to Persephone, Psyche and Ophelia. Then she remembered that Ophelia wasn't a character from classical mythology, but Hamlet's girlfriend, driven mad by his violent rejection of her. She remembered studying the play at school and finding it rather too long and dense for her taste at the time. She had seen several film versions since then, including one with Mel Gibson as Hamlet and another with Marianne Faithfull as Ophelia, and she remembered from somewhere the image of Ophelia floating down a river surrounded by flowers. Did Luke feel guilty about rejecting someone, then? Had he been killed out of revenge, by 'a woman scorned'? And if so, who? Liz Palmer? Lauren Anderson? Rose Barlow?

Of course, the repeated references to 'sweet white breasts', 'pale cheeks' and 'soft white thighs' in Luke's fragments of songs and poems could have been mere adolescent fantasy. Luke certainly had a romantic imagination and, if Banks were to be believed, adolescent boys thought of nothing but sex. But they could also point to the fact that Luke had been involved in a sexual relationship. Liz Palmer looked a likely candidate, despite her denials. Annie also shouldn't forget that according to the head teacher's daughter, Rose Barlow, there might have been something going on between Luke and Lauren Anderson. Rose was unreliable, but it might be worth talking to Lauren again if she got nowhere with Liz and Ryan. Rose had been involved with Luke, in however slight a way, and she had no doubt felt jilted when he spent more time with Liz or Lauren. Or was there someone else Annie was overlooking, some connection she was missing? She felt that she was, but no matter how she tried, the missing link still eluded her.

Her phone rang just as she was turning off Luke's computer.

'Annie, it's Stefan Nowak. Don't get your hopes up too high, but I might have a bit of good news for you.'

'Do tell. I could do with some good news round about now.'

'The lab hasn't finished trying to match your DNA samples with the blood on the drystone wall yet, so I can't tell you about that, but my team *did* find blood at the flat.'

'Liz Palmer's flat?'

'Yes.'

'How much?'

'Only a small amount.'

'Where?'

'Not where you'd expect. Smeared under the bathroom sink.'

'As if someone gripped it while leaning over?'

'Could be, yes. But there are no prints or anything, just a small smear of blood.'

'Is it enough for analysis?'

'Oh, yes. We're working on it now. All the lab has been able to tell me so far is that it matches Luke Armitage's blood type and that it doesn't match the samples we took from Liz Palmer or Ryan Milne.'

'But that's fantastic, Stefan! Don't you see? It puts Luke Armitage bleeding in Liz Palmer's flat.'

'Maybe. But it won't tell you *when*.'

'For the moment, I'll take what I can get. At least that gives me some leverage in the next interview.'

'There's more.'

'What?'

'I've just been talking to Dr Glendenning, and he tells me the tox screen on Luke shows an unusually large amount of diazepam.'

'Diazepam? That's Valium, isn't it?'

'That's one name for it. There are many. But the point is that it was mostly undigested.'

'So he died very soon after taking it, and his system didn't have time to digest it?'

'Yes.'

'But it's not the cause of death?'

'No way.'

'Would it have been enough to kill him?'

'Probably not.'

'Anything else?'

'In the flat? Yes. Drugs. Some marijuana, LSD, Ecstasy.'

'Dealing?'

'No. Not enough. Just for personal use, I'd say. And no diazepam.'

'Thanks, Stefan. Thanks a lot.'

Annie hung up and pondered what she had just heard. Luke had bled in Liz and Ryan's flat, and he had undigested diazepam in his system. Where did he get it? She didn't remember anything about medication in the information they'd gathered on him. She wasn't even sure that doctors prescribed diazepam to someone that young. She should at least check with Robin. Even though Stefan's team hadn't found any in the flat, the first thing to do, Annie thought, getting to her feet and reaching for her jacket, was to find out if either Liz or Ryan had prescriptions for diazepam.

•

According to his file, Des Wayman lived in a two-bedroom council house on Hazel Way, just off the crescent at the Wilmer Road end of the estate. It was mid-morning when Michelle and DC Collins parked outside and walked down the path. The sky was covered in grey cloud and the air was so saturated with moisture it felt like warm drizzle. Michelle's clothes were sticking to her, and DC Collins had taken off his suit jacket and loosened his tie. Even so, there were damp patches under his arms. She was glad Collins was with her. He played second row for the police rugby team, and his solid presence was enough to put anyone off trying anything. As far as Michelle could make out, nobody had followed them, and she hadn't seen any beige vans in the area.

Michelle knocked at the scratched red door of Number 15. The man who opened it seemed surprised to see her. It was Des Wayman, no doubt about it. The pug nose gave him away, and the piggy eyes. He was wearing grubby jeans, with his shirt hanging out.

'Who are you? I thought it was a mate of mine,' he said, with a leer. 'I'm off out. But seeing as you're here, how about coming with us for a drink?'

Michelle showed her warrant card and DC Collins followed suit. The man's expression became wary.

'Mr Wayman?' Michelle said.

'And what if it is?'

'We'd like a word, sir. Mind if we come in?'

'Like I said, I'm just on my way out. Can't we talk down the pub?' He licked his lips and nodded towards the pub at the bottom of the street, the Lord Nelson. Then he looked at Collins. 'And you can leave your chaperon behind.'

'It'd be better here, sir,' Michelle insisted. When Wayman made no move, she walked past him into the house. He stood and looked at her for a moment, then followed her into his living room, DC Collins right behind him.

The place was a tip, to put it mildly. Empty beer cans littered the floor, along with overflowing ashtrays. The heavy curtains were closed, allowing just enough light to illuminate the mess. The medley of smells was hard to define. Accumulated dust, stale beer and smoke, with overtones of used socks and sweat. But there was more: something vaguely sexual that turned Michelle's stomach. She flung the curtains open and opened the window. The latter took a bit of doing, as it hadn't been opened in a long time and had jammed. DC Collins lent a hand, and the two of them finally got it open. The still, humid air outside didn't help much, and the room looked even worse in full light.

'What are you doing?' Wayman protested. 'I value my privacy. I don't want the whole fucking estate looking through my window.'

'We value our health, Mr Wayman,' Michelle said. 'It's already at risk just by being here, but a little fresh air might help.'

'Sarky bitch,' said Wayman, sitting down on a worn and stained sofa. 'Get to the point, then, love.' He picked up a can of beer from the table and ripped the tab. Foam spilled over the top and he licked it off before it fell to the floor.

Michelle looked around and saw no surface she felt comfortable sitting on, so she stood. By the window. 'First off, don't call me "love",' she said, 'and second, you're in a bit of trouble, Des.'

'What's new? You lot are always trying to fit me up.'

'This isn't a fit-up,' said Michelle, aware of DC Collins paying careful attention to her. She hadn't explained much to him in the car; all she had said was not to take notes. He hadn't a clue what this was all about, or how it linked to the Graham Marshall case. 'It's cut and dried.'

Wayman folded his arms. 'So tell me what I'm supposed to have done.'

'Last night at approximately ten fifty-five, you and another man assaulted a man outside a riverside flat.'

'I did no such thing,' said Wayman.

'Des,' Michelle said, leaning forward. 'He saw you. He picked you out of the villains' album.'

That seemed to stop him for a moment. He frowned, and she could almost see the wheels spinning, cogs turning in his addled brain, looking for a way out, an explanation. 'He must be mistaken,' he said. 'His word against mine.'

Michelle laughed. 'Is that the best you can do?'

'His word against mine.'

'Where were you?'

'Matter of fact, I was having a bevvy or two in the Pig and Whistle.'

'Anyone see you?'

'Lots of people. It was very busy.'

'That's not far away from where the attack took place,' said Michelle. 'What time did you leave?'

'Dunno. After closing time.'

'Sure you didn't sneak out a few minutes early and then go back for last orders?'

'And waste good drinking time? Why would I do that?'

'That's what I'm trying to find out.'

'Not me, Miss.'

'Show me your hands, Des.'

Wayman stretched his hands out, palms up.

'Turn them over.'

Wayman did as she asked.

'Where'd you get that skinned knuckle?'

'I don't know,' said Wayman. 'Must have brushed it against the wall or something.'

'And that ring you've got,' Michelle went on. 'Sharp, I'll bet. Sharp enough to cut someone. I bet there'll still be traces of blood on the metal,' she said. 'Enough to identify as your victim's.'

Wayman lit a cigarette and fell silent. Even with the window open the air soon became thick with smoke.

'Right,' said Michelle, 'I'm sick of pissing about. DC Collins, let's take Mr Wayman down the station and organize an identity parade. That should settle things once and for all.'

Collins moved forward.

'Just a minute,' said Wayman. 'I'm not going to no station. I've got an appointment. People are expecting me.'

'In your local. I know. But if you want to enjoy a nice pint this lunchtime, or any lunchtime for the next little while, you'd better tell us what we want to know.'

'But I've already told you. I didn't do anything.'

'And I've told you you were identified. Stop lying, Des. Do yourself a favour. Think about that nice, thirst-quenching pint sitting there on the bar at the Lord Nelson, just waiting for you.' Michelle paused to let the image sink in. She could do with a pint, herself, even though she rarely drank beer. The air was fast becoming unbreathable, and she didn't know if she could stand it much longer. She had one last card to play before she would have to take Wayman in. 'Trouble is, Des,' she said, 'the man you attacked, the man who recognized you . . .'

'Yeah? What about him?'

'He's a copper. He's one of us.'

'Come off it. You're trying it on. Trying to fit me up.'

'No. It's true. What was it you said earlier? His word against yours? Whose word do you think the judge is going to believe, Des?'

'Nobody told me—'

'Told you what?'

'Shut up. I've got to think.'

'You've not got long. Assaulting a police officer. That's a serious charge. You'll go down for a lot longer than nine months on that one.'

Wayman dropped his cigarette stub in the empty beer can, tossed it on the floor and opened another one. His fleshy lips were wet with foam and beer. He reached for another cigarette.

'Please don't light another one of those, Des,' Michelle said.

'What do you mean? Surely it's not got so bad a bloke can't even smoke in his own house these days?'

'When we're gone you can smoke yourself silly,' said Michelle. 'That's if we leave without you. Up to you. There's no smoking in the holding cells any more.'

Wayman laughed. 'You know,' he said, puffing out his chest, 'I'm practically one of you lot, myself. I don't know where you get off coming and pinning this assault on me when it's police business to start with.'

Michelle felt a little shiver up her spine. 'What are you talking about?'

'You know damn well what I'm talking about.' Wayman touched the side of his pug nose. 'I told you, I was on police business. Undercover. Sometimes a little tap on the head and a few words of warning work wonders. It's the way they used to do things in the old days, so I hear. And don't tell me you don't know what I'm talking about. Your boss certainly does.'

'Boss?'

'Yes. The big ugly bloke. *Numero uno*. Detective bloody Superintendent Ben Shaw.'

'*Shaw?*' Michelle had been more than half-suspecting that Shaw was behind the attacks on her and Banks, but found herself stunned to have it confirmed.

Wayman tilted the can and took a long swig, then he wiped his mouth with the back of his hand and grinned. 'Don't look so surprised, love.'

'Superintendent Shaw told you to do this? Wait a minute. Are you telling me you're an undercover police officer following Detective Superintendent Shaw's orders?'

Wayman shrugged, perhaps sensing he'd gone too far. 'Well, maybe I'm not exactly what you'd call an under-cover officer, but I've done your boss a little favour from time to time. You know, like giving him the nod where the stuff from the Curry's warehouse job was stashed. That sort of thing.'

'So you're Shaw's snitch?'

'I've been happy to help out now and then. He'll see me all right. So do us a favour and bugger off, then just maybe I won't tell your boss you've been round upsetting me.'

'Do you own a beige van?' Michelle asked.

'What? I don't own a van at all. Dark blue Corsa, if you must know.'

'Ever done time for burglary?'

'You've read my form. Did you notice anything about burglary?'

Michelle hadn't. So Wayman most likely wasn't respon-sible for the damage to her flat and the attempt on her life. Somehow, she sensed he didn't have the subtlety to do what had been done with the dress, even if his employer had told him about Melissa. He clearly wasn't the only vil-lain on Shaw's payroll. Michelle sensed DC Collins paying rapt attention beside her. She glanced at him and he raised his eyebrows. 'Look,' she said, wishing she could sit down. Her shoes were killing her. But it wasn't worth catching something. 'You're in a lot of trouble, Des. GBH is bad enough in itself, but against a copper, well . . . you don't need me to tell you . . .'

For the first time, Wayman looked worried. 'But I

didn't know he was a copper, did I? Do you think I'd have done something like that if I'd known who he was? You must think I'm crazy.'

'But you did it, didn't you?'

'Where's this going?'

'Up to you, Des.'

'What do you mean?'

Michelle spread her hands. 'I mean it's up to you where it goes from here. It could go to the station, to the lawyers, to court eventually. Or it could end here.'

Wayman swallowed. 'End? How? I mean . . . I don't . . .'

'Do I have to spell it out?'

'You promise?'

'Only if you tell me what I want to know.'

'It goes no further?'

Michelle looked at DC Collins, who looked lost. 'No,' she said. 'This bloke you and your friend assaulted last night, what did Shaw tell you about him?'

'That he was a small-time villain from up north looking to get himself established on our patch.'

'And what did Detective Superintendent Shaw ask you to do?'

'Nip it in the bud.'

'Can you be more specific?'

'Shaw didn't want to know. I mean, he'd just asked me to handle the situation, do something about it. He didn't tell me how, and he didn't want to know.'

'But it usually meant violence?'

'Most people understand a thump on the nose.'

'That's your understanding of the situation?'

'If you like.'

'So that's what you did?'

'Yes.'

'How did you find out he was in town?'

'I've been keeping an eye out. I recognized his car from when he was down here last week.'

'And how did you know where he was that evening?'

'I got a call on my mobile in the Pig and Whistle.'

'From who?'

'Who do you think?'

'Go on.'

'He said our mutual friend was drinking in a pub down the street, and if an opportunity presented itself . . . well, I was to have a quiet word, like.'

'But how did he . . . Never mind.' Michelle realized that Shaw must have been using his whole network of informers to keep an eye on the comings and goings in the Graham Marshall investigation. But why? To hide the truth, that the great local hero Jet Harris was a murderer?

'So what did you do?'

'We waited outside and followed the two of you back to the riverside flats. We were a bit worried because we thought he might be going in to get his end away, like, no disrespect, and we might not get back to the Pig and Whistle till they'd stopped serving, so it was all sweetness and joy when he came straight down those stairs and into the street. We didn't muck about.'

'And the beating was your idea?'

'Like I said, it gets the point across. Anyway, we wouldn't have hurt him too much. We didn't even get a chance to finish. Some interfering bastard walking his dog started making a lot of noise. Not that we couldn't have dealt with him, too, but the bloody dog was waking the whole street up.'

'And that's everything?' Michelle asked.

'Scout's honour.'

'When were you ever a scout?'

'Boys' Brigade, as a matter of fact. What's going to happen now? Remember what you promised.'

Michelle looked at DC Collins. 'What's going to happen now,' she said, 'is that we're going to go away, and you're going to the Lord Nelson to drink yourself into a stupor. And if you ever cross my path again, I'll make sure they put you somewhere that'll make the Middle East look like an alcoholic's paradise. That clear?'

'Yes, ma'am.' But Wayman was smiling. The prospect of a drink in the present, Michelle thought, by far outdid any fears for the future. He wouldn't change.

'Do you think you can tell me what all that was about?' asked DC Collins when they got outside.

Michelle took a deep breath and smiled. 'Yes,' she said. 'Of course, Nat. I'm sorry for keeping you in the dark so long, but I think you'll understand when you hear what I have to say. And I'll tell you over a pie and a pint. My treat.' She looked around. 'But not in the Lord Nelson.'

17

'**Glad you could come**, Alan,' said Mrs Marshall, sticking out her black-gloved hand. 'My, my. You've been in the wars.'

Banks touched his lip. 'It's nothing,' he said.

'I hope you'll come back to the house for drinks and sandwiches.'

They were standing outside the chapel in the light drizzle after Graham's funeral. It had been tasteful enough, as such things went, Banks thought, though there was something odd about a funeral service for someone who has been dead over thirty years. They had the usual readings, including the 23rd Psalm, and Graham's sister gave a short eulogy throughout which she verged on tears.

'Of course,' Banks said, shaking Mrs Marshall's hand. Then he saw Michelle walking down the path under her umbrella. 'Excuse me a moment.'

He hurried along after Michelle. During the service, he had caught her eye once or twice and she had looked away. He wanted to know what was wrong. She had said earlier that she wanted to talk to him. Was it about last night? Was she having regrets? Did she want to tell him she'd made a mistake and didn't want to see him again? 'Michelle?' He put his hand gently on her shoulder.

Michelle turned to face him. When she looked him in the eye, she smiled and lifted the umbrella so it covered his head too. 'Shall we walk a while?'

'Fine,' said Banks. 'Everything okay?'

'Of course it is. Why do you ask?'

So there was nothing wrong. Banks could have kicked himself. He'd got so used to feeling that his every move, every meeting, was so fragile, partly because they *had* been – like walking on eggs – with Annie, that he was turning normal behaviour into perceived slights. They were police officers in public – in a bloody chapel, for crying out loud. What did he expect her to do? Make doe eyes at him? Walk over to his pew and sit on his knee and whisper sweet nothings in his ear?

'This morning, in the station, I wanted to tell you that I enjoyed last night, but I could hardly say that in the cop shop, could I?'

She reached over and touched his sore lip. 'I enjoyed it, too.'

'Are you coming back to the house?'

'No, I don't think so. I don't like that sort of thing.'

'Me neither. I'd better go, though.'

'Of course.'

They walked down one of the narrow gravel paths between graves, carved headstones dark with rain. Yews overhung the path and rain dripped from their leaves onto the umbrella, tapping harder than the drizzle. 'You said you wanted to talk to me.'

'Yes.' Michelle told him about Dr Wendell's tentative identification of the Fairbairn-Sykes commando knife and Harris's wartime record.

Banks whistled between his teeth. 'And you say Jet Harris was a commando?'

'Yes.'

'Bloody hell. That's a real can of worms.' Banks shook his head. 'It's hard to believe that Jet Harris might have killed Graham,' he said. 'It just doesn't make any sense. I mean, what possible motive could he have had?'

'I don't know. Only what we speculated about yesterday, that he was somehow connected with Fiorino and the porn racket and Graham fell foul of them. Even so, it's hard to imagine someone in Harris's position doing a job like that himself. And we don't really have any hard evidence; it's all just circumstantial. Anyway, he's not the only candidate. I remembered Mrs Walker – you know, the woman in the newsagent's – said something about Donald Bradford being in a special unit in Burma. I checked. Turns out it was a commando unit.'

'Bradford, too? That complicates things.'

'Well, at least we know that Bradford had some sort of involvement with pornography. We don't even have any evidence that Harris was bent yet,' said Michelle. 'Only Shaw's behaviour. Which brings me to our interview with Des Wayman.'

'What did he have to say for himself?'

Michelle told him about Wayman's assertion that Shaw was behind last night's attack. 'He'd deny he ever said it if we challenged him, and I'm sure Shaw will deny it, too.'

'But *we* know it's true,' said Banks. 'That gives us an edge. It was a stupid move on Shaw's part. It means he's worried, getting desperate. What about the burglary at your flat and the van that tried to run you down?'

Michelle shook her head. 'Wayman knows nothing about them. Shaw must have got someone else, maybe someone a bit brighter. My impression is that Wayman is okay for the strong-arm stuff but couldn't think his way out of a paper bag.'

'Like Bill Marshall?'

'Yes.'

'You think we should have a chat with Shaw?'

'Soon. It'd be nice to know a bit more about Harris first.'

'I'll call you later.'

'Okay.' Michelle turned and carried on walking down the path.

'Where are you going now?' Banks asked.

She slowed, turned and smiled at him. 'You're a very nosy fellow,' she said. 'And you know what happens to nosy fellows, don't you?' Then she walked on, leaving Banks to gape after her. He could swear he saw her shoulders shaking with laughter.

•

'Okay, Liz, are you going to tell us the truth now?' Annie asked once the interview room was set up and the tapes turned on.

'We didn't do anything wrong, Ryan and me,' Liz said.

'I have to remind you that you're entitled to a lawyer. If you can't afford one we'll get a duty solicitor for you.'

Liz shook her head. 'I don't need a lawyer. That's like admitting I did it.'

'As you like. You know we found drugs in your flat, don't you?'

'There wasn't much. It was only . . . you know, for Ryan and me.'

'It's still a crime.'

'Are you going to arrest us for that?'

'Depends on what you have to tell me. I just want you to know that you're in trouble already. You can make it better by telling me the truth, or you can make it worse by continuing with your lies. What's it to be, Liz?'

'I'm tired.'

'The sooner we're done with this, the sooner you can go home. What's it to be?'

Liz nibbled at her trembling lower lip.

'Maybe it would help,' said Annie, 'if I told you we found traces of Luke's blood under your bathroom sink.'

Liz looked at her, wide-eyed. 'But we didn't kill Luke. Honest we didn't!'

'Tell me what happened. Convince me.'

Liz started crying. Annie passed her some tissues and waited till she calmed down. 'Did Luke call at your flat the day he disappeared?' she asked.

After a long silence, Liz said, 'Yes.'

'Good,' breathed Annie. 'Now we're getting somewhere.'

'But we didn't do him any harm.'

'Okay. We'll get to that. What time did he arrive?'

'Time? I don't know. Early in the evening. Maybe six-ish.'

'So he must have come straight from the market square?'

'I suppose so. I don't know where he'd been. He was a bit upset, I remember, because he said some of the kids from the school had pushed him around in the square, so maybe he *had* come straight from there.'

'What happened in the flat?'

Liz looked down at her chewed fingernails.

'Liz?'

'What?'

'Was Ryan there?'

'Yes.'

'All the time? Even when Luke arrived?'

'Yes.'

So that put paid to Annie's theory that Ryan had

interrupted something between Liz and Luke. 'What did the three of you do?'

Liz paused, then took a deep breath. 'First we had something to eat,' she said. 'It must've been around teatime.'

'Then what?'

'We just talked, went through a few songs.'

'I thought you did your rehearsals in the church basement.'

'We do. But Ryan's got an acoustic guitar. We just played around with a couple of arrangements, that's all.'

'And then?'

Again, Liz fell silent and her eyes filled with tears. She rubbed the back of her hand across her face and said, 'Ryan rolled a joint. Luke . . . he'd . . . like he was a virgin, you know, when it came to drugs. I mean we'd offered to share before but he always said no.'

'Not that night?'

'No. That night he said yes. The first time. It was like he . . . you know . . . *wanted* to lose his virginity. I don't know why. I suppose he just felt it was time.'

'What happened?'

'Nothing much at first. I think he was disappointed. A lot of people are the first time.'

'So what did you do?'

'We smoked some more and it seemed to work. It was pretty strong stuff, opiated hash. He got all giggly at first, then he went sort of introspective.'

'So what went wrong?'

'It was when Ryan put that Neil Byrd CD on. You know, that new compilation, *The Summer that Never Was*.'

'He did *what*?' Annie could imagine what effect something like that might have on Luke if he was under the influence of strong cannabis. Maybe it wasn't a seriously dangerous drug, but it could cause paranoia in people, and it intensified and exaggerated emotions. Annie knew; she'd smoked it more than once in her teenage years. Reining in her temper, she asked, 'How did Luke react to the music?'

'He freaked. He just freaked. Ryan was thinking it would be a neat idea to do a Neil Byrd song, you know, with Luke singing. I mean, it'd get a lot of attention.'

'Didn't you realize how confused Luke was about his real father? Didn't you know he *never* listened to Neil Byrd's music?'

'Yes, but we thought this was a good time to try it,' Liz protested. 'We thought his mind was, you know, open to new things, mellow from the dope, that it was more likely he'd see how *beautiful* his father's work was.'

'When he was disoriented, ultra-sensitive?' Annie shook her head in disbelief. 'You're a lot more stupid than I thought you were. Stupid or so selfish and blinkered it amounts to much the same thing.'

'But that's not fair! We didn't mean any harm.'

'Fine,' said Annie. 'Let's just say you were guilty of poor judgement and move on. What happened next?'

'Nothing at first. It seemed as if Luke was just listening to the song. Ryan was playing the chords along with it, trying a little harmony. All of a sudden Luke just went crazy. He knocked the guitar out of Ryan's hand and went over to the CD player and took the CD out and started trying to break it in two.'

'What did you do?'

'Ryan struggled with him, but Luke was, like, *possessed*.'

'What about the blood?'

'In the end Ryan just punched him. That was where the blood came from. Luke ran into the bathroom. I was just behind him, to see if he was all right. There wasn't much blood, it was only like a nosebleed. Luke looked in the mirror and started going crazy again and banging the mirror with his fists. I tried to calm him down, but he pushed past me and left.'

'And that was it?'

'Yes.'

'Neither of you went after him?'

'No. We figured he just wanted to be by himself.'

'A disturbed fifteen-year-old having a bad drug experience? Oh, come on, Liz. Surely you can't be *that* stupid?'

'Well, *we* were stoned, too. I'm not saying we were, like, the most *rational* we could be. It just seemed . . . I don't know.' She lowered her head and sobbed.

Though she believed Liz's story, Annie found it hard to dredge up any sympathy. Legally, however, any charges that could be brought against them were minor. If reckless negligence could be proven, then they could, at a stretch, be convicted of manslaughter, but even though they had given Luke drugs, Annie reminded herself, she still didn't know how he had died, or why.

'Do you know where he went after he left your flat?' Annie asked.

'No,' said Liz between sobs. 'We never saw him again. I'm sorry. I'm so sorry.'

'Did you or Ryan give Luke any Valium, to calm him down, perhaps?'

Liz frowned and looked at Annie through her tears. 'No. We didn't do stuff like that.'

'So you never had any Valium in the house?'

'No.'

'And there's nothing more you can tell me?'

'I've told you everything.' She looked up at Annie with red eyes. 'Can I go home now? I'm tired.'

Annie stood up and called for a uniformed officer. 'Yes,' she said. 'But don't wander too far. We'll be wanting to talk to you again.'

When Liz had been escorted away, Annie closed the interview-room door behind her and sat down again and held her throbbing head in her hands.

•

'Another drink, Alan?'

Banks's beer glass was half full, and he had just arranged to go out drinking that evening with Dave Grenfell and Paul Major, so he declined Mrs Marshall's offer and ate another potted meat sandwich instead. Besides, the beer was a neighbour's home brew and it tasted like it.

'You know, I'm glad we did this,' Mrs Marshall went on. 'The service. I know it probably seems silly to some people, after all this time, but it means a lot to me.'

'It doesn't seem silly,' said Banks, looking around the room. Most of the guests were family and neighbours, some of whom Banks recognized. Dave's and Paul's parents were there, along with Banks's own. Pachelbel's 'Canon' played in the background. Graham would have hated it, Banks thought. Or probably not. If he'd lived, his tastes would no doubt have changed, as Banks's had. Even so, what he really wanted to listen to was 'Ticket to Ride' or 'Summer Nights' or 'Mr Tambourine Man'.

'I think it meant a lot to all of us,' he said.

'Thank you,' Mrs Marshall said tearfully. 'Are you sure you won't have some more?'

'No, thank you.'

Mrs Marshall wandered off. Banks noticed Bill Marshall in his armchair by the fireplace, a blanket over his knees despite the muggy day. The windows were all open, but it was still too stuffy in the house. Banks saw Paul talking to a couple he didn't recognize, probably old neighbours, and Dave was chatting with Graham's sister, Joan. His own parents were talking to Mr and Mrs Grenfell. Feeling the call of nature, Banks set his glass down on the sideboard and went upstairs.

When he had finished in the toilet, he noticed that the door to Graham's old room was open, and he was surprised to see that the space-rocket wallpaper he remembered from years back was still on the walls. Drawn by the odd sight, he wandered into the small bedroom. Of course, everything else had changed. The bed had gone, along with the small glass-fronted bookcase Banks remembered, mostly full of science fiction. The only familiar object stood in a case leaning against the wall. Graham's guitar. So they had kept it all these years.

Certain that no one would mind, Banks sat down on a hard-backed chair and took the guitar out of its case. Graham had been so proud of it, he remembered. Of course, he had wanted an electric one, a Rickenbacker like the one John Lennon played, but he had been chuffed to death with the second-hand acoustic his parents had bought him for Christmas 1964.

Banks remembered the fingering, even after so long, and strummed a C chord. Way out of tune. He grimaced. Tuning it would be too much of a job for the moment. He wondered if Mrs Marshall wanted to keep it as a memento, or if she would consider selling it. If she would, he'd be glad to buy it from her. He strummed an out-of-tune G seventh, then moved to put the guitar back in its case. As he did so, he thought he heard something slip around inside it. Gently, he shook the guitar, and there it was again: something scraping inside.

Curious, Banks loosened the strings so that he could slip his hand inside. With a bit of juggling and shaking he managed to grab hold of what felt like a piece of stiff, rolled-up paper. Carefully, he pulled it out, noticing the dried Sellotape Graham had used to stick it to the inside of the guitar. That made it something he had tried to hide.

And when Banks unrolled it, he saw why.

It was a photograph: Graham sprawled on a sheepskin rug in front of a large, ornate fireplace, arms behind him, hands propping him up, legs stretched out in front. He was smiling at the camera in a flirtatious and knowing manner.

And he was absolutely stark naked.

•

Michelle was lucky to find a parking spot about a hundred yards from the former Mrs Harris's pretentious pile of mock Tudor on Long Road, Cambridge, opposite the grounds of Long Road Sixth Form College. It was still drizzling outside, so she took the umbrella from the back of her car.

It hadn't been too hard to track down Jet Harris's ex-wife. The biographical pamphlet told Michelle that her maiden name was Edith Dalton and that she had been married to Harris for twenty-three years, between 1950 and 1973, and that she was ten years his junior. A few discreet enquiries around the office yielded the information that a retired civilian employee, Margery Jenkins, visited her occasionally, and she was happy to give Michelle the address. She also told her that the former Mrs Harris had remarried and was now called Mrs Gifford. Michelle hoped that the nature of her enquiries didn't get back to Shaw before she got the information she needed, whatever that was. She wasn't even sure what Mrs Gifford could, or would, tell her.

A slim, elegantly dressed, grey-haired woman answered the door, and Michelle introduced herself. With a puzzled but interested expression, Mrs Gifford led Michelle to her large living room. There was no clutter, just a white three-piece suite, various antique cabinets stuffed with crystal and a large sideboard against the wall. Mrs Gifford offered nothing in the way of refreshments but sat, legs crossed, and lit a cigarette from a gold lighter. She had a calculating look about her, Michelle noticed, around the eyes, in the eyes themselves, in the strict set of her jaw and sharp angles of her cheeks. She was also very well preserved for her seventy-plus years and had a deep tan, the sort she couldn't have got in England so far this summer.

'The Algarve,' she said, as if she had noticed Michelle looking. 'Got back last week. My husband and I have a nice little villa there. He was a doctor, a plastic surgeon, but he's retired now, of course. Anyway, what can I do for you? It's been a long time since the coppers came to call.'

So Edith Dalton had landed on her feet after twenty-three years of marriage to Jet Harris. 'Just information,' said Michelle. 'You've heard about the Graham Marshall case?'

'Yes. Poor lad.' Mrs Gifford tapped her cigarette against the side of a glass ashtray. 'What about him?'

'Your husband was in charge of that investigation.'

'I remember.'

'Did he ever talk about it, tell you any of his theories?'

'John never talked about his work to me.'

'But something like that? A local boy. Surely you must have been curious?'

'Naturally. But he made a point of not discussing his cases at home.'

'So he didn't have any theories?'

'Not that he shared with me.'

'Do you remember Ben Shaw?'

'Ben? Of course. He worked closely with John.' She smiled. 'Regan and Carter they used to think of themselves. *The Sweeney*. Quite the lads. How is Ben? I haven't seen him for years.'

'What did you think of him?'

Her eyes narrowed. 'As a man or as a copper?'

'Both. Either.'

Mrs Gifford flicked some ash. 'Not much, if truth be told. Ben Shaw rode on John's coat-tails, but he wasn't half the man. Or a quarter the copper.'

'His notebooks covering the Graham Marshall case are missing.'

Mrs Gifford raised a finely pencilled eyebrow. 'Well, things do have a habit of disappearing over time.'

'It just seems a bit of a coincidence.'

'Coincidences do happen.'

'I was just wondering if you knew anything about Shaw, that's all.'

'Like what? Are you asking me if Ben Shaw is bent?'

'Is he?'

'I don't know. John certainly never said anything about it.'

'And he would have known?'

'Oh, yes.' She nodded. 'John would have known. Not much got by him.'

'So you never heard any rumours?'

'No.'

'I understand your husband was a commando during the war.'

'Yes. A real war hero, John was.'

'Do you know if he owned a Fairbairn–Sykes commando knife?'

'Not that I saw.'

'He didn't have any mementos?'

'He gave everything up when he was demobbed. He never talked about those days much. He just wanted to forget. Look, where is all this leading?'

Michelle didn't know how to come straight out with it and ask her if her ex-husband was bent, but she got the impression that Mrs Gifford was a hard one to deceive. 'You lived with Mr Harris for twenty-three years,' she said. 'Why leave after so long?'

Mrs Gifford raised her eyebrows. 'What an odd question. And a rather rude one, if I may say so.'

'I'm sorry, but—'

Mrs Gifford waved her cigarette in the air. 'Yes, yes, you've got your job to do. I know. It doesn't matter now, anyway. I waited until the children left home. It's amazing how much one will put up with for the sake of the children, and for appearances.'

'Put up with?'

'Marriage to John wasn't a bed of roses.'

'But there must have been some compensations.'

Mrs Gifford frowned. 'Compensations?'

'The high life.'

Mrs Gifford laughed. 'The high life? My dear, we lived in that poky little semi in Peterborough almost all our married life. I'd hardly call that the high life.'

'I don't know how to say this diplomatically,' Michelle went on.

'Then bugger diplomacy. I've always been one to face things head on. Come on, out with it.'

'But there seem to be some anomalies in the original investigation into the Graham Marshall disappearance. Things seem to have been steered in one direction, away from other possibilities, and—'

'And my John was the one doing the steering?'

'Well, he was senior investigating officer.'

'And you want to know if he was being paid off?'

'It looks that way. Do you remember Carlo Fiorino?'

'I've heard the name. A long time ago. Wasn't he shot in some drug war?'

'Yes, but before that he pretty much ran crime in the area.'

Mrs Gifford laughed. 'I'm sorry, dear,' she said, 'but the image of some sort of Mafia don running crime in sleepy old Peterborough is . . . well, to say the least, it's *ridiculous*.'

'He wasn't Mafia. Wasn't even Italian. He was the son of a POW and a local girl.'

'Even so, it still sounds absurd.'

'Where there are people, there's crime, Mrs Gifford. And Peterborough was growing fast. The new town expansion. There's nothing anyone likes better than a quickly expanding market. People want to gamble, they want sex, they want to feel safe. If someone supplies them with all these needs, there's quite a tidy profit to be made. And the job's made all the easier if you have a senior policeman in your pocket.' She didn't mean it to come out so bluntly, but she wanted to get Mrs Gifford to take her seriously.

'So you're saying John was on the take?'

'I'm asking you if you noticed anything that might indicate he was receiving extra money, yes.'

'Well, if he was, I never saw any of it. I can tell you that much.'

'So where did it all go? Wine, women and song?'

Mrs Gifford laughed again and stubbed out her cigarette. 'My dear,' she said, 'John was strictly an ale and whisky man. He also had a tin ear, and you can forget the women. I've not told anyone except my present husband this, but I'll tell you now, John Harris was queer as a three-pound note.'

•

'Another round?'

'My shout,' said Banks.

'I'll come with you.' Dave Grenfell got up and accompanied Banks to the bar. For old times' sake, they were in the Wheatsheaf, where the three of them had drunk their very first pints of beer at the age of sixteen. The place had been tarted up over the years, and now it seemed a lot more upmarket than the shabby Victorian backstreet boozer it had been all those years ago. Probably got the lunchtime crowd from the new 'business park' over the road, Banks guessed, though now, early in the evening, it was practically deserted.

Over the first pint, they had caught up with one another to the extent that Banks knew Dave, as his father had said, still worked as a mechanic in a garage in Dorchester and still lived with his first wife, Ellie, whereas Paul was cheerfully unemployed and gay as the day is long. Coming hot on the heels of hearing Mrs Gifford's revelations about Jet Harris over the phone from Michelle, this last discovery shocked Banks only because he had never spotted any signs of it back when they were kids. Not that he would have recognized them. Paul had seemed to leer over the porn just as much as the others, laugh at the jokes about poofs, and Banks was sure he remembered him having a steady girlfriend at one point.

Still, back in 1965 people denied, pretended, tried to 'pass' for straight. Even after legalization, there was so much stigma attached to it, especially on the more macho working-class estates where they had all lived. And in the police force. Banks wondered how hard it had been for Paul to come to terms with himself and come out. Clearly Jet Harris had never been able to do so. And Banks was willing to bet a pound to a penny that *someone* had known about it, and that someone had used the knowledge to advantage. Jet Harris hadn't been bent; he'd been blackmailed.

As Dave prattled on about how gobsmacked *he* was to find out Paul had turned into an 'arse-bandit', Banks's thoughts returned to the photo he had found in Graham's guitar. He hadn't told Mr or Mrs Marshall, hadn't told anyone except Michelle, over his mobile phone when he took the photo up to his room before meeting the others in the Wheatsheaf. What did it mean, and why was it there? Graham must have put it there, Banks assumed, and he had done so because he wanted to hide it. But why did he have it in his possession, why had he posed for it, who took it, and where was it taken? The fireplace looked distinctive enough. Adam, Banks guessed, and you didn't find those just anywhere.

Banks could begin to formulate a few answers to his questions, but he didn't have enough pieces yet to make a complete pattern. Two things he and Michelle had agreed on for certain during their phone conversation: the photo was in some way connected with Graham's murder, and Donald Bradford and Jet Harris were involved in whatever nasty business had been going on. Maybe Carlo Fiorino and Bill Marshall, too. But there were still a few pieces missing.

They carried the drinks back to the table, where Paul sat glancing around the room. 'Remember the old juke-box?' he said.

Banks nodded. The Wheatsheaf used to have a great jukebox for a provincial pub outside the city centre, he remembered, and they spent almost as much money on that as they did on beer. The sixties of familiar, if senti-mental, memory was in full bloom then, when they were sixteen: Procol Harum's 'A Whiter Shade of Pale', the Flowerpot Men singing 'Let's Go to San Francisco', the Beatles' 'Magical Mystery Tour'.

'What do you listen to now, Alan?' Dave asked Banks.

'Bit of everything, I suppose,' Banks said. 'Jazz, classical, some of the old rock stuff. You?'

'Nothing much. I sort of lost interest in music in the seventies, when we had the kids. Never really got it back. Remember Steve, though, the kind of stuff he used to make us listen to on Sunday afternoons? Dylan and all that.'

Banks laughed. 'He was ahead of his time, was Steve. Where the hell is he, anyway? Surely he must have heard, someone must have been in touch with him.'

'Hadn't you heard?' Paul said.

Banks and Dave both stared at him. 'What?'

'Shit. I thought you must know. I'm sorry. Steve's dead.'

Banks felt a shiver up his spine. *The Big Chill.* It was one thing to get to an age when the generation ahead started dying off, but another thing entirely to face the mortality of your own generation. 'What happened?' he asked.

'Lung cancer. About three years ago. I only know 'cos his mum and dad kept in touch with mine, like. Christmas cards, that sort of thing. I hadn't actually seen him for years. Apparently he had a couple of kids, too.'

'Poor sod,' said Dave.

After a brief silence, they raised their glasses and drank a toast to the memory of Steve, early Dylan fan. Then they toasted Graham again. Two down, three to go.

Banks looked closely at each of his old friends and saw that Dave had lost most of his hair and Paul was grey and had put on a lot of weight. He started to feel gloomy, and even the memory of Michelle naked beside him failed to dispel the gloom. His lip burned and his left side ached from where his assailant had kicked him. He felt like getting pissed, but he knew when he felt that way that it never worked. No matter how much he drank he never reached the state of oblivion he aimed for. Even so, he didn't have to watch what he drank. He wasn't driving anywhere that night. He had thought he might try to get in touch with Michelle later, depending on how the evening went, but they hadn't made any firm arrangements. Both needed time to absorb what had happened between them, Banks sensed. That was okay. He didn't feel that she was backing off or anything, no more than he was. Besides, she had a lot to do. Things were moving fast.

Banks looked at his cigarette smouldering in the ashtray and thought of Steve. Lung cancer. Shit. He reached forward and stubbed it out even though it was only half smoked. Maybe it would be his last. That thought made him feel a bit better, yet even that feeling was fast followed by a wave of sheer panic at how unbear-able his life would be without cigarettes. The coffee in the morning, a pint of beer in the Queen's Arms, that late evening Laphroaig out by the beck. Impossible. Well, he told himself, let's just take it a day at a time.

Banks's mobile rang, startling him out of his gloomy reverie. 'Sorry,' he said. 'I'd better take it. Might be important.'

He walked out into the street and sheltered from the rain under a shop awning. It was getting dark and there wasn't much traffic about. The road surface glistened in the lights of the occasional car, and puddles reflected the blue neon sign of a video rental shop across the street. 'Alan, it's Annie,' said the voice at the other end.

'Annie? What's happening?'

Annie told Banks about the Liz Palmer interview, and he could sense anger and sadness in her account.

'You think she's telling the truth?'

'Pretty certain,' said Annie. 'The Big Man interviewed Ryan Milne at the same time and the details check out. They haven't been allowed to get together and concoct a story since they've been in custody.'

'Okay,' said Banks. 'So where does that leave us?'

'With a distraught and disoriented Luke Armitage wandering off into the night alone,' Anne said. 'The thoughtless bastards.'

'So where did he go?'

'We don't know. It's back to the drawing board. There's just one thing . . .'

'Yes.'

'The undigested diazepam that Dr Glendenning found in Luke's system.'

'What about it?'

'Well, he didn't get it at Liz and Ryan's flat. Neither of them has a prescription and we didn't find any in our search.'

'They could have got it illegally, along with the cannabis and LSD, then got rid of it.'

'They could have,' said Annie. 'But why lie about it?'

'That I can't answer. What's your theory?'

'Well, if Luke was freaking out the way it seems he was, then someone might have thought it was a good idea to give him some Valium to calm him down.'

'Or to keep him quiet.'

'Possibly.'

'What next?'

'We need to find out where he went. I'm going to talk to Luke's parents again tomorrow. They might be able to help now we know a bit more about his movements. I'll be talking to Lauren Anderson, too, and perhaps Gavin Barlow.'

'Why?'

'Maybe there was still something going on between Luke and Rose, and maybe her father didn't approve.'

'Enough to kill him?'

'Enough to make it physical. We still can't say for certain that anyone *murdered* Luke. Anyway, I'd like to know where they both were the night Luke disappeared. Maybe it was Rose he went to see.'

'Fair enough,' said Banks. 'And don't forget that Martin Armitage was out and about that night, too.'

'Don't worry. I won't.'

'What's happened with him by the way?'

'He appeared before the magistrates this afternoon. He's out on bail till the preliminary hearing.'

'What about Norman Wells?'

'He'll mend. When will you be back?'

'Tomorrow or the day after.'

'Getting anywhere?'

'I think so.'

'And what are you up to tonight?'

'School reunion,' said Banks, walking back to the pub. An approaching car seemed to be going way too fast, and Banks felt a momentary rush of panic. He ducked into a shop doorway. The car sped by him, too close to the kerb, and splashed water from the gutter over his trouser bottoms. He cursed.

'What is it?' Annie asked.

Banks told her, and she laughed. 'Have a good time at your school reunion,' she said.

'I'll tell you all about it when I see you.' He ended the call and returned to his seat. Dave and Paul had been making uneasy small talk in his absence, and Dave seemed glad to see him come back.

'So you're a copper,' said Paul, shaking his head when Banks sat down again. 'I still can't get over it. If I'd had to guess, I'd have said you'd end up a teacher or a newspaper reporter or something like that. But a copper . . .'

Banks smiled. 'Funny how things turn out.'

'Very queer, indeed,' muttered Dave. His voice sounded as if the beer was having an early effect.

Paul gave him a sharp glance, then tapped Banks's arm. 'Hey,' he said, 'you'd have had to arrest me back then, wouldn't you? For being *queer*.'

Banks sensed the tension escalating and moved on to the subject he'd been wanting to talk about from the start: Graham. 'Do either of you remember anything odd happening around the time Graham disappeared?' he asked.

'You're not working on the case, are you?' asked Dave, eager to be given a change of subject.

'No,' said Banks, 'but I'm interested in what happened. I mean, I *am* a copper, and Graham was a mate. Naturally, I'm curious.'

'Did you ever tell them about that bloke by the river?' Paul asked.

'It didn't lead anywhere,' Banks said, explaining. 'Besides, I think it's a lot closer to home.'

'What do you mean?' Paul asked.

Banks didn't want to tell them about the photograph. Apart from Michelle, he didn't want anyone to know about that if he could help it. Maybe he was protecting Graham's memory, but the idea of people seeing him like that was abhorrent to Banks. He also didn't want to tell them about Jet Harris, Shaw and the missing notebooks. 'Do you remember Donald Bradford?' he asked. 'The bloke who ran the newsagent's.'

'Dirty Don?' said Paul. 'Sure. I remember him.'

'Why did you call him Dirty Don?'

'I don't know.' Paul shrugged. 'Maybe he sold dirty magazines. It's just something my dad called him. Don't you remember?'

Banks didn't. But he found it interesting that Paul's dad had known about Bradford's interest in porn. Had his own father known? Had anyone told Proctor and Shaw all those years ago when they came to conduct the interviews? Was that why the notebooks and action allocations had to disappear, so that suspicion wouldn't point towards Bradford? Next to the family, Donald Bradford should have come under the most scrutiny, but he had been virtually ignored. 'Did Graham ever tell you where he got those magazines he used to show us inside the tree?'

'What magazines?' Dave asked.

'Don't you remember?' Paul said. 'I do. Women with bloody great bazookas.' He shuddered. 'Gave me the willies even then.'

'I seem to remember you enjoyed them as much as the rest of us,' said Banks. 'Do you really not remember, Dave?'

'Maybe I'm blanking it out for some reason, but I don't.'

Banks turned to Paul. 'Did he ever tell you where he got them?'

'Not that I remember. Why? Do you think it was Bradford?'

'It's a possibility. A newsagent's shop would be a pretty good outlet for things like that. And Graham always seemed to have money to spare.'

'He once told me he stole it from his mother's purse,' said Dave. 'I remember that.'

'Did you believe him?' Banks asked.

'Saw no reason not to. It shocked me, though, that he'd be so callous about it. I'd never have dared steal from *my* mother's purse. She'd have killed me.' He put his hand to his mouth. 'Oops, sorry about that. Didn't mean it to come out that way.'

'It's all right,' said Banks. 'I very much doubt that Graham's mother killed him for stealing from her purse.' On the other hand, Graham's father, Banks thought, was another matter entirely. 'I think there was more to it than that.'

'What?' Paul asked.

'I don't know. I just think Graham had something going with Donald Bradford, most likely something involving porn. And I think that led to his death.'

'You think Bradford killed him?'

'It's a possibility. Maybe he was helping distribute the stuff, or maybe he found out about it and was blackmailing Bradford. I don't know. All I know is that there's a connection.'

'Graham? Blackmailing?' said Dave. 'Now, hold on a minute, Alan, this is our mate Graham we're talking about. The one whose funeral we just went to. Remember? Stealing a few bob from his mum's purse is one thing, but blackmail . . . ?'

'I don't think things were exactly as we thought they were back then,' said Banks.

'Come again,' said Dave.

'He means none of you knew I was queer, for a start,' said Paul.

Banks looked at him. 'But we didn't, did we? You're right. And I don't think we knew a hell of a lot about Graham, either, mate or not.' He looked at Dave. 'For fuck's sake, Dave, you don't even remember the dirty magazines.'

'Maybe I've got a psychological block.'

'Do you at least remember the tree?' Banks asked.

'Our den? Of course I do. I remember lots of things. Just not looking at those magazines.'

'But you did,' said Paul. 'I remember you once saying pictures like that must have been taken at Randy Mandy's. Don't you remember that?'

'Randy Mandy's?' Banks asked. 'What the hell's that?'

'Don't tell me *you* don't remember, either,' said Paul, exasperated.

'Obviously I don't,' said Banks. 'What does it mean?'

'Randy Mandy's? It was Rupert Mandeville's place, that big house up Market Deeping way. Remember?'

Banks felt a vague recollection at the edge of his consciousness. 'I think I remember.'

'It was just our joke, that's all,' Paul went on. 'We thought they had all sorts of sex orgies there. Like that place where Profumo used to go a couple of years earlier. Remember that? Christine Keeler and Mandy Rice-Davies?'

Banks remembered Christine Keeler and Mandy Rice-Davies. The newspapers had been full of risqué photographs and salacious 'confessions' around the time of the Profumo scandal. But that was in 1963, not 1965.

'I remember now,' said Dave. 'Rupert Mandeville's house. Bloody great country mansion, more like. We used to think it was some sort of den of iniquity back then, somewhere all sorts of naughty things went on. Whenever we came across something dirty we always said it must have come from Randy Mandy's. You must remember, Alan. God knows where we got the idea from, but there was this high wall and a big swimming pool in the garden, and we used to imagine all the girls we fancied swimming naked there.'

'Vaguely,' said Banks, who wondered if there was any truth in this. It was worth checking into, anyway. He'd talk to Michelle, see if she knew anything. 'This Mandeville still around?'

'Wasn't he an MP or something?' said Dave.

'I think so,' Paul said. 'I remember reading about him in the papers a few years ago. I think he's in the House of Lords now.'

'Lord Randy Mandy,' said Dave, and they laughed for old times' sake.

Conversation meandered on for another hour or so and at least one round of double Scotches. Dave seemed to stick at a certain level of drunkenness, one he had achieved early on, and now it was Paul who began to show the effects of alcohol the most, and his manner became more exaggeratedly effeminate as time went on.

Banks could sense Dave getting impatient and embarrassed by the looks they were receiving from some of the other customers. He was finding it harder and harder to imagine that they had all had so much in common once, but then it had been a lot easier and more innocent: you supported the same football team, even if they weren't very good, you liked pop music and lusted after Emma Peel and Marianne Faithfull, and that was enough. It helped if you weren't a swot at school and if you lived on the same estate.

Perhaps the bonds of adolescence weren't any more shallow than those of adulthood, Banks mused, but it had sure as hell been easier to make friends back then. Now, as he looked from one to the other – Paul growing more red-faced and camp, Dave, lips tight, barely able to keep his homophobia in check – Banks decided it was time to leave. They had lived apart for over thirty years and would continue to do so without any sense of loss.

When Banks said he had to go, Dave took his cue, and Paul said he wasn't going to sit there by himself. The rain had stopped and the night smelled fresh. Banks wanted a cigarette but resisted. As they walked the short distance back to the estate, none of them said much, sensing perhaps that tonight marked the end of something. Finally, Banks got to his parents' door, their first stop, and said goodnight. They all made vague lies about keeping in touch and then walked back to their own separate lives.

•

Michelle was eating warmed-up chicken casserole, sipping a glass of sauvignon blanc and watching a television documentary on ocean life when her telephone rang late that evening. She was irritated by the interruption but, thinking it might be Banks, she answered it.

'Hope I didn't disturb you,' Banks said.

'No, not at all,' Michelle lied, putting her half-eaten food aside and turning down the volume with the remote control. 'It's good to hear from you.' And it was.

'Look, it's a bit late, and I've had a few drinks,' he said, 'so I'd probably better not drop by tonight.'

'You men. You take a girl to bed once, and then it's back to your mates and your beer.'

'I didn't say I'd had *too* much to drink,' Banks replied. 'In fact, I think I'll phone for a taxi right now.'

Michelle laughed. 'It's all right. I'm only teasing. Believe me, I could do with an early night. Besides, you'll only get in trouble with your mother. Did you find out anything from your old pals?'

'A bit.' Banks told her about Bradford's 'Dirty Don' epithet and the rumours they used to hear about the Mandeville house.

'I've heard of that place recently,' Michelle said. 'I don't know if Shaw mentioned it, or if I read about it in an old file, but I'll check up on it tomorrow. Who'd have thought it? A house of sin. In Peterborough.'

'Well, I suppose, strictly speaking, it's outside the city limits,' said Banks. 'But going by the photo I found in Graham's guitar and the information you got from Jet Harris's ex-wife, I think we'd better look into anything even remotely linked with illicit sex around the time of Graham's murder, don't you?'

'That's it!' Michelle said. 'The connection.'

'What connection?'

'The Mandeville house. It was something to do with illicit sex. At least it was illicit back then. Homosexuality.

There was a complaint about goings on at the Mandeville house. I read about it in the old logs. No further action taken.'

'Tomorrow might turn into a busy day, then,' said Banks.

'All the more reason to get an early night. Can you stick around to help, or do you have to head back up north?'

'One more day won't do any harm.'

'Good. Why don't you come to dinner tomorrow?'

'Your place?'

'Yes. If I can tempt you away from your mates in the boozer, that is.'

'You don't have to offer dinner to do that.'

'Believe it or not, I'm quite a good cook if I put my mind to it.'

'I don't doubt it for a moment. Just one question.'

'Yes?'

'I thought you told me you hadn't seen *Chinatown*.'

Michelle laughed. 'I remember saying no such thing. Goodnight.' And she hung up, still laughing. She noticed the photo of Ted and Melissa from the corner of her eye and felt a little surge of guilt. But it soon passed, and she felt that unfamiliar lightness again, a buoyancy of spirit. She was tired, but before calling it a night she went into the kitchen, pulled out a box of books and flipped through them before putting them on her shelves. Poetry for the most part. She loved poetry. Including Philip Larkin. Then she hefted out a box full of her best china and kitchenware. Looking around at the mostly empty cabinets, she tried to decide where would be the best place for each item.

18

All the way to Swainsdale Hall Annie worried about what she was going to say to the Armitages. Their son had lived a good part of his life unknown to them, mixed with people they didn't know and wouldn't approve of, especially Martin. But don't all kids? Annie had grown up in an artists' commune near St Ives, and some of the people she had mixed with would have made Martin Armitage's hair stand on end. Even so, she hadn't told her father about the wild group she took up with one summer, whose idea of fun was a Saturday afternoon shoplifting expedition in town.

The view over Swainsdale looked gloomy that morning in the low cloud and impending rain, dull gradations of grey and green. Even the patches of yellow rapeseed on the far hillsides looked jaundiced. As Annie rang the doorbell, she felt a surge of anxiety at the thought of seeing Martin Armitage again. It was foolish, she knew; he wasn't going to assault her – not in front of his wife – but she still had an aching jaw, two loose teeth and an upcoming dentist's appointment by which to remember their last meeting.

Josie opened the door and the dog sniffed Annie's crotch as she walked in. Josie collared it and took it away. Only Robin Armitage sat on the large living-room sofa in jeans and a navy blue top, flipping through a copy of *Vogue*. Annie breathed a sigh of relief. Maybe Martin was out. She'd have to talk to him, but a little procrastination wouldn't do any harm. Robin wore no make-up and seemed to have grown older since Luke's death. She looked as if a strong gust of wind would blow her away. She stood up when Annie entered, gave her a thin smile and bade her sit down. She asked Josie to bring in some coffee.

'Is your husband not home?' Annie asked.

'He's in his study. I'll ask Josie to send for him when she brings the coffee. Are you making any progress?'

'Some,' said Annie. 'That's why I wanted to talk to you both again, ask you a few questions.'

'Are you all right? Your mouth still looks bruised.'

Annie put her hand up to her jaw. 'I'm fine.'

'I'm really sorry for what happened. I know Martin is absolutely guilt stricken.' She managed a weak smile. 'It'll take him all his courage to come down and face you again.'

'No hard feelings,' Annie said, which wasn't exactly the truth, but there was no point in taking it out on Robin.

Josie came in with the coffee and digestive biscuits on a tray and Robin asked her to call Mr Armitage down. When he walked into the living room a couple of minutes later, Annie felt a wave of panic. It passed, but it left her heart pounding and her mouth dry. This was ridiculous, she told herself, but her body couldn't help but respond that way to whatever aura of violence Martin Armitage emitted. It just seemed closer to the surface in him than in most people.

Naturally, he was contrite and embarrassed. 'Please accept my apologies,' he said. 'I don't know what came over me. I've never laid a finger on a woman before.' Robin patted his knee.

'It's all right,' said Annie, eager to move on.

'Of course, if there are any medical expenses . . .'

'Don't worry about it.'

'How's Mr Wells?'

Annie had talked with the hospital and discovered that, while Norman Wells's physical injuries were healing well, the psychological damage went a lot deeper. He seemed, they said, to be suffering from depression. He couldn't sleep, but he didn't want to get out of bed, had no interest in food and seemed unconcerned about his future. Hardly surprising, Annie thought, given what the poor sod had been through over the past week or so. And now the newspapers had got hold of the story, there'd be no more bookshop for Wells. Once everyone knew what he had been accused of, nobody would go down there, or if they did it would only be to cause damage. Norman Wells would become a pariah.

'He'll be fine,' Annie said. 'Actually, I have a few more questions for the both of you.'

'I can't imagine what more we can tell you,' said Robin. 'But please go ahead.'

'First of all, do either you or your husband have a prescription for Valium or any other form of diazepam?'

Robin frowned. 'Martin doesn't, but I do. Nerves.'

'Have you noticed any missing lately?'

'No.'

'Would you?'

'Of course.' Robin reached for her handbag on the sofa beside her and took out a small plastic container. 'Here they are,' she said. 'Look. Almost full. Why do you ask?'

Annie looked, then dunked her digestive biscuit in her coffee. Though she had to eat it carefully, avoiding the loose teeth, it tasted good, and it gave her a moment to phrase her response to avoid using images that might upset Robin. 'It's just that the pathologist found traces in Luke's system,' she said – it sounded better than stomach contents. 'We were wondering where he got it from.'

'Luke? Valium? Certainly not from us.'

'And I assume he didn't have a prescription of his own?'

Martin and Robin looked at one another, frowning. 'Of course not,' said Robin. 'Someone else must have given it to him.'

'Is that what killed him?' Martin Armitage asked.

'No,' said Annie. 'It's just another complication I'd like to get out of the way, that's all.'

'I'm sorry we can't help you,' said Robin.

Annie struggled to phrase her next question, too. Talking to these two was like walking on eggs, but it had to be done. 'Mrs Armitage, Robin, you know Luke was confused about his biological father, don't you?'

'Neil? Well, yes, I suppose . . . But, I mean, Luke never knew him.'

'Surely you knew he must have wondered what happened, why his father didn't want him?'

'It wasn't like that. Neil just couldn't cope. He was a child himself in so many ways.'

'And a drug addict.'

'Neil wasn't an addict. He used drugs, but they were just a sort of tool for him, a means to an end.'

Annie didn't bother arguing that that was what they were for most people; it would be easier if she took Neil Byrd's exalted artistic status in her stride, especially when talking to Robin. 'But you knew Luke couldn't listen to his music, didn't you?'

'I never asked him to. I don't listen to it myself any more.'

'Well, he couldn't,' Annie said. 'Any reference to Neil Byrd or his music upset him. Did he ever talk to either of you about any friends of his called Liz and Ryan?'

'Not to me, no,' said Robin. 'Martin?'

Martin Armitage shook his head.

'He was in a band with them. Didn't you know?'

'No,' said Robin. 'He didn't tell us.'

'Why would he keep it from you?'

Robin paused and looked at her husband, who shifted in his seat and spoke. 'Probably because we'd already had arguments about that sort of thing.'

'What sort of thing?'

'I thought Luke was devoting far too much of his time to poetry and music, and that he ought to get more involved in team sports, get more exercise. He was starting to look pasty-faced from spending all his time indoors.'

'How did he react to this?'

Martin looked at Robin, then back at Annie. 'Not well. We had a bit of an argument about it. He insisted he was the best judge of how to spend his time.'

'Why didn't you tell me any of this earlier?'

'Because it didn't seem relevant. It still doesn't.' Martin sat forward and stared at her with that intense, disconcerting look of his. 'Someone kidnapped Luke and murdered him, and all you can do is ask questions about Neil Byrd and my relationship with Luke.'

'I think I'm the best judge of what questions I should be asking, Mr Armitage,' said Annie, aware of her heart pounding again. Surely they could hear it? 'Did you agree with your husband?' she asked Robin.

'Sort of. But I didn't want to stand in the way of Luke's creative development. If I'd known about the band, I would have been concerned. I wouldn't have wanted him getting into that kind of life. Believe me, I've seen it at first-hand. I've been there.'

'So you wouldn't have been thrilled, either, if you'd known that Luke was playing in a group?'

'No.'

'Was drug use a concern?'

'We warned him about drugs, of course, and he swore he didn't take them.'

'He didn't,' Annie said. 'At least not until the day he disappeared.'

Robin's eyes widened. 'What are you saying? You know how he died?'

'No. No, we don't know that yet. All we know is that he was with two friends, that he took some drugs and they played him his father's music. Luke got upset and left. We still don't know where he went after that.'

Robin put her coffee cup down in the saucer. Some of the coffee spilled. She didn't notice. 'I can't believe it,' she said.

'Who are these people?' Martin butted in.

'And what will you do if I tell you, Mr Armitage?' Annie said. 'Go and beat them up?'

Armitage's chin jutted out as he spoke. 'It's no less than they deserve if what you say is true. Giving my son drugs.'

'Mr Armitage,' Annie said. 'What did you do when you went out for two hours the night Luke disappeared?'

'I told you. I just drove around looking for him.'

'Drove where?'

'Eastvale.'

'Any particular areas or streets?'

'I don't remember. I just drove around. Why is it important?'

Annie's chest felt tight, but she forged ahead. 'Did you find him?'

'Of course I didn't. What are you talking about? If I'd found him, he'd be here safe and sound right now, wouldn't he?'

'I've seen a demonstration of your temper, Mr Armitage.' There, it was out. 'I also know from talking to several people that you and your stepson didn't get along very well.'

'What are you suggesting?'

Armitage's tone chilled Annie, but it was too late to stop now. 'That if anything happened that evening. Some sort of . . . accident . . . then it's better to tell me now than have me find out by some other means.'

'Accident? Let me get this straight. Are you asking me if I found Luke, picked him up in my car, then lost my temper and killed him?'

'I'm asking you if you did see him that night, yes, and if anything happened between you that I should know about.'

Armitage shook his head. 'You really are a piece of work, DI Cabbot. First you act rashly and probably cause my son's death, then you accuse *me* of killing him. For your information, I did exactly what I told you. I drove around Eastvale looking for Luke. It was probably pointless, I know, but I had to do something. I needed to act. I couldn't just sit around and wait. I didn't find him. All right?'

'Fine,' said Annie.

'And I resent your accusation.'

'I haven't accused you of anything.'

Martin Armitage stood up. 'It shows how little progress you've made, scraping the bottom of the barrel like this. Will that be all? I'm going back to my study now.'

Annie felt relieved when Armitage had left the room.

'That was cruel,' said Robin. 'Martin loved Luke like his own son, did his best for the boy, even if they didn't always agree. Luke was no angel, you know. He could be difficult.'

'I'm sure he could,' said Annie. 'All teenagers can. And I'm sorry I had to ask those questions. Police work can be uncomfortable at times, but the solution often lies close to home, and we'd be derelict in our duty if we didn't pursue such lines of enquiry. Did you know that Luke had a girlfriend?'

'Certainly not.'

'He never said anything to you?'

'I don't even believe he had a girlfriend.'

'Everyone says he was mature for his age, and he was a good-looking boy, too. Why shouldn't he?'

'He just never . . .'

'It might have been someone he didn't feel he could bring home to meet his parents. Maybe even Liz Palmer, the girl in the group.'

'You think that's why he was killed? Because of this *girl*?'

'We don't know. It's just one possibility we've been looking at. What about Lauren Anderson?'

'Miss Anderson? But she was his English teacher. You can't think . . .'

'I don't know. It's not as if these things don't happen. Rose Barlow?'

'Rose? The headmaster's daughter. Well, she came round to the house once, but it was all perfectly innocent.'

'Rose Barlow came to your house? Why didn't you tell me?'

'But it was ages ago.'

'February? March?'

'Around that time. Yes. How do you know?'

'Because somebody else noticed Luke and Rose were spending time together then, thought maybe they were going out together.'

'I don't think so,' said Robin. 'It was something to do with a school project.'

'Did she visit often?'

'Only the once.'

'And she never came back?'

'No.'

'Did Luke ever talk about her?'

'Except to say that he'd ended up doing most of the project himself, no. Look, I don't understand all this, all your questions. Don't you think he just wandered off and someone kidnapped him?'

'No,' said Annie. 'I don't think that's what happened at all.'

'Then what?'

Annie stood up to leave. 'Give me a little more time,' she said. 'I'm getting there.'

•

Michelle had made three important discoveries before lunch that day and it seemed a nice goal to set oneself. Who was it, she tried to remember, who had made it a point to believe six impossible things before breakfast? Was it Alice in *Through the Looking Glass*?

Well, the things Michelle had discovered were far from impossible. First, she had gone back to the logbook for the summer of 1965 and found the reference to the Mandeville house. On 1 August that year, an anonymous informant had telephoned the station with allegations of under-age sex and homosexuality. The possibility of drug taking was also mentioned. A young DC called Geoff Talbot had gone out to make enquiries and had arrested two men he said he found naked together in a bedroom there. After that, nothing more appeared on the case except a note that all charges were dropped and an official apology issued to Mr Rupert Mandeville, who, she discovered from an Internet search, had served as a Conservative Member of Parliament from 1979 to 1990 and was granted a life peerage in 1994.

It took Michelle a bit longer to track Geoff Talbot down, as he had left the police force in 1970 to work as a consultant with a television company. Eventually, through a patient personnel officer, she managed to find his address in Barnet, a North London suburb. She had rung him and he had agreed to talk to her.

After that, Michelle had enlisted DC Collins's aid and discovered through local land registry records that Donald Bradford's shop had been owned by a company linked to Carlo Fiorino, the late but unlamented local crime kingpin. The company had also owned Le Phonographe discotheque and several other newsagents' shops in the Peterborough area. Ownership of Bradford's shop went to the Walkers when he sold, but many of the other shops remained under Fiorino's control well through the new town expansion and into the seventies.

What it all meant, Michelle wasn't too sure, but it looked very much as if Carlo Fiorino had set up the perfect retail distribution chain for his wholesale porn business, and who knew what else besides? Drugs, perhaps? And maybe even some of those advertising cards in the news-agents' windows weren't quite so innocent after all.

All this she told to Banks as she drove through a steady drizzle down the A1 to Barnet. As they talked, she kept a keen eye on her rear-view mirror. A grey Passat seemed to stay on their tail a bit too long and too close for comfort, but it finally turned off at Welwyn Garden City.

'Bradford must have got Graham involved somehow, through the magazines,' said Banks. 'But it didn't stop there. He must have come to the attention of Fiorino and Mandeville, too. It helps to explain where all that extra money came from.'

'Look, I know he was your friend, Alan, but you have to admit that it looks as if he was up to some unsavoury stuff, as if he got greedy.'

'I admit it,' said Banks. 'The photo must have been Graham's insurance. Evidence. He could use it to black-mail Bradford into paying him more money, only he didn't know what he'd got himself into. Word got back to Fiorino and he signed Graham's death warrant.'

'And who carried it out?'

'Bradford, most likely. He didn't have an alibi. Or Harris. I mean, we can't rule him out completely. Despite what his ex-wife told you, he could have kept the com-mando knife, and if he was being threatened with exposure as a homosexual, he might have been driven to kill. Remember, it wouldn't only have meant his career back then, but jail, and you know how long coppers survive behind bars.'

'Jet Harris searched Graham Marshall's house person-ally just after the boy disappeared,' said Michelle.

'Harris did that? Searched the house? How do you know?'

'Mrs Marshall mentioned it the first time I went to talk to her. I didn't think anything of it at the time, but now . . . a superintendent conducting a routine search?'

'He must have been after the photo.'

'Then why didn't he find it?'

'He obviously didn't look hard enough, did he?' said Banks. 'Adolescents are naturally very secretive. Sometimes, of necessity, they have an uncanny knack for hiding things. And at the time, if that photo had been securely Sellotaped to the inside of Graham's guitar, nobody could know it was there without taking the guitar apart. It was only because the adhesive had dried out and the Sellotape had stiffened over the years that the photo broke free and I found it.'

'I suppose so,' Michelle said. 'But does that make Harris a murderer?'

'I don't know. It's not proof. But he was in it. Deep.'

'I also rang Ray Scholes this morning,' Michelle said. 'Remember, the detective who investigated Donald Bradford's murder?'

'I remember.'

'It turns out there was a Fairbairn-Sykes knife among Bradford's possessions.'

'What happened to it?'

'Forget it. It's long gone. Sold to a dealer. Who knows how many times it's changed hands since then?'

'Pity. But at least we know it was in his possession when he died.'

'You said the photo was evidence,' Michelle said. 'But what of? How?'

'Well, there might have been fingerprints on it, but I think it was more dangerous because people would have known where it was taken. I doubt there are that many Adam fireplaces around, and probably none quite as distinctive as that one. The rug, too.'

'You're thinking of the Mandeville house?'

'Sounds a likely place to me. I'm certain it was all connected: Fiorino's porn business, his escort agency, the Mandeville parties, Graham's murder. I think this is where we turn off.'

Michelle kept going.

'The junction's coming up,' Banks said. 'Here. Move over or you'll miss it. Now!'

Michelle waited and made a last-minute lane change. Horns blared as she sped across two lanes of traffic to the off ramp.

'Jesus Christ!' said Banks. 'You could have got us killed.'

Michelle flashed him a quick grin. 'Oh, don't be such a pussycat. I knew what I was doing. This way we can be certain no one's following us. Where now?'

When his heart rate slowed, Banks picked up the street guide and directed Michelle to the pleasant suburban semi where ex DC Geoff Talbot enjoyed his retirement.

Talbot answered the door and asked them in. Michelle introduced herself and Banks.

'Miserable day, isn't it?' Talbot said. 'One wonders if summer will ever arrive.'

'Too true,' said Banks.

'Coffee? Tea?'

'A cup of tea would be nice,' Michelle said. Banks agreed.

Michelle and Banks followed Talbot into the kitchen,

which turned out to be a bright, high-ceilinged room with a central island surrounded by tall stools.

'We can talk here, if it's all right with you,' Talbot said. 'My wife keeps pestering me for a conservatory, but I don't see the need. On a nice day we can always sit outside.'

Michelle looked out of the window and saw the well-manicured lawn and neat flower beds. Someone in the family was obviously a keen gardener. A copper beech provided some shade. It would indeed have been nice to sit outside, but not in the rain.

'You didn't give me much of an idea what you wanted to talk about over the telephone,' Talbot said, looking over his shoulder as he dropped a couple of teabags into the pot.

'That's because it's still a bit vague,' Michelle said. 'How's your memory?' She and Banks had agreed that, as it was her case and he had no official capacity, she would do most of the questioning.

'Not so bad for an old man.'

Talbot didn't look that old, Michelle thought. He was carrying a few pounds too many and his hair was almost white, but other than that his face was remarkably unlined and his movements smooth and fluid. 'Remember when you served on the Cambridge Constabulary?' she asked.

'Of course. Mid-sixties, that'd be. Peterborough. It was called the Mid-Anglia Constabulary back then. Why?'

'Do you remember a case involving Rupert Mandeville?'

'Do I? How could I forget. That's the reason I left Cambridgeshire. If it comes right down to it, it's the reason I left the force not long after, too.'

'Could you tell us what happened?'

The kettle boiled and Talbot filled the pot with boiling water, then carried it on a tray along with three cups and saucers to the island. 'Nothing happened,' he said. 'That was the problem. I was told to lay off.'

'By whom?'

'The super.'

'Detective Superintendent Harris?'

'Jet Harris. That's the one. Oh, it was all above board. Not enough evidence, my word against theirs, anonymous informant, that sort of thing. You couldn't fault his arguments.'

'Then what?'

Talbot paused. 'It just didn't feel right, that's all. I can't put it any other way than that. There'd been rumours for some time about things going on at the Mandeville house. Procurement, under-age boys, that sort of thing. It was the start of what they called the permissive society, after all. Ever heard of Carlo Fiorino?'

'We have,' said Michelle.

Talbot poured the tea. 'Rumour has it he was the supplier. Anyway, the problem was that Rupert Mandeville was too well connected, and some of the people who attended his parties were in the government, or in other high-level positions. Real Profumo stuff. Of course, I was the naive young copper fresh from probation, proud to be in CID, thinking he could take on the world. Not a care had I for rank or sway. We were all equal in the eyes of God as far as I was concerned, though I wasn't a religious man. Well, I soon learned the error of my ways. Had my eyes opened for me. When the super found out I'd been out there and caused a fuss, he had me in his office and told me in no uncertain terms that Mandeville was off-limits.'

'Did he say why?' Michelle asked.

'He didn't need to. It's not difficult to add up.'

'An operation like that, and one like Fiorino's, would need police protection,' Banks said. 'And Harris was it. Or part of it.'

'Exactly,' said Talbot. 'Oh, he was clever, though. He never admitted it in so many words, and he got me transferred out of the county before my feet even touched the ground. Cumbria. I ask you! Well, I ran into one or two nice little gentleman's agreements between local villains and constabulary up there too, so I called it a day. I mean, I'm no saint, but it just seemed to me that no matter where I went I found corruption. I couldn't fight it. Not from my position. So I resigned from the force. Best move I ever made.'

'And you told no one of your suspicions about Harris?' Michelle asked.

'What was the point? Who'd believe me? Jet Harris was practically a god around the place even then. Besides, there were implied threats of what might happen to me if I didn't do as he said, and some of them were quite physical. I'm not a coward, but I'm no fool either. I cut my losses.'

'Was anyone else involved?'

'Might have been,' said Talbot. 'The chief constable himself might have been a regular at Mandeville's parties, for all I know.'

'But no one you knew of?'

'No. I didn't even *know* about Harris. Like I said, it just felt wrong. I just guessed from his attitude, his wording. It was only him and me in his office. Even by the time I got outside I was thinking I'd been reading too much into it.'

'What happened that day?'

'From the start?'

'Yes.'

'It was a warm Sunday morning, end of July or beginning of August.'

'It was was the first of August,' Michelle said.

'Right. Anyway, I was by myself, not much on, I remember, when the phone call came and the switchboard patched it through to the office.'

'Do you remember anything about the voice?'

Talbot frowned. 'It's so long ago, I don't . . .'

'Man? Woman?'

'It was a woman's voice. I remember that much.'

'Did she sound upset?'

'Yes. That's why I headed out there so impulsively. She said there'd been a party going on since the previous night, and she was convinced that some of the girls and boys were under-age and people were taking drugs. She sounded frightened. She hung up very abruptly, too.'

'So you went?'

'Yes. I logged the details and drove out there like a knight in shining armour. If I'd had half the sense I have now, I'd at least have taken the time to organize a small raiding party, but I didn't. God knows what I thought I was going to do when I got there.'

'Did you meet the woman who'd phoned?'

'Not that I know of. I mean, if she was there she never came forward and admitted she was the one who phoned. But then she wouldn't, would she?'

'Who opened the door?'

'A young man. He just opened it, glanced at my identification and wandered off. He didn't seem interested at all. I thought he was on drugs, but I must admit I didn't know much about them at the time. I'm not even sure we had a drugs squad back then.'

'What did you find inside?'

'It was more like the aftermath of a party, really. Some people were sleeping on the sofa, a couple on the floor . . .'

'How many?'

'Hard to say. Maybe twenty or so.'

'What kind of people?'

'A mix. Young and old. Businessmen. Mods. One or two of the girls looked like swinging London types, mini-skirts and what have you. There was a funny smell, too, I remember. At the time I didn't know what it was, but I smelled it again later. Marijuana.'

'What did you do?'

'To be honest, I felt a bit out of my depth.' He laughed. 'Like Mr Jones in that Bob Dylan song, I didn't really know what was happening. I wasn't even sure if any of it was illegal. I mean, the girls and the men didn't *look* under-age to me, but what did I know? I talked to a few people, took names. A couple of the girls I'd seen before at Le Phonographe. I think they also worked for Fiorino's escort agency.'

'You used your notebook?'

'Yes.'

'What happened to it?'

'Same as usual, I suppose.'

'You also found two men together?'

'Yes. I looked in some of the rooms, and in one bedroom I saw two men in bed together. Naked.'

'Were they doing anything?'

'Not when I opened the door. They were just . . . very close together. I'd never seen anything like that before. I mean, I knew about homosexuality, I wasn't that naive, but I'd never actually seen it.'

'Did either of them look under-age?'

'No. One I pegged at early twenties, the other older, maybe forty. But it didn't matter how old you were back then.'

'So what did you do?'

'I . . . er . . . I arrested them.'

'Did they resist?'

'No. They just laughed, put their clothes on and went back to the station with me.'

'What happened then?'

'Jet Harris was waiting for me. He was furious.'

'He was at the station waiting for you? On a Sunday morning?'

'Yes. I suppose someone from Mandeville's house must have phoned him.'

'Probably dragged him out of church,' Banks said.

'What did he do?' Michelle asked.

'He had a private talk with the two men, let them go and had his little chat with me. That was the end of it. No further action.'

'Just out of interest,' Michelle asked, 'how old was Rupert Mandeville at the time?'

'Quite young. In his thirties. His parents had been killed in a plane crash not too long before, I remember, and he'd inherited a fortune, even after tax. I suppose he was just doing what many young people would have done if they'd gained their freedom and had unlimited funds.'

'Ever hear of Donald Bradford?' Michelle asked.

'The name doesn't ring a bell.'

'Bill Marshall?'

'He was one of Fiorino's musclemen. I ran into him a

couple of times in Le Phonographe. Tough character. Thick as the proverbial pigshit.'

'Thank you, Mr Talbot.'

'You're welcome. Look, I can't see as I've been any help, but . . .'

Banks placed the photograph of Graham Marshall in front of him. 'Do you recognize that boy?'

Talbot paled. 'My God, isn't that the boy who . . . ? His photograph was in the papers only a few weeks ago.'

'Did you see him at the Mandeville house?'

'No . . . I . . . but that's the room. Mandeville's living room. I remember the sheepskin rug and the fireplace. Does that mean what I think it means? That the boy's death is somehow connected with Mandeville and Harris?'

'Somehow,' said Michelle. 'We're just not quite sure how yet.'

Talbot tapped the photo. 'If we'd had something like that back then, we'd have had some evidence,' he said.

'Possibly,' said Banks. 'If it ever saw the light of day.'

They stood up and Talbot showed them to the door. 'You know,' he said, 'I felt at the time that there was more going on than met the eye. I've always wondered what would have happened if I'd pushed it a bit harder, not let go too easily.'

'You'd have probably ended up under a field with Graham Marshall,' said Banks. 'Bye, Mr Talbot. And thank you.'

•

Gavin Barlow was in his study when Annie called, and he invited her to sit with him there while they talked. It was a light, airy room, with plenty of space, and the bookcases didn't feel as overwhelming as the ones in Gristhorpe's office. Barlow pushed his laptop aside on his desk and smiled. 'It might be summer holidays for most,' he said, 'but some of us still have work to do.'

'I won't take up much of your time,' Annie said. 'It's about your daughter.'

'Rose? I'm afraid she's out.'

'Perhaps you can answer my questions, then.'

'I'll try. But look, if Rose is in any sort of trouble . . .'

'What?'

'I don't know. Maybe I should call my solicitor or something.'

'Why would you want to do that?'

'Just tell me what you've come to say.'

'Your daughter came to the station and made some pretty serious allegations about Lauren Anderson and Luke Armitage.'

'She did what?'

'And now it turns out that she was seeing Luke earlier this year. She even visited him at Swainsdale Hall on at least one occasion. Do you know anything about that?'

'Of course. It was a school project the students were asked to partner up on. To promote working together, task sharing. Rose worked with Luke.'

'Her choice or his?'

'I don't know. I should imagine the teacher assigned them.'

'Lauren Anderson?'

'No, actually. It was a science project. It would have been Mr Sawyer.'

'Do you know if Luke and Rose had any sort of romantic involvement?'

'Not as far as I know. Look, Ms Cabbot, I'm not so naive

as to think that teenagers their age don't form liaisons. I've been a head teacher too long to think otherwise. I've even come across my share of teenage pregnancies. But I also know my own daughter, and believe me, I would have known if she'd been seeing Luke Armitage.'

'They were seen talking together in and around the school. Did she ever talk to you about Luke?'

'She might have mentioned him once or twice, yes. It was only natural. I mean, they were in the same class, he was a little odd and something of a minor celebrity. At least his parents are.'

'Was she obsessed with him?'

'Don't be ridiculous!'

'Would you have approved if they had been going out together?'

Barlow pursed his lips. 'I can't say that I would, no.'

'Why not?'

'She's my daughter, for crying out loud. You don't think I'd have wanted her going out with that . . .'

'That what, Mr Barlow?'

'I was going to say that *boy.*'

'Oh, were you?'

'Yes. But I'll admit that, as a father, I thought Luke Armitage just a little too weird for my daughter.'

'How far would you have gone to stop them going out together?'

'Now, hold on a minute. I won't have you—'

'Where were you and Rose the night Luke disappeared? That's a week ago last Monday, in case you don't remember.'

'Here.'

'Both of you?'

'As far as I know. My wife will remember.'

'Why would Rose want to make trouble for Ms Anderson?'

'I don't know.'

'How well does your daughter do at English?'

'It's not her best subject, or her favourite.'

'Was she jealous?'

'Of what?'

'Of the attention Luke got from Lauren Anderson?'

'Why don't you ask Lauren?'

'I will. But I'm asking you first.'

'And I'm telling you I don't know.'

They stared at one another, and Annie tried to weigh up whether he was telling the truth or not. She decided he was holding something back. 'What is it, Mr Barlow?' she asked. 'If it's nothing to do with Luke's death, it will go no further than these walls, I promise.'

Barlow sighed and stared out of the window. The clouds had split in places and shafts of light lanced the distant hills. The laptop hummed on his desk.

'Mr Barlow?'

He turned back to face her, and his facade of benevolent authority had disappeared. In its place was the look of a man with a burden. He stared at her a long time before speaking. 'It was nothing,' he said, finally, his voice little more than a whisper. 'Really. Nothing.'

'Then tell me.'

'Ms Anderson. Lauren. If you've seen her, you must have noticed she's an attractive woman, quite the Pre-Raphaelite beauty,' Barlow said. 'I'm only as human as the next man, but everyone expects me to be above reproach.'

'You're a head teacher,' said Annie. 'You're supposed

to be *responsible*. What happened? Did you have an affair? Did Rose find out?'

'Oh, good lord, no. Nothing like that. I might have flirted a bit, as one does, but Lauren wasn't interested in me. She made that quite clear.'

Annie frowned. 'Then I don't understand.'

A thin smile twisted his lips. 'Don't you? Sometimes things can seem other than they are, and any attempt to explain them away only makes you seem more guilty.'

'Can you elaborate on that?'

'Lauren came to see me in my office shortly after Christmas. A family problem. Her father had been diagnosed with Alzheimer's and she was upset, needed some time off. I put an arm around her, just to comfort her, you understand, and Rose chose that moment to come barging in with some family matter. It's one of the disadvantages of being the head of the school your daughter attends. Rose was usually pretty good about observing the boundaries, but on this occasion . . . Well, she misread the situation and went running off.'

'I see,' said Annie. 'Did she tell your wife?'

'No. No, thank God. I managed to talk to her. I'm not sure she quite believed in my innocence, but she agreed not to say anything.'

'And that's the root of her animosity towards Lauren Anderson?'

'I should imagine so. Maybe she had a crush on Luke Armitage, too, at one time, but believe me, I'd have known if there was more to it than that.'

'Are you sure there's nothing else?'

'Not that I can think of.'

'You *were* attracted to Lauren, though, weren't you? What did you call her? A Pre-Raphaelite beauty?'

'Yes. As I said, I'm only human. And she *is* a very attractive woman. You can't arrest a man for his thoughts. At least not yet. The damn thing is, I'd done nothing wrong, but because I wanted it I felt as guilty as if I had, anyway.' He gave a bitter laugh. 'Funny, isn't it?'

'Yes,' said Annie. 'Very funny.' But her thoughts were elsewhere. Barlow might not have given her the answers she was hoping for, but he had certainly given her plenty to think about.

•

'Well, if it isn't our two lovebirds,' said Ben Shaw, opening the door to Banks and Michelle. 'What the fuck do you two want?'

'A few words,' said Banks.

'And why should I want a few words with you?'

'Des Wayman,' said Michelle.

Shaw squinted at her, then shut the door, slid off the chain and opened it, walking away from them, leaving Banks to shut the door behind them and follow.

The house was far neater than Banks had expected. He had pegged Shaw as an alcoholic living alone, and that usually meant chaos. At least Shaw probably hired a cleaning lady, and his personal habits seemed tidy enough. The only booze in sight was a half-empty bottle of Bell's on the living-room table, a full glass beside it. Shaw sat down and took a slug without offering his guests anything. Well, Banks thought, why should he?

Grieg's *Peer Gynt* Suite was playing on the radio, another surprise for Banks. He wouldn't have guessed Shaw to be a man of classical tastes. Or maybe it didn't matter what was on as long as there was sound.

'So what porkies has Mr Wayman been telling today?'

'Stop pissing around,' said Banks. 'You told Wayman and a mate to work me over and get me out of the picture. It backfired.'

'If he told you that, he's lying.'

'He told me, sir,' said Michelle, 'and, with all due respect, I think he was telling the truth.'

'*All due respect?* You don't know the meaning of the term.' Shaw lit a cigarette and Banks felt a wave of pure need surge inside him. He was already feeling light-headed and edgy from not smoking but this . . . this was ten times worse than he'd imagined. He took a grip. 'Wayman's nothing but criminal scum,' Shaw went on. 'And you'd take his word over mine?'

'That's neither here nor there,' Banks went on. 'DI Hart has done a bit of digging into your Regan and Carter days with Jet Harris, and we were just wondering how much the two of you took in from Carlo Fiorino.'

'You bastard!' Shaw lurched forward to grab Banks's lapel but he was already a bit unsteady with drink, and Banks pushed him back down into his chair. He paled, and a grimace of pain passed over his face.

'What is it?' asked Banks.

'Fuck you.' Shaw coughed and reached for more whisky. 'John Harris was worth ten of you. You're not worth the piss stains in his underwear.'

'Come off it, Shaw, the two of you were as bent as the day is long. He might have had a good excuse for it, but you . . . ? You couldn't remove every scrap of evidence from the archives. All your arrests were for burglary, assault, fraud and the occasional domestic murder. Doesn't that tell you something?'

'What, smart arse?'

'That all the time Carlo Fiorino was running prostitution, escort agencies, illegal gambling, protection, porn
and drugs with absolute impunity. Sure, you had him
or one of his henchmen brought in once or twice for
questioning, just for the sake of appearances, but guess
what – either the evidence disappeared or witnesses
changed their statements.'

Shaw said nothing, just sipped more whisky.

'Fiorino fed you his opposition,' Banks went on. 'He
had eyes and ears out on the street. He knew what jobs
were going down. Small fry, or competition. Either way it
made you look good and deflected attention from his own
operations, which included supplying Rupert Mandeville
with as many bodies as he wanted for his "parties", male
and female.'

Shaw slammed the tumbler down on the table so hard
the whisky slopped over the side. 'All right,' he said. 'You
want the truth? I'll tell you. I'm not stupid. I worked with
John for too many years not to have my suspicions, but –
know what? – I never took a fucking penny in my life. And
maybe I blinkered myself, maybe I even protected him,
but we did our jobs. We brought down the bad guys. I
loved the man. He taught me everything. He even saved
my life once. He had charisma, did John. He was the kind
of bloke everybody noticed when he walked in the room.
He's a fucking hero around these parts, or hadn't you
noticed?'

'And that's why you've been doing everything in your
power to scupper DI Hart's investigation into Graham
Marshall's murder? To protect your old pal's memory. To
protect Jet Harris's reputation. To do that you get
someone to break into her flat, try to run her down, have
me beaten up.'

'What the fuck are you talking about?'

'You know what I'm talking about.'

He looked at Michelle, then back at Banks, a puzzled expression on his face. 'I certainly never had anyone intimidate DI Hart in any way. I wasn't worried about her. It was you I was worried about.'

'Why's that?'

'You're the loose cannon. It was you I needed to keep an eye on. It was different for you. Personal. You knew the victim. I could tell the first time I saw you that you weren't going to let go.' He shook his head and looked at Michelle again. 'No,' he said. 'If anyone had a go at you, DI Hart, it wasn't down to me.'

Banks and Michelle exchanged glances, then Banks moved on. 'Are you asking us to believe that you worked with Harris all those years and you hadn't a clue what he was up to?'

'I'm saying I had my suspicions, but I buried them. For the sake of the force. For John's sake. Listen, squash a bug like Fiorino and another one takes his place. You can no more stop prostitution, porn and drugs than you can stop sex and drinking. They're always going to be there. Policing was different then. Sometimes you had to rub shoulders with some pretty nasty bedfellows to do the job.'

'And what about Graham Marshall?'

Shaw looked surprised. 'What about him?'

'Did you know what really happened to him? Have you been covering that up all these years, too?'

'I don't know what the fuck you're talking about.' Shaw's voice was little more than a whisper now.

'Well, let me tell you a story,' said Banks. 'We can't prove it, but this is what DI Hart and I believe happened.

Donald Bradford most likely killed Graham. He owned the kind of knife that was used and Graham trusted him. All Bradford had to do was drive down Wilmer Road around the time Graham would be heading for the other side and tell him something else had come up, to get in the car. That's why he took his bag of newspapers with him. He thought he would be going back to finish his round later.'

'What possible motive could Bradford have?'

'That's where it gets complicated, and that's where your boss comes in. Donald Bradford distributed porno-graphic magazines and blue films for Carlo Fiorino. Fiorino had quite a network of newsagents working for him. I'm surprised you didn't know about it, you being a vigilant copper and all.'

'Sod you, Banks.' Shaw scowled and topped up his glass.

'Somehow or other,' Banks went on, 'Graham Marshall became involved in this operation. Maybe he found some of Bradford's stock by accident, showed interest. I don't know. But Graham was a street-smart kid – he grew up around the Krays and their world, and his father was a small-time muscleman – and he had an eye for the main chance. Maybe he worked for Bradford to earn extra money – which he always seemed to have – or maybe he blackmailed him for it. Either way, he was involved.'

'You said yourself you can't prove any of this.'

'Graham came to the attention of one of Fiorino's most influential customers, Rupert Mandeville,' Banks went on. 'I know he posed for some nude photos because I found one at his house. Whether it went any further than that, I don't know, but we can tie him to the Mandeville house, and we know what went on there. Under-age sex, drugs, you name it. Mandeville couldn't afford to come under scrutiny. He was an important person with political goals to pursue. Graham probably asked for more money or he'd tell the police. Mandeville panicked, especially as this came hot on the heels of Geoff Talbot's visit. He got Fiorino to fix it, and Jet Harris scuppered the murder investigation. You knew that, knew there was something wrong, so you've been trying to erase the traces to protect Harris's reputation. How am I doing?'

'You're arguing against your own logic, Banks. What would it matter if he told the police, if we were all as corrupt as you make out? Why go so far as to kill the kid if Bradford thought we could control the outcome anyway?'

Banks looked at Michelle before continuing. 'That puzzled me for a while, too,' he said. 'I can only conclude that he knew which police officer *not* to tell.'

'How do you mean?'

'Graham had definitely been to the Mandeville house. What if he saw someone there? Someone who shouldn't have been there, like a certain detective superintendent?'

'That's absurd. John wasn't like that.'

'Wasn't like what? Mandeville's parties catered to all tastes. According to his wife, John Harris was homosexual. We don't know if Mandeville or Fiorino found out and blackmailed him or if they set him up. Maybe that's how he took his pay-offs from Fiorini and Mandeville, in young boys. Or drugs. It doesn't matter. Point is, I think Graham saw him there or knew he was connected in some way and made this clear to Bradford, too, that he'd go elsewhere with his story.'

Shaw turned pale. 'John? *Homosexual?* I don't believe that.'

'One of my old schoolfriends has turned out to be gay,'

said Banks. 'And I didn't know that, either. John Harris had two damn good reasons for keeping it a secret. It was illegal until 1967 and he was a copper. Even today you know how tough it is for coppers to come out. We're all such bloody macho tough guys that gays terrify the crap out of us.'

'Bollocks. This is all pure speculation.'

'Not about John Harris,' Michelle said. 'It's what his ex-wife told me.'

'She's a lying bitch, then. With all due respect.'

'Why would she lie?'

'She hated John.'

'Sounds like she had good reason to,' Banks said. 'But back to Graham. He threatened to tell. I don't know why. It could have been greed, but it could also have been because Mandeville wanted him to do more than pose for photos. I'd like to think that was where Graham drew the line, but we'll probably never know. It also explains why he was preoccupied when we were on holiday in Blackpool just before he disappeared. He must have been worrying about what to do. Anyway, Graham knew he'd better go further afield than the local nick. And he had the photo as evidence, a photo that could incriminate Rupert Mandeville. He compromised the whole operation. Mandeville's *and* Fiorino's. That was why he had to die.'

'So what happened?'

'The order went down to Donald Bradford to get rid of him. Bradford had to be at the shop by eight o'clock, as usual, that morning. That gave him an hour and a half to abduct Graham, kill him and dispose of the body. It takes a while to dig a hole that deep, so my guess is that he planned it in advance, picked the spot and dug the hole.

Either that or he had help and another of Fiorino's henchmen buried the body. Either way, with Harris on the payroll, Bradford could at least be certain that no one was looking too closely at his lack of an alibi.'

'Are you saying that John Harris ordered the boy's death because—'

'I don't know. I don't think so. I'd say it was Fiorino, or Mandeville, but Harris had to know about it in order to misdirect the investigation. And that makes him just as guilty in my book.'

Shaw closed his eyes and shook his head. 'Not John. No. Maybe he didn't always play by the rules, maybe he did turn a blind eye to one or two things, but not murder. Not a dead kid.'

'You have to accept it,' Banks went on. 'It's the only thing that makes sense of later events.'

'What later events?'

'The botched investigation and the missing notebooks and actions. I don't know who got rid of them – you, Harris or Reg Proctor, but one of you did.'

'It wasn't me. All I've done was discourage DI Hart here from digging too deeply into the past.'

'And set Wayman on me.'

'You won't get me to admit to that.'

'It doesn't matter anyway,' said Banks. 'So Harris took them himself when he left. That makes sense. It wasn't his finest hour, and he wouldn't want the evidence hanging around for anyone to see if Graham's body ever did turn up. Insurance. Cast your mind back. You were there in the summer of 1965. You and Reg Proctor covered the estate. What did you find out?'

'Nobody knew anything.'

'I'll bet that's not true,' said Banks. 'I'll bet there were one or two references to "Dirty Don" in your notebooks. One of my old mates remembered referring to him that way. And I'll bet there was a rumour or two about porn.'

'Rumours, maybe,' said Shaw, looking away, 'but that's all they were.'

'How do you know?'

Shaw scowled at him.

'Exactly,' said Banks. 'You only know because Harris told you so. Remember, you were just a young DC back then. You didn't question your superior officers. If anything showed up in your interviews that pointed you in the right direction – Bradford, Fiorino, Mandeville – then Harris ignored it, dismissed it as mere rumour, a dead end. You just skimmed the surface, exactly as he wanted. That's why the action allocations are missing, too. Harris was in charge of the investigation. He'd have issued the actions. And we'd have found out what direction they all pointed in – the passing paedophile theory, later made more credible by Brady and Hindley's arrest – and, what's more important, what they pointed *away* from. The truth.'

'It's still all theory,' said Shaw.

'Yes,' Banks admitted. 'But you know it's true. We've got the photo of Graham, taken at Mandeville's house, Bradford's connection with the porn business and the possible murder weapon, and the missing notebooks. Go ahead, see if it adds up any other way.'

Shaw sighed. 'I just can't believe John would do something like that. I know he gave Fiorino a lot of leeway, but I thought at the time that he got his reward in information. Fair exchange. That's all I was trying to protect. A bit of tit for tat. All those years I knew him . . . and I still can't fucking believe it.'

'Maybe you didn't really know him at all,' said Banks.

'No more than I knew Graham Marshall.'

Shaw looked over at Banks. His eyes were pink and red-rimmed. Then he looked at Michelle. 'What do you think about all this?'

'I think it's true, sir,' Michelle said. 'It's the only explanation that makes sense. You didn't want me to look too closely at the past because you were worried I'd find out something that might tarnish Harris's reputation. You suspected he was bent, you knew he gave Fiorino a wide berth in exchange for information, and something about the Graham Marshall case bothered you. You didn't want it stirring up again because you didn't know what would come to the surface.'

'What next?' Shaw asked.

'There'll have to be a report. I'm not going to bury this. I'll report my findings and any conclusions that can be drawn to the ACC. After that, it's up to him. There might be media interest.'

'And John's memory?'

Michelle shrugged. 'I don't know. If it all comes out, if people believe it, then his reputation will take a bit of a knock.'

'The lad's family?'

'It'll be hard for them, too. But is it any better than not knowing?'

'And me?'

'Maybe it's time to retire,' Banks said. 'You must be long past due.'

Shaw snorted, then coughed. He lit another cigarette and reached for his drink. 'Maybe you're right.' His gaze went from Banks to Michelle and back. 'I should have known it would mean big trouble the minute those bones were found. There wasn't much, you know, in those notebooks. It was just like what you said. A hint here, a lead there.'

'But there was enough,' said Banks. 'And, let's face it, you know as well as I do that in that sort of investigation you first look close and hard at the immediate family and circle. If anybody had done that, they'd have found one or two points of interest, some lines of enquiry that just weren't followed. You dig deepest close to home. Nobody bothered. That in itself seems odd enough.'

'Because John steered the investigation?'

'Yes. It must have been a much smaller division back then, wasn't it? He'd have had close to absolute power over it.'

Shaw hung his head again. 'Oh, nobody questioned Jet Harris's judgement, that was for certain.' He looked up. 'I've got cancer,' he said, glancing towards Michelle. 'That's why I've been taking so much time off. Stomach.' He grimaced. 'There's not much they can do. Anyway, maybe retirement isn't such a bad idea.' He laughed. 'Enjoy my last few months gardening or stamp collecting or something peaceful like that.'

Banks didn't know what to say. Michelle said, 'I'm sorry.'

Shaw looked at her and scowled. 'You've no reason to be. It won't make a scrap of difference to you whether I live or die. Come to think of it, your life will be a lot easier without me.'

'Even so . . .'

Shaw looked at Banks again. 'I wish you'd never come back down here, Banks,' he said. 'Why couldn't you stay up in Yorkshire and shag a few sheep?'

'You wouldn't understand.'

'Oh, wouldn't I? Don't you be too sure I'm as corrupt

as you think I am. Now if you're not going to charge me or beat me up, why don't the two of you just bugger off and leave me alone?'

Banks and Michelle looked at one another. There was nothing else to say to Shaw, so they left. Back in the car, Banks turned to Michelle and said, 'Do you believe him?'

'About not being responsible for the burglary and the van?'

'Yes.'

'I think so. He seemed genuinely horrified by the idea. What reason has he to lie about it now?'

'It's a serious crime. That's reason enough. But I think you're right. I don't think he was behind it. He was just doing his best to protect Harris's reputation.'

'Then are you thinking who I'm thinking?'

Banks nodded. 'Rupert Mandeville.'

'Shall we pay him a visit?'

'You want me along?'

Michelle looked at Banks and said, 'Yes. I feel we're getting near the end. Graham Marshall was your friend. You deserve to be there. I'd just like to stop off at the station and check a few things out first.'

'He won't tell us anything, you know.'

Michelle smiled. 'We'll see about that. It certainly won't do any harm to yank his chain a bit.'

19

It didn't take Annie long to drive to Harrogate and find the small terraced house off the Leeds Road. Vernon Anderson answered the door and, looking puzzled, invited her into his spartan living room. She admired the framed Vermeer print over the fireplace and settled down in one of the two armchairs.

'I see you have an eye for a good painting,' Annie said.

'Art appreciation must run in the family,' said Vernon. 'Though I confess I'm not as much of a reader as our Lauren is. I'd rather see a good film any day.'

On the low table under the window a couple of lottery tickets rested on a newspaper open at the racing page, some of the horses with red rings around their names.

'Any luck today?' Annie asked.

'You know what it's like,' Vernon said with an impish grin. 'You win a little, then you lose a little.' He sat on the sofa and crossed his legs.

Vernon Anderson didn't look much like his sister, Annie noted. He had dark hair, short tight curls receding a little at the temples, and he was thickset, with a muscular upper body and rather short legs. With his long lashes, dimples and easy charm, though, she imagined he would be quite successful with the opposite sex. Not that any of those things did much for her. If there was any resemblance, it was in the eyes; Vernon's were the same pale blue as Lauren's. He wore jeans and a T-shirt advertising Guinness. And sandals over white socks.

'What's all this about?'

'I'm looking into the kidnapping and murder of Luke Armitage,' Annie said. 'Your sister was his teacher.'

'Yes, I know. She's very upset about it.'

'Did you ever meet Luke?'

'Me? No. I'd heard of him, of course; of his father, anyway.'

'Martin Armitage?'

'That's right. I've won a few bob on teams he played for over the years.' Vernon grinned.

'But you never met Luke?'

'No.'

'Did your sister tell you much about him?'

'She talked about school sometimes,' Vernon said. 'She might have mentioned him.'

'In what context?'

'As one of her pupils.'

'But not how exceptional he was and that she gave him private tuition?'

'No.' Vernon's eyes narrowed. 'Where are we going here?'

'Lauren said she was visiting you the day Luke disappeared. That'd be a week ago last Monday. Is that true?'

'Yes. Look, I've already been through all this with the other detective, the one who came by a few days ago.'

'I know,' said Annie. 'That was one of the locals helping us out. It's not always possible to get away. I'm sorry to bother you with it, but do you think you could bear to go through it again with me?'

Vernon folded his arms. 'I suppose so. If you think it's necessary.'

'If you don't mind.'

'It's just as I told the chap the other day. We had rather too much to drink and Lauren stayed over.' He patted the sofa. 'It's comfortable enough. Safer than trying to drive.'

'Admirable,' said Annie. People always seemed to make nervous comments about drinking and driving when police officers were around, as if that were the only crime they had time to pursue, all they were interested in. 'Where were you drinking?'

'Where?'

'Which pub?'

'Oh, I see. We didn't go to a pub. She came here for dinner and we had wine.'

'What kind?'

'Just an Australian Chardonnay. On sale at Sainsbury's.'

'Did your sister visit you often?'

'Fairly often. Though I can't see what that's got to do with anything. Our father's ill and mother's not coping too well. We had a lot to talk about.'

'Yes. I know about the Alzheimer's. I'm sorry to hear it.'

Vernon's jaw dropped. 'You know? Lauren told you?'

'It's surprising the information you pick up sometimes in this job. Anyway, I just wanted to make sure I'd got all the times right, for the record, you know. You'd be amazed if you knew how much of our job is just paperwork.'

Vernon smiled. 'Well, as I remember, she arrived at about six o'clock, and that was it. We ate at around half-past seven.'

'What did you cook?'

'Venison in white wine. From Nigella Lawson.'

It didn't sound very appetizing to a vegetarian such as

Annie, but to each his own, she thought. 'And no doubt there was a fair bit of wine to wash it down with?'

'A couple of bottles. That's why Lauren ended up staying. That and the Grand Marnier.'

'Liqueurs, too. You were really pushing the boat out.'

'I'm afraid we both got a bit upset. Over Father. Lauren had paid a brief visit home at half-term and he hadn't recognized her. I know alcohol doesn't help solve problems, but one does tend to reach for it in times of trouble.'

'Of course,' said Annie. 'So you went to bed around what time?'

'Me? I'm not sure. It's a bit of a blur. Probably around midnight.'

'And your sister?'

'I don't know how late she stayed up.'

'But she did stay all night?'

'Of course.'

'How do you know?'

'I remember going to the toilet once. You have to go through the living room. She was asleep on the sofa then.'

'What time was that?'

'I don't know. I didn't look at my watch. Dark, though.'

'But she could have been gone for a few hours and returned, couldn't she?'

'I'd have heard her.'

'Are you certain? If you'd had that much to drink you probably slept quite heavily.'

'Don't forget, we *both* had too much to drink.'

'Did she receive any phone calls during the evening?'

'No.'

'What time did she leave?'

'About eleven o'clock the following morning.'

'It must have been a bit of a rough morning for you at work, after all that drink. Or did you take the day off?'

'I'm presently unemployed, if it's any of your business. And I can handle the drink. I'm not an alcoholic, you know.'

'Of course not.' Annie paused for a moment. 'Did you ever get any hints that Lauren's relationship with Luke might have been a bit more than the normal teacher–pupil one?'

'I certainly did not.'

'She never talked about him in an affectionate way?'

'I've had quite enough of this,' Vernon said. 'It's one thing checking up on times, but quite another to suggest that my sister had some sort of affair with this boy.' He stood up. 'Look, I've told you what you want to know. Now why don't you just go and leave me alone.'

'What's wrong, Mr Anderson?'

'Nothing's wrong.'

'You seem a bit agitated, that's all.'

'Well, wouldn't you feel agitated if someone came into your house and started flinging accusations around?'

'What accusations? I'm simply trying to make certain that your sister didn't see Luke Armitage the night he was killed. Can't you see how important this is, Vernon? If she did see him, he might have told her something. She might have had some idea of where he was going, who he was seeing.'

'I'm sorry. I still can't help. Lauren was here all night.'

Annie sighed. 'All right, then. Just one more thing before I leave you in peace.'

'What?'

'I understand you have a criminal record.'

Vernon reddened. 'I wondered when that would come

out. Look, it was a long time ago. I forged my boss's signature on a cheque. I'm not proud of it. It was a stupid thing to do, okay, but I was desperate. I paid the price.'

'Well, that's all right, then, isn't it,' said Annie, who was thinking it was amazing what people would do when they were desperate. 'Thanks for your time, Mr Anderson.'

Vernon said nothing, just slammed the door behind her. Annie had noticed a bookie's on the main road, just around the corner from Vernon's street. She glanced at her watch. Time for a quick call before it closed. In her experience, bookies' shops were always full of smoke, so she took a deep breath and went inside.

•

If this was the face of evil, then it was remarkably bland, Banks thought as he and Michelle were ushered into Rupert Mandeville's presence by a young man who looked more like a clerk than a butler. In fact, Mandeville reminded Banks of the old prime minister, Edward Heath, who came to lead the party in opposition in 1965. Casually dressed in white cricket trousers, a cream shirt open at the collar, and a mauve V-necked pullover, he had the same slightly startled, slightly befuddled, look about him as Heath, the same silver hair and pinkish skin. Why was it, Banks wondered, that every politician he had ever seen had skin like pink vinyl? Were they born that way?

The sheepskin rug was gone, replaced by a carpet with a complex Middle Eastern design, but the fireplace was the same one as in Graham's photograph. Being in the room where the picture had been taken all those years ago made Banks shiver. What else had happened here? Had Graham been involved in sex acts, too? With Mandeville? He realized that he would probably never know.

Reconstructing the past after so long was as faulty and unreliable a process as memory itself.

At least they now had some idea how Mandeville knew about the progress of Michelle's investigation, even if they couldn't prove anything. According to a local reporter Michelle had rung from the station, Mandeville had spies everywhere; it was how he had managed to survive so long in such a ruthless world as politics. It was also rumoured that he had close contacts within the police force, though no names were mentioned. That must have been how he knew so much about the investigation into Graham's death, and the threat that it was beginning to pose for him.

Mandeville was courtesy personified, pulling out a chair for Michelle and offering refreshments, which they refused. 'It's been many years since I had a visit from the police,' he said. 'How can I help you?'

'Would Geoff Talbot's visit have been the one you're thinking about?' Michelle asked. It was still her case, Banks knew, and he was only present because she had invited him; therefore, she got to ask the questions.

'I can't say I remember the young man's name.'

'You ought at least to remember the month and year: August 1965.'

'So long ago. How time flies.'

'And the reason for the visit.'

'It was a mistake. An apology was offered, and accepted.'

'By Detective Superintendent Harris?'

'Again, I must confess I don't remember the person's name.'

'Take my word for it.'

'Very well. Look, I sense a little hostility in your tone.

Can you please either tell me why you're here or leave?'

'We're here to ask you some questions relating to the Graham Marshall investigation.'

'Oh, yes. That poor boy whose skeleton was uncovered some days ago. Tragic. But I don't see how that has anything to do with me.'

'We're just tying up a few loose ends, that's all.'

'And I'm a loose end. How fascinating!' His glaucous eyes gleamed with mockery.

Banks took the photo from his briefcase and slid it across the table to Mandeville, who looked at it without expression.

'Interesting,' he said. 'But, again . . .'

'Do you recognize the boy?' Michelle asked.

'I'm afraid I don't.'

'Do you recognize the fireplace?'

Mandeville glanced towards his own Adam fireplace and smiled at her. 'I'd be a liar if I said I don't,' he said. 'Though I hardly imagine it's the only one of its kind in existence.'

'I think it's unique enough for our purposes,' Michelle said.

'Photographs can be faked, you know.'

Michelle tapped the photo. 'Are you saying this is a forgery?'

'Of course. Unless someone has been using my house for illicit purposes in my absence.'

'Let's get back to 1965, when this photo was taken, in this room,' Michelle said. 'You were quite famous for your parties, weren't you?'

Mandeville shrugged. 'I was young, wealthy. What else was I to do but share it around a bit? Maybe I was foolish, too.'

'Parties that catered for every taste, including drugs, prostitutes and under-age sex partners, male and female.'

'Don't be absurd.'

'This boy was fourteen when that photo was taken.'

'And he was a friend of mine,' said Banks, catching Mandeville's eye and holding his gaze.

'Then I'm sorry for your loss,' said Mandeville, 'but I still don't see what it has to do with me.'

'You had him killed,' said Michelle.

'I did what? I'd be careful, if I were you, young lady, going around making accusations like that.'

'Or what? You'll have your chauffeur break into my flat again, or try to run me over?'

Mandeville raised his eyebrows. 'I was actually going to warn you about the possibility of slander.'

'I did a bit of homework before I came out here,' Michelle said. 'Checked into the background of your employees. Derek Janson, your chauffeur, served a prison sentence for burglary fifteen years ago. He came to be regarded as somewhat of an expert at picking locks. I'm sure he knows how to drive a van, too.'

'I know about Derek's background,' Mandeville said. 'It's very difficult for ex-convicts to get employment. Surely you can't fault me for doing my little bit for Derek's rehabilitation? I happen to trust him completely.'

'I'm sure you do. When the investigation into Graham Marshall's disappearance was reopened, after we found his remains and discovered that he had been murdered, you did everything in your power to put me off.'

'Why would I want to do that?'

'Because he was using the photo to blackmail you, and you asked Carlo Fiorino to take care of him. You paid Fiorino well for his various services, so he obliged.'

'This is absurd. You have no evidence for any of this.'

'We've got the photograph,' Banks said.

'As I said before, photographs can be faked.'

'They can be authenticated, too,' Banks said.

Mandeville stared at them, assessing the damage. Finally, he stood up, put his hands on the table, palms down and leaned forward. 'Well,' he said, 'that's quite a story the two of you have concocted. It's a pity that none of it will stand up in court, or anywhere else for that matter.'

'Maybe you're right,' Michelle said. 'But you still have to admit that it doesn't look good. Some mud's bound to stick.'

'I'm not without influence, you know.'

'Is that a threat?'

'I don't stoop to threats.'

'No, you get someone else to do that for you.'

'What do you intend to do now?'

'Whatever I can to make sure you pay for what you did. For a start, we'll have a nice chat with Mr Janson.'

Mandeville walked over and leaned against the fireplace, smiling. 'Derek won't tell you anything.'

'You never know. We're not without influence, either, especially with ex-cons. Then there's Geoff Talbot's notebook. Jet Harris didn't bother to remove that from the archives. No reason to. There was no investigation.'

'I don't know what you're talking about.'

'Names,' said Banks. 'Talbot made a note of the names of the people he talked to when he came up here. I'm sure if we dig around a bit, we'll find one or two people who remember the old days: partygoers, perhaps, or club patrons.'

Mandeville's face darkened and he went back to sit at

the table. 'I'm warning you,' he said, 'if you attempt to spread these vicious lies about me, I'll have your jobs.'

But Michelle was already out of the room, striding towards the front door.

Banks took the opportunity of a few seconds alone with Mandeville to lean in close, smile and lower his voice. 'And if DI Hart so much as trips on a banana skin, I'll be right back here to rip out your spine and shove it down your throat. Your lordship.'

He couldn't swear to it, but judging by the change in Mandeville's expression, he thought he had got his point across.

•

It was already the evening of a long day, and the shadows were lengthening when Lauren Anderson led Annie into the book-lined living room. Classical music was playing, a violin concerto, but Annie didn't recognize it. Banks would have done, she thought. Lauren was barefoot, wearing ice-blue jeans and a white sleeveless top. Her shoulders were pale and freckled, like her face. Her mane of auburn hair was fastened behind her head by a leather barrette. 'What do you want?' she asked. 'Have you caught them?'

'I think so. But first sit down and listen to what I have to say. You can correct me if I'm wrong about anything.'

'I don't know what you mean.'

'You will in a minute. Sit down, Lauren.' Annie crossed her legs and leaned back in the armchair. She had worked out how to approach Lauren on the drive back from Harrogate, then made a couple of phone calls and picked up DC Winsome Jackman, whom she had instructed to stay outside in the car for the time being. She didn't expect any trouble, and it would be easier for her to talk to Lauren alone. 'We know where Luke was shortly before he was killed,' she began. 'Did he ever mention a girl called Liz Palmer to you?'

'No. Why?'

'Are you sure? She meant a lot to Luke.'

Lauren shook her head. 'No, that can't be true. I don't believe you.'

'Why not, Lauren? Why can't it be true?'

'Luke . . . he didn't . . . he wasn't like that. He was devoted to art.'

'Oh, come off it, Lauren. He was just a randy adolescent, like any other. This Liz was a bit older than him and she—'

'No! Stop it. I won't listen to this.'

'What's the problem, Lauren?'

'I won't have you tarnishing Luke's memory.'

'Tarnishing? What's so wrong about a fifteen-year-old boy losing his virginity to an older woman? It's a time-honoured tradition, even if it is technically having sex with a minor. Who cares about a few petty rules and regulations? Especially if it's the boy who's under-age and not the woman. At least we know now Luke got to enjoy the pleasures of sex before he died.'

'I don't know why,' Lauren said, looking into Annie's eyes, 'but you're lying to me. There is no "Liz".'

'Yes there is. I can introduce you.'

'No.'

'What is it, Lauren? Jealous?'

'Luke meant a lot to me. You know he did. He was so talented.'

'It was more than that, though, wasn't it?'

'What do you mean?'

'You were lovers, weren't you?'

Lauren hesitated for a moment, then said, 'What if we were? Are you going to arrest me for that?'

'No. I'm going to arrest you for murder.'

Lauren jerked upright. 'You can't be serious.'

'I'm serious all right. You see, Liz and her boyfriend live about five minutes' walk away from here, and Luke was distraught when he left their flat. I asked myself, where would he go? Maybe it took me too long to come up with the right answer, the *only* possible answer, but that was because of the clever smokescreen you put up. The kidnapping. We thought we were looking for a man or someone closer to home. But Luke couldn't have gone home because the last bus had gone and we checked all the taxis. We suspected his music teacher, Alastair Ford, too. But Luke couldn't have gone to his house because it's so remote, and he had no means of getting there. That leaves you, Lauren. Luke didn't have a wide circle of friends and acquaintances. Also, he was very upset. You're the one he talked to about his emotional problems. How long had you been lovers, Lauren?'

Lauren sighed. 'Near the end of term. It just happened. It was so . . . so natural. I wasn't trying to seduce him or anything like that.' Annie could see tears clouding her eyes. 'We were looking at some pictures. Pre-Raphaelites. He remarked on my resemblance to one of the models.'

'Elizabeth Siddal, Dante Gabriel Rossetti's first wife. You do look a lot like her, Lauren. Or a lot like the paintings of her. A typical Pre-Raphaelite beauty, as someone said.'

'You know?'

'I should have made the connection sooner,' Annie said. 'My father's an artist, and I do a bit of painting myself. I've picked up a thing or two over the years.'

'But how could you have known?'

'We found Luke's shoulder bag at the other flat, too. I read over his recent writings and found a lot of classical references I didn't understand. One thing I did understand is that they were of a sexual nature, very intimate, and they stressed a kind of Pre-Raphaelite look. There were also references to Ophelia, but I don't think it was Shakespeare Luke had in mind. It was John Everett Millais. He painted Ophelia and used Elizabeth Siddal as a model. She caught pneumonia lying in a tepid bath every day posing as Ophelia floating down the river. Very romantic. But what I don't understand is why. Why did you do it, Lauren? Why did you kill him? Was he going to leave you?'

'You don't understand anything. I didn't kill him. You've got no proof. I've got an alibi. Talk to Vernon.'

'I've already talked to Vernon,' said Annie, 'and I'd trust him about as far as I could throw him. Your brother lied for you, Lauren. Only natural. But I'm willing to bet that he's the one who helped you get rid of the body. You couldn't have done it all by yourself. And he's the one who hatched the kidnapping scheme. That had all the hallmarks of an afterthought. It wasn't the reason for Luke's disappearance and death. Your brother thought he'd try and cash in on it and he's small-time enough to ask for only ten thousand. Besides, you'd probably talked about Luke and told him the family wasn't quite as wealthy as people assumed. He's a gambler, Lauren. And a loser. He needs the money. I talked to his bookie. Your brother's in debt up to his eyeballs. Did you even know what he'd done after he'd helped you?'

Lauren looked down into her lap. Her fingers were

twined together, grasping so tightly all the knuckles were white. She shook her head. 'I don't believe Vernon would do anything like that.'

'But you must have suspected, after you heard about the kidnap demand?'

'It confused me. I didn't know what was going on. Maybe I had my suspicions, I don't know. I was too upset to think about it.'

'The thing is,' Annie went on, 'that our Scene-of-Crimes Officers found minute traces of blood on the wall where Luke was shoved over into Hallam Tarn. Minute, but enough to provide a DNA profile. I think that profile would match you or your brother. I'm also certain that when our men come in here and go over your place, they'll find traces of Luke's blood. Now that might not be conclusive in itself, as we know Luke was punched in the nose before he came here, but it's all starting to add up, Lauren.'

Lauren looked at Annie, her eyes red-rimmed and almost unbearably sad. 'I didn't kill him,' she said, in a small, distant voice. 'I would never have harmed Luke. I loved him.'

'What happened, Lauren?'

Lauren reached for her cigarettes and lit one. Then she eyed Annie sadly and began her story.

•

'Do you think I might have a word alone with your husband?' Banks asked Mrs Marshall at her house that evening.

'Bill? I don't know what he can tell you,' she said. 'You know he can't talk.'

'There might be one or two little things.' Banks looked

at the invalid who, judging by the hard expression in his eyes, certainly knew he was being talked about. 'Can he write?'

'Yes,' said Mrs Marshall. 'But he can't hold a pencil properly. He can only grasp it in his fist and scribble a few letters.'

'That'll do,' said Banks. 'Can you get me a pad and pencil, if it's no trouble?'

Mrs Marshall brought Banks a lined pad and a pencil from the sideboard drawer.

'Come on,' said Michelle, taking her arm and leading her towards the kitchen. 'Let's go make some tea. I've got a few things to tell you.' Banks and Michelle had agreed on a sanitized version of events to tell Mrs Marshall. If the media dug too deeply and the story hit the news, then she might find out more than she wanted about her son's life and death, but that was for the future. Now, maybe it was enough for Michelle to tell her that Donald Bradford killed Graham because he found out something about Bradford's illegal activities.

When they had gone into the kitchen and closed the door, Banks put the pad and pencil on Bill Marshall's knee and settled in front of him, gazing into the expressionless eyes. 'I think you know why I want to talk to you,' he said.

Bill Marshall made no sign that he understood.

'You used to spar with Reggie and Ronnie Kray in your younger days,' he said. 'Then, when you came up here, you fell in with Carlo Fiorino and did a few strong-arm jobs for him. Am I right? Can you nod or write something down?'

Bill Marshall did nothing.

'Okay, so that's how you want to play it,' Banks said.

'Fine. I'm not saying you had anything to do with Graham's death. You didn't. You'd never have done anything like that. But you knew who did it, didn't you?'

Bill Marshall just stared at Banks.

'See, the trouble with people like you, Bill, is they insist on working outside the law. You've no use for coppers, have you? Never have had, I shouldn't think. Just like my own dad. Want to know what I think happened? Well, I'll tell you anyway. I think Donald Bradford just wasn't cut out to be a killer of young boys. I don't think he had much choice in the matter, though. Fiorino pushed him into it. After all, Graham was *his* responsibility, and Graham was in a position to do a lot of serious damage. There was just too much at stake. Not just the empire as it existed then, but the future. The city was expanding, becoming a new town. Soon it would double in population. What an opportunity for a man like Fiorino. He supplied what people always seem to want, for a good price. Are you with me so far?'

Marshall just glared at Banks. A little drool slid down his stubbly chin.

'Fiorino had no use for the law, either, unless it was in his pay, so he used other people to do his dirty work. Shortly after the killing, Bradford sold up and moved out. Fiorino didn't like that. Didn't like people escaping his control, being out of his line of sight. Especially if they knew as much as Bradford did and were fast becoming unstable and unreliable. Bradford was guilt-ridden by what he had done. Also, I think he took some of Fiorino's goods with him, though that's just a minor matter. What really counted was that Bradford was out of sight and untrustworthy. And he knew too much.'

Marshall still showed no reaction. Banks could hear

muffled voices from the kitchen. 'So what does he do when he has a problem with Bradford? Well, he could pay for a hit, I suppose, and that's one option. But he knows you. That's an easier one. He knows that whatever you do, you'll do it yourself, you won't go running to the police. So he tells you that Bradford killed your son, though not on *his* orders. He convinces you that Bradford was a pervert. He also gives you Bradford's address. Easy. All he had to do next was leave the rest up to you. Am I right so far, Bill?'

Banks could tell by the anger and hatred in Bill Marshall's eyes that he was right. 'You went up to Carlisle, didn't you? Probably told everyone you were looking for work. Then you broke into Donald Bradford's flat and waited for him to come home. You knew Bradford was a tough customer, so you attacked him from behind with a cosh. I don't blame you, Bill. The man murdered your son. I'd want to do the same to anyone who harmed either of my children. But you let your wife suffer all those years. You *knew* Graham was dead and you knew who killed him. Maybe you didn't know where the body was, but I'll bet you could have found out. Instead, you went up there and murdered Bradford and said nothing to your wife or your daughter. All these years they've lived not knowing what happened to Graham. That's unforgivable, Bill.' Banks nodded towards the pad. 'What do you have to say about that? Come on, tell me something.'

Marshall held his gaze for a while, then grasped the pencil, moved his hand with difficulty and scrawled on the pad. When he had done, he handed it to Banks. There were three words in capital letters: FUCK OFF COPPER.

•

'He came to me, like you said,' Lauren Anderson began. 'He was in a terrible state. He was upset because . . . well, you know why. I tried to calm him down and we went to . . . We just lay down on the bed together and I held him. I'd already realized I had to end it. I just hadn't been able to find the courage. But I knew that it couldn't go on. Someone would find out eventually and that would be it. My career, reputation . . . everything. A fifteen-year-old boy and a twenty-nine-year-old woman. Taboo. I thought I'd got him calm enough, so I started talking about it, you know, how we should probably cool things for a while.'

'Did he tell you he'd been smoking cannabis earlier?'

'Cannabis? No. He never told me that. But that must be why he seemed so disoriented and excitable. I'd never seen him like that before. He scared me.'

'How did he react when you told him you wanted to finish the affair?' Annie asked, remembering that it hadn't been too long ago when she had told Banks the same thing.

'He didn't want to accept it. He said he couldn't bear to lose me.' Lauren started crying. 'He said he'd kill himself.'

'What happened next?'

She dabbed her eyes with a tissue. 'He stormed off to the bathroom. I gave him a couple of minutes, then I heard all the things falling out of the cupboard into the sink, glass breaking, so I went after him.'

'Was the bathroom door locked?'

'No.'

'He was after the Valium?'

'You know?'

'We know he took some Valium shortly before he died, yes.'

'I have a prescription. But I suppose you know that, too?'

Annie nodded. 'I checked.'

'He had the bottle open, and he poured some tablets into his hand and swallowed them. I went to him and struggled with him over the bottle. We fought, pulling and pushing each other, and then he went down. Just like that. He was in his socks, and the floor tiles can be slippery. His feet just went from under him and he hit his head on the side of the bath. I did what I could. I tried to revive him, mouth to mouth. I checked for a pulse and listened for his heartbeat, and then I even tried holding a mirror to his mouth. But it was no use. He was dead. So much blood.'

'What did you do then?'

'I didn't know what to do. I panicked. I knew if any of it came out I'd be finished. I didn't know where to turn, so I called Vernon. He said he'd come right away and not to do anything until he got here. The rest you know.'

'What happened to Luke's mobile?'

'It fell out of his pocket in the car. Vernon took it.'

That explained the call to Armitage's mobile. Vernon had looked up Martin's number on Luke's phone. He wasn't to know that Luke would be unlikely to call his stepfather for anything. Vernon could easily have driven up to Eastvale and made the call there to avoid detection. Harrogate wasn't that far away.

'*Did* you know about the ransom demand?'

Lauren shook her head. 'No. I'd never agree to anything like that. And as I said, I was too upset to think about it. If anything, I thought it must be some sort of cruel practical joke. I'm so sorry for what happened.' She reached out and grasped Annie's wrist. 'You've got to believe me. I'd never have harmed Luke. I loved him. Maybe if I hadn't been so insensitive, so selfish, and not tried to end it when he was so upset, or just held him the way he wanted, it might not have happened. I've relived that moment over and over again ever since it happened. I can't sleep. I don't know how I'm going to go back to work. Nothing seems to matter any more.'

Annie stood up.

'What are you going to do now?'

'I'm going to call in my partner from the car outside, and we're going to make sure you know your rights before we take you to the police station to make a formal statement. We'll also be sending a message to the Harrogate police to pick up your brother.'

'What's going to happen to me?'

'I don't know, Lauren,' Annie said. Again, she was feeling shitty about doing her job. Harden up, she told herself. Maybe Lauren Anderson didn't deliberately kill Luke, but she was at least partly responsible for his death, along with Liz Palmer and Ryan Milne. All adults who should have known better than to tamper with the feelings of a confused and disturbed fifteen year old. All of whom were selfish and used Luke for their own ends. Even if that end, at least in Lauren's case, was love. A romantic imagination and adolescent lust could be a dangerous combination.

But maybe, Annie thought, if she *didn't* feel pity for a woman in Lauren's position, then she would lose some of her humanity. One of the things working with Banks had taught her was how to do the job without becoming callous and cynical, the way she had been going before she met him. Lauren would probably get off quite lightly,

Annie told herself. If Luke had died during a struggle, the object of which was to stop him taking an overdose of Valium, and if Lauren had not known of her brother's botched ransom demand, then she wouldn't get a very stiff sentence.

Lauren would lose her job, though, and, like Norman Wells, she would become a pariah for some – the seductress and corrupter of youth. And the family would suffer – Robin and Martin – as it was all dragged into the open. Because this would be a high-profile trial, no doubt about it. Neil Byrd's son, a famous model and a sports star. Not a chance of escaping the media circus. It was a damn shame they couldn't prosecute Liz and Ryan, Annie thought as she walked Lauren, head hung low, out to the car. They were at least as much to blame for what happened as Lauren was, if not more so. But it wasn't her judgement to make.

•

'Jet Harris *bent*? I can't believe it,' said Arthur Banks in the Coach and Horses early that evening. Banks had dragged him out there to tell him the full story, and they sat over their pints in the dreary, half-empty pub. Banks felt a craving for nicotine rush through his cells like a desperate need for air, but he pushed it aside. One day at a time. One craving at a time. It passed. People said the cravings got less and less powerful as time went on. But others said you were never rid of the habit. He knew people who had started again after they'd been off for ten years. One day at a time.

Arthur Banks stared at his son in disbelief. 'Is this going to come out?' he asked.

'Probably,' said Banks. 'We don't actually hand our

reports to the press, but they have their ways. Depends on the media interest.'

'Oh, there'll be media interest around here, all right. Jet Harris, homo and bent copper.' He eyed Banks warily. 'You sure you're not going to hush it up, then?'

'Dad,' said Banks. 'We don't go in for cover-ups. At least *I* don't, and nor does DI Hart. This investigation has cost her a lot. She's only been at the division a couple of months and here she is, debunking the legend. Imagine how popular that's going to make her around the place.' It had nearly cost Michelle her life, too, Banks thought. She would be safe from now on, he was certain, and not because of his melodramatic threat. Now Mandeville knew there were more people involved, he could hardly scare or kill off everyone. He would just have to take his chances that time had hidden his secrets.

'Why are you telling *me*?' Arthur Banks asked.

Banks sipped some beer. 'Dad, you and mum have never really given me a chance, you know, ever since I joined the force. You've always pointed out the negative side of the job. I just wanted you to know that some of us aren't crooked, that some of us take our work seriously. Even if it never comes out in public, at least *you'll* know the truth, and you'll know *I* told you.'

Arthur Banks paused for a moment, looking his son in the eye, then he said, 'And did you also find out what happened to your friend Graham after all these years?'

'Yes. Well, DI Hart did most of the work. I just filled in the blanks.' Banks leaned forward. 'But yes, Dad, I found out. It's what I do. I don't go around waving rolls of fivers at striking miners, I don't beat up suspects in the cells, I don't botch investigations into murdered black youths, and I don't steal confiscated drugs and sell them back on the street. Mostly, I push paper. Sometimes I catch murderers. Sometimes I fail, but I always do my damnedest.'

'So who did it?'

Banks told him.

'Donald Bradford! You'd have thought that would've been the first place they'd look.'

'That's what made us suspect some sort of mis-direction.'

'And Rupert Mandeville. That'll make a nice headline.'

'If we can pin anything on him. Remember, it was a long time ago, and he's hardly likely to confess.'

'Even so . . . your pal Graham was up to no good, wasn't he?'

'Why do you say that?'

'I don't know. He always seemed a bit shifty to me, that's all. Like his father.'

'Well, Graham wasn't exactly walking the straight and narrow, but that's no excuse for killing him.'

'Course not.' Banks senior fell silent for a moment, contemplating his son through narrowed eyes. Then he let slip a thin smile. 'You've stopped smoking, haven't you?'

'I wasn't going to tell anyone.'

'There's not much you can slip past your own father.'

'Dad, have you been listening to me? All I've been trying to demonstrate to you all these years,' Banks went on, 'is that I've been doing a decent, honest day's work, just like you did.'

'And Jet Harris, local legend, was a bent copper?'

'Yes.'

'And you're going to expose him.'

'Something like that.'

'Well,' said Arthur Banks, rubbing his hands together. 'That's all right, then. You'll be having another pint, I suppose? On me, this time.'

Banks looked at his watch. 'Better make it a half,' he said. 'I've got a date.'

> Was it the age of my innocence,
> Or was it the lost land of Oz?
> Was it only a foolish illusion,
> The summer that never was?
>
> Did I walk through the fields with the child in my
>   arms
> And the golden wheat over my head?
> Did I feel my heart breaking under the weight?
> Was my sweet sleeping boychild a burden, like
>   lead?
>
> I remember him crying the day he was born
> And his hand like a spider that wouldn't let go
> And he wouldn't let go and he wouldn't let go
> And the pain tore my heart out and filled me with
>   woe.
>
> Can a dreamer take hold of reality
> And become a responsible man?
> Can a killer become a lover
> Or is he forever damned?
>
> You can't follow me where I'm going now
> And you can't go to the places I've been
> Don't listen to the demons I've listened to
> Or look into the darkness I've seen.

*There's a field and a boy and the tall golden
    wheat
And eternity held in a day
But it's so hard to hold and it's so hard to reach
And forever rushing away.
Was it the age of my innocence,
Or was it the lost land of Oz?
Was it only a foolish illusion,
The summer that never was?*

Banks lay in bed late that night listening to Neil Byrd's CD on his Walkman after dinner with Michelle and a phone call from Annie. 'The Summer that Never Was' was the first song on the CD, though the liner notes said it was the last song Byrd had recorded, just weeks before his suicide. As Banks listened to the subtle interplay of words and music, all set against acoustic guitar and stand-up bass, with flute and a violin weaving in and out, like Van Morrison's *Astral Weeks,* he felt the despair and defeat of the singer. He didn't understand the song, didn't know what all the tortured phrases meant, only that they were tortured.

Here was a man at the end of his tether. And he was thinking of his child, or of his own childhood. Or both.

Banks couldn't even begin to imagine what this had meant to Luke Armitage when, his mind disoriented with strong cannabis, he had heard it for the first time in Liz and Ryan's flat. Annie was right. How callous could the bastards be? Or stupid. It no doubt never even entered their addled minds what damage they might be doing. All they could think of was opening up Luke's mind to his father's music to further their careers, and everyone knew that drugs opened the doors of perception.

Banks remembered the Rimbaud quote written in silver on Luke's black wall: 'Le Poëte se fait voyant par un long, immense et raisonné dérèglement de tous les sens.'

Well, had Luke become a seer? What had he seen? Was he trying to kill himself with the diazepam, or was he just trying to stop the pain?

In Banks's mind, Luke Armitage and Graham Marshall became one. They might have died in different ways for different reasons – not to mention in different times – but they were just two kids lost in a grown-up world, where needs and emotions were bigger than theirs, stronger and more complex than they could comprehend. Graham had tried to play the big leagues at their own game and lost, while Luke had tried to find love and acceptance in all the wrong places. He had lost, too. Accident though his death was, according to Annie, it was a tragic accident made up of many acts, each one of which was like a door closing behind Luke as he moved towards his fate.

Banks put the CD player on the bedside table, turned over and tried to go to sleep. He didn't think it would be easy. The song had left him with such a feeling of desolation and loneliness that he ached with need for someone to hold and found himself wishing he had stayed at Michelle's after their love-making. He almost took out his mobile and rang her, but it was past two in the morning, way too late. Besides, how would she react if he showed such neediness so early in their relationship? She'd probably run a mile, like Annie. And quite rightly.

He could hear his father snoring in the next room. At least there had been a reconciliation of sorts between the two of them. Though Arthur Banks would never actually admit anything, his attitude had changed since their drink together that evening. Banks could tell that his father had been proud of him for his success in solving Graham's murder – though he insisted Michelle had done most of the work – and for not trying to cover up Jet Harris's role. Proud for perhaps the first time in his life.

How strange it was to be at home in his old bed. As he drifted towards sleep, he imagined his mother calling him for school in the morning: 'Hurry up, Alan, or you'll be late!' In his dream, he fastened his tie as he dashed downstairs for a quick bowl of cornflakes and a glass of milk before picking up his satchel and meeting the others out in the street. But when he walked out of the door, Dave and Paul and Steve and Graham all stood there waiting for him with the bat, the ball and the wickets. The sun shone in a bright blue sky and the air was warm and fragrant. There was no school. They were on holiday. They were going to play cricket on the rec. 'It's summer, you fool,' Graham said, and they all laughed at him. *The summer that never was.*